The barman said nothing as she slipped out of the pub, and no one else saw her leave. On the pavement, in the fresh air, she suddenly felt very confused. What was she doing here? Where the hell was she? She thought about going back inside the pub and calling for a taxi, but her mind wasn't working with any logic or sense and the idea evaporated the instant it came into her head. She fastened her coat and began to walk.

Halfway up the road, a car pulled alongside her and Claire stopped. She leant forward as a window was wound down and spoke to the man inside. She recognized him but couldn't think how.

'D'you need a lift?' he asked.

She nodded; it was a long walk back.

'Where to?'

'The university.' It was an effo̶r̶ ̶ ̶ ̶ ̶ ̶ ̶ds out clearly.

'Hop in.'

Claire opened ̶ ̶ ̶ ̶ ̶ ̶ ̶ ̶ ̶ ̶ ̶ ̶ seat. Her feet knocked ̶ ̶ ̶ ̶ ̶ ̶ ̶ ̶ ̶ed it aside.

'Careful, you'll break the bulb.'

Claire bent and picked up a powerful flashlight. 'Sorry,' she mumbled, letting it rest on her lap. She put her head back against the seat and closed her eyes. The car moved off. Moments later it had turned the corner and was gone. There was no witness at all to the disappearance of the eighteen-year-old history student; no one even knew she had gone.

Also by Maria Barrett

STILL VOICES

MARIA BARRETT

timewarner
paperbacks

A *Time Warner* Paperback

First published in Great Britain in 2002 by Little, Brown
This edition published by Time Warner Paperbacks in 2003

A CIP catalogue record for this book
is available from the British Library.

ISBN 0 7515 3057 3

Typeset by Palimpsest Book Production Limited,
Polmont, Stirlingshire
Printed and bound in Great Britain by
Clays Ltd, St Ives plc

Time Warner Paperbacks
An imprint of
Time Warner Books UK
Brettenham House
Lancaster Place
London WC2E 7EN

www.TimeWarnerBooks.co.uk

For William, Lily and Edward.
With love.

ACKNOWLEDGEMENTS

As always, in writing this novel I am indebted to the people who have contributed to my research. They have tirelessly answered my questions, read bits and pieces of the script and helped to shape this book. I should like to thank the following: D.I. Del Cuff for his inside knowledge of the police and his patience (any mistakes are mine), Victoria Kingston for her historical accuracy, Megan Farringdon for talking to me about her lovely house, Laura Royall and Siobhan Taylor for frank and open discussion about divorce, and Jon Iredale for reading the first draft of this novel and for his inspirational ideas for the cover. I should also like to thank Sarah Domonick, who works in the background, thus leaving me free to occupy the foreground – I simply could not write as I do without her hard work and support. Thank you to the team at Time Warner Books for the edit, Mic for her confidence in this book and finally my children, the best in the world, and JB for being JB.

Maria Barrett
January 2002

Chapter 1

It was Monday morning, seven a.m., and Gordon had left for Glasgow on business on the last flight out Sunday night. It annoyed Lotte that he couldn't go first thing Monday, of course it did, she'd had to drive him to Heathrow at six that evening, having prepared an early lunch of roast beef and apple crumble and got the children bathed and ready for bed by five so that the baby-sitter – a fifteen-year-old from up the road who she didn't really trust but who could stand in at short notice on a Sunday night – didn't have much to do except put them to bed. But she hadn't said anything, she never did. Lotte had gone past saying things, she had been beaten down so often by Gordon's clever, aggressive mind, and outwitted so easily, that she couldn't be bothered any more. She was tired, worn out by two young children who rarely slept and often whined, and worn down by one husband who rarely thanked and often criticized. She was, as her friends said, the proverbial doormat. They all joked about it and often Lotte joined in, but the truth was that it was far from a joke. She was too bullied and too depressed to see anything even remotely funny in the situation.

So, after an exhausting Sunday – Gordon was out at tennis in the morning while she prepared the lunch; he watched sport on Sky while she packed for him and snoozed in the car while she drove him to the airport – this morning,

Monday, seven a.m., Lotte was having a lie-in. She could hear Milly playing in her bedroom as she lay in the dark, luxuriating under the warm, solitary duvet; she could hear Freddie moaning gently for his milk, but she didn't get up, she stayed where she was and lulled herself into a false sense of security. The next thing she knew there was an almighty scream, a stomach-churning series of thumps, then silence. She jumped out of bed, ran to the stairs and saw Milly lying on the floor at the bottom of them, her arm bent back under her, her long blonde hair fanned out around her still, pale face. The childgate was open.

'Milly!' she screamed, running down the stairs. She knelt at the bottom by her daughter and put her fingers to Milly's neck. The pulse was there. She gently patted her cheeks. 'Milly? Oh God, Milly, please, please speak to me.' Panicked, not having the first clue what to do, she jumped up and ran to the phone. Upstairs, Freddie had started to wail. She dialled 999, spoke to the operator and asked for an ambulance. She was told there would be an immediate response. Then she called Gordon's mobile, waited the forty seconds or so for it to connect, then heard his voice and said: 'Oh God, Gordon, Milly's fallen down the stairs, she's . . . oh God, I can't get her to open her eyes Gordon, I . . .'

'Call an ambulance, Lotte, do it now!'

'I've done it, they're on their way.'

'Right. Don't move her, don't do anything until the ambulance arrives, OK? I'll get the next plane home. Ring me as soon as you know what's going on.'

Lotte hung up and ran back to Milly. She knelt down again and tried to get some response. Nothing. Freddie's wail became a howl. She put her face close to Milly's: 'Oh Milly, oh God, please be all right, Milly, please speak to me, please.' Freddie was howling and screaming upstairs and

Milly was sickeningly silent downstairs. A minute passed. Lotte struggled to breathe properly, not to hyperventilate. She stroked her daughter's brow with the tip of a finger and with her entire being willed her child to be all right. A moment later, Milly opened her eyes. She blinked several times and started to cry.

By the time the immediate-response ambulance arrived, twenty minutes later, Milly was sitting up, whimpering in pain, her arm swollen and distended. Lotte was still in her nightdress and Freddie had whipped himself into a hysterical frenzy in his cot. Lotte opened the door with Milly in her arms; two paramedics came in and she handed her daughter over. Then she ran upstairs, heaved Freddie out of his cot and tried to calm him down. She carried him into the bedroom, pulled on a pair of jeans and a sweater over her nightie, slipped her feet into shoes and hurried back downstairs. She was so upset that she could hardly think straight.

'She's broken her arm,' one of the paramedics said. 'Looks quite nasty. We'd better take her in.' He had wrapped Milly in a blanket and was directing the other paramedic, who had just come back in with a stretcher.

'Yes, yes, of course. I'd better come with you, I'd, erm . . .' Lotte looked up as her neighbour put her head round the door.

'You OK, Lotte? I saw the ambulance and . . .' Mrs Prior was sixty-eight, not a particularly nice neighbour, always criticizing the kids, always moaning at the noise and the fact that the front garden wasn't kept as neat as it should be.

'No, no, I'm not. Madge, could you have Freddie for me? I've got to go in the van with Milly to hospital. She's fallen down the stairs.'

'Oh, I, oh dear, I'm not sure I . . .'

Lotte held out a still wailing Freddie and Mrs Prior simply had to take him.

'I really appreciate it, thank you so much.' Milly was being wheeled out of the house and Lotte was about to follow. 'There's cereal in the cupboard,' she called, 'formula in the fridge, warm it in the microwave. Do anything you like, thanks so much . . .'

As she disappeared out of the house, Mrs Prior came to the door. 'Lotte dear, what time . . .?'

The ambulance door was slammed shut and Lotte was out of earshot.

'Oh well, Freddie, we'd better have some breakfast, hadn't we?' And Freddie, who was in a complete state by now, screamed for Lotte then threw up all down Mrs Prior's front.

It was eleven thirty, and Lotte sat in the A & E reception, with Milly on her lap, waiting for someone to set her daughter's arm. Milly had been X-rayed and examined: she had mild concussion and a break just above the elbow of her right arm, but of course it was Monday, and after the weekend they were rushed off their feet, so Milly, a non-urgent case, had to wait. Lotte was watching Richard and Judy, with the sound turned down; a celebrity chef was doing something terrific with tofu and she let the image on the screen pass before her eyes without it even registering. Then a phone-in came on. Richard and Judy and their resident agony aunt were talking about mistresses and inviting viewers to call in with their experiences. This should be good, Lotte thought, and the woman next to her stood on a chair to turn the volume up. Lotte shifted Milly on her lap to get a better view.

And it was good. It was bloody interesting. Lotte

wondered how the women who rang got themselves into such complicated relationships for the sake of sex and someone to watch the telly with. Was it really love? Lotte wasn't sure she believed in love any more; she thought it was just another name for exploitation.

'Silly cow,' she muttered to a caller from Macclesfield who'd spent five years waiting for a married man to leave his wife. The woman beside her gave her a look and she piped down. The next caller was anonymous, calling on a mobile. Lotte shook her head but resisted making another remark.

'I've been having an affair with a married man for three years,' the caller said. 'It's been a very fulfilling and loving relationship and I think I've provided him with the love and warmth that he doesn't get at home. Recently we've become very close indeed and he's talked of his problems at home and how he's been thinking about leaving . . .' At this point, the caller, who was noticeably upset, stopped, and Richard said: 'Are you all right?'

'Yes, fine,' came the reply. 'I'm just about keeping myself together.'

'May we ask where you're calling from?'

'Glasgow, but I live in London,' came the reply. 'Three years we've been together, I accompany him on all his business trips, we even manage to spend some time together at weekends, and although I've never initiated it, recently he's been saying that he thinks we might have a future together. He's led me to believe that one day we might . . .'

'Ouch!' Lotte was leaning on Milly's head as she strained to hear the programme.

'Sorry, darling.'

'This must be very difficult for you,' said Judy, 'but can you tell us what's happened?'

'This morning,' the caller said, 'this morning, at seven a.m., despite a wonderful night in bed and some very tender moments, he got a call from his wife, who told him that his daughter had had an accident, and he upped and left, just walked out. Within ten minutes he'd gone, without a word of comfort or explanation. All that stuff last night about leaving his wife and about how I mean everything to him was all rubbish, it was just lies. All he said this morning was "I have to go." Nothing else, not another word; he just packed and walked out.'

'I see,' said Judy,

'Do you?' asked the caller. 'I mean nothing to him, I'm just his mistress, to be used whenever it suits him, I . . .'

Lotte didn't hear any more. She snatched Milly off her lap, took a lunge forward to the bin, missed it and was sick all over the floor.

Chapter 2

Charles Meredith, Professor of History at Wessex University (specialist subject – the Victorians), poured himself a coffee from the jug on the hot plate behind Marian, department secretary, and added sugar, two cubes, but no milk. He stirred his drink with an already dirty teaspoon, left it where he'd found it and made his way over to the door, mug in hand.

'You're taking in too much caffeine,' Marian said, still typing.

Charles turned. 'I need it, I've got a tutorial in ten minutes.'

Marian took the audio piece out of her ear and looked at Charles. 'You should change to herbal tea, Charlie, you'll get brown teeth and high cholesterol on that stuff.'

'Right.'

'I mean it, you'll lose your looks and then where would we ladies in the administration team be?'

'Worshipping some other unlikely Adonis, I should think.' He smiled. 'Or maybe you'd just get on with some work, like the rest of us.'

'Ha ha.' Marian put her ear piece back in and continued typing. Charles left the office and made his way down the corridor towards his room. He glanced at his watch: still seven minutes to go and Claire Thompson was there already.

'Afternoon, Claire.' He passed the student – short gelled

7

hair, baggy jeans, vest top, trainers – and went into his office. He didn't ask her in, but closed the door behind him and sat down to drink his coffee. If it had been anyone else he might have suggested they get a coffee from the machine and join him, but not Claire Thompson.

He took out a book, read half a chapter, glanced at his watch again and stood to open the door.

'Oh, Claire? Is it just you?' His tutorials usually consisted of five students, sometimes seven if everyone turned up. 'What's happened to everyone else?'

'Don't know.'

'Hang on.' Charles walked up the corridor to the office. He put his head round the door.

'Marian? Is there something going on that I don't know about? No one's turned up for my tutorial.'

'Flu,' Marian answered, her fingers never leaving the keyboard. 'Everyone's got it. The medical centre is inundated.'

Charles walked back towards his room. 'I'm sorry, Claire, but we'll have to postpone this afternoon. It seems there's a flu epidemic.'

'Oh.'

'We'll rearrange it when everyone is back. I've got your last essay here, I'll give it to you to look over my comments and we can discuss it next week. OK?' He went into his office, lifted the essay off the top of the pile on his desk and handed it over. Claire seemed reluctant to leave. 'I'll see you next week then.'

Eventually she nodded.

'Thanks, Claire.' Charles smiled, then gently closed the door on her. She had been about to say something but he wasn't going to give her the chance. He waited, heard her walk off, then glanced at his watch. It was five past three.

He'd been given a reprieve, half a day free of hormonal youths talking about the Franco-Prussian War, and he wasn't going to waste it here. He stuffed some papers into his case, grabbed his jacket off the back of his chair and left. It wasn't that he didn't like the job, but this afternoon, he couldn't wait to leave.

Charles stopped at the farm shop on the way home and bought venison sausages, some local green beans and a frozen raspberry mouse. He liked to cook, when he had the time; when he didn't, they ate salad, pasta and ready meals from M & S. Mia wasn't a cook, she was more domestic nightmare than goddess, but that had never worried Charles. She was good for him, they had a lot in common. The relationship worked in the way that many relationships work, founded on common interests, comfort more than passion, security and the belief that it is always better to be with someone than alone.

He arrived home at twenty to four and let himself into the house, thinking that he would prepare supper then get on with some work on his book before Mia came home. But he saw her coat over the banister, her shoes kicked off by the bottom of the stairs, and went up to find her. She was asleep in the bedroom, curled up under the duvet with her clothes on, the paracetamol bottle by the side of the bed, an open packet of sanitary towels on the dressing table. Charles bent and kissed the side of her face. It was that time of the month and she suffered with it. Tenderly, he stroked her hair. He loved Mia, or at least he cared for her a great deal. He didn't really know what love was, having never experienced it in its full intensity, and he supposed that this was his lot, a good, stable relationship with a kind, attractive woman. A good lot it was too, he wasn't complaining, never had; but sometimes, like now for instance, he did wonder what it would be like to feel that pull in the guts, that need, that rush of sexual desire that came with real love, the sort of love he was certain existed, if not for the likes of him. He sat on the edge of the bed for a moment and wondered about waking her. She hated to sleep for too long in the middle of the day, it made her feel groggy, worse almost than if she hadn't slept at all, but he didn't have the heart. She looked peaceful, so he left her and went along to the bathroom to wash his hands before he started on supper.

The bathroom was a mess. Charles hated mess. He picked up the dirty clothes off the floor and put them in the laundry basket, then bent to collect up the rubbish that Mia had left under the sink. There was a box, he looked at it: Clear Blue pregnancy test. He sat on the edge of the bath. Mia's diary fell on to the floor and Charles picked it up. In the sink there was another testing kit. An ovulation kit. Charles looked at the diary, then did something totally against his nature: he began to flick through the pages. The only thing that he took in was that in the right-hand corner of six or seven pages of each month was a red dot – this, he supposed, not being entirely thick in the ways of conception, was Mia's fertile period. He held the diary, the ovulation kit and the pregnancy test, which was negative, for several moments, not sure what to do, then he stood, took them into the bedroom and put them on the bed next to the sleeping Mia, and went downstairs to prepare supper, even though he had completely lost his appetite.

He was sweating the onions when Mia appeared in the doorway. He had chopped them, crushed the garlic, peppercorns and juniper berries, peeled the potatoes and celeriac for the mash and prepared the beans in a fug, a haze of anger, hardly conscious of what he was doing. Mia said: 'You've found me out then,' and Charles replied: 'I have no idea why it was a secret.' He didn't look at her.

She came into the kitchen. 'Of course you do, Charles, you'd never agree to trying for a baby, you know that.' Her voice was hot and angry.

'But you went ahead anyway, whether or not I agree.' He looked up. His hair had fallen over his forehead and Mia had the urge to nudge it away for him, in a motherly gesture. 'What were you going to do, present me with a fait accompli? Tell me when you'd gone too far down the line for me to object?'

'God, that's a disgusting comment. Am I hearing this right? By object, do you mean force me to have an abortion?'

'No!' He stopped and looked away. 'I don't know what I mean. I'd never force you to do anything, you know that, Mia, but this, this is underhand and low and it's not worthy of you. You should have told me, I have a right to know.'

'But you'd never agree! You're terrified of the whole subject, I dare not mention it. You are completely baby-phobic. You won't discuss it, even think about it, you go deaf when any kind of talk of children comes up. Tell me, Charles, tell me how I should have mentioned it? What should I have done, pinned you to the floor and shouted in your ear?'

'You could have talked to me, quietly, reasonably, instead of going behind my back, testing, planning, orchestrating sex, presumably on your fertile days so that you might conceive. Can't you see how awful that is? It's like loving me under false pretences, it's . . . it's deceit, plain and simple. You've been deceiving me, and from the look of your diary it's gone on for quite some time.'

11

Mia crossed the room. 'This is ridiculous, Charles, you're making a big deal out of nothing. I was not deceiving you, I was merely helping nature along.'

'Rubbish!' Charles dropped the spoon into the saucepan and walked out of the room.

Mia followed him. 'You don't see it, do you, you don't see how desperate I must be for a baby,' she said, 'how difficult it is to communicate that to you. All you can see is your own view: I was going behind your back, so I'm in the wrong. Christ, you can be so bloody self-righteous, Charles.'

'But you still want me to father your baby.' Charles sat on the edge of the sofa. His look challenged her.

'That's unfair.'

'Is it?'

'God, what is wrong with you? I'm thirty-eight years old and time is running out for me. You are thirty-nine. What have you got against having kids? We're together, aren't we? We're happy, stable, we have a future. So what's so wrong with wanting a family in that future?' Mia stopped. Her chest was heaving with the clot of emotion that lay inside it, heavy and desperate. 'Or don't you see a future? Is that it? That you don't see a future with me?'

Charles stared down at his hands. He could hardly bear to look at her. 'I don't know,' he said quietly.

She stared at him, aghast. 'You don't know?' She shook her head. 'After two years, a mortgage, a life together, and you don't know?' She turned away. Her hands trembled and she clasped them together, supporting herself.

'Mia, look, I'm shocked, confused, that's all. Please, you're upset, we're both upset, we don't have to talk about this now.'

She spun round. 'Yes we do! We've spent far too long dodging it!'

'Now isn't the right time.'

'Then when *is* the right time?' she cried.

Once again he couldn't look at her.

A sob caught in the back of her throat, and she put her hand up to her mouth to stifle it. Charles moved towards her. 'Don't!' she cried. 'Don't come near me, just get out of here, leave me alone and get out, go on, go!' She turned and walked out of the sitting room.

Charles sat where he was. He heard her in the kitchen running the tap, splashing her face with icy water, he guessed, trying to numb the pain. He looked at his hands again. So many questions he couldn't answer. Did he see a future with Mia, did he want children with her, or at all? He rose and went upstairs. He didn't know, that was the truth; he thought he loved her, but he yearned for something more, only he had no idea what that something more was. He stood in their bedroom and thought about packing a bag, but he was drained, the emotion had exhausted him, and he couldn't be bothered. So instead he walked back downstairs, put his coat on and left the house.

In his car, he sat for ages, just looking out of the window at the street, taking nothing in. Then he started the engine and drove. He was headed for London; he'd stay with Rob, his brother, get away for a night, give himself some time to think, some time to find some answers. He dialled Rob's mobile and glanced at his watch.

'Rob, it's me.'

Rob was at home, flinging shirts into a suit bag. He packed badly, always had someone press everything for him when he arrived at his destination. 'Charlie, hi. How are you?'

'Not good. Can I come and stay tonight?'

'Sure. I'm not here, I'm leaving for the States in about

13

fifteen minutes, but I'll leave the keys with the doorman, you can pick them up from him. What's up?'

'It's too complicated to explain.'

Rob stopped his packing in the bedroom of number 9, Nelson House, Dolphin Square, and sat on the bed. 'You sound crappy, mate. You sure you don't want to talk about it?'

Charles smiled. 'Thanks, Rob, but no. Anyway, you'd miss your flight.'

'Right. Well, there's clean sheets in the cupboard, cold beer in the fridge.'

'Thanks.'

'I'll call you when I get back, OK?'

'Yeah, sure. Bye.' Charles disconnected. For a moment he envied Rob his executive bachelor lifestyle, jetting off to New York, sleeping where and with whom he wanted. The money, the freedom, a life where he didn't have to think too hard or for too long about anything. Then he shook his head, pulled on to the A27 and put his foot down to London.

Claire Thompson finished writing in her diary and closed it, almost ceremoniously, tying the ribbon she bound it with into a bow, sliding it into the top drawer of her desk and locking it safely away. She stood up and went to the window, looking down at the group of people gathered by the entrance to the hall of residence. They were laughing, mucking around, secure in their numbers. Up here, in her room, she was alone. She opened the window and felt a rush of pleasure as the cold air hit her face, but their voices upset her so she shut it again immediately. She sat down on the bed. She looked at her hands, picked at her finger-nails, felt depressed. The fact was that Claire Thompson found life a struggle. It didn't fit her, this life, or any other life really. She was apart, alone, she didn't mix well, had few friends, none actually, not close ones. She was a loner, that was what they called her, too involved in her dreams and the private world of her fertile imagination to have much of a grip on reality.

Claire leant forward and reached under the bed for the bottle of vodka she kept there. She stood, took a mug from the desk and poured herself a big measure of clear, tasteless liquid. She took a gulp and slipped a CD into the machine. Marianne Faithfull, not light pop, something low and complex. Lying on the bed, she stared at the ceiling and let her mind drift. She had some decent Moroccan black in her drawer but she would save that until later. There was a party on her floor tonight to which she hadn't been invited, so she'd put on her headphones and get stoned, have her own private wild time. She smiled and closed her eyes. The music enveloped her and the vodka worked its magic.

Charles arrived in Pimlico and drove around the block several times, looking for a parking space reasonably near to Rob's flat. He found one, eventually, and parked up, but when he got to Dolphin Square he saw the garage with twenty-four-hour parking and cursed himself; he'd thought it closed at six. He almost went back for the car, but couldn't be bothered. Besides, he was saving himself ten quid, and it did seem pointless to walk back three streets and re-do the whole procedure, this time having to pay for it. He left the car where it was and went in to collect the keys from the doorman.

Rob's flat was OK, nothing special, a man-about-town's flat, somewhere to kip, to relax in, not for entertaining –

Rob always took people out. It was comfortable, but not fashionable; it wasn't a converted loft space, that was for sure. Charles walked round it, the kitchen, the bedroom, the small functional bathroom, and settled in the sitting area with a bottle of cold beer from the fridge. He reached for the remote, turned the TV on and channel-hopped for a while, not interested in anything he saw. He stood up again and did another tour of the flat. Odd, he thought, how few possessions Rob had, how little real comfort there was here. There were no photographs, just a framed montage in the kitchen that Charles had given him last year of their skiing trip together with Mia. There were few pictures, only a couple of decent paintings, but they hardly filled the walls. There were no cushions, no curtains, just two roller blinds; certainly no ornaments or collectibles. There were a great deal of books, though, and a huge number of CDs, the only things that gave any indication of Rob's personality. Without these, the flat could have belonged to anyone.

Charles came back to the sofa. He wondered how much of himself there was in his own house, how much there was of Mia. He didn't really think there was a great deal of either of them. It was a comfortable home, but when he analysed it, it lacked something, it lacked permanence. He finished his beer, then opened another one, standing in the kitchen to drink it. Why, he wondered did his life contain so little passion, so little commitment to the future? If this flat was anything to go by, then Rob's life was the same. They'd had a very happy childhood, growing up in a house that was passionate about many things: music, art, literature. His parents loved each other, had argued, fought, kissed and made up in front of the children. Or maybe that was it: maybe subconsciously Charles realized that he could never match what his parents had, the life he'd grown up with, so he'd never even bothered trying.

He finished his second bottle of beer and gave up thinking; it was doing his head in. He picked up the keys to the flat and went out. There was a bar up the road that Rob had taken him to several times, five minutes' walk away, and despite the fact that he hated bars and hated drinking alone, he felt the need to get hammered. Swiftly, he made his way towards this, went in and ordered himself a large measure of Scotch over ice.

Claire had finished the bottle of vodka by the time the party, two rooms down from her, got under way. Admittedly it had only been a quarter full, but she wasn't a big girl and alcohol affected her badly. She rolled herself a joint, not too heavy, just enough to mellow out a bit, but used her last match to heat the dope and realized that she would have to go along to the kitchen to see if she could borrow some matches to light it. She slipped the joint into the drawer and made her way along towards the noise and hubbub of the party.

The communal kitchen, as is always the case at parties, was full. Claire squeezed herself into a space and poured herself a glass of cheap plonk. She turned, spotted someone she knew and said: 'Jen, lend me a box of matches, will you? I've run out.' She was hoping it sounded cool, off-hand and casual, but when Jen, deep in conversation with a young man with a shaved head, turned in surprise, Claire knew she'd got it wrong. 'If you've got any, that is, that you can spare, I mean.'

Jen nodded. 'Here.' She handed Claire a packet of Marlboro lights, tucked inside which was a slim packet of matches from some restaurant or other. Claire took the matches and returned the cigarettes.

'Thanks.'

'Sure.' Jen looked at her. 'Enjoying yourself?'

'I only came for the matches, I can't stop.'

'Oh?'

Claire flushed. 'Yes, I've got a date with Charles, I mean Professor Meredith. We're going into town for a drink and, erm . . . some supper.'

Jen stared at Claire, but Claire knew she was looking right through her. She smiled, drank her wine down in one and was about to leave when Jen caught her arm. 'Claire,' she said. 'Don't bullshit me. I'm not stupid, you know, and nor is anyone else. Get real, Claire, get a life.' She dropped Claire's arm and turned back into the throng of people.

Claire put her hands up to her face and hurried through the crush. Back in her own room, she slammed the door and immediately lit her joint, taking a long, deep pull, holding the dope-filled smoke in her lungs for as long as she could. She felt instantly better, calmer; her head was light, the room had lost its hardness. 'I am going out with Professor Meredith,' she said, 'I'm going out for a drink with him.' She took another drag of the joint, a third, then turned and carefully knocked the end of it into the ashtray and put it out. She picked up her bag, pulled her coat on and left the room, not even thinking to lock the door behind her. She was stoned when she made her way down the stairs and out into the cold night air. She was stoned, drunk and retreating fast into another world, a far nicer one than this, a world she had invented all for herself.

Charles too was drunk. He knew it; by the third double Scotch he had that fishbowl view of the world, that nice, comfortable, insulated view that blotted out the things he didn't like and elevated the things that he did to unlikely heights. He saw a woman across the bar, an attractive woman, late twenties, maybe early thirties, and as the bar was almost empty and the barman wasn't in the least bit interested in listening to him talk about the book he was planning to write, Charles walked across and sat down next to her, offering to buy her a drink.

She looked at him for quite some time, as if trying to make up her mind, and finally said, 'I'd love a margarita, but without the salt, because I've had three already and the salt has made my mouth go all bumpy.' At this point she gently lowered her bottom lip and put her finger on the soft pink flesh of the inside of her mouth. 'See, here,' she said, and Charles only just managed not to raise his own finger to the tiny ridges in her mouth.

'It's OK,' he said, 'I'll take your word for it.'

'Will you? Take the word of a complete stranger? How trusting you are.' She leant towards him and looked right into his eyes. Hers were the oddest brown colour, with flecks of blue, and very slightly slanted. 'I am very trusting too, you know, too trusting in fact, but that's a long story and one that I don't wish to tell you.' Then she burped and laughed at her rudeness. 'Please forgive me, I don't usually drink,' she said. 'No, that's a lie, I do usually drink, I don't usually burp when I drink.' She was drunk, possibly more so than Charles. 'I'm far too polite. Polite and trusting and, well . . .' She stopped mid sentence and stared down at her hands. She looked suddenly vulnerable and Charles wanted to take her hand in his. 'I'm too nice, wouldn't say boo to a goose. I get walked all over . . .' She looked at him and shrugged. 'I might say fuck off to a duck, though,' she giggled, thinking herself awfully funny. 'But probably not, I don't say fuck off, perhaps that's my problem, perhaps

19

I should.' She *was* funny, Charles thought, funny and vulnerable and ridiculously exciting. He was drunk, he had to be.

The barman came across and Charles ordered the drinks: one Scotch, single measure this time, and a margarita without the salt. The woman had her elbow on the bar, propping up her chin.

'Are you nice too, Mr . . .'

'Professor.'

'Mr Professor. That's a nice name, sounds very important. You can call me Mrs Teacher. There, we match.' Her elbow slipped off the bar and she toppled precariously for a few moments on the stool. Charles thought he was going to have to catch her and leant forward ready, but she managed to right herself and laughed. 'Oh dear,' she said, 'I think I might be pissed.'

The drinks arrived and Charles handed her the cocktail glass. 'So am I,' he said. 'I'm drowning my sorrows.' The woman put out a hand and touched his fingers, very gently, with her own. She was wearing a pale grey sleeveless dress, fitted, Jackie O style, and her arms were long and slim, the perfect length and shape. She smelled of amber and jasmine, rose and sandalwood, like an Indian garden. 'Oh,' she said softly, 'how could someone as beautiful as you ever have sorrows?' Then she laughed. 'Of course I mean that in a purely aesthetic sense.'

'Of course,' Charles said, and for the first time in his life he felt a shift in the ground under him, a tremor, a sudden piercing of desire so strong that it took his breath away. He took her fingers in his own and said: 'You are the most extraordinary woman I have ever met.'

'And you,' she replied, 'by your own admission, are drunk.' She swallowed down her margarita in two large gulps and almost dropped the glass on to the bar. 'One more,' she said, 'for the road.'

'The road?'

'To oblivion.'

Charles called the barman over and ordered another drink. The situation was unreal; he felt unnerved, excited by it. He said: 'So we're both drinking to forget. How sad.' And she replied: 'Is it? I think it's rather sensible actually. Why keep all sorts of crap in your head when you can obliterate it with large quantities of alcohol.' She smiled, but it wasn't sincere, it was a smile that covered the cracks. 'And I have lots of crap that needs blasting, believe me; I have years' worth of it.'

Claire Thompson walked the back way into town, past the station, through the narrow dark streets, on her own, not focusing properly, not in control of her senses. Twice she crossed the road without looking and narrowly missed being run over by a car; once she fell off the pavement and twisted her ankle. She hadn't smoked very much Moroccan black but it was enough. Her state of mind was somewhere between carelessness and paranoia. She didn't really know what was going on.

When she reached town she walked on past the usual student haunts – the pub, the wine bar – and made her way right down the high street, watching the lights reflected in the windows. She kept on walking, not thinking about where she was going, not conscious of very much outside her head. She walked for five miles and eventually found herself in a part of the city she didn't recognize. It was half industrial, run down, dark and deserted. She stopped, trying for a few moments to orientate herself; she had no idea where she was. There was a pub at the end of the street, a grim-looking, shabby place, but she made her way to it and went in, a stale smell hitting her hard in the face. She ordered a double vodka and took it to a corner. She sat, lit up a cigarette and put her head back on the stained, worn velvet seat.

'You on your own?'

She opened her eyes; the lids were heavy, she was barely able to lift them. A man in a grubby sweater stood over her, too close. She could smell him.

'Can I buy you a drink?'

She shook her head.

'Sure? A nice girl like you shouldn't drink alone, you know.'

Claire focused on the man. 'Piss off,' she said quietly. He blinked several times, stood where he was for a few seconds more, then wandered off. She saw him go through to the other side of the bar and picked up her drink. She closed her eyes again and sipped. The vodka was ice cold in her mouth, burning hot inside, and she savoured the contradiction. She was alone, anonymous and stoned. She felt OK, more relaxed than she had done for ages. Of course she wasn't going to meet Professor Meredith, not really, but it was good to pretend. It was always good to pretend, especially about Professor Meredith. Some lines popped into Claire's head and she whispered them under her breath:

'Life may change, but it may fly not:
Hope may vanish, but can die not:
Truth be veiled, but still it burneth;
Love repulsed, but it returneth.'

It was closing time, and Charles helped the woman off her stool, holding on to her arm while she searched on the

22

floor under the bar for her pashmina. She was very unsteady on her feet, feet slipped neatly into kitten-heeled strappy sandals that did up round her ankles, feet that Charles had the sudden urge to unwrap, slowly and carefully. She wobbled a bit as she straightened and knocked several glasses over on the bar with a back-lash of cashmere as she threw her pashmina over her shoulders.

'Oh God, sorry . . .'

Charles righted the glasses and bent to retrieve her handbag. He didn't think she'd stay standing if she bent down a second time. 'Come on, let me put you in a taxi and send you home,' he said as he gently propelled her out of the bar.

'What a good idea,' she said. 'Might be a bit expensive, though.' She exploded into laughter at this as they came out on to the pavement, and Charles stood and looked at her. There was something ferociously attractive about her, the combination of irreverence, vulnerability and humour. She pushed her hair back off her forehead and stopped laughing as suddenly as she'd started. 'Why are you looking at me?' she asked.

'Because you deserve to be looked at, you're a very lovely woman.'

She shook her head. 'I am too drunk for charm, I will fall for it all, every word of it.' She turned away from him and looked up the road. 'I must get a taxi,' she declared, slurring her words. 'I will stand in the road until one comes . . .' Stepping forward off the pavement, arm out, she misjudged the height of the kerb, and Charles, in what he later thought was a rather heroic lunge forward, caught her just as she toppled. So she fell, as in all great romances, literally into his arms. 'Oh shit, sorry, I . . .' He didn't give her a chance to finish. He put his mouth on hers, first just

23

to see what it felt like, and then, after a momentary jolt that went though his entire body, to kiss her. He kissed her and she kissed him back. They stood like that, on the kerb, oblivious to the passing cars and the light drizzle that had started to fall, in the sort of screen kiss that even Richard Curtis would have been proud of, before Charles broke off and said: 'Come home with me?' She nodded. 'We can walk, it's Dolphin Square.'

She opened her eyes. 'How bizarre!'

'What is?'

She smiled and put her hands either side of his face, bringing his mouth down on to hers again. 'Nothing,' she whispered. 'Don't talk . . .'

They walked the three blocks to Dolphin Square, stopping every now and then, locked together in a kiss. They continued the kiss as they entered the building and made their way along to Rob's front door, where Charles leant her back against the wall and felt the shape of her wonderful body against his. He dug in his pocket, found the key and unlocked the door without moving his mouth off hers, something he had never done before and was sure he would never do again. Inside, in the hall, he lifted her legs, wrapped them round his waist and carried her into the bedroom. He laid her on the bed, moved over her and lowered his body on to hers.

The phone rang.

They stopped kissing for the first time in almost twenty minutes, both breathing hard, and waited for the trilling to cease. After six rings the answer phone came on, and Rob's voice filled the small flat.

'Charlie, it's me. I'm sorry to call so late, but can you do me a favour, mate? I need some information off my PC for the presentation that I'm working on, thirty-five thousand feet in the air and halfway across the bloody Atlantic. I didn't think I'd need it, but it would appear that I do, so if you're there can you pick up, and if you're not can you give me a ring back on the mobile when you get in? Thanks, mate, we'll speak soon . . .'

Charles sat up and grabbed the phone. 'Rob, hi. I'm in the bedroom, is this stuff urgent? Oh God, OK, I'll just go into the sitting room and you can talk me through what I have to do. No, no, it's fine, I was asleep, that's all. Hang on.'

He stood and looked down at the woman. She really was exquisite. 'I'm sorry. I won't be long.' She shrugged, smiled sleepily and blew him a kiss as he walked into the sitting room. There he picked up the phone and carried on his conversation with his brother.

Twenty minutes later, he exited Rob's system, hung up and took a deep breath, then made his way back to the bedroom. 'Sorry about that,' he said, 'I couldn't get out of it, I . . .' He looked down at the woman on the bed, who was curled into the foetal position, fast asleep fully clothed, her pashmina wrapped round her.

'I hope you didn't mind,' he said lamely. He sighed, reached out to stroke her hair, and then, drunk and exhausted himself, lay down next to her and passed out.

By closing time Claire had drunk two more double vodkas. She heard last orders and wondered about another, but she was drunk enough, so got unsteadily to her feet. She couldn't find her scarf – it had slipped down under the seat and she didn't bother to try and look for it; she was in no fit state to do so. She made her way over to the door. The barman said nothing as she slipped out of the pub, and no one else saw her leave. On the pavement, in the fresh air, she suddenly felt very confused. What was she doing here? Where the hell was she? She thought about going back inside the pub and calling for a taxi, but her mind wasn't working with any logic or sense and the idea evaporated the instant it came into her head. She fastened her coat and began to walk.

Halfway up the road, a car pulled alongside her and Claire stopped. She leant forward as a window was wound down and spoke to the man inside. She recognized him but couldn't think how.

'D'you need a lift?' he asked.

She nodded; it was a long walk back.

'Where to?'

'The university.' It was an effort to get the words out clearly.

'Hop in.'

Claire opened the car door and sank into the seat. Her feet knocked against something and she kicked it aside.

'Careful, you'll break the bulb.'

Claire bent and picked up a powerful flashlight. 'Sorry,' she mumbled, letting it rest on her lap. She put her head back against the seat and closed her eyes. The car moved off. Moments later it had turned the corner and was gone. There was no witness at all to the disappearance of the eighteen-year-old history student; no one even knew she had gone.

Chapter 3

Charles woke at five a.m. with a raging thirst. He opened his eyes, rolled over on to his back and stared at the ceiling, momentarily confused. In a matter of seconds, his brain made all the right connections, his thought process followed a logical pattern, and holding his breath, he swivelled his eyes to the right to see the woman he had slept next to. She wasn't there. Charles sat up. He looked at the bed, saw the dent in the pillow, the crumpled cover, then he stood, felt nauseous and sank back on to the bed again.

'Hello? Are you in the bathroom?' he called feebly. There was no answer. He eased himself gradually on to his feet again, one hand on his throbbing head, the other holding the table for support.

'Hello?' He made his way to the bathroom, expecting at any moment to bump into the woman, then to the kitchen and finally the sitting room. There was no sign of her. He sat down on the sofa, rubbed his hands over his face and said: 'Shit.' He was both relieved and disappointed. Relieved because he'd made a mistake but had been saved from making a much bigger one. He was in a committed relationship and he'd almost, very nearly, let both himself and Mia down. He hadn't, but it was a close-run thing. Charles was a man who believed in trust, in doing what was right, and getting involved with another woman while in a relationship was not, in his book, right. But he was disappointed too, disappointed because he had to admit to himself that despite the throbbing head, the shakes, the mouth like a monkey's ass, he felt an incredible sexual pull when he thought about the woman. She was in his head, the smell of her was on his skin, and when he closed his eyes he could taste the sour sweetness of tequila and lime with an edge of salt. 'Shit,' he said again, because now he wanted something that he had never before really been sure existed. He wanted to feel again what he felt last night, and that thought made him shrivel inside with dread, because it meant that he no longer wanted Mia, and that he just wasn't ready to face it.

Half an hour later, Charles was back in his car, having made a note of the name of the bar he'd been to last night. He would ring them when he got home and try and trace the woman. He convinced himself that it was the polite thing to do, to check that she had got home all right, had come to no harm, and then he would have nothing more to do with her. He drove the A27 fast and not very well. He felt lousy, hadn't bothered to shower at Rob's or even make a coffee. He'd simply straightened the bed covers and left, making sure there was no trace of his guest. He wanted to get home, he wanted a hot bath in his own house and a cup of steaming Colombian coffee, he wanted to normalize things, to pretend that yesterday hadn't happened. And yet every one of his senses told him that it had; he remembered the kiss with every nerve in his body. It had happened and he was going to have to lie to Mia, something he had never done before, but something that couldn't be avoided, because the truth was no good. The truth, Charles thought, wasn't what either of them wanted to hear.

Claire woke with a start. The first thought that registered

was pain, the second was panic. It was dark, she was cold, freezing cold, and her hands were bound together in front of her. She felt the air inside her chest constrict as if someone had also bound her body in a tight corset, and she had to make a conscious effort to breathe in and out. She started to cry. She was in a small space, her body forced into the foetal position, and her limbs ached with cramp. 'Help,' she called out, over and over. 'Someone, help me, please!' But the effort of shouting exhausted her and she was using up the air in the confined space. Her cries fell to whimpers. She was alone, trapped and frightened. No one heard her.

Cat Collins climbed out of bed at five thirty and pulled on her tracksuit top and bottoms. She found a pair of socks at the end of the bed and bent to put them on.

'You all right, love?' Jeff Collins rolled over and looked at his wife for a few moments of consciousness.

'Just off. See you later.'

He drifted back to sleep and Cat left the bedroom and went to check on the kids, two girls, Hayley aged five and Kylie, seven. Downstairs she found her trainers, yanked a fleece over her head and left the house. It was a twenty-minute walk to work and she moved at a brisk pace. At the pub she let herself in, then locked the door behind her; you couldn't be too sure in this area. She took her cleaning basket from under the bar, put her overall on and started on the tables. It was a daily routine: tables first, then bar, then windows; hoover the seats with the attachment and finally hoover the floor. She was thorough and quick and she was usually home by eight fifteen to get the girls break-fast and take them to school.

At the table in the far corner, Cat bent to retrieve someone's scarf off the floor. She looked at it – silk velvet, very nice – and turned it over in her hands. There was a name tape on it, like the ones she put on the girls' school uniforms. It belonged to a Claire Thompson. She wondered briefly how likely it was that this Claire Thompson would come back to the pub for her scarf, and reckoned on not very. She rubbed the wonderful fluid fabric between her fingers and then held it against her cheek. It was a fabulous colour, a deep red, burgundy she would have called it. She folded the scarf and neatly tucked it into the pocket of her overall. 'Finders keepers,' she murmured, and that was the last thought she gave it. The scarf went home with Cat at eight o'clock that morning, and very nice too it looked with her overcoat for the school run.

Charles pulled up in front of the house he shared with Mia just after eight. He could see a light on in the bedroom and knew that Mia was up. That made him feel worse. He parked, went in and straight upstairs. She was sitting up in bed, the lamp on, her face haggard from lack of sleep and tears.

'Where the hell have you been?' she demanded. 'I've been worried sick.'

'At Rob's,' Charles replied. 'I went out, got hammered and crashed out about eleven thirty. I'm sorry, I should have called.'

Mia nodded and turned her face away. Tears streamed down her cheeks and Charles, wretched, sick with remorse, sat down on the bed, pulled her towards him and held her tightly. 'I'm sorry, Mia,' he said quietly. 'I'm sorry we argued and I'm sorry I was so angry with you. Please, let's forget it, let's put it behind us and get on with our lives.' He eased back and gently turned her face to his. 'Hmm? Can we?' Again she nodded, and he held her once more, burying his face in her hair and kissing her soft neck. Comforting her calmed his troubled conscience and he felt better. 'Oh, Mia,' he whispered, 'why did we do it?' But it was a question that he didn't want an answer to, and nor, in her heart, did Mia.

Chapter 4

It was Thursday morning, early, and Lotte sat at the kitchen table with her friend Liz, who had called in unannounced just to see if she was all right. The last time they had spoken, Monday night, Lotte had been almost hysterical and Liz had been worried sick. Of course she'd seen it coming, hadn't they all? Gordon was a first-class prick, but it was always the wife who was the last to know.

Liz had never understood why Lotte had married him in the first place. Darling Lotte, clever, chaotic, creative Lotte, who seemed to do everything her own eccentric way and would never be told, going out with, and then engaged to, the egocentric, boorish Gordon, much older than her, wealthy of course, but not rich enough to excuse his terrible behaviour. Then married, always doing and caring, never being done for or cared about. Always being told.

Lotte had changed over the six years of her marriage to Gordon. She had become less apparently Lotte; her originality hadn't dimmed, but had shifted, gone underground almost. Liz still saw glimpses of it, but it was well covered now.

'So,' Liz began, 'have you heard from him since Monday?' Lotte shook her head. 'Bloody hell!' Liz exploded. 'How can you be so accepting? I'd have cut his bloody dick off by now!' And she would have done too.

Liz was the first person Lotte had called from the hospital

on Monday morning and she'd told Lotte to telephone the hotel in Glasgow and ask for Gordon's room. This Lotte had done, and got some woman on the line. The same woman? Obviously, Liz had told her, without a doubt. Confront the bastard, tell him you want it finished or he's out. But Lotte hadn't. She'd let Gordon berate her for being irresponsible and not getting up with the children; she'd let him criticize the way she cared for them and reminded her, graphically, of all the dangers that a careless mother exposes her children to. Then he'd called the airline and booked himself a ticket back to Glasgow that evening. 'You don't need me here,' he'd told Lotte. 'Milly is fine, it's only a broken arm, and I have to earn us a living.' He'd gone by six and Lotte had called Liz again, distraught to the point of hysteria.

'So what are you going to do? Monday you were inconsolable, now you seem oddly calm. Are you going to ignore it?' Liz couldn't keep the note of anger out of her voice, but it wasn't necessarily aimed at Lotte. There is nothing worse than seeing your friends badly treated and knowing you are unable to help. 'Are you going to just get on with things and pretend that it didn't happen?' Lotte didn't answer. 'The man is having an affair, for God's sake, Lotte, he's been doing it behind your back for, how long did she say? Three years?'

Lotte stared at the oiled tablecloth and traced one of the flowers in the pattern with her fingertip. 'Yes, three years,' she murmured.

'So?' Liz felt like jumping up from her chair and shaking her friend, her dearest and oldest friend, but a friend too much trodden on to be able to get up and fight back.

'So,' Lotte said, looking up at Liz, who had a glint of steel in her eyes that sometimes frightened Lotte despite her good intentions. 'I am going to ask him for a divorce once I have established who this woman is and where she lives. I need to name the co-respondent and so far all I know her as is Anonymous from Glasgow.'

Liz couldn't help smiling – this was the old Lotte talking. Lotte smiled back.

'When Gordon comes home tomorrow,' she went on, 'I'm going to check through his briefcase, see if I can find any reference to her and then contact a solicitor. I want a divorce, but not a long-running, messy, acrimonious one.'

'I didn't know there were any other ones,' Liz said. She narrowed her eyes. 'You sound very calm, Lotte, very reason-able. What's happened since Monday to turn you from hysterical housewife into cool divorcee?'

Lotte stood and picked up the coffee pot. 'D'you want more coffee?' she asked.

'Yes please.' Liz watched her friend, saw how she was studiously avoiding her eye. 'Lotte? How can you have changed so much in two days?'

Lotte turned. 'I've finally realized what I should have worked out years ago. This man has done me more harm than good, he has put me down, demoralized me, used me, and his affair is my escape route. I took some time out this week, got one of our more responsible baby-sitters to look after the children and had a few hours to myself. I did quite a bit of thinking and it's marked out the only clear path for me to take.'

'Alleluia.'

Lotte looked down at the ground and a blush spread over her face. 'Besides, I met someone else.' Liz started so violently that she almost fell off her chair. She stared at Lotte speechless for several moments, all the time thinking, of course she's met someone else, she's beautiful, why wouldn't she meet someone else? But finally, when she did manage to speak, all she could utter was: 'I don't believe it!'

'Nor do I really. It's not a relationship or anything like that, it's more of a . . .' Lotte searched for the right explanation. 'More of a reassurance that I am still who I always was, before I met Gordon, I mean. It's an assertion of my power as a woman, an attractive woman, a woman who's still desirable.'

'It's a good fuck, plain and simple, by a man who thinks you're gorgeous,' Liz said.

Lotte burst out laughing. 'Not quite, Lizzie, but it's very flattering that you think I've still got that sort of pull.'

'At least he's put a smile back on your face.' Liz stood and emptied the dregs of her coffee into the sink while Lotte made another pot. 'So who is he? Anyone I know?'

'No, and I shouldn't think I'll see him again.'

'No?'

Lotte filled the cafetière and came back to the table. 'No.' She looked at Liz's face. 'And there's no need to look like that! He's given me confidence, that's all.'

'It's enough,' Liz said, reaching across the table to give Lotte's hand a squeeze. 'For the moment, anyway, it's enough.'

Detective Inspector Annie Taylor reversed out of the drive in her red convertible Mazda MX5 and swung the car back and round to the right to let the removals van behind her park in the drive of her new house. It was a small, pristine cottage-style semi on the brand-new Belle View development, and she had the keys in her handbag. As she climbed out of the car, the driver of the van gave her the thumbs-up and drove forward, parking the van as close to the house as he could get it.

'All right, love?' he said, jumping down from the cab. 'It's a fair old drive from London. You must have been shifting it a bit.'

Annie had arrived at the house an hour earlier than the van, even though they'd set off from Croydon at exactly the same time. 'The speed limit and no more,' she replied.

'Yeah, right.' The driver went round to the back of the van and Annie looked up at the house. It wasn't really her style, but hopefully it wasn't permanent either: a year, maybe two, then a quick resale for a good profit and on to the next promotion. She dug in her bag for the keys to let the removals men in.

'Where d'you want this, love?' the driver's mate asked. Annie turned from opening the front door. 'Sitting room, please.' She walked into the little house, which smelled of fresh paint and newly fitted carpet. She didn't really want to be here, in a boxy little house, on a nondescript housing estate, too close to her mother for comfort, but she was ambitious and she knew the route to success was littered with empty tea chests.

She moved out of the way as two pairs of heavy-duty boots trod over her carpet, wishing she'd remembered to put something down to protect it, and watched as the men carried the sofa into the small open-plan living area. They dumped it in the middle of the room and left Annie staring at it. She had never been a great home-maker; she tended to live in a rather haphazard way, preferring a takeaway curry and a video on nights off to knitting or needlepoint and a home-cooked casserole. She wondered if she should move the sofa, rearrange it, try it in different parts of the room, but decided against it. She shoved it into the nearest space, against the wall, and that was where it would stay, providing it was opposite the telly point.

'Books?' the removals man shouted out.

'In here,' Annie called back. He came in with a box, dropped it on the floor and shifted it against the wall.

'We're just delivering and you're unpacking, aren't you, love?'

'Eventually,' Annie said. She looked at the box and wondered how long she could leave it before her mother came round and forced her to put some shelves up to house its contents. Two months, maybe three. 'All the books in here,' she said, 'and everything else as marked.'

'Okey-doke.'

'Would you like a cup of tea?' She felt she had to ask.

'Love one. Two sugars for me, none for him.'

'Right.' Annie went into the kitchen, looked around and realized that of course she didn't have a kettle, tea bags, milk or sugar. 'Tea's off, I'm afraid,' she called out. She opened the fridge and checked in all the cupboards, with no idea what she was looking for – a leftover from the builders, perhaps – then went back into the sitting room. 'I'll get us a couple of cans from the corner shop. Any preference?'

'I'll have a Coke, he'll have a Tango. Awright, Billy? Tango?'

'Cheers, mate.'

'Right. Won't be long.' Annie glanced at the growing pile of boxes accumulating in the sitting room, felt eminently depressed and left the house. There was no thrill for her at the thought of her own little home, no feeling of belonging. To be honest, she'd have been just as happy in rented. She pressed the alarm pad for the MX and three sharp bleeps rang out, almost in greeting. She climbed in and started the engine. If she was really honest, it was a relief to get away.

*   *   *

Charles Meredith opened the door of his room at the university and let in the four students who had been waiting outside. They shuffled around and seated themselves, his immaculate study suddenly a muddle of bags, coats and gangly post-pubescent bodies that didn't seem to fit anywhere with ease. He stepped over a pair of large trainers on the end of long, thin legs encased in faded khaki combats and sat down at his desk.

'No Claire Thompson today?'

The tutorial group looked at each other.

'Anyone know where she is? She hasn't sent an apology.'

'Haven't seen her since Monday,' one of the girls said. 'She might have gone home.'

Charles looked at them; they were uncomfortable talking about someone he guessed they didn't like. 'Did she say anything about that? Amanda, you have three tutorials a week with Claire, don't you? Did she tell you she was going home?'

'No, but she . . .' Amanda stopped short and Charles raised an eyebrow.

'She what?'

'She doesn't talk much.'

'She's a bit of a loner, Professor Meredith, she doesn't join in much. Keeps to herself,' one of the boys filled in.

'Right.' Charles opened the file on his desk and looked over the work in it. 'Well, maybe one of you might just see if she's all right on your way back to hall this afternoon. OK?' There was a murmur of assent. 'So,' he began, 'essays . . .' And he started on the pile in front of him, a rather sorry lot of attempts, in his opinion, at a discussion of the Married Women's Property Acts.

At lunchtime Charles left the campus and went into town to Mia's office. There had been a silence in the house for the past two days; it wasn't a deliberate not speaking, more a sense of having nothing to say. They needed to talk, there were issues to address, but in the evenings Charles worked on his book and during the day Mia worked office hours. How could two people who lived together find so little time to talk? he wondered, climbing the stairs to her office. He knocked on the glass panel of the door and went in.

'Hi, Julie, is Mia in? I thought I'd surprise her for lunch.'

'Hello, Charles, she's with a client but she won't be long.' She went to stand up. 'Can I get you a coffee?'

'No thanks, Julie, you carry on.' Charles picked up a copy of *Country Life* and sat down on a chair to flick through it. A whole different life, he thought, glancing at the houses. At last Mia came out of her office, following her client. She saw Charles but said nothing, finishing off her business before she acknowledged him. When the client had left, Charles said: 'D'you fancy lunch? I've booked a table at the wine bar. Can you manage an hour?'

Mia turned to Julie. 'What time are the Perkinses coming in, Jules?'

'Three.'

'Then I can manage an hour,' she said to Charles. 'I'll get my coat.'

In the wine bar they took their usual table by the window and Charles ordered a bottle of wine. It was a place they used often. He looked at Mia while they waited for the wine to arrive but she didn't look back at him. She was avoiding his gaze.

'Mia?'

She picked a matchbook out of the ashtray and fiddled with it, flipping it open and shut.

Charles leaned forward across the table. 'Mia, look at me,'

he said. She faced him. 'We have to talk, you know, we can't go on in this way.'

'I wasn't aware that we . . .' She stopped, thinking better of the denial. 'No, we can't,' she said. 'But I don't know what there is to talk about.'

'Us?'

She shook her head. 'Us? Haven't we said all there is to say about that?'

Charles reached out and took her hand in his, thus stopping her flicking the book of matches. 'We've hardly said anything.' He paused and took a breath. 'Why did you deceive me in that way, Mia? Why didn't you talk to me about it, at least give me the chance to comment?'

'To comment? What does that mean? To let me know, as you always have in the past, that you're not cut out for children, that they're, what's your expression, too permanent?' She took a gulp of her wine. 'And I'm not, presumably, I'm temporary, until you find someone better.'

'No, God no, it's not like that at all. It's just . . .' He broke off as a sudden memory of the woman in the bar pierced his brain. His response to it was physical and he had to look away from the pain on Mia's face. 'It's just that I'm not ready,' he finished.

'Well I am.'

He turned back to her. 'And that's your excuse for deceiving me?'

Mia's face changed. The hurt in her eyes hardened into something different, something Charles didn't understand. Defiance, perhaps? 'I don't need an excuse, Charles, I didn't deceive you. What I do with my body is my business. If I want a baby, then it's up to me, it would be my responsibility, I would be its carer and provider.'

'And I would be its father!' Charles burst out. 'The child

would be half mine and I would have a responsibility too, a practical and moral responsibility. Can't you see that? How can you do that to me without my agreement?'

Mia drank her wine down and moved her chair back. 'We make love, Charles, and you assume there will be no outcome. Isn't making love to me your moral responsibility as well, then?'

'I don't know, I . . .'

'You are prepared to make love to me, but not to take responsibility for the natural result of that act. Aren't the two irrevocably entwined? If you love me enough to do something that might result in the creation of a baby, then you should love me enough to want that baby.'

'God, what is this? Suddenly we've elevated a good fuck out of all proportion.'

Mia stood up. 'Is that what our relationship is? A good fuck?' Her voice was tight with anger and her face burned.

'No, I just don't want to get all moral about sex. This isn't the fifties. You have as much right to the freedom of sex as I do.'

'The freedom of sex! Are you trying to tell me something, Charles?'

Charles was angry too now. This discussion had got right out of hand. What the hell was going on in Mia's head; where did all this crap come from? 'Sit down, Mia,' he snapped. 'People are looking.'

'Go to hell, Charles!' she said, and turning on her heel, she strode out of the wine bar.

Embarrassed, Charles looked round the restaurant, but he'd been wrong: no one was looking, no one was interested in him and Mia. He poured himself another glass of wine and picked up the menu. He might as well eat, having made the effort to come, but glancing down the list of dishes he couldn't find anything that appealed. Charles had lost his appetite.

Claire came round in darkness. She moved her head to the right and realized that she was on her stomach in a much bigger space than she had been in before. Her legs were straight and the pain in them had gone. She opened her eyes, but the darkness was too dense to be able to make anything out clearly. She could just about see her own shape, and put her hand down to touch her thigh, then up to her face, to reassure herself. She sat up. She was covered with a blanket – it smelt stale, damp – and she was lying on some kind of padded slippery fabric, a nylon sleeping bag she guessed. She was cold, and she pulled the blanket up round her shoulders. She sniffed. The air was putrid and it made her gag. She moved on to all fours and crawled forward a few feet, feeling her way with her hand out. The flesh on the inside of her thighs chafed against the stiff urine-soaked denim of her jeans. It hurt, and she stopped, feeling inside her trousers. The skin was hot and inflamed. Claire sat back. She was still frightened, but the fear had ossified; it was less fluid, less consuming, it lay rigid in the pit of her stomach. She wanted to cry but willed herself not to.

'Shelley,' she said aloud. Her voice wobbled and she had to clear her throat. She tried again. 'Percy Bysshe Shelley, born 1792, died 1822.' He was one of her favourite poets. Her words rebounded off the dank walls, and the small amount of courage that she had gained from waking safe and unharmed began to recede. She hugged her knees under her and buried her face in her hands. 'Oh God,' she murmured. 'Please God, let me be all right . . .' She felt tears and swallowed them back. 'We know,' she began in a whisper, 'that we have power over ourselves to do . . .' She stopped and took a deep breath; it calmed her. 'And suffer what, we know not till we try . . .' Her voice grew in strength. 'But something nobler than to live and die.'

Mia wasn't in when Charles got home at seven that night. He wasn't usually back this late but he'd returned to the university after lunch to do some research work on his book and had lost track of time. The house was empty as he entered it; no more empty than it had been that morning, yet it felt so. He checked the answer phone for messages, nothing from Mia, then rang her office; it was closed. In the kitchen he got himself a glass of water and wondered what to do. There was a chicken in the fridge; he'd been planning to roast it with lemon and garlic for supper, only now he had a sense that she wouldn't be in. He couldn't be bothered to cook it for himself; he would rather work.

Upstairs, he looked in the bedroom, just to reassure himself that her clothes were still there, and hung up the jacket he'd left slung over the back of the armchair. Before putting it away, he checked in the pockets, as he always did, for loose change or anything that he might have forgotten, and pulled out a slip of paper. It had the name of a bar on it, the bar that he'd been to on Monday night. He sat on the edge of the bed and looked at it. He hadn't called the place, of course he hadn't, though he'd thought about it again after that morning, twice actually. His guilt about Mia had paralysed him and he'd done nothing. He looked at the name of the bar again, then scrunched the paper up into a little ball and pushed it into his trouser pocket. He thought about the woman, about her long bare arms, and closed his eyes. Why did some experiences stay with you for ever, perfect images in your head, and others just fragment into hundreds of seconds' worth of memory that you could never put together again to form a whole? There were some things in Charles's life that he was sure at the time he would remember always, and yet they'd slipped into oblivion; others he wanted to forget and couldn't. Oblivion – she'd used that word: ignorance, nothingness. What had she wanted to reduce to nothing? Do we have any control at all over what we want to forget and what we are able to? Charles thought. He doubted it. God, if only he could wipe out all memory of her, if only he could stop this endless wanting something he couldn't have.

He heard the door open downstairs and went on to the landing. 'Mia?'

But it wasn't Mia, it was her friend Helen, who said: 'Sorry, Charles, I've come to get a few of Mia's things. She's staying with me for tonight. I hope you don't mind.'

Of course I mind, Charles wanted to say, I mind a lot, I want Mia, but he didn't say that, just shrugged. 'D'you want to do it or shall I?'

Helen came up the stairs. 'I've got a list,' she offered, holding it out. 'You probably know where most of these things are.'

Charles took the slip of paper and read it. 'Just for tonight?' He took a bag from under the bed and went into the bathroom. He found her face things, her make-up bag, her toothbrush and the special paste she used for sensitive teeth. He opened the cupboard and saw the ovulation kit; it made him wince. 'Toiletries,' he said, coming back into the bedroom and dropping them into the bag. 'Shirts, shoes and suits are in the wardrobe, jeans, sweaters, T-shirts and gym kit are all in the chest of drawers. Perhaps you'd be better at choosing what she might want to wear.'

He dug his hands in his pockets as he watched Helen

open the chest and take out a pair of combats, a T-shirt and a cashmere cardigan, the one he'd bought Mia for her birthday. She laid them on the bed and went to the wardrobe for a silk shirt, a pair of navy court shoes and a navy suit.

'She'll be back tomorrow?' Charles asked.

Helen turned. 'I think so. Look, I'm sorry, Charles,' she said. 'This isn't easy for me either, you know.'

Charles walked out of the bedroom and went downstairs. He was in the kitchen when Helen came down. She looked in and said: 'I'm off.'

'Right,' Charles answered. He walked to the door with her. 'Can you ask Mia to call me,' he said. 'I'd like to speak to her.'

Helen nodded. She opened the front door and left the house. Charles watched her go, then went into the dining room, which he had commandeered as his study. He sat down at his desk, switched on his PC, and took his notes out of his briefcase.

Charles was an historian, specializing in the Victorian age, and his fascination was with Victorian crime. Mia thought it odd, macabre almost, but she'd had to admit, when he'd hit on this idea two years ago, that if he was ever going to write a book, then this was the one to write. It was the story of a crime of passion, the murder by the Right Honourable Henry Chatten of his lover, Daisy Burrows, a servant girl who had worked for his family. Chatten had been convicted and hanged for the murder, but the case, when Charles came across it, seemed to be littered with gaping holes, the main one being the fact that they had never found a body. Henry and his parents had protested his innocence to the end, but he was still convicted. A blood-soaked knife and nightdress found in his room were enough for the jury and judge to hang him.

But Charles had never been convinced. He had worked on this, on and off, for over two years, and he was now as sure as he could be that Henry Chatten was innocent. He still hadn't worked out all the details, but he needed to start writing in order to classify his thoughts and make sense of his research. He was hoping, as most writers do, that the ending would somehow work itself out.

He pulled the keyboard closer to him and took a breath, wondering if every writer found the first few words so difficult. Then he typed: *The murder of Daisy Burrows by the Right Honourable Henry Chatten, 1897. A case of thwarted love and revenge, but whose revenge?* He stopped, read it twice, then deleted it and tried again: *When Henry Chatten was hanged for the murder of his lover Daisy Burrows in 1897, it was a scandal that shocked Victorian society and ruined the Chatten family name. But was it a scandal that should never have happened? Henry Chatten was a murderer convicted purely on circumstantial evidence, he protested his innocence to the end and the case was a murder investigation without a body. Could he have been innocent? Could Scotland Yard and the great British justice system have been wrong?*

After reading through what he'd written, Charles deleted that too, then sat back and stared at the blank screen and thought hard about what he wanted to say. I want, he thought, to give some sense of their love, to somehow evoke what Henry felt so that I can understand what he did. He closed his eyes, and once again the image of the woman in the bar came into his head. She was under him and above him and her hair fell over his face and touched his skin like silk. He snapped his eyes open again.

'I want,' he said aloud, 'to write a love story.' And he began to type.

Chapter 5

The first time that Henry Chatten saw Daisy Burrows was in the woodland that bordered the Chatten estate. It was May 1896, and the woods were carpeted with thousands and thousands of deep lilac bluebells. The scent was sharp and sweet and the canopy overhead was a bright, translucent green. Against this colour, this dappled sunlight, stood Daisy, naked to the waist and drying her pale creamy-white skin, the colour of blanched almonds, on a piece of cloth. She had been bathing in the small fresh-water pool. She loved the feel of the cool air and the warm sun on her body, and she was smiling. Completely alone and completely content, she was smiling at the pleasure of it.

Henry stood for a few moments, unseen, on the other side of the pool. He stood absolutely still, awestruck by her beauty. He was twenty-one, a thoughtful young man, a scholar and an academic. He was not at all what his father had hoped for – he was a bad shot and loathed fishing, he preferred to ride alone than to hunt, was shy, reluctant to argue, and worst of all, he was an aspiring poet. But Henry was his mother's perfect son. He was sensitive and kind, truthful and loving. His mother adored him; she was, they said later, the only one ever to believe wholeheartedly in his innocence.

Daisy finished drying herself and wrapped her damp hair in the cloth, tying it under at the back. She took her stockings from the branch of a tree and rolled them slowly up over her legs, her movements a half caress, then she sat, still naked to the waist, and pulled on her boots, lacing them swiftly with dextrous fingers. She stood and stretched, almost provocatively, and Henry started, thinking for a moment that she knew she was being watched. Then she turned and took her chemise off the branch, eased it over her head and tied the ribbon at the front. She had no corset on, just a shirt and a skirt, over which she wore a brown serge jacket fitted to the waist. She buttoned the jacket, took the cloth off her head and unloosed her hair. It was auburn, long, heavy, fluid, and it dropped down her back like a velvet curtain. She moved off, treading carefully through the flowers, and walked round the pool towards Henry. Panicked, he crouched behind a mossy tree stump and tucked his chin down on to his chest. He heard her begin to whistle, then to sing, and her tune was clear and high. He closed his eyes, somehow thinking childishly that if he didn't see her, she wouldn't see him, but there was a rustle of cotton, the moist crunch of a footstep on the undergrowth, and he looked up.

'Hello.' She was smiling. He put his hand up to his forehead to shield his eyes from the sun, and saw that her face was even paler than her body.

'Oh, erm, yes, hello.' He stood, brushing the moss from his trousers. 'I was looking for specimens, wild flowers, I collect them. They sometimes live, erm, gather, sprout near fallen trees.'

Daisy continued to smile, and Henry had the oddest sense that she knew him. She knew that he had been watching her and that he was on fire with the thrill of it. He thought that she knew he had never seen another woman, and that her body was perfect to him.

'Henry Chatten,' he said, holding out his hand. Daisy took it and they shook, politely. Her skin was cooler than his, soft and cool. 'And you are?'

She turned and glanced into the distance. 'I must go,' she said, 'I'm late,' and she went to move off.

'No, wait,' Henry cried. 'I don't know your name, you can't

leave. Where do you live, who are you?' He stopped and silently cursed himself for sounding so gauche.

Again Daisy smiled. 'I'll see you, Henry Chatten,' she said, and she walked away, crisply and smartly, the back of her skirt moving with the sway of her hips.

It was a week before Henry saw Daisy again, a whole week of thinking about her, remembering her, imagining her and wanting her. He had never known a want like it; it consumed him, left him weak, uninterested in anything. He had no experience of these things, but he thought, felt, sensed, that he might be in love.

The next time he saw Daisy Burrows was at breakfast in the dining room of Bicester House, his family home. He was eating alone, the first one up, unable to sleep in late, and one of the servants came in to check that the breakfast on the sideboard was in good order. He didn't look up; he was reading the paper and drinking tea. He heard the sharp swish of starched cotton and the click of boots on the floor. Several lids were lifted from serving dishes and replaced, noisily in his opinion, and he raised his head to make a reprimand. Daisy stood in her parlourmaid's uniform looking straight at him. He couldn't be sure afterwards, but he thought he could see the faint trace of a smile on her lips.

'My God! It's you, it's . . .' Henry's tea spilt, he dropped the newspaper on to the floor and stood up. 'It is you, isn't it?' He took a pace forward, came round the table and looked at her.

Daisy stared right back at him. She shouldn't have done, she should have lowered her eyes out of respect, but she didn't. She was as good as Henry Chatten.

'I said I'd see you, didn't I?'

'How long have you worked here? I haven't seen you before, have I?'

'Three weeks, sir, been undermaid for the last two, just been promoted.' She curtsied as she said this, and Henry smiled.

'And when is your afternoon off?'

49

'This afternoon, sir.'

'Would you like to walk out with me this afternoon? In the woods? It's a lovely day, I'm sure the rain will hold off.'

Daisy glanced away without answering and on impulse Henry said: 'We could have tea afterwards, there's a tea shop across the woodland in Wick Village. I could take you there if you'd like.'

Suddenly Daisy smiled. 'That would be very nice, thank you.' Her eyes flashed. 'Sir.' She turned back to the sideboard and raised the lids on the remaining three serving dishes, this time replacing them silently, which made Henry smile even more.

'I'll meet you at the gate to the field on Paterson's Farm,' he said. 'We can take the footpath from there. What time do you finish?'

'Two o'clock, sir.'

'Would two thirty be acceptable?'

'Two thirty will be fine.' Daisy walked towards the door, then stopped and turned when she reached it. 'I'll look forward to seeing you then,' she said.

Henry nodded; he didn't trust himself to speak. He was so delighted that he was concerned about making a fool of himself. Daisy left the room and closed the door behind her and Henry turned back to his paper. Two thirty, he thought, then he stood up abruptly and hurried to the door, opening it and calling after her: 'Excuse me? Hello?' As he went out into the hall, Daisy turned by the door to the scullery and saw Henry's father, Sir Lionel, coming down the stairs. She scurried away, leaving the hall empty and Henry alone to greet his father.

'Good morning, Father.'

'Henry? After something, were you? We'll go back and ring, you can order it with my eggs.'

Sir Lionel always liked his eggs freshly boiled. He strode ahead of Henry into the dining room and Henry stood for a few moments, confused, feeling foolish, both exalted and terrified by what he'd just done. Then he followed his father back to the dining room and continued his breakfast, for once deeming it lucky that almost all the meals in this house were eaten in complete silence.

At ten past two that afternoon, Henry was waiting by the gate with an umbrella and an air of fevered anticipation. He felt he was about to embark on something, although the exact nature of that something he couldn't, or didn't dare, imagine. It was hot, and he was sweating in his grey wool suit with its starched white collar and blue tie. He had bathed again after lunch, using the excuse to his mother of a hard morning's ride. Not that it would matter, of course, this was just a walk, an amble in the bluebell woods and there would be no physical contact to speak of. But perhaps, if the pool was cool and they were very hot, they might . . . Henry swallowed hard. The image that had haunted him for days sprang into his mind as fresh as if he'd just seen it, and his body reacted with a sudden lurch. He turned, looked up the road and saw her, in pale blue linen, a dress far too smart for a parlourmaid, her tiny waist cinched in tight, her hair piled high on her head, and the same half-smile on her lips when she saw him, as if she knew, just knew what he was thinking.

'Good afternoon, Mr Chatten,' she said.

'Good afternoon, Miss . . .?'

'Burrows. Miss Daisy Burrows.'

At last, her name. Daisy, like the flower: fresh, sweet, pure and simple. Henry took the hand she offered and held it for a few moments before pressing it very lightly to his lips. He could feel the coolness of her skin through the lace of her gloves. 'How do you do, Miss Burrows.' He stepped back. 'Would you care to join me for a walk?'

She smiled. 'I'd love to.' He opened the gate for her and she took his arm. They walked on through the field, on a footpath cut into knee-high green corn that rustled either side of them in the breeze.

'So, Miss Burrows, do you enjoy working at Bicester House?'

Daisy looked at him, her eyes narrowing and her face clouding for a moment. 'What a queer question,' she said at last. 'I'm a servant, it's a job. That's all.'

Henry flushed. 'Of course,' he stammered. 'I didn't think.'

'No,' Daisy said, 'you didn't.'

They walked on in silence, Henry now painfully embarrassed, aware of his age and inexperience, stuck for conversation, wishing he'd never suggested this; Daisy silent and frowning.

'I was in a school before,' she offered at last. 'I was brought up there. It was run by two sisters, Miss Mary and Miss Eliza Chase.'

'Were they relations?'

'No, they took me in after my mother died; she was their dressmaker. I was an orphan, so Miss Mary took pity on me. I worked for them, domestic things, and when I wasn't working, Miss Mary schooled me. She taught me everything, much to Miss Eliza's annoyance. I was there for eleven years. They were kind – well, at least Miss Mary was; Miss Eliza was a bugger.'

Henry's step faltered. Shocked, he glanced sidelong at Daisy, not sure that he had heard right.

She walked on unabashed. 'She was mean,' she went on. 'As mean and withered as an old stick. She'd never have let me out of the kitchen if she'd had her way; I'd never have learnt to read and write or play the piano.'

'You play the piano?'

'Yes,' she answered, 'I play very well.' She glanced at him momentarily, then looked away. 'And I have a neat hand and draw admirably, Miss Mary said, although I find portraits difficult.'

Henry's mind was somersaulting. This he had not expected.

It seemed that Daisy was as surprising as she was beautiful, and his body, in such close proximity to her, was reacting in a way that he had no control over.

'And what do you like to read, Miss Burrows?' he asked.

'My favourite is Dickens, but I couldn't possibly afford to buy books.'

Henry was suddenly embarrassed by his own pomposity. 'Perhaps you might allow me to lend you some of mine, Miss Burrows,' he said.

'Perhaps I might,' Daisy replied.

They reached the woods and Henry let Daisy walk in front of him, as the path wasn't wide enough for them both. They went on deeper into the woods, and the cool air filtered through Henry's mind and relieved it. The verdant green and velvet blue took them over and they were silent for a while. Then Daisy stopped and turned. She said: 'The bluebells fill me with joy. They are the most beautiful flowers in the world; wild and simple. They're like a rich blue velvet cloth, don't you think?' She took a deep breath. 'They make me want to lie down in the middle of them and drink in their colour and their scent.'

Henry smiled.

'What is so funny, Mr Chatten?'

'Such rapture over bluebells.'

'And what is wrong with that?'

'Well, I'm surprised, that's all. They're hardly roses or lilies or orchids, are they?'

Daisy frowned and bit her bottom lip. 'No, they may not be exotic hothouse flowers, but they are free, in the woods, for every man to enjoy,' she answered forcefully. 'And they have a purity, a simplicity that your hothouse blooms could never achieve.' She looked at him, and once more there was a faint smile on her lips. 'Besides which, they are the colour of my eyes.' And she moved closer to him so that he could see for himself.

'Nothing,' Henry said quietly, 'is the colour of your eyes. They are the most intense blue I have ever seen.'

Daisy lowered her eyelids and moved away. She knew at that moment that he was in love with her. She had been on a path since she saw him that day in the woods, watching her bathe; she had been on a path set out for her, moving towards this end. She hadn't known it then, but she recognized it now. Great love, love that transcended everything, was as random and arbitrary as the natural world; it had chosen her, and she was certain, as certain as there is a God, that nothing that she could ever do would stop it.

Chapter 6

Freddie called out to Lotte at six thirty, and for a minute she lay in bed with her eyes closed and just prayed that Gordon would hear him. But he snored on gently beside her, so she climbed out of bed, pulling on her dressing gown, and staggered bleary-eyed across the landing to Freddie's room. There she took him out of his cot and cuddled him for a few minutes, then lay down on the spare bed with him and pulled the duvet over them both. She closed her eyes and within seconds had drifted off to sleep. She woke again an hour later, the sound of Gordon's voice booming from the bedroom.

'For Christ's sake, it's seven thirty on a Saturday morning, child! Why the hell can't you go and do that somewhere else?'

Lotte sat up, eased her arm out from under Freddie's small body and hurried into her bedroom. Milly was sitting on the floor with a harmonica in her mouth, playing loudly and clearly 'Three Blind Mice'.

'Jesus, Lotte! Can't you keep them quiet?' Gordon sat up and glared at Lotte, then slumped back down on the pillows and pulled the duvet up over his head.

'Milly, love, let's do that downstairs in the kitchen. Daddy's trying to sleep.' She picked up Milly, who protested loudly that Lotte was hurting her broken arm, and carried her out of the bedroom, closing the door firmly behind her.

Out on the landing she sighed, pushed her hair out of her eyes and checked on Freddie before taking Milly downstairs. 'Another weekend,' she said to Milly, filling the kettle. 'Not that I'd notice, of course; the last time I had a lie-in was . . .' She turned and looked at her daughter. 'How old are you, Milly?'

'Oh, Mummy, can't you remember?'

'No, darling, it's too early.'

'Four and a little bit.'

'Four and a half years ago, including all the sleepless nights with heartburn from about thirty weeks onwards, of course.'

'Who are you talking to, Mummy?'

Lotte shrugged. 'Anyone who'll listen to me, Milly,' she said.

Tea made and drunk, Freddie washed and changed, both children sitting, albeit not at all quietly, at breakfast, Lotte found her handbag and fished out the piece of paper with the name of the solicitor that Liz had found for her on it. They ran a legal clinic on a Saturday morning, Liz had told her. She'd said: 'Dump the kids with Gordon and go get your divorce, baby.' But of course it wasn't going to be quite as simple as that.

Gordon had arrived home late last night from Glasgow, just in time for dinner, a dinner that Lotte had made despite begrudging him every mouthful. They had eaten it watching television, so she'd not had to speak to him, but her body language had been aggressive and resentful, to the point that Gordon had actually asked her what was up. He'd looked across the sofa while the news flickered on the screen in the corner and said: 'You've been a right bloody grump all night, Lotte. What the hell is the matter with you?' And Lotte, so used to this type of subtle abuse, had said: 'I'm just tired, Gordon, it's been a difficult week, what with the accident and Milly in plaster.'

He had nodded and gone back to the screen, then said, not looking at her: 'Of course, if you'd got up with them on Monday morning instead of lounging in bed, then the accident wouldn't have happened, would it, Lotte? Milly wouldn't have opened the gate unnoticed.'

Lotte had gritted her teeth then and gripped her fork tightly in the hope that she could stop her sudden urge to stab him to death with it. But all she said was: 'No, of course not, Gordon.'

That was the thing about being worn down, slowly, carefully and cleverly, by abuse. It was a detailed procedure: sometimes it took years, but it worked. Bit by bit the victim got devalued, they began to think that they deserved to be told what they were told, treated the way they were treated. Lotte was like this. She was so far gone down the victim line that she took everything Gordon said on the nose, and now, looking at the piece of paper that might just be her way out of here, she panicked. She folded it up into a tiny square and pushed it right down into the side pocket of her jeans. Guilt. Abusers were very good at guilt. They took it and played with it and doled it out. What if I really am a bad mother? Lotte thought. What if Milly had broken her back, her neck, not survived, while I was lying in bed, too lazy to be bothered to get up and see to my children? I must be mad to be thinking what I am; if I divorced Gordon I could lose custody of the children, he would paint me as irresponsible, uncaring. I should leave it, say nothing, at least for the time being. She removed the remains of the mashed banana from Freddie's high chair and replaced it with a slice of home-made bread and butter.

*   *   *

Later that morning, after Lotte had done a good deal of pleading, finally having to implore in a humiliating way, using the lure of earning some money, Gordon took Milly and Freddie out on some errands and she sat in her studio at the top of the house, looking at her watercolour paints. She was supposed to be painting; she was working on a commission from a publisher to illustrate a gardening book and had almost finished a botanical painting of the Hyacinthoides non-scriptus, or English bluebell. It needed a wash for the leaves and some more sketching-in for detail, but she couldn't concentrate on the work; she was too muddled, too upset to paint.

She dug in her pocket, lifting her hips off the chair and feeling around for the tiny square of paper with the telephone number of the solicitor on. She located it, took it out and unfolded it. Her scrawl looked up at her accusingly. She left her work and went downstairs, the slip of paper in her hand. She was stupidly nervous, her stomach churning. Going into the kitchen, she picked up the phone and dialled the code. She was just punching in the rest of the number when Gordon's car pulled up outside the house. 'Shit,' she said aloud. She slammed the phone down and went to the front door, stuffing the paper back into her pocket. Milly was there first, smiling and shouting at Freddie, who had only just mastered walking proficiently, to hurry up.

Gordon followed them in with flowers. He held them out and said: 'For you.'

Lotte took them. They were magnificent, white lilies and roses surrounded by silver tissue and tied with white ribbon. 'Thank you. They're . . .' Lotte had never been able to lie. They were, she thought, no, knew now, a guilt buy. 'Incredible,' she finished.

Milly had gone dancing into the kitchen and Lotte

followed her in. 'Lunch?' Lotte asked, glancing at her watch. 'It's half past twelve, you were ages.'

Milly avoided her eye and nodded. 'Freddie would like chips,' she said. 'He won't eat anything else.' Freddie was her alter ego.

'Well, Freddie can have pasta, and if he doesn't eat it then he'll be hungry, won't he?'

Freddie toddled into the kitchen and plopped down on to the floor. Lotte took a vase out of the cupboard for the flowers. 'What books did you get from the library, Milly?' she asked as she cut through the tissue paper and cellophane. 'I hope you got a few for Freddie as well, not all for yourself.'

There was a silence while Milly studiously avoided the question and paid particular attention to her brother – something she rarely did. Lotte turned and watched her for a few minutes. 'Didn't you go to the library, Milly?'

Milly was building a tower out of bricks and wouldn't look up. 'Nope.'

Lotte's stomach lurched. It was something that she would never usually have given a second thought to: so they didn't go to the library, they ran out of time, big deal. But now she came across the kitchen and knelt down by Milly and Freddie. 'Why didn't you go to the library, Milly? Did shopping take too long?' Milly concentrated hard on the bricks. 'Did you go somewhere else?'

Milly nodded, still not looking at Lotte.

'Can you tell me where, sweetheart?'

Milly pulled a face and finally looked at her mother. 'Daddy said not to say anything, that it was a little secret, but we went to see a friend of his. Freddie and I weren't allowed in, so Daddy left us in the car and we listened to *Percy the Park Keeper*.'

Lotte's face burned. 'Did Daddy introduce you to his friend?' she asked, her voice unsteady.

Milly frowned. 'She was quite pretty but she only said hello. She had her nightie on.'

Lotte jumped up. She stood for a moment to try and calm herself, but her anger was so intense that she had to move around. As she paced the floor of the kitchen, Milly said: 'Mummy? What's wrong?' But Lotte couldn't answer.

After a while she stopped and clenched her hands together. She was shaking, her whole body was shaking, and she had the urge to throw up. Walking out of the kitchen, she snatched the car keys off the hall table and went into the sitting room, where Gordon was checking his share prices on Ceefax. 'I have to go out,' she snapped. 'Sorry, I need to get to the chemist.' She walked back into the hall, looked at Milly and Freddie and shouted: 'They need lunch, Gordon, it's in the fridge!' That was a first. Then she slammed out of the house, got into the car and accelerated off. At the end of their road, she stopped, took the slip of paper out of her pocket and rang the solicitor. She got the address and drove straight there.

Charles was working when he heard the front door. He was reading what he had written last night and making corrections. He wasn't sure how the story was going to develop, but he had made a start and that was exhilarating in itself. He went into the hall and saw Mia with her overnight bag. She was taking her coat off.

'Hi.' She looked terrible, her face wretched from crying. 'Are you all right?'

She shrugged and hung the coat on a hanger, slotting it into the hall cupboard. 'Do I look all right?'

'No, you look upset.'

'Are you surprised?'

Charles moved towards her, but she walked away into the kitchen. 'Mia,' he said, following her in, 'we can't go on like this. This is no way to live, you storming out of restaurants, staying with friends, us not talking. Please, can't we get over this?'

'And what?' She switched the kettle on and reached up for the tea bags. 'Forget it ever happened? Ignore the fact that I am desperate for a baby and you are not? Or perhaps,' she turned, 'perhaps go ahead and have a baby, and you can just pretend it isn't there, then we've both got what we want, haven't we?'

'Mia this is ridiculous!' All the joy at having written the first two thousand words of his book evaporated. 'If you are still so angry, so unresolved about this, why did you come back?'

Mia slammed down the tea bags. 'Because we have to go to a dinner party tonight, hosted by Leo Chandler. Remember him? One of the bigwigs at the university, your great champion. Or had you forgotten? You may be totally self-absorbed, Charles, but I am not. We accepted the invitation and it would be very bad form to let them down at the last minute.'

Charles was humbled. He came into the kitchen and pulled out a chair. 'I'm sorry, Mia,' he said. 'I had forgotten and I'm glad that you hadn't. Thank you, for coming back.'

Mia softened. 'D'you want tea?' she asked.

He nodded, and she made two mugs, bringing them over to the table. It was peculiarly British, Charles thought, to be able to drink a cup of tea in the midst of such emotional angst. He reached out and touched her hand. 'We will sort it,' he said.

Mia slid her hand out from under his and cupped it round the hot mug of tea. 'One way or another,' she said.

Charles didn't reply; there was nothing more to add.

Roper & Co., Solicitors, ran a drop-in legal clinic on a Saturday morning which was unusual and cheap and as a result always packed to capacity. Lotte had only just managed to get a space, and now sat in a crowded waiting room leafing through an old copy of *OK!* magazine, agog at Posh and Becks and the terrible purple wedding. She wondered if the accumulation of money automatically required the forfeiture of sense. Certainly she'd never been stupid until she met Gordon. But with him she'd been a prize klutz. All those times he had popped out on a Saturday morning to run his personal errands, and she'd never asked where to or what for. All those times he'd been away on business and she'd never rung to check his room, just waited until he called her. All those times he'd been on the phone in the office and she'd assumed it was business; or played tennis that had lasted an hour longer than usual. Had he been with this woman then? She had to live close by or he wouldn't have been able to manage the trip this morning. In her nightie! For God's sake! The thought of it made Lotte's blood boil. And leaving the children in the car unattended while he whipped the said nightie off and had a quick one in the front room . . .

Lotte heard her name called and stood up to go through. In Mr Roper's office, she took a seat and looked at the grey, worn-down, exhausted man in front of her, and thought, I'm in better shape than he is; how is he going to help me?

Mr Roper said: 'Mrs Graham, you're here about a divorce, is that right?'

'Yes, my own.' Stupid, stupid, of course it was her own

divorce; it was hardly likely to be anyone else's. 'I was wondering what the first steps are.'

'Well, we need grounds for divorce, and then we serve papers on your husband and take it from there.'

'Adultery,' Lotte said.

'Excellent.'

'Excellent? Why is my husband's affair excellent?'

Mr Roper sighed. He had been here, single-handed since nine a.m. – the other two solicitors were off sick – and it was now two p.m. and he had another four people to see. 'Your husband's affair isn't excellent, Mrs Graham, but as grounds for divorce it couldn't be better.'

'Couldn't be better?'

'It's quick, easy and relatively painless.'

Lotte swallowed. 'Painless?'

'Legally, I mean.'

'I see.'

Mr Roper turned to a fresh page in his notebook. 'So,' he said, 'I need your husband's name and address and the name and address of the co-respondent.'

'Ah.' Lotte opened her handbag, pretended to look inside it, then clipped it shut again. 'I don't have that,' she said.

'Then I can't proceed. I must have the co-respondent's name in order to do the paperwork. I'm sorry, but there it is.'

'I see,' Lotte said again. She did see. It was a shambles. She was upset today, angry and confused. It was a ridiculous mistake coming here. She stood. 'Thank you, Mr Roper,' she said. 'I'll be in touch.'

'Mrs Graham,' Mr Roper said, rising from his chair. 'Please, don't scurry off, let me explain.' He didn't usually, but there again, a great number of his clients didn't have English as a first language, so explaining was often a waste of time. Besides, women like Mrs Graham didn't come into his sphere very often. She was lovely, and in his overworked, grey old world, this splash of vibrant loveliness wasn't to be let out of the door too soon. Lotte sat down again. 'If you can get the name and address of the woman your husband is having an affair with, then I can serve papers on him, notably a letter telling him that you are filing for divorce on the grounds of adultery with Miss X. Does that sound OK? All I need is her name and address and we can take it from there.'

'Yes.' Her name and address. Simple. Ha!

'So if you'd like to give me a ring,' Mr Roper swiped a business card from the holder on his desk and held it out with a flourish, 'then we can get going.'

Lotte took the card. 'Thank you.' She tucked it into her bag and stood for the second time. 'I'll be in touch,' she said again. She left the office and walked through the waiting room, down the stairs and out into the fresh air.

Maybe this was a mistake, maybe she should forget the whole thing. She was comfortable, well looked after, she had the children. Maybe she and Gordon could work things out, maybe it would all just blow over. Maybe, maybe, maybe. She stopped and looked around her. Everywhere in the high street on a busy Saturday morning people were getting on with their lives, and here she was just thinking about it. Maybe nothing. Lotte knew that she had to stand up for herself; she knew in her heart that living with Gordon was no longer an option. She knew, and of this she was absolutely certain, that this affair would not blow over. She tightened the belt round her jacket and stepped into the throng of people going about their business. Lotte knew it was time to go about hers.

*   *   *

Annie Taylor was just finishing the washing-up from the night before, one knife, one fork and one glass – she'd had a ready meal from M & S and had eaten it out of the silver foil container – when her phone rang. It was her mother. She looked at her watch and estimated at least five minutes, if not ten.

'Yes, it went very well, thanks, Mum.' She yawned. 'A pretty standard move, I'd say . . . Yes, I know you think it's a lot for a woman on her own . . . Yes, I know you worry, but worrying won't help much, Mum, there's not a lot we can do about it.' She took a deep breath. 'Believe me, if I knew where all the nice men were, I'd be there in a flash. Anyway, it doesn't bother me much, so I wouldn't let it get you down.' Annie held the phone away from her ear. Big mistake, saying it didn't bother her much. 'But I love the job,' she put in a minute or so later. 'It's a big part of my life . . . Yes, I know you think that, but it's what I wanted to do and I'm good at it, very good in fact . . . Oh? Golf? This morning? Oh, well, that's a wonderful idea, Mum, but I, erm, I'm afraid that I've, erm, I've got to work . . .' She shook her head and slumped against the wall. Again she held the phone aloft. She watched a minute and a half tick by, then said: 'Yes, I do know it's a Saturday, yes, I know if I got out more or played a round of golf I might just meet a company director with his own home and good prospects, but I've got to go through some files, Mum. This is a big promotion and I want to be up to speed when I meet my team on Monday. My God, is that the time? I was due in the office ten minutes ago. Sorry, Mum, I've got to dash. Shame about the golf, another time perhaps. Love to Dad.' Without waiting for a reply, Annie hung up, then let out a sigh and wandered back into the kitchen to make herself a coffee. Day one, she thought, and a narrow escape from a Saturday round of golf with my mother. This, she suddenly knew with conviction, was going to be much harder than she had imagined. She just hoped the job was worth it.

Lotte served Gordon his lunch much later than usual but couldn't even force herself to sit down with him. She made herself a couple of pieces of toast whilst cooking his Spanish omelette, but her throat had closed up and she couldn't swallow any of it down. He ate, making no comment on why she wasn't eating with him, then stood and said he was tired and was going to snooze on the sofa for half an hour.

'Tired?' Lotte said. 'I'm not surprised, you've had a very busy morning.'

Gordon looked at her. 'Meaning?'

Lotte's heart hammered in her chest. 'Meaning that you seemed to be out a long time with the children.'

Gordon's face relaxed. 'Was I? I didn't notice.'

Go on, Lotte told herself, go on, confront him, tell him that you know. 'Didn't you? I'm not . . .'

She stopped as Milly trooped into the kitchen, followed closely by Freddie, who was crying loudly. 'I had it first,' Milly declared. 'He tried to get it off me but I had it first!' She turned to her brother. 'You've got to learn to share, Freddie, or you'll never have any friends.' Freddie howled loudly and pulled Milly's hair from behind, very hard.

Swiftly Lotte bent and swiped the offending toy, a bright blue bit of plastic, out of Milly's hand and put it up on the shelf. 'If you can't play nicely with it, then no one has it,' she said. Gordon had walked out of the room. 'Freddie,' she announced, 'time for your nap, and Milly, you can watch a video and have some quiet time with Daddy.' That was unheard of. She took Freddie up to his room, changed him, closed the curtains and put him down, then she took Milly into Gordon and said, in her best *Playdays* voice, 'Milly would like to spend some time with Daddy. Here's *Pinocchio* to watch; perhaps, Gordon, you can sing along.' Milly, delighted by this turn of events, climbed on to the sofa next to Gordon and Lotte walked out of the room. She heard Gordon call her, but she was on her way up the stairs and pretended not to hear him.

In the bedroom she locked the door, took Gordon's brief-case from beside the chest of drawers and placed it on the bed. She would start here, then go through his wallet and his suits if need be. She wanted a name, and, if possible, an address. It could be anywhere, evidence of Gordon's mistress: on a slip of paper, a receipt, anywhere. But Lotte knew one thing for certain: it had to be somewhere.

She opened the case and carefully rifled through the papers. She didn't need to look any further. There was a list of people from Gordon's company who had attended the conference in Glasgow, three men and one woman; her name was Eve Francis. It had to be her. Lotte didn't know why she thought so, but she could sense it. She continued to look, in every pocket, every file. Then she found it, in one of the zipped compartments, a card for Gordon's birthday, 14 March, signed: *With all my love always, Eve*. It was her. Eve Francis.

Lotte sat on the bed and fought the urge to cry. She looked at the card; it was hand-made, a red cotton padded heart stitched on to a white background, with a tiny silver heart stitched on to that. Two hearts together. The urge to cry disappeared and was replaced by an urge to rip the card up. Lotte dropped it on to the bed and stood up. She went to the door, then walked back to the bed, picked up the card and ripped it in half, then in half again, and suddenly the feeling was so good, so liberating, that she ran to the bathroom, grabbed a pair of scissors and stabbed the red cotton padded heart right in the centre. She stabbed it and gouged a great hole in it, then cut it up, into twenty or thirty little pieces. Then she looked at what she'd done, took a deep breath and bent to pick up the pieces. She put them in the top drawer of her chest, closed it firmly and went back to the door. Now for the address.

Up in her studio, Lotte sat at her drawing board and stared out of the window, hoping that the huge expanse of sky might free her mind up for some lateral thinking. Eve Francis, she had just discovered, was ex-directory, and Lotte could think of no other way of tracing her. She rang Mr Roper, the solicitor.

Roper was about to lock up when Lotte rang. It was five in the afternoon and he had just finished with his last client, a Bengali family who wanted to buy the lease on a small shop in the Park Rise area. Translation had been a problem, but at least the eldest son had spoken enough English to just about make sense of it all. That had taken him two hours. Now he was starving, his diverticulitis was playing up and frankly he'd had enough. When Lotte's call came in he was tempted to ignore it, but when he heard her voice on the answer phone the memory of her pale, fine-featured face sprang to mind and he lunged forward to take the call.

'Mrs Graham, you've got a name, very good, very good indeed.'

'I was wondering, Mr Roper, if you might be able to tell me where I might find an address. The woman is local, I think, but she's ex-directory. I've just tried looking her up. Have you any idea how I might track her down?'

Roper loved Mrs Graham's voice. He could have listened

to it all day; it was so clear and concise and had a softness that roused his masculinity.

'I would try the local library, Mrs Graham, they keep a copy of the electoral roll and they might be able to pass on the information.'

'Oh, right, thanks.' Mr Roper sounded exhausted, Lotte thought.

'Call me with your success,' he said, almost cheerfully.

'Right.' Her success? Was he enjoying this? What an odd way to make a living, out of other people's pain and misfortune. 'Thank you,' she said, and rang off. She called the library. Normally on a Saturday afternoon it would have been shut, but today was an open day, luckily for Lotte, and the librarian who answered her call was having a thoroughly good time showing people round, explaining the machinations of the library system and eating the special M & S Florentine biscuits that they'd bought in for the occasion. He was in buoyant form.

'I wonder if you might be able to help,' Lotte asked. 'It's just that I'm trying to trace a friend for a reunion and I know she lives in the area but don't have her address. Is there any way I can look at the electoral roll, perhaps?'

'I'm afraid the electoral roll is listed by address,' the librarian said. 'If you had the address I could give you the name, although technically speaking I'm not allowed to, of course.'

'Oh, I see. How very disappointing.' Lotte *was* disappointed, too; she sounded the genuine article. 'I was so hoping to get hold of this person.'

'Well,' said the librarian, 'I shouldn't really tell you this, and if anyone asks you don't tell them I said, but if you look up the electoral roll on the Internet, you can cross-match the name with the address.'

'Really?' Lotte said.

The librarian picked another Florentine off the plate and put it in front of him, ready to pop into his mouth when he hung up. 'Absolutely,' he said. 'You have to register your own name and address for security purposes, but I'm sure that won't be a problem for you if she's a good friend.'

'Not at all,' Lotte replied. 'Thanks. Thanks a lot.' She rang off and immediately called Liz. 'Do me a favour, Lizzie,' she said. 'I need the address of one Eve Francis off the Internet and I need you to register in order to get it for me. I don't want to put my name in, in case I can be traced. I don't want Gordon to know anything about this.'

'Why not?' Liz asked, not daring to hope.

'Because I'm certain now that I want to file for divorce,' Lotte replied. 'And I want to take him by surprise.'

'Alleluia!' Liz said. 'Bloody Alleluia!'

It was five to eight. Charles sat in the car with the engine running, waiting for Mia to put the alarm on and lock up the house. She came out pulling her coat on, and as she climbed into the car he said: 'You look lovely, Mia.'

She glanced at him. 'Thanks,' she replied, and slammed the door shut. They drove for a while in silence, then, 'How far is it?' she asked, smoothing her dress over her lap so that it wasn't creased by the seat belt.

'About twenty-five minutes,' Charles answered.

'Nice house?'

'Lovely. Beautiful, in fact. It's in a perfect location, just up from the Bicester estate and Ludwell Ponds.'

'Very nice.' Mia pulled down the sun visor and looked at her reflection in the mirror. 'Will I like them?'

'I should think so, they're both very charming.'

'Age?'

Charles looked at her. 'What is this? Twenty questions?'

'I just want to know what to expect,' she said. 'Whether it's going to be late fifties middle-class intellectual, early forties child-rearing commuterville, or thirties up-and-thrusting career climbers.'

'For what purpose?'

'So that I can arm myself mentally.'

'Is that really necessary?'

Mia snapped the visor back. 'I think so,' she said. She turned to look at him. 'You see, at the moment, Charles, I feel so devalued, so low in morale, that I have to rehearse my personality before I do it for real, because if I act the way I really feel then I'd be about as much fun as a wet weekend.'

Charles pulled up at traffic lights and stopped. He was helpless. Mia wanted something from him that he couldn't give, and it rendered him powerless in the face of her distress. He was about to say something when Mia interrupted with: 'Anyway, let's change the subject, Charles. I'm sure you're as bored with it as I am by now. How's the book?'

The lights changed and Charles accelerated off. 'The book,' he replied, 'is actually off to a reasonable start.'

'You've started it? But I thought your notes were inconclusive. How can you start when you don't know the ending?'

'A philosophical question of life, I think,' he replied, and grudgingly, Mia smiled. 'That's better,' Charles said.

'Don't get your hopes up,' Mia retorted. 'It's only a smile.'

It was after eight by the time Annie Taylor decided that she'd had enough and that it was safe to go home without having to dodge an invitation to join her parents for

Saturday night supper and a hand of bridge. She was the last of the day shift to leave. She packed a selection of files into her briefcase, replaced the rest and pulled on her coat. She was wearing jeans, a white T-shirt and high-heeled black suede boots, and as she looped and tied a velvet leopard-print scarf round her neck, she caught a glimpse of her reflection lit up in the plate-glass window. Not bad, she thought, and definitely not like a copper. She flicked her hair over her shoulder – brown with blonde streaks, courtesy of a very expensive hairdresser in Chelsea – and left the office.

On the way out she smiled at the duty sergeant, who barely returned the compliment, then muttered under her breath: 'Miserable git.' She crossed the car park to her car and pressed the alarm pad. Nothing happened. 'Bugger!' she said aloud. She unlocked the door manually, threw her case on to the passenger seat and slotted the key into the ignition. Again, nothing happened.

Annie tried once more, but it didn't even tick over. She climbed out, opened the bonnet and peered inside, more for effect than anything else; she didn't have a clue about engines. She fiddled with the car battery connection to check nothing was loose, then stood up. She would have to ring the AA and suffer the smirks of the duty sergeant, who had clearly taken against her. She dug in her pocket for her phone.

'Hello. You in trouble?'

Annie looked round.

'I'm not a whiz at cars, but I could have a look if you like.'

A man, interesting-looking, taller than her – important when you were five foot ten – slim build, probably professional; a copper? She couldn't see it somehow.

'Thanks, I would like.'

'Problem?'

'It won't start, not even a catch. Dead as a dodo.'

'Did you leave your lights on?'

Annie shot him a look.

'No, of course not. You don't seem like the sort of person who leaves their lights on.' He smiled. Crooked, sexy smile, she thought. 'Mind if I try?'

She held the keys out for him, and he took them and slid inside the car. A small red light winked at him from the dashboard. He put the key in the ignition; all the lights came on, but the engine wouldn't connect.

'It's immobilized,' he said, climbing out. 'Your alarm's still on. Is there something wrong with the alarm pad?'

'Oh, bloody hell!' She shook the alarm pad and aimed it at the receiver, pressing frantically. 'The battery must be dead! Great! That's all I bloody need on a Saturday night!'

He raised an eyebrow. 'Hot date, I expect.'

Annie shrugged. 'Something like that.'

'Well, let's open it up, see what sort of battery it is and if mine will fit it just for now.' He took the key out of the ignition, ran his thumbnail along the edge of the plastic casing and opened the alarm pad. 'Three-volt Duracell. We might be lucky.' He took the back off his own alarm pad. 'Perfect.' Removing his battery, he slotted it into Annie's alarm pad. This time, the little red light went off and he started the engine. 'How about that for service?'

'Five-star,' Annie said. She returned the battery and started the car again. 'Thanks, thanks a lot.'

'No problem. Have you got a spare battery at home?'

'I've got a spare alarm pad, I think. The car's pretty new.'

'Yes, nice motor.' He grinned and, almost imperceptibly, looked her up and down. 'Suits you.'

73

She smiled back. 'Thanks.' She climbed into the car, pressed the window down and looked up at him. 'I appreciate your help.' He was more than interesting; he was actually pretty well made.

He grinned again. 'Think nothing of it. But maybe if you're around here again you could buy me a drink, to thank me properly.'

Annie revved the engine. 'Yes, maybe,' she replied. She shifted gear and accelerated off. Maybe indeed, she thought. And I didn't even have to get my golf clubs out.

It was eight thirty when Gordon came in from tennis. It had been a hard match, he'd told Lotte on the phone from the car; they had only just won, and of course the drink afterwards in the bar was obligatory. Entering the kitchen, he came across, kissed the top of her head as she bent to load the washing machine and said: 'Fancy a glass of wine before supper?'

Lotte stood straight. She looked at him. All thoughts of a civilized divorce, a reasonable divorce, went out of her head. She was incensed by him. For the first time in six years she felt all the anger of being downtrodden well up inside her; all the fury of her meek acceptance of a situation that was at best difficult, at worst intolerable explode inside her head. It wasn't that she was deeply hurt – she'd given up on love several years ago; it was the injustice of it, the sheer cheek of her alone at home cooking and cleaning and caring for Gordon, running his life, and he couldn't give a fuck. Or rather he could, only it was to someone else. She saw red. She said: 'You don't get it, Gordon, do you? You just don't get it.'

Gordon stopped opening the bottle of wine he had in his hands. 'I'm sorry?' His face had set and something in his eyes changed. Lotte could see it and held on to the edge of the washing machine to support herself. Her hands shook. 'There isn't any supper. If you want supper, then I suggest that you run over to Eve's house, I'm sure she'd cook you something.'

Gordon put the wine down and took a step forward; Lotte took a step back. 'I don't know what you're talking about,' Gordon said. 'I don't know any Eve.'

In her mind Lotte could see a woman in a nightie; the image was so strong it was almost as if she'd seen it herself. 'Eve Francis? You don't know her?' She saw Milly and Freddie locked and strapped in the car, alone, vulnerable. 'Don't insult me, Gordon. You've been having an affair with her for three years now. I don't think she'd be very happy to hear you deny her existence.' Lotte licked her lips, but it made no difference; her mouth was bone dry. 'She certainly wants the world to know; she rang Richard and Judy and talked about your affair live on morning television to what is it? Three million viewers?'

Gordon narrowed his eyes. 'Have you gone mad, Lotte? I don't know what the hell you're talking about!'

'Don't you?' Lotte stormed out of the kitchen and ran upstairs. She snatched the pieces of birthday card out of the drawer and ran back down again. 'Here!' She threw them on to the kitchen table, where they scattered. 'Your birthday card, from Eve. All my love always, it says. A bit much from a perfect stranger, isn't it? Two hearts, one encased in the other. All my love always, Eve!' She was breathing hard and her chest ached with the effort of it. 'And you say you don't know her. Bullshit!'

'All right, I know her, but it's not what you think!'

'Not what I think? You spent a week in Glasgow with her, Gordon, she rang a national television station and told them on air that you'd shared some very tender moments in bed, and it's not what I think! What is it then, if it's not what I think?'

'For Christ's sake, Lotte, calm down! You've got it all wrong. This is stupid, you've never been good at deciphering things, you don't understand . . .'

'Actually, Gordon, I understand perfectly, and I haven't got it wrong. For years you've been telling me that I've got it wrong, that it's my fault when things go awry, that I'm useless and unattractive and stupid. But I'm not. Finally I've realized that I'm not stupid, I'm not any of those things. This isn't stupid, this is you being caught out, and I haven't got it wrong. By God, I've hit the nail absolutely on the head!'

'You're hysterical! You're not making any sense!'

'Oh, for pity's sake, Gordon! I am not hysterical, I am filing for divorce on the grounds of adultery and naming Miss Eve Francis of 18 Perry Road as co-respondent!'

'You are bloody well not!' Gordon bellowed, moving towards her.

'I bloody well am!' she shouted back. She gripped the washing machine so tight that it hurt her fingers, but she was going to stand her ground; even if he hit her she was going to stand her ground. Fear clutched her insides.

'I forbid you to file for divorce, Lotte, I absolutely forbid it! If you go ahead and do it then you'll see the full extent of my fury. I will take you to court and make sure that your life is a misery. You will not ruin me in this way, Lotte. I forbid it!'

'Ruin you, Gordon? What the hell does that mean?' Lotte stared at him, but he turned away so that she couldn't see his face. 'It is you who have ruined me! All these years of being put down, all these years of no affection, virtually no sex, nothing, not a marriage, just me being walked all over, and now I know why! Three years, Gordon! Three years you've been having an affair. God, you've hardly looked at me the past year, hardly noticed I was there.'

'Are you surprised?' Gordon spat. 'You've got nothing to offer me, Lotte, you've had nothing for years. My affair is simply a symptom, and the cause is the misery of living with a woman who doesn't excite me in the slightest, either mentally or physically.'

Lotte gasped, at the violence of this attack, at his bitterness. It was as though he'd hit her; she felt weak, suddenly defeated.

'You are not to name Eve as co-respondent, I will not have it.' His voice had changed; there was an underlying note of triumph in it. 'You can file for divorce, but I won't have Eve involved.' He thought he had knocked her out of the contest, that he had won.

Lotte pulled herself up and lifted her head. She looked straight at him, and for the first time in a long while Gordon could see the incredible fire in her eyes that had once attracted him. The brown flecks in the pool of blue almost burned, turning gold. Her weakness drained away. 'What you will or won't have is no longer up to you, Gordon,' she said coldly. 'It is in the hands of my solicitor.' She let go of the edge of the washing machine and took a step forward. 'There is nothing more you can do to me.'

Suddenly Gordon lunged forward and grabbed her shoulders. He shook her so hard that she was frightened her neck would break. 'How dare you go behind my back, how dare you . . .'

With a strength Lotte hadn't known she had, she brought her arms up with such force that she freed herself and shunted him back into the table. Her head burned, her vision was blurred, but her mind was perfectly clear. 'If you ever touch me again,' she said, 'I will kill you.'

Gordon stared at her, with such hatred that it bored into her and left her breathless.

'I am going to pack,' she said. 'I will go and stay with my mother, because I am not safe in this house.' She moved past him out of the kitchen and he let her go.

Upstairs in the bedroom, she threw a few of her own things into a case, bundled up armfuls of the children's clothes, nappies, wash things, and clicked it shut. She staggered down the stairs with it and put it straight into the car. Then, as gently as she could, she woke the children, carried them out to the car, strapped them in and went back for her handbag. Within ten minutes she had gone, and Gordon hadn't even moved from where she'd left him.

In the car, she started the engine and drove off. She made it to the post office three roads down before she had to stop. Pulling into the kerb, shaking uncontrollably, she put her hands up to her face and wept.

Chapter 7

It was nine thirty p.m., and Meg Chandler was collecting up the plates from the first course and taking them through to the kitchen. There the caterer was deglazing the pan for the sauce to go with the rack of lamb and had laid out eight large white dinner plates with garnish, ready to carve and arrange the lamb on to.

'Everything all right, Mrs Chandler?'

'Delicious, thanks, Fiona. How long before we're ready to go?'

'Ten minutes.'

'Great.' Meg took two more bottles of white wine from the fridge and two bottles of red from the sideboard, where Leo had left them to breathe. In the dining room she handed them to Leo, who rose to pour.

'So you've made a start, then, have you, Charlie?' Leo said, coming round the table with the wine. 'Mia was telling me you're quite pleased with it.'

'Yes, yes, I have, Leo, but it's the fact that I've finally got some words on paper that I'm pleased about more than anything else. I've no idea how good they are.'

'Oh,' said the woman on Charles's right. 'Are you writing a book?'

'Well, trying to.'

'How exciting! What's it about?' Charles looked to Mia for support. 'I'm sure it's not terribly interesting . . .'

'Of course it is, Charles, it's bloody interesting,' Leo interrupted. 'And it's local. Tell Mary the story. It's fascinating, Mary, you'll love it.'

'Well,' Charles began, 'I'm trying to prove that a local man, Henry Chatten – his family owned the Bicester estate . . .'

'What, where Lord and Lady Beatty live?'

'Yes.'

'Sorry for interrupting, do go on.'

'Well, I'm trying to prove that Chatten, who was hanged in 1897 for the murder of his lover, Daisy Burrows, a servant working for his family, was in fact innocent. I think he was framed for her murder and wrongly convicted.'

'My God, that sounds like a bit of a task. Are you a lawyer?'

'No, a historian. I specialize in the Victorian era. Mia's the lawyer.' Mary glanced across at Mia. The whole table had now focused their interest on Charles.

'Well, I take my hat off to you,' the woman to Charles's left said. 'How on earth you can concentrate on writing a book with a baby in the house, I have no idea. It must take enormous concentration . . .'

'We don't have a baby,' Charles said.

The woman blinked, embarrassed. 'Oh, I'm sorry, I thought your wife said that you had a baby . . .'

'I'm not his wife,' Mia interrupted. 'And I said we were *trying* to have a baby, not that we have one.' Her cheeks burned as she spoke and her voice wavered.

There was a moment's embarrassed silence, then someone said: 'So how did you first meet Leo, Charles?' A wave of relief seemed to wash over the table at the change of subject.

'We met through my brother, Rob,' Charles answered. He tried to focus on the conversation, but Mia had excused herself from the table and was on her way out of the dining room. 'Rob and Leo are neighbours in Dolphin Square. Rob introduced us a couple of years ago, Leo and I got talking, and he ended up in an advisory role at the university.'

'Advisory?' Leo laughed. 'More like non-executive director, and there's no bloody share options!' Everyone laughed, the caterer came in with the vegetable dishes for the main course and the front door bell rang. Charles glanced at the door to the dining room; there was no sign of Mia.

'Excuse me,' Leo said. He stood and left the room. A couple of minutes later he was back, whispering in Meg's ear.

Meg rose. 'Do carry on, everyone,' she said. 'I have an unexpected visitor.' Charles watched her leave.

'Lotte!' Meg went to her daughter and folded her into an embrace. 'Darling, what on earth is wrong?'

Lotte, who had wept for most of the journey to her mother's, was still tearful. 'I've left Gordon,' she said.

'Where are the children?'

'They're in the car, asleep.'

'Oh God, poor Lotte.'

She broke off as Mia came across the hall and the caterer put her head out of the kitchen.

'I'm ready with the lamb when you are, Mrs Chandler!'

Meg released Lotte, squeezed her shoulders and said: 'Get the children in out of the car and let's put them to bed. I have to carry on with this dinner, I'm afraid, but I'll get you settled first.' She turned to the caterer and said: 'Give me five minutes, will you, Fiona?'

'No problem.'

Mia stepped forward. 'Can I help, Meg? Can I bring one of the children in?'

'Lotte?'

'Thanks, that would be great.' Aware of how she must look after so much weeping, Lotte avoided eye contact with the other woman.

'I'll whiz up and get their beds ready for you,' Meg said. 'See you up there.'

Lotte went out to the car, which she'd had to park on the road as the drive was full.

'Let me move ours and you can bring your car right up to the house,' Mia said. She opened her handbag, which she'd taken with her to the loo to repair her face, and took out her car keys. Once she'd moved the car and Lotte had driven into the space, Mia came round to the back passenger seat to help.

'Could you take Freddie?' Lotte asked. 'He sleeps like a brick and won't wake up if you lift him.'

'Of course.' Mia reached into the car and struggled for a few moments with the car seat. Lotte unclipped the harness for her and she lifted Freddie's small, warm body up and into her arms. She held her breath and cupped his head with her hand, gently laying it on her shoulder. He smelt wonderful, a smell she could never have described, and the feel of his warmth, his vulnerability, his child's body against her made her want to weep. Carefully she carried him into the house and up the stairs. She followed Lotte into a bedroom with a bed and a travel cot in it, and laid him in the travel cot, bending awkwardly to place him without the smallest jolt. Then she covered him with a sheet and a cotton blanket and stood back. 'He's beautiful,' she said to Lotte.

Lotte came and stood next to Mia for a few moments, and looked down at her son. 'Yes, he is,' she answered quietly, and thought: whatever else I've lost, I've got them, and they are worth all the pain and heartache. 'D'you have children?' she asked Mia.

'No. I'd like to, but it's difficult, I . . .' Mia broke off and turned away, and Lotte touched her arm, to try in some way to comfort her. We all have our own private sorrows, she thought.

In the guest suite, Lotte sat down on the bed and kicked her shoes off. It was a long drive to her mother's, and coupled with the stress and emotion of the past few days, she felt quite exhausted. She put her feet up and curled on to her side. Meg found her like that a few minutes later, eyes closed and almost asleep. She covered Lotte with a rug and went to turn the lights off.

'I'm not asleep, Mum,' Lotte said. Meg came and sat down on the bed next to her. 'I'm sorry to just pitch up like this, in the middle of your dinner. I should have called, but I . . .' She broke off and dug in her pocket for her handkerchief, already damp and crumpled. Meg fetched some tissues and handed them to Lotte, who blew her nose. 'Gordon's been having an affair, for three years. I just found out.'

'Dear God, Lotte! That . . . that . . .' Meg struggled to find the right word. She wanted to say *that bastard*, it was what she thought, what she called Gordon privately, but she couldn't say it to Lotte. 'That man is having an affair? I'm stunned! With someone like you at home?' Agitated, Meg stood up. 'Christ,' she burst out, unable to stop herself, 'I've always thought he was a sod, but this really takes the biscuit!'

Lotte sat up. 'Have you?'

'God, yes!' Meg sat down again. 'Leo can't stand him, and if your father had ever met him, well, I'm sure he'd have been horrified.'

'But you never said.' Lotte stared at her mother. 'All this time you've never said anything, nothing, not a word, and God knows I could have done with some support at times!'

Meg looked down at her hands. 'What could I say, Lotte? I tried, I tried to talk to you when you wanted to marry him in the first place, but we were all so upset, grieving so much for Daddy, and you said you knew exactly what you were doing, you . . .'

'I told you not to interfere,' Lotte said.

'Yes.' They fell silent. Meg reached out and took Lotte's hand in hers. She held it tight. 'I think when your father died that we were, all of us, so shocked and upset that we didn't know what to do. You took refuge in Gordon.'

'I thought he'd look after me.'

'How wrong you were.' Meg kissed Lotte's hand, then stood. 'I hope Fiona has had the initiative to serve the lamb without me, or our guests will be eating charcoal for dinner.' She moved towards the door. 'Would you like something on a tray?'

Lotte shook her head.

'We'll talk more tomorrow,' Meg said. 'Goodnight, Lotte darling.' She left the room and closed the door behind her. Lotte got up to open it again so that she could hear the children across the corridor, then peeled off her clothes and crawled under the covers. She didn't even bother to wash or clean her teeth. She fell straight asleep.

Claire sat in the darkness and listened to the sounds outside. She was somewhere rural, she knew that; she had heard the scrape and scurry of small animals above her, on the roof, outside, and she'd heard birdsong, she could just make it out through the thick, damp walls of her prison and it was a sound so powerful and so full of hope that she strained every nerve to catch just a few moments of it. She had lost track of time, she had no idea how many days she had been here; her watch had been taken and she could only sense the night because of the nocturnal activity, the constant, fevered running of tiny feet above her.

She was still frightened, but the fear was no longer all-consuming. She was more hopeful every day that she was being kept alive for a purpose. She figured that if he had wanted her dead he would have killed her already. He fed her daily, leaving a bowl of dry breakfast cereal and some bread; and he left water, a plastic bottle of it, but she could eat very little, her stomach had closed up with fear. He wanted money, that was what she thought, but she had tried to tell him where to go for it, to contact her parents, and he'd hit her across the face, shouting at her to shut up. It didn't make any sense, but she couldn't afford to dwell on it. If she had thought about it, in all the hours she sat and lay in the darkness, she would have gone insane. Instead, she concentrated her mind on what she loved most. She had worked her way through Shelley and was on to Byron. Every time she recited his verse she began with the same words. 'George Gordon, Lord Byron, born 1788, died 1824.' It was reassuring to remember the poet, his dates, the verses, to say the lines that she had learnt by heart, over and over in her head and out loud. It reassured her that she was holding on, that she was clinging, if only by her fingernails, on to her sanity. That he hadn't, despite her being here, frightened and alone, got her yet.

Charles drove home. Mia was drunk; not visibly so, but enough for Charles to know it. She had been downing cognac at the end of the evening in a way that indicated she was beyond caring about how she felt tomorrow morning. When she said goodbye to Meg and Leo she was effusive in her thanks, almost slurring her words, and by the time she climbed into the car she was fumbling with her seat belt.

A few yards up the road, she said: 'I met Meg's daughter tonight.'

'Did you?' Charles glanced sidelong at her as if she'd gone mad. 'Really?'

'That's what all the fiasco was about, at dinner,' she said. 'Why Meg went missing. She turned up unannounced, in trouble I'd say. She was pretty upset.' Mia pulled her coat round her and laid her head back against the seat. The headlights of the other cars hurt her eyes. 'She's lovely, Meg's daughter, beautiful, long and sleek-looking, with these amazing eyes. And she has beautiful children, two of them.'

Charles thought: Oh God, here we go, but he said nothing; he didn't want to get into a fight, not now, with Mia in this state.

'I carried the little one up to his cot,' Mia said. She lifted her head, a bit unsteadily, and stared out of the window. 'He felt wonderful in my arms, warm and soft . . .' Her voice trailed away and Charles realized that she was crying. 'I think,' she said at last, after a long, protracted silence, 'that I should leave.' Still Charles said nothing.

Eventually, they pulled up outside the house and he came round to help her out. 'Thanks,' she murmured, and led the way to the front door. Inside, she turned to him as if to say something, then changed her mind and went upstairs to bed without another word.

Charles went into his study and sat down. He thought about Henry Chatten, about loving someone so completely that nothing else really mattered, and then instinctively he thought about the woman in the bar. It was impossible, he told himself, to fall in love with someone in one night, after one meeting. It just couldn't happen; love took time and patience. But as he picked up his notes taken from Lady Chatten's diary and looked over them again, he wondered, not for the first time since Tuesday, if his long-held view might be wrong.

Chapter 8

The next time that Henry saw Daisy was on Saturday. She had managed to get a day off by telling the housekeeper she had a sick friend she needed to visit. It was the middle of May, the weather was warm – blue skies with a mild south-westerly breeze – and he had organized a day out at the seaside. His family had a house in Brighton and Henry knew the town well. They wouldn't be able to visit the house; his aunt was there for the month, and although Henry was infatuated, he knew the boundaries. But they would promenade, go on the electric line along the seashore, see the Royal Pavilion, picnic, take tea in one of the smart hotels along the front, maybe even have a swim in the sea. They would have, as Daisy told one of the girls she worked with, 'A right proper day out.' Of course she didn't tell the girl who was taking her for this day out. Daisy was clever; she had set her sights unrealistically high and she had no intention of telling anyone about Henry, at least not until there was something to tell.

Henry met Daisy at Brierly railway station at ten thirty. She had borrowed a bicycle from one of the lads on the estate and rode to the station feeling liberated and modern, arriving with her cheeks flushed and her wonderful auburn hair in wild, untidy wisps around her face. She locked the bicycle to the railing and ran into the station to meet him. Henry, who had been watching out for her, felt a surge of excitement. Only Daisy would arrive for a day out in such style.

'Good morning, Miss Burrows. How was your bicycle ride?'

Daisy swiftly tucked her hair back into place and smiled at Henry. 'It was marvellous,' she said. 'The wind on my face and in my hair, and my heart racing. It was pure exhilaration.'

'It looked it,' Henry answered. 'Shall we?' He proffered his arm and Daisy took it. He showed their tickets and they walked up on to the platform, Daisy carrying a parasol, Henry the picnic basket and a rug. It was busy; Brighton was a popular destination for a day out on a Saturday in summer. Henry walked Daisy to the end of the platform, away from the crowd, and glanced surreptitiously, he hoped, over her head to check there was no one there he knew.

'I don't think I'll let you down, Mr Chatten,' Daisy said. 'There's no need to look so worried at the crowd.'

Henry turned his gaze back to her. He was about to protest, but she was smiling and he knew there was no point. 'Do you know everything I am thinking, Miss Burrows?'

'No, not everything, that would be boring, but it was obvious to me, if you don't mind me saying, that you'd be a trifle worried about being with me in public, what with your position and mine being so, how shall I put it, disparate.'

Henry laughed. 'You put it very nicely, but I am not worried; I am charmed and delighted to be with you in public.'

Daisy rolled her eyes, her beautiful deep blue eyes. 'How very kind, I'm sure. Not that I believe a word of it, of course.'

'Well you should. You look quite lovely this morning.'

She looked at him. She was about to smile, to make some witticism, to impress him with her cleverness, but the sight of his earnest face showed her there was no need. 'Thank you,' she said simply.

Suddenly there was the clear, shrill sound of a steam locomotive from up the track, and everyone strained to get a glimpse of the train approaching. The station master blew his whistle, guards walked the platform announcing the train and Daisy clapped her hands in excitement. As it drew in, belching out a cloud of steam, the crowd bustled and surged towards the carriages and Henry positioned himself to open the door. In a burst of noisy excitement from the crowd, the two of them climbed aboard. Henry stowed the picnic basket away on the overhead shelf and Daisy took her seat. They were in a first-class carriage; it was the only time she had ever been out of steerage, but she gave no indication of that. She sat neatly on her seat by the window and waited for Henry to sit next to her. He took out his pocket watch as he did so and glanced at the dial. 'Exactly on time,' he said as the guards began closing the carriage doors ready for departure. 'We shall be at the coast in just over an hour.'

'I do hope the sunshine lasts,' Daisy said, peering out at the sky.

'I am certain that it will,' Henry replied. He was, too. He looked at her face, which even in the harsh sunlight had a softness that he had never seen on any woman before. 'For us it will last.' And because the carriage was empty but for them, and because he was filled with such longing that he could no longer control, he took her hand and held it in his own, just for a few moments, just until she drew it away. It was enough; the day could only get better.

The first thing they did when they arrived in Brighton was to promenade along the sea front. The sun was high in the sky and Daisy kept her parasol up to protect her face. She noticed as they passed the other ladies and gentlemen promenading that fine as her parasol was – actually the finest thing she owned, and a present from Miss Mary Chase – it was terribly old-fashioned, and these things, in Daisy's mind, mattered.

'Do you think, Mr Chatten,' she said, as they strolled, 'that my parasol is looking a bit tired and frayed at the edges?'

'Your parasol? Good Lord, I hadn't even thought to look.' They stopped, and Henry took a step back and regarded the item. 'It is old, that is certain, but it is lovely, Miss Burrows. I think it quite fine.'

'Yes, it's fine, but is it in keeping with the rest of the ladies' parasols, Mr Chatten? I am beginning to think that I shouldn't have brought it with me. I am concerned that it is letting you down.'

'Letting me down? Not at all.'

They walked on.

'I really do think it is most old-fashioned.' Daisy stopped again. 'And I think that I should take it down for fear of embarrassing you.'

As she went to release the catch on it, Henry said, 'But you might get a pink nose, Miss Burrows, and it would be very uncomfortable in the glare of the sun. You must not be without a parasol.' He took a few moments to think it through, then said: 'But I have an idea. Why don't we make our way up to the new department store off the sea front and purchase another one? I would love you to choose one that you would consider more fashionable.'

It was exactly the right thing to say; Daisy beamed. 'That is a charming idea, Mr Chatten,' she said. 'Let's do it at once.' She took Henry's arm and they walked on in the direction of Hannington's department store.

The new parasol purchased, along with some linen handkerchiefs and some lavender soap, Daisy and Henry took their picnic on the lawn in front of the bandstand. Cook had wanted to prepare something special for Master Chatten's day out, but he did not want to embarrass Daisy and had been insistent that she keep it simple. When he opened the basket and saw Daisy's face, he was pleased with his decision. Henry might have been

91

in love, but he wasn't naive. He was separated from Daisy by class, and that class divide involved a whole different set of experiences, of values and judgements. For Daisy it would have been bad form to let Cook go to extraordinary lengths for a seaside picnic for her, one of the underlings in the household below stairs. She would have been overwhelmed by what normally would be prepared for a family picnic; she would have felt guilty and in awe of the food. But this, a pork pie, some bread and good cheese, some home-made pickle, some fresh tomatoes, cold chicken and strawberries, was perfect. A feast without pretension. They sat on the rug and Henry opened the bottle of lemonade and poured the drinks, while Daisy laid out the food.

'Let me do that,' Henry said, handing her a glass.

'Not at all, sir,' she replied. 'It's no bother. I've had a great deal of practice at it.'

Henry flushed. He didn't want to be reminded of Daisy's station, not now, not at all today in fact; but she seemed to slip from one accent to another as effortlessly as she made conversation. To her it was a joke; to Henry it was far from it. But he recovered himself and noted her pleasant manners and forgot once again the gulf that separated them.

After lunch they took a ride on the electric line along the sea front, then they walked up to the Royal Pavilion and around the outside, admiring the architecture. Of course Henry did all the admiring, the pointing-out of features, the explaining of the building's appeal. Daisy walked quietly by his side, nodding, looking, paying attention.

'So,' Henry asked, when they had made it around the exterior of the building and through the gardens, 'do you like it, Miss Burrows?'

'Yes, I like it, but I have to confess that I think it's a shocking waste. Why, they could have housed half the poor in London for

92

what it cost to build this, and for what? It is empty most of the time now, a building with no use except to be looked at and admired.'

'But isn't that use enough?'

'Not if you're poor it isn't, Mr Chatten. Not if you live in a filthy room, with five other people, where the air is putrid and damp and your chances of ever getting out of it are slim.'

Henry turned to her. 'Are you a new woman, Miss Burrows? One of these daughters of the revolt? You certainly seem to have very strong opinions on things.'

'Do I? I just speak the truth, Mr Chatten. It's got nothing to do with opinions, it's just what I know. And I would love to be one of the women you mention, were I of a different class and education. I would so love to be independent.'

Henry was again reminded of what lay between them, and hated it. It seemed that each moment he spent with her he felt closer to her, not further apart. He didn't want to think about who she really was and where she came from. He was captivated by her, by her capriciousness, her intellect, her sheer vivacity. He knew that Daisy Burrows was unique, much as Miss Mary Chase had known the day she took a homeless eleven-year-old girl into her school for domestic help. She had a quality that elevated her above so many: a wonderful intelligence and a love of life, a desire for it, which shone out of her in every-thing she said and did, lighting Henry's predictable grey life and putting everything else in the shade. Daisy, he had no doubt, was his equal, in all but the most important thing of their time: her status.

'Would you like to take tea?' he asked, wanting so desper-ately to bridge the gap.

'I would love to.'

'Then we'll go to the Grand.'

Daisy looked at him; this was not a wise decision. 'The Grand?

Wouldn't a small tea shop in the Lanes be cosier?'

'Not at all.' He held out his arm and she took it. 'We will go to the Grand and have a sumptuous tea and finish our day out properly.'

Daisy said nothing. The Grand was out of her league and she knew it, but if Henry was prepared to take the risk then so was she; she had never been short of courage. So they walked back along the sea front to the imposing building opposite the pier.

The hotel was packed. They were asked to wait, and Daisy saw the maître d' cast a glance in her direction that told her that he knew her place, even if she didn't. She smoothed the skirt of her dress with her hand and picked at the fringed edge of her new parasol. The dress was her best, a pale blue linen, not the height of fashion, but decent enough, except not decent enough for the Grand, where the most affluent women were dressed in tea gowns and the less affluent in summer dresses. Daisy began to fret. The women around her were highly fashionable, their hats adorned with silk and feathers, to which Daisy's hat, a small straw affair with a pale blue linen bow, just didn't compare. She had stepped into a world dominated by attention to detail, and the ability to be fashionable was a sign of social status, a status it was clear that she simply didn't have.

'I wonder if it isn't a bit too long to wait, Mr Chatten,' Daisy said quietly, after the couple who had come in after them were given a table. 'They seem to be terribly busy and I wonder if somewhere else might not be better.'

Henry, who had noticed the slight by the maître d', had determined that they would have tea here. He did not like the fellow's attitude and he would stand his ground. 'We'll wait,' he said. 'They will have a table free shortly.'

Daisy looked away. She had noticed that a group of ladies by the palms were whispering and staring in their direction, and a creeping blush spread over her face.

94

'Excuse me?' Henry said, stopping the maître d'. 'Have you any idea how long it might be until a table becomes free?' The waiter looked at his list, then up at the vast tea room, then back at his list again. He seemed to be taking a long time over it, procrastinating Henry would have said, when he spotted a departing party approaching the exit.

'Right now, sir,' he replied. 'There is a party leaving now and I will have their table prepared for you immediately.' Henry followed his gaze. A matronly woman leading her two young daughters was heading his way. His heart sank and he swallowed hard, looked down at the floor and shifted very slightly away from Daisy. The woman saw him.

'Henry?' she called. 'Henry, it is you, isn't it?'

His head jerked up and he flushed. 'Aunt Dehlia! Yes, of course it's me. What a pleasure to see you, and Cecily and Alice. How nice!' He stepped forward and kissed the ladies, then stood back, another pace away from Daisy.

'Are you here alone, Henry? You should have said, my dear boy, you could have taken tea with us. We always take tea at the Grand when we're in Brighton, don't we, girls?'

The two girls nodded, and Cecily looked across at Daisy. Then Aunt Dehlia did the same. There were a few moments of embarrassed silence before Henry said: 'Miss Langley, let me introduce you to my aunt, Lady Heaton, and to my cousins, Miss Cecily and Miss Alice Heaton. Miss Elizabeth Langley.'

Lady Heaton nodded at Daisy, whose face was scarlet. Cecily and Alice gave her the briefest of glances, and she nodded back, then all three ladies looked away. Daisy was quite clearly not of the right class.

'We must be on our way, Henry,' Lady Heaton said. 'Give my love to your parents, we will look forward to seeing them in London at the end of the month. Girls.' And she swept out, the two girls trailing behind.

Henry stared down at the marble-tiled floor.

'Your table, sir?'

Henry glanced up again, but Daisy had gone. He spun round and saw her figure hurrying across the lobby of the hotel. 'Excuse me,' he said to the waiter, and rushed off after her.

'Miss Burrows? Daisy?' He caught up with her on the pavement and jumped in front of her to stop her in her path. 'Miss Burrows, please, please wait.' Daisy stopped, but she did not look at him. 'Miss Burrows, I do beg your pardon, that was intolerable of me. I didn't know what else to do, I didn't want to embarrass you by revealing who you are, I wouldn't want anyone to talk, to gossip, I . . .'

'You didn't want to embarrass yourself by telling anyone who I am, and that's the truth.'

Henry shook his head. 'No! No, I don't care who you are or where you come from . . .'

'Then more fool you, because you should!'

Daisy began walking off again and Henry trotted alongside her. 'I'm sorry I didn't introduce you, I should have done, but my aunt is . . .'

Daisy stopped and faced him. 'Your aunt is Lady Heaton and you are the Right Honourable Henry Chatten, son of Sir Lionel and Lady Margaret Chatten of Bicester House; and I am Daisy Burrows, orphan, housemaid, working class. I don't know what I am doing here, this is quite, quite ridiculous. Please, Henry, leave it as it is, let me alone, I want to go home.'

Henry placed both his hands on her shoulders and gazed down at her face. 'I can't leave you alone, Daisy, you know it and I know it. What has happened between us, this, this love, it's bigger than we are, it's better than all that in there.' He nodded back at the Grand Hotel. 'It transcends everything, it is more than both of us . . .'

'No!' Daisy shrugged his hands away. 'That is upper-class

romanticism and I haven't got time for it, Henry Chatten. I am working class, I sweat and scrub and empty your mother's chamber pot. I cannot afford love.' She turned away from him.

'Everyone can afford love, Daisy. Love is God's currency and we have no right to deny God.'

She looked back at his face and saw the truth in his eyes. She felt elated and at the same time pitifully sorry for him. 'You really believe it, don't you?' she asked.

Henry took her hand and pressed it to his lips. For the second time he marvelled at how cool her skin was. 'Of course. Don't you?'

Daisy let him hold her hand; she let him leave his lips on her flesh longer than she should have done, and she could feel the pulse of love in him. She did not answer him; she could not. What could she tell him of love? How, in all her struggle, could she have found time to open her heart and understand the meaning of the word? She knew that he felt it, but did she? Henry moved his lips to kiss her fingertips, and she shivered.

'Shall we go home, Daisy?' he asked. She nodded. He released her hand and offered his arm. She took it, and in awed silence they made their way back to the station.

Chapter 9

At the university hall of residence a team of cleaners came in every Monday morning to do through the students' bedrooms, bleach the bathrooms and restore the small kitchens on each floor to a state of reasonable hygiene. There were five of them, and they worked together, starting at the top and moving down the building. On each floor they swapped duties so that everyone got a go at the bathrooms or the bedrooms or the gruelling task of cleaning the floors. This morning, on the second floor, it was Magda who went to unlock Claire Thompson's room, number 201B, to clean it and found the door already unlocked. She went inside.

The first thing she noticed was the smell of rancid milk. She removed the offending carton – it must have been over a week old – opened the window to let some air into the room and began on the sink in the corner. It was pretty clean, lacking the usual hard globules of toothpaste and soggy soap; in fact it looked as if it hadn't been used. Magda lifted the things on the glass shelf under the mirror to clean it. The dust was thick; none of the toiletries or cosmetics had been moved for days. She picked up a packet of contraceptive pills; they didn't seem to have been taken since last Tuesday.

Magda went to the door. 'Dorrie,' she called, 'could you come in here for a mo?'

Dorrie headed the team. She got paid a bit extra by the company to motivate the ladies and act as team leader. She joined Magda in Claire Thompson's room.

'Dorrie, it looks like Claire hasn't been here for a few days.'

'She might just be away.'

'She left her milk open on her desk, and all her wash things are here and her contraceptive pills haven't been taken.'

Dorrie frowned. They knew most of the students by name, it made for a nicer working relationship, but they knew very little else about the girls' lives. 'Maybe she went away suddenly, she might have just jumped on a train and headed home because she was feeling homesick.'

'Might have done.'

Dorrie cast her eye over the room. Magda did have a point; it didn't have the usual lived-in feel about it. 'Ask her neighbour in 202, see if she's seen her around. If you're still worried at the end of the shift, I'll go and see the warden.'

Magda nodded and followed Dorrie out of the room. She knocked on the door next to Claire's room and it was opened by a small, plump girl who had obviously still been in bed.

'Can you come back and clean next week?' she asked Magda. 'I'm not feeling too good.'

'No, but I can work round you, it won't take long. I was wondering if you'd seen Claire Thompson around?'

'No, not much, not at all actually, but then she might have had what I've got and gone home. It's the flu, I feel bloody awful.'

'Right, I'll check.' Magda looked at the girl. 'Have you been to the doctor?'

'No, I've been in bed for two days.'

'Then ring him and ask him to come out. You look awful.'

The girl closed the door and Magda went back to Claire's room. She finished the sink area, wiped over the desk and the woodwork and finally mopped the floor. As she came out Dorrie said: 'Any luck?'

'No, I think you'd better go and see the warden, just to be on the safe side.'

'Right.' Dorrie sighed irritably. She'd be late home at this rate, and although she was paid a bit more for the position of responsibility, she certainly wasn't paid ruddy overtime.

Jill Hooper, the warden, had a flat on the ground floor of the hall of residence. Dorrie rang the bell at lunchtime, hoping that she wouldn't be in and that she could scribble a note, posting it through the letter box. But Jill was at home, and she invited Dorrie in for coffee, which, despite making her even later home, it would have been rude to refuse. Dorrie reported Magda's thoughts on Claire Thompson, and after coffee they both went up and had a quick look in Claire's room. Jill said she would ring Claire's parents and ask them if she was there. She thanked Dorrie for her concern, asked her to thank Magda, and reassured her that there was very probably a simple explanation for the whole thing. Dorrie left twenty minutes later than she should have done and felt that it had all been a bit of a waste of time.

Jill Hooper went straight to her file and found Claire Thompson's home address. She rang the number and spoke to Claire's mother, trying to keep the concern out of her voice. She asked if Claire was at home; Claire's mother said no, she was at college, she had spoken to her last Tuesday before her tutorial. Jill could hear the anxiety in Mrs Thompson's voice when she said: 'Is anything wrong, Miss Hooper?'

'No, I shouldn't think so,' Jill replied. 'It's just that we haven't seen Claire for a couple of days and I was just checking that she hadn't gone home with this awful flu.'

'She is around, isn't she? She's not the sort of girl to go off without telling anyone.'

'I'm sure she's on campus somewhere, please don't worry.' God, why did students have no sense of responsibility? Jill thought. Silly girl had probably bunked off with a boyfriend and hadn't bothered to tell anyone. 'I'll get Claire to ring you when I catch up with her,' she said. She hung up, made herself a sandwich and decided to pay a quick call to the history department after lunch, just to see if anyone there knew where Claire might have gone to.

Charles was in his office when Jill Hooper came to the department. She asked in the office, Claire was looked up on a list and Jill was sent down to see Professor Meredith, her tutor. She knocked lightly on the half-open door.

'Professor Meredith?'

'Yes?'

Jill came into the room and Charles stood. 'I'm Jill Hooper, I'm the warden for Norton Hall.' They shook hands. 'I'm sorry to bother you, Professor Meredith, but I'm trying to locate one of your students, Claire Thompson. It doesn't look as if she's been in her room for several days and I was wondering when you had seen her last.'

'Claire Thompson?' Charles blinked. He liked most of his students, put up with some and disliked one or two. Claire made him distinctly uneasy. 'Well, I'm not sure . . .' He appeared quite vague for several moments, then went to his desk and looked at his diary. 'I make a note of my tutorials here.' He flicked back over the pages. 'She was here on Tuesday, last Tuesday, but I cancelled the tutorial as no one else turned up: flu epidemic. She wasn't here on Thursday. I asked the group if anyone had seen her; most students usually send an apology, but there wasn't one. She hasn't been absent before, so naturally I asked after her, but she . . .' He broke off and considered his words. 'She doesn't seem to have many close friends. No one knew where she was – one of them called her a bit of a loner, as far as I can remember – but I did ask someone to go and check on her.'

'I see.' A bit of a loner would have been Jill's description too.

'So has anyone seen her since Tuesday?'

Jill shrugged. 'I don't know yet. Can you give me a list of the students she shares tutorials with? I think I'll ask around this afternoon.'

Charles walked back to his desk and went into his system. 'I'll print one off for you,' he said.

'She's probably just taken off somewhere on some sort of whim,' Jill said. 'Or maybe she's met someone and is having a bit of a fling.' Jill knew as she spoke that she was trying to convince herself more than anyone else. She was beginning to get a bad feeling about this. A loner wasn't the sort for a whim or a fling. Charles handed her the list; she glanced at it and said: 'I know three of these girls. I'll pop over to the Union bar and see if I can find them.'

'You can find anyone and everyone in the SU bar,' Charles replied.

Jill smiled. 'Thanks.' She tucked the list in her bag. 'When's Claire's next tutorial?'

'Tomorrow.'

'That's a week, then, since anyone's actually seen her.'

'Yes.' Charles dug his hands in his pockets. 'But she does keep herself to herself. I'm sure it won't be as sinister as it appears now.'

Jill went to the door. 'I'm sure you're right,' she answered. But it wasn't true; she wasn't sure at all.

The Student Union bar was packed. As if they haven't had enough leisure time over the weekend, Jill thought, here they all are again, Monday lunchtime, drinking pints and smoking themselves to death. She went in and walked the length of the bar but couldn't spot the two students she was looking for, so went out on to the terrace. She saw one of the girls immediately, sitting with two boys in the sunshine. Jill approached her.

'Sarah?'

The girl lowered her sunglasses, in what Jill thought was a rather theatrical and pretentious way.

'Hello, Miss Hooper.' She took the glasses off. 'D'you want to sit down?'

'Thanks.' The lads moved round a space and created a vacancy for Jill. She sat on the bench and said: 'Sarah, I'm trying to find out where Claire Thompson is. No one seems to have seen her this week. Have you seen her around at all?'

The girl shook her head. 'She wasn't at Charlie's tutorial on Thursday, so no, I haven't seen her. We don't really move in the same circles, Miss Hooper.'

'Who does Claire hang out with, have you any idea?'

The boys exchanged glances.

'Am I missing something?' Jill asked.

'She doesn't really hang out with anyone,' one of them offered. 'She's kind of weird, like not really in this world.'

'What d'you mean?' Jill asked.

'She lies a lot,' Sarah cut in. 'Can't seem to differentiate between truth and fantasy.'

'It's like she's got no life so she has to make it up . . .'

'And boy does she make it up!' The other lad smiled at this. Jill was always amazed at the cruelty of young people. They were very ungiving.

'So none of you have seen her and you have no idea where she might be?' Jill's voice was sharp and Sarah picked up on it.

'She is all right, isn't she?'

Jill stood. 'Thank you for your concern, though it might be a little late. We'll have to wait and see.' She walked away, back through the bar and out on to campus. She would give it until later that day, then she would have to get a bit more thorough, maybe even go to the vice-chancellor.

Annie Taylor had had her first shift in the new job with the new team and had found a whole lot of new problems that needed to be dealt with. Sure, she had accepted a more downbeat posting so as to get a promotion, but she didn't expect hicksville in terms of attitudes, archaic in terms of work patterns and almost Neolithic in terms of male egos. As she sat alone in the pub, nursing a lime and soda water and a soggy lasagne – which would serve as her supper – she wondered, not for the first time since she had taken occupation of her small house on the Belle View Estate on Friday, whether this was the best move forward for her.

First there had been Saturday. Her colleagues in CID had been staggered when she had turned up at the weekend unannounced, unpaid, in her free time, to get to know the team and to collect a bootload of files to read up over the weekend. She meant business, that was why she'd joined the police, but no one there seemed anything other than resentful at her attempt to make sure she was up to speed when she started today. Then today, a catalogue of mutterings in corridors, withheld information, snide remarks, no invite at lunchtime, barely concealed resentment and at times the odd bout of hostility. OK, so she had swanned in and walked off with the top job, but she had better qualifications and experience and results than anyone else applying for it, hadn't she? But it seemed that wasn't good enough. They had their own golden boy of CID, who she had yet to meet – he hadn't bothered to turn up – and if he couldn't have the job then nor, it would appear, could anyone else. God, it was so provincial! This was going to be hard, far harder than she'd thought, and on top of all that crap was the fact that she had moved home, back to a county that she had been desperate to escape from ten years ago, and to Sunday lunch with her parents and her mother thinking that any moment she would meet Mr Right and it would be a hop, skip and a jump to a white dress and two weeks in Mauritius.

She fiddled with her lasagne, ate another mouthful, then abandoned it. She wasn't hungry, she didn't want a drink, but she didn't want to go home either. Pubs were lonely places; they were full of people, but without a companion, in such a jovial atmosphere one's social inadequacies seemed far more apparent. What am I doing? Annie thought. I don't want to be here. She stood, gathered up her bag and jacket and made her way to the door. Her phone rang, and she scrabbled around in her bag for it, but it went on to messaging before she had a chance to answer it. It was her mother, checking she was all right on her own. All right on her own? Annie swore. She was thirty, independent, professional, and it was her choice to be alone, she liked it that way. She tossed the phone back into her bag and headed out to her car. Back to the office, she thought; there was nothing like paperwork to soothe the temper.

*   *   *

Jill Hooper was looking through Claire Thompson's file when there was a ring at her door. She hadn't yet decided what to do, but she was worried. She didn't know if she was over-reacting, but she had a duty of pastoral care and so was beginning to think that it would be better to report this to the authorities, to at least be on the safe side. She went to the door and opened it. Sarah, the girl she had spoken to earlier, stood there with another girl, Jen, a rather hard-nosed character from the same floor as Claire. Sarah said: 'Miss Hooper, Jen wanted to have a word with you about Claire.' Jill noticed a small, discreet prod, and Jen said: 'Erm, yeah, I, erm, spoke to her on Tuesday night, that was the last time I saw her.'

'You'd better come in,' Jill said. She opened the door and the two girls shuffled into the flat, standing uneasily in the small sitting room. 'You saw Claire on Tuesday, is that right, Jen?'

'Yes, she was pretty pissed, she came to the floor party and asked me for some matches. I asked her if she wanted to stay, but she said she was going out with Professor Meredith for a drink and some supper. I didn't believe her, of course . . .'

'Of course?'

'No, she's always telling stories like that. She reckons Charles Meredith's got a thing for her.' Jen smiled. 'None of us believe her. I mean, look at Professor Meredith and look at Claire. I don't think so.'

'Have you seen her since Tuesday?'

'No. I did knock on her door late on Tuesday night, or rather Wednesday morning, about three a.m. I was desperate for a fag and wanted my matches back, but she wasn't there.'

'So she left the party having borrowed some matches off

you and went out into town, supposedly with Professor Meredith, and she still hadn't returned by three a.m.'

'No.'

'And neither of you have seen her since. Is that right?'

The girls looked at each other.

'Have you bothered to knock, to see if she was all right?'

They stared at the floor.

'And you didn't think to tell anyone about this? How long did you intend to leave it?' No answer. Jill went into the hall and took her jacket out of the cupboard. She slipped it on. 'OK, what I suggest is that you two go back to your rooms and stay there for the time being so that I can get hold of you easily if I need to. I am going to see the vice-chancellor to ask his advice on what to do next. All right?'

They nodded. Jill moved towards the door, but both girls stayed where they were.

'Is there something else?'

Sarah looked up. 'Apparently Claire told a friend of Jen's that she was having counselling. She said that she was going to the university practice to see one of the therapists there. She told this girl that Professor Meredith was causing her a real problem and that she needed help with it. We just thought it was bullshit, but, well, I don't know now, perhaps there was something in it.'

Jill patted Sarah on the arm. 'You've been very open, Sarah, I appreciate it, thank you. Both of you have.' She wanted to add: about bloody time too, but she didn't. She ushered them towards the door. 'I must get going. I know that the vice-chancellor works late tonight, but I don't know how late. I don't want to miss him.' She opened the door and all three went out. 'I'll be up to see you both later.' Jill waved and headed towards her car.

* * *

107

Annie Taylor had worked her way through a file of paper-work and calmed her temper sufficiently to go home. She finished off, tidied everything away and left the office. On her way out of the door, she called goodbye to the duty sergeant on the front desk and suddenly realized her mistake as his face lit up.

'Ah, DI Taylor, you might be able to help us on this one, if you can spare a minute.'

Annie felt her spirits sink; she was about to be stitched up.

'This lady here, Miss Hooper, is a warden at the university and she wants to report a missing person. I think it would be better handled by CID. Would you mind?'

Annie sighed. She looked at the woman at the desk, late twenties, smart but not expensively dressed, obviously professional, concerned. 'Sure,' she said. 'We'll take the small interview room. Can you bring some forms through, please, Sergeant.' She smiled at Miss Hooper and opened the door back into the bowels of the station.

'I'm Detective Inspector Taylor. Please, have a seat.'

'Jill Hooper. I'm the warden for Norton Hall, it's one of the girls' halls of residence up at the university.' Jill sat. She was pleased she was dealing with a woman; the sergeant on the desk hadn't seemed in the least bit bothered by her concern.

Annie sat down opposite her and said: 'We have a check list now, Ms Hooper, a guide for reporting a missing person. When the sergeant brings in the forms, if it's all right with you we'll go through the list. This will give us an indication of how high a priority the case is. Very often, you see, missing persons go missing of their own accord and there's really not very much we can do about that.'

'I see. I don't think that is the case here.'

The sergeant came in with the forms. He smiled at Annie but she didn't return it. Smug bastard, she thought.

'Right, let's go down the list and we'll discuss each point as it comes up. Name.'

'Claire Thompson. Her date of birth is twenty-five, six, eighty-two. Her address is Norton Hall, at the university.'

'Right, thanks.' Annie looked up. 'OK, the first question I need to ask is: is she vulnerable at all?'

'Vulnerable?'

'Yes, emotionally insecure, depressed, just split up with a boyfriend, lacking in confidence. Anything like that?'

Jill hesitated. 'I would describe her as self-contained; she didn't have many close friends, and some of the other students called her a bit of a loner, but I don't think she is emotionally insecure. I certainly don't know of any relationship failure and I don't think she's depressed. She didn't show any of the classic signs, her work was good, she belonged to various societies, like the cinema society, the art society. She seemed to participate in university life, but she didn't have a lot of friends. That's not unusual; some students take much longer to settle away from home than others. She has apparently been seeing a counsellor, but I haven't spoken to the university practice yet.'

'So she's in counselling.' Annie made several notes. 'Do you know why?'

'She has been having a bit of a problem differentiating between fantasy and reality. Or so some of the other students seem to think.'

'What, she tells lies?'

'Apparently, yes, to her peer group.'

'Her work? You said it was good, but might there have been any recent problems? Did she attend tutorials regularly?'

'Yes, her attendance record is very good and I believe her work is exemplary. She is a very clever girl, an A-grade student.'

'Has there been a break in routine? Something that wouldn't normally happen?'

'She has missed a tutorial, and she's never done that before. Her tutor commented on it at the time, apparently.'

'Has she argued with anyone?'

'No, not that I know of.'

Annie put down the list and looked at Jill Hooper. Procedure was not always appropriate. 'Why do you think she has gone missing, Ms Hooper? What makes you think something has happened to her? I'm not sure that this list is going to tell us what we want to know.'

'Claire hasn't been in her room for six days now; it was left unlocked and looked as if she'd just walked out of it and not come back. She is a meticulous girl, she would not have gone away leaving things as they were. She left her contraceptive pills, a carton of milk open; none of her clothes have gone, all her wash things are there, and no one has seen her since last Tuesday. I telephoned her parents but she is not at home.'

Annie continued to make notes. She found missing persons cases so difficult to evaluate. Who could honestly say what was going on in someone else's mind at any one moment in time? People did vanish; normal, sensible people simply walked away from their normal, sensible lives and started again in Scotland, or Spain, or wandered aimlessly around the country for a few years. Could this Claire Thompson have done that? She was a loner; perhaps she wanted more solitude?

'Is there anything else you can tell me that might add to this profile?'

110

'Claire was drunk when she left the hall of residence on Tuesday night, and she told one of the other girls that she was going to meet Professor Meredith, her history tutor, in town for drinks and supper.'

'Was this the case?'

'No. I asked him this evening and he was apparently in London on Tuesday night. The same girl went to Claire's room at three o'clock the following morning but she hadn't returned home. That is very unusual; she doesn't have a reputation for staying out late, and we have a midnight curfew during the week at the hall. To my knowledge Claire has never broken the curfew.'

Annie looked up from her page of scribble. 'I can understand your concern,' she said. 'I'll organize for one of our uniformed officers to come to Norton Hall tomorrow to have a look at Claire's room and speak to one or two of the other students. Meanwhile, I'll file this report and we'll put Claire on our missing persons list.'

Jill stared at DI Taylor. 'Is that it?'

Annie braced herself. 'Yes, I'm afraid for the moment it is. There is nothing yet to indicate that there is any sort of crime behind this disappearance, so we will follow procedure for missing persons and keep you updated on our progress.'

'But that's not good enough,' Jill said sharply. 'I have come here to report a missing person and all you are going to do is put my report on file. What if something has happened to her?'

Annie stopped collecting her papers up. 'If something has happened to her then we will find out soon enough. We circulate this report to all the hospitals in the area.'

'No, I mean what if something else has happened to her!'

'Like what?'

Jill stood up. 'Look, I don't want to be funny, but I came down here because I think that something might have happened to one of my students, I think she might have been abducted, and you want to fob me off with forms and reports. I'd like to see a senior CID officer, please, right away!'

Annie stood as well. 'I am the senior CID officer appropriate to the case. I wouldn't normally be involved at this point; I'm usually only called in when we are sure a crime has been committed. I will follow this report up myself, but that's all I can do and it is better than most people get. I'm sorry.'

'But I am sure something has happened to her!'

'You may be right, but we have to wait and see. I really am sorry.'

Jill walked out of the interview room. Annie glanced at the form and sighed, then she stood and hurried out after her.

'Miss Hooper?'

Jill turned.

'I'll look into it personally,' she said. 'I'll send two officers round tomorrow and I'll keep a watching brief on this one myself. If I see anything that looks even remotely suspicious we'll be on to it immediately. OK?'

Jill nodded. 'Thank you,' she said. Annie shrugged. She smiled, turned and walked back into the nick.

The children were asleep. Lotte, wrapped in a towelling robe, sat on her mother's bed watching Meg pack for a couple of days in Vienna.

'Shall I take two pairs of linen trousers or just the one? I'm not sure if they might not be a bit too casual.'

'I'd take them both. You can always bring them home again clean, can't you?'

Meg smiled at this advice and folded two pairs of linen trousers into the case. It was typical of Lotte to advise on both pairs; she had never been cautious, organized or careful, she had always rushed headlong into things and lived to regret it. She had certainly rushed into marriage with Gordon, but Meg knew there were many complicated reasons for that. She went to the drawer, took out a couple of linen shirts to match the trousers and packed those too.

'I wish you weren't going,' Lotte said.

Meg came and sat on the bed next to her. 'I have to go,' she replied. 'This is business, I'm Leo's wife and I have to go with him.' She picked up Lotte's hand and marvelled at how a mother never loses the joy of physical contact with her child, whatever the child's age. She squeezed it and said: 'You can stay here for a while, Lotte, as long as it takes you to get yourself on your feet, but this isn't your home, it's Leo's house, and mine. You do understand that, don't you?'

Lotte didn't answer. In a way she understood it, and in another she resented it. When do those ties cut loose, she wondered; at what point do children have to be independent? She couldn't imagine Freddie and Milly ever separate from her, but then perhaps that was because they were her life, the only life she had at the moment.

Meg broke into her thoughts. 'Lotte, I hope you don't mind, but I want to say something about what's happened.'

Lotte nodded, though she didn't particularly want to listen.

'Lotte, I never gave you advice when your father died, I was too distraught myself to offer you comfort and I realize, I have realized for a long time, that I failed you. You weren't able to stand on your own two feet and so you fell into the path of the first man who offered to look after you. It was a disaster and I admire you for sticking it so long once you fell pregnant with Milly. But . . .' She tilted Lotte's chin up so that her daughter was forced to look at her. 'But you are vulnerable again, vulnerable and grieving and lonely, and this time you must stand up for yourself, you must learn to be your own person, Lotte, whatever it takes.'

Lotte looked at her mother. She could see the change in Meg, the change from a widow to a woman who was loved again, and she envied her that flowering.

'I love you, Lotte, but if you are going to leave Gordon, you have to do it on your own, for yourself.'

Lotte moved off the bed. She tightened the dressing gown cord and stood looking down at her mother. 'I have left Gordon, I have instructed my solicitor today and I will see that decision through, independently. You know, I've always felt, all my life, that I needed someone or something else to rely on, and now I've finally come to the conclusion that there is only me, there is no one and nothing else. I am the only one I can rely on.' She bent to kiss her mother's cheek. 'What time is your flight again?'

'Early, seven a.m. We have to leave at about four thirty. We'll be long gone by the time you get up.'

'Have a safe trip,' Lotte said, walking to the door. 'And a good time.' She blew Meg a kiss and went into the guest bedroom. In her bed, propped up on too many pillows and cushions, was Milly, who had crept in there for reassurance. Lotte took off her robe, removed all the pillows bar one and slipped into bed next to her daughter. She wouldn't bother to put Milly back in her own bed, there was no point. Besides which, the child needed comfort. Lotte reached out and held her daughter's tiny hand under the duvet, and closed her eyes. Milly wasn't the only one, she thought.

*　　*　　*

Mia finished packing her case and shut it firmly, then shifted it out on to the landing. She checked the chest of drawers was empty, then did a last recce of the bathroom to make sure she had everything. She left the room, but then remembered the bedside table and went back to take her hand cream and a novel she was reading out of the drawer next to her side of the bed. She was ready.

She carried the case downstairs, struggling with the weight of it, and took it straight out to her car. That done, she came back for the two bags she had left by the front door and packed them into the boot of the car with the case. In the hall she took her coat off the peg and put it on, and finally went into the dining room they had turned into a study, to see Charles. He was engrossed in his work. She coughed and he looked round.

'Mia! Sorry, I didn't hear you.'

She shrugged. 'How's it going?'

He turned round on his chair and faced her. 'It's going pretty well actually,' he said. 'These letters and diaries of Lady Chatten have made the most enormous difference to the work. Every time I read through them, the whole inflexibility of the Victorian class system comes alive for me, and so, funnily enough, does Henry. She really loved him, you know, he was her only child. She brings him to life, with her reports of their conversations and the things he said. She's a very good writer, very descriptive. She makes that sister Dehlia out to be a bit of a battleaxe.' Charles laughed, 'She sounds like a real matron of the Empire.' He spun back to the desk, took up one of the letters and turned round to Mia again. 'Here, have a look at this.'

Mia took the letter and skimmed down it. The script was hard to read and she was in no mood to try and decipher it. 'It looks great.' She handed it back and wondered if Charles had even noticed that she had her coat on.

'It is,' he said. 'It's such a help. I'm really beginning to get a feel for the situation now, I only hope my writing is doing it justice.'

'I'm sure it's fine,' Mia said quietly.

Charles was re-reading the letter Mia had just passed back to him and hardly heard her. He suddenly remembered she was there, glanced up and said: 'Did you want something, Mia?'

'No, nothing at all.'

He went back to the letter, head bowed, the long curve of his spine bent forwards over his work. She left the study, held back the urge to cry and walked out of the house. In the car she sat for a while and stared up at the home she had shared with the man she honestly thought she would live happily ever after with. Then she started the engine, tore her gaze away and drove off. Don't, she told herself, ever look back. She had left Charles, and he didn't even know that she had gone.

Chapter 10

Letter to Lady Dehlia Heaton, dated June 1896

> 12 Cadogan Square
> London
> WCI

My dear sister,

We are here in London for the season; at home 'the problem' rumbles on and I am afraid I am at a loss as to what to do. I am so indebted to you for your letter in May; I honestly don't know what I would have done without that information. What was Henry thinking of, taking a servant girl to the Grand for tea? Imagine if he had met someone of consequence. I shudder to think of the embarrassment.

I think that Henry is behaving in an unforgivable way, but he is my dear boy and I suppose, if I really think about it, I can remember such feelings myself in my young days. I know you will despair of me, Papa always did, but we are different, Dehlia, we have always been different. I am shocked by Henry's affair, but I do understand it. Is that so terrible of me? I wish of course that I hadn't had to come to London. Lionel was insistent, he does so love the Season here, being out and about with everybody who is some-body. I have to say that I don't care for it much myself. I find it a bit of a bore constantly dressing up, making the

117

same conversation three times a day, having to be seen. I long to be at home, walking the dogs along by Ludwell Ponds, staying down at the lodge to watch the deer graze. I think I am becoming closer to nature as I get older; I have certainly grown tired of the human side of things. And if I were at home, of course, I could be with Henry, distract him, take him to the house in Brighton perhaps.

I did want to dismiss this Daisy Burrows, but Henry made such a terrible fuss, threatening to leave Cambridge and run off with her, that I thought it best to leave things as they are. He is a normal young man, and despite the ideas of our day, we are both married women and we know the desires of men. Perhaps, and this is my private view, he will satisfy his yearning and lose interest in a young woman who is beneath him in every way. I have to say that I can see the attraction. She is a handsome young woman, and has a certain voluptuousness that is quite apparent, but looks are not everything. Henry is bright, and modern too, and he knows that he has to one day make a solid partnership, a partnership for life, which will require a meeting of minds and values as much as anything else. He knows that we have already singled out several girls from the right families. He may be in love – no, I will qualify that, he is certainly in love – but I do not think that will render him careless. Do you? I know that taking this girl to the Grand was foolish, reckless even, but I did speak to him and I am certain that he will not repeat the mistake. Let us hope so.

So, all I can do is continue the round of calling and parties and dinners that is London and hope that my dearest boy is using some sense and coming to terms with what is expected of him.

Do let me know when you are coming up to town, Dehlia.

I miss your company and was so disappointed to hear that you wouldn't be here for the first two weeks of the Season. Let me know your thoughts on the Henry situation too. I always feel better for your advice, it is so eminently sensible.

My love to Cecily and Alice, and to you of course.

Yours,

Madeleine.

Lady Chatten's diary, June 1896

It is Monday and the rain is lashing down outside my window, grey and cold. It chills me to the bone. I feel sad and lonely and I miss my home. Bicester House seems so far away. There is only a scant covering of green here in London; everything is dirty, coal-soaked, grime-laden, and the poor that we pass on the street fill me with such pity that it makes my heart heavy. Of course Lionel says that he doesn't see them, but I do, and the children especially move me almost to tears. I do so admire these women who are able to go out and do something for the people. I wish I were that sort. Dehlia could do it, she has that courage and steadfastness, but I am weak, I have nothing of her confidence.

I miss my garden. I do not mind the rain at home when it falls through the canopy of leaves in the woodland at the edge of the estate and makes that wonderful light, echoing sound, or when it creates an ever-moving pattern of circles on the water of the pond. I love the smell of the rain, fresh and cleansing, making the earth offer up its scents. Sometimes when it rains at home I go out in it. I never tell Lionel. I slip out of the house and walk with the water beating against my face and soaking my hair. I don't care if I am wet through, although if Lionel ever knew he would

119

be shocked at the state I have sometimes returned in. Maisie knows, of course; she is always chastising me and telling me that I will catch a chill as she strips me and dries my wet, clammy skin. But I really don't mind it; I like it, in fact, the rain taking me over, drenching me. It makes me feel real, alive.

It was the beginning of June, and Henry had not seen Daisy for two weeks. He thought about her so much that he wasn't able to sleep. He had gone to stay with friends just outside Cambridge after his exams, but by the second week he was miserable and knew that he had to return to Bicester House, just to see Daisy. He thought about her constantly, about the shape of her mouth, the taste of her breath, her skin, so cool and smooth against his lips. He wanted Daisy, he wanted to take her, possess her, but he had no idea how. He knew that she manipulated him, he could see it, but he was powerless to stop it. So on the last Saturday in June, Henry Chatten took the train from Cambridge to London and then from London to Brierly, and went home.

He should have stopped in London to see his parents, but he knew that his mother would be disappointed in him, and he so hated to upset her. He arrived at Bicester House late on Saturday night, and realized as the butler let him in that he would have to wait for Daisy to come to him. It was purgatory, not knowing when, or even if, she would acknowledge his presence. He ate a solitary supper in the drawing room by the fire, wandered around the house for a while, and then decided, because it was a full moon, to take a walk around his mother's garden. But it was a full moon chased by thick cloud; it threatened rain. He lit a cigar on the terrace, stepped down on to the lawns and wandered across the damp grass towards the rose garden. The light was extraordinary, refulgent, it touched the petals of the roses, marking their colour with luminosity. Henry stopped. He bent to touch the bud of a deep burnt-pink rose, held it in his fingers for a moment and closed his eyes. It felt like her skin.

'You came back then,' she said.

He turned. She was standing beneath the rose arch, and she was smiling.

Henry went to her and took her hands in his. 'Of course I came back. How could I not?' He kissed her hand, her fingers, and felt her shiver. He held her palm against his mouth, not caring that it was rough and chapped.

'Will you stay long?' she asked.

'Do you want me to?'

She continued to smile.

'I will stay with you as long as you want me to,' he said. 'I will cover you with devotion, clothe you with kisses and envelop you with love.'

Daisy pulled her hand away. 'You speak wildly, Mr Chatten.'

'I speak the truth, Miss Burrows.'

Daisy had stopped smiling. 'You must not make promises that you cannot keep, Henry. It is not honourable.'

'I make no promises that I cannot keep.'

She looked at him. The moonlight had vanished under cloud and it was suddenly dark. She could only just make out his face from the lighted tip of his cigar. They were locked together in this warm, heavy night. It began to rain.

'Here.' Henry slipped off his jacket and held it up for Daisy.

'No, I don't want it,' she said. 'I love the rain, it will cool my soul.' She stepped out from under the bower, and the drops of rain fell on to her white shirt, staining it.

'You'll get soaked,' he said. 'I think it's going to pour.'

'I don't care. I want to be soaked, I want to be drenched.'

Henry suddenly laughed. 'You are insane.'

'No,' she said, 'I am burning inside and I want the rain to chill me to the core.'

He looked up at the sky. The rain had intensified; it fell in great leaden drops. Henry ground his cigar under his heel and took her hand. 'Come on,' he said. He pulled her with him and strode through the rose garden, past the hedge, into the kitchen garden and across it, through the door in the kitchen garden wall. They were on open grass now. He walked fast and she struggled to keep up with him. It was raining heavily, and Daisy could feel the wet penetrating the thin cotton of her shirt. It clung to her and felt like a second skin. There was virtually no light and she stumbled a few times, but it didn't matter. At the gate to the wood, he stopped.

'Listen,' he said. Daisy was breathless; her heart beat so fast that the vein on her neck pulsed with blood. 'Can you hear it?'

Daisy looked at him. He was leaning forward towards the trees. 'Hear what?'

Henry opened the gate and led her into the wood.

'The rain,' she murmured. 'It echoes, it sounds like . . .' She listened hard. 'It sounds like music; percussion music.'

Henry smiled. 'I knew you would hear it, Daisy,' he said. 'I knew it. My mother used to bring me here when I was a boy, and we'd sit under the trees and listen to the sound of the rain. I would be wet through and Nanny was always furious, but I didn't care, nor did my mother.'

Daisy's hair was flat against her scalp, the water ran down her cheeks and off her nose, her shirt and skirt were saturated. She laughed. 'This,' she said, 'is wonderful.'

Henry laughed as well. 'It is, isn't it?'

Daisy stepped into a clearing in the wood, put her face up to the rain and parted her lips to let it run into her mouth. Then she unfastened her blouse and took it off so that she stood in her corset, the white skin of her shoulders just visible in the darkness. Henry caught his breath. She looked at him and began to unbutton her corset. He moved forward, caught her hand and *pulled her to him. For a moment he closed his eyes and heard his heart and the rain beat a rhythm together, then he heard nothing. He heard nothing but her.*

Later, dripping with water, he led her up to his room in the semi-darkness of an empty house, and took her into his bed. He warmed her icy skin with his hot caresses and wrapped her in linen sheets perfumed with lavender. They made love and they slept until the first light of day, when Daisy rose and walked naked to her clothes by the fire, unashamed of her body but not unaware of the intense eroticism of her act.

'Come back to bed,' Henry called to her.

'I can't, I have to work.'

'But it's Sunday.'

She came across and bent to kiss him, her loose hair trailing on to his chest. He touched her breast and felt her shudder.

'Please come back to bed.'

'I have to work,' she said again, moving out of reach. She went back to the drying rack, took her stockings from it and began to pull them on. Henry sat up to watch her. Next she slipped her clothes on, still damp, and fastened them quicker than Henry could ever have done his own. She went back to him and kissed him once again, opening her mouth on to his. He caught her wrist and tried to pull her down on to him, but she broke away and took a step back.

'That is unfair,' she said, smiling.

'No, you are unfair, to leave me like this.'

Daisy slipped her hand under the cover and touched him. 'You only have yourself to blame, sir,' she said. She turned and walked towards the door, but Henry threw back the covers and caught her before she opened it.

'Daisy, wait! Please!' He held her shoulders. 'This afternoon, can you steal a few hours off?'

123

'Yes, but . . .'

'No buts. You must meet me down at the lodge by Ludwell Ponds, the fishing lodge. I will be there from two onwards. Please. We'll have the place to ourselves.'

Daisy hesitated. She glanced down at the hands on her shoulders, hands that were so soft and smooth that they made her own look like those of a man; hands that had never done a hard day's labour. But they were hands that gave her pleasure, and that she loved.

'I'll be there, but it won't be until after five.'

'OK, five.' He kissed her and she turned to go. 'Daisy?'

She stopped a second time and rolled her eyes. 'Yes?'

He smiled. 'I love you.'

She shook her head. 'You are a romantic, Henry Chatten,' she said, but she smiled back. Of course he loved her; that was what they had been moving towards, it was inevitable. Henry Chatten loved Daisy Burrows, and the gulf that separated them had been bridged. For now.

Chapter 11

Charles rolled over in bed, looked at the luminous dial on the clock and decided to get up and make a cup of tea. It was pointless lying there any longer; he had been awake most of the night worrying about Mia, and there was no way he was going to get to sleep now. It was five a.m. He climbed out of bed, pulled on a bathrobe and went downstairs. The house was empty, no more empty than it usually was when she was away on business or staying with friends, but it felt worse, suddenly lonely.

In the kitchen he switched on the kettle and reached into the cupboard for the tea bags. He plonked one into a mug, thought that looked too sad, and took the tea pot from the draining board. He'd never drink a pot of tea, of course, but at least it wouldn't feel pathetic. He supposed that eventually he would have to get those round bags that slotted perfectly into his mug for just one cup; along with small tubes of toothpaste, single pints of milk and prepared vegetables, because there was nothing worse than peeling carrots for one person. He heated the pot, plonked a couple of tea bags into it and filled it with boiling water, then put it on a tray along with the milk bottle, the sugar bowl and his mug and carried the whole thing into the sitting room. He switched on the TV, poured himself a cup of tea and slumped on to the sofa to watch breakfast news. That was another thing, he thought, unlimited TV. No one to talk to, nothing better to do, just mindless broadcasting for company. He sipped his tea and closed his eyes. He was feeling bitterly sorry for himself, and for the moment, nothing was going to distract him from it.

It was seven a.m. and Lotte was feeding Freddie small pieces of toast with jam and butter on. Meg and Leo didn't have a high chair, and she hadn't brought one with her – frankly it was the last thing she had thought about in her flight from Gordon – so she was having to do everything she could to minimize the risk to upholstered surfaces, walls, carpets; everything, in short, in Meg and Leo's house. Of course Lotte was very lucky to be there and it was comfortable in the extreme, but with two small children, the last three days had been an unnerving experience.

Leo was wonderful, and Lotte loved him for loving her mother, but he had never had children and he was convinced that they should be able to play quietly in one place with one toy for stretches of up to eight hours at a time. Impossible, unless bound and gagged, and impossible particularly for Freddie, who had a voice like a foghorn and a tendency to overwhelming mess. And of course, with a great deal of money and no children, almost all the colour schemes in the house involved cream – cream linen sofas, cream carpets, cream counterpanes, cream silk dining chairs, cream gauze drapes, cream cushions – all of which was like a magnet to both Freddie and Milly. Every time they saw anything cream, they seemed to be armed with a felt pen, a lipstick stolen from Lotte's bag or a chocolate biscuit.

As Lotte watched the last piece of buttery jammy toast go down, she thought about the immediate future. She would have to find somewhere to rent, and quickly if she was going to remain on good terms with her mother and

Leo. Apart from which, she wanted to go, she wanted to get on with her life now that she had made the decision to do it. She was in limbo here, albeit comfortable limbo, and she needed to find out what was what financially, then start her life again.

She wiped Freddie's hands and face, checked him over for anything that might leave a stain, and let him get down from the table. Then she shouted for Milly, who had somehow managed to disappear while she was feeding Freddie.

'Milly? You need to come and finish your Weetabix, darling,' she called, following Freddie into the TV room. Milly wasn't there. 'Milly?' She walked out across the hall and peered into the sitting room – as immaculate as ever – then the study – empty – then the dining room. She was about to go out when she noticed the door to the conservatory open. Lotte walked across the Persian rug into the hothouse. She took a deep, warm breath and listened hard. There was a rustle in amongst the ferns.

'Milly,' she said softly, 'this is not a room for playing in, it is Leo's conservatory, a special glasshouse where he keeps all his rare plants. You must come out, darling, before you damage something.' She looked round the place. It really was spectacular, if you liked that sort of thing, and Leo obviously did. It was big, about twenty foot by twenty-five, and tall, a great high glass ceiling to house his collection. It was a proper conservatory, containing some wonderful tropical plants, an atmosphere heavy with heat and moisture, and only one set of basket-weave furniture, where sometimes he would sit and admire his collection.

'Milly,' Lotte said again, 'you really must come out now, because if Granny and Leo find you in here then you could be in big trouble.'

'But they've gone away,' came a little voice from behind a collection of leafy ferns, 'so they can't find me, can they?'

'All right, smart alec,' Lotte said. 'Out now!'

Milly crawled out from her hiding place, soil all over her leggings, leaving a trail of it behind her.

'I'll have to sweep up after you now, and I don't want to find you in here again! OK?' Milly pulled a face. 'I mean it, this place is very . . .' Lotte searched for the right word. 'Very precious.' That was all she could think of. 'Come on now, let's go and finish your breakfast, then we can go out into the garden and water Granny's plants.' She held out her hand, Milly took it and they turned towards the dining room. 'Ah, here's Freddie come to see us,' Lotte said, smiling as Freddie toddled towards them. 'Oh my God,' were her next words. He had a pot of raspberry jam in one hand and a spoon in the other, the lid was off the jam and his face was covered in red sticky mess. 'Freddie, give that here now!' Lotte cried. She snatched the jam, grabbed Freddie and with one hand vice-like round Milly's wrist, the other firmly on jam-stained son, marched them back to the kitchen to assess the damage.

At seven forty-five, still early for most people, but late for mothers with tiny children, Lotte took off her rubber gloves, put the 1001 carpet stain remover back in the cupboard and unlocked the TV room door. She walked in, turned off the video and collected up Milly and Freddie.

'We are going for a walk,' she announced, knowing that if she didn't get them out of the house before they did some more damage she would really lose it. She took their coats off the peg by the back door, picked up their wellies and found the pushchair. Ten minutes later they were ready to go. She opened the front door, met the postman, took the letters and signed for a recorded delivery for herself.

'Bugger,' she murmured under her breath. It was from Millard, Fraser and Tims, Gordon's business lawyers. Lotte gulped; this was going to hurt.

'Come on, you two,' she said, far more cheerily than she felt. She would open her letter down by Ludwell Ponds and read it while the children fed the ducks; or maybe she'd just throw it in the water. She smiled at that; as if she would. The three of them set off in the hope that the removed raspberry jam stains would be dry by the time they returned.

Lotte stopped halfway down the lane, the letter burning a hole in her pocket, and opened the gate to the paddock that adjoined Meg and Leo's house. She ushered the children in, went in after them and closed the gate. Then she glanced at the envelope, slit it open and pulled out the contents. Milly and Freddie ran around insanely, shrieking at the tops of their voices, while Lotte read the letter.

Dear Mrs Graham, it began, *we have been instructed by our client, Mr Gordon Graham* . . . and so it went on, difficult, complex legal speak designed to confuse and intimidate, and in this case completely successful. Lotte read it, folded it away, then promptly burst into tears. She wept for several minutes, then thought that perhaps she had got it wrong, Gordon surely wasn't going to act like that. She unfolded it and read it again. Yes he bloody well was – the bastard! He was offering her a small lump sum for her share in the house – a house (his lawyers proposed) purchased with his capital and paid for with his salary – plus a generous hundred pounds a month for the children – had he tried to feed a family on twenty-five pounds a week, let alone clothe them? – and nothing, the huge sum total of nothing for herself, because (his lawyers proposed) Lotte was self-employed and could pay her own way – had they any idea of the rates of pay for producing watercolour illustrations

129

for botanical magazines? She read the letter again, wept some more, then read it a fourth time, at which point Milly came over and clung to her legs.

'Don't cry, Mummy,' she said. 'Granny won't be cross about the jam, honestly.'

'I'm fine, darling,' she said, 'I've just got something in my eye.' Ridiculous, she thought. Why do we tell such stupid lies to our children? Pull yourself together, she told herself. For God's sake, Lotte, don't go to pieces now; ring Mr Roper, get it sorted. Gordon can't, he simply cannot, do this!

'Why are you crying, Mummy?' Milly asked.

'I'm a bit unhappy, that's all, Milly. Please don't worry about me.'

'But I do.' Milly looked up at her mother. 'I love you, Mummy.'

Lotte picked her up and hugged her very tight. 'I love you too,' she said. There was a howl; she looked up. Freddie had fallen head first into a cow pat.

Later on, after they had been home and cleaned Freddie up, and Lotte had made herself a strong, reviving coffee, they set out again to walk to the ponds. It was still only eight thirty and it was quiet, hardly a person in sight. They walked along the road until they found the footpath to the ponds, through the woodland and along a far from easy path. Lotte had one of those snazzy rough-terrain pushchairs, which Gordon had insisted on buying, but instead of being relieved, it irked her now that she was using it for what it was designed for. Somehow it just rubbed salt in the wound. She would almost have preferred to struggle with a totally inappropriate buggy.

When they reached Ludwell Ponds, Lotte stopped. She

stood and watched the sun and the leaves overhead reflected in the clear still water; it never failed to calm her. It was quiet, peaceful, there was a background of birdsong and rustling trees in the breeze, but apart from that nothing else, nothing human. She bent to let Freddie out of the pushchair. 'Why don't we all walk right the way round the pond to the other side and feed the ducks?' she suggested. 'I've got some bread in my pocket.'

'Hooray!' Milly responded. Freddie hooted. They set off, Freddie on a wrist strap, Milly having to be warned every two minutes or so to keep away from the edge of the water. The circumference of the pond was over four miles, and it was taking ages to make it even halfway round. Lotte had never done it before, and it was clear to her now why not. It would be a miracle if she had the energy to get the bread out, let alone keep the children from falling into the rushes at the edge of the water. She stopped a quarter of the way round and looked through the trees for somewhere to sit down. It was warm in the woods; the children were grumpy and they needed a rest. She spotted a clearing, saw it had once been fenced off and went nearer to gauge whether she might be able to scramble over bits of broken fence and find somewhere to sit.

'Milly, Freddie, look over here, we can make a camp in the woods here. Come on, let's sit down in this little space and pretend we're having a picnic.' She gathered up Freddie, carried him into the clearing and called to Milly to follow on. The clearing, Lotte found out as she went into it, must once have been the entrance from a garden to the pond. She stopped, dropped Freddie on to his feet and looked up the long, sloping lawn to a small ramshackle cottage, run-down and empty. Milly took her hand and Lotte said: 'Shall we go on up and see the house?'

'Are we allowed?' Milly asked.

Lotte glanced down at her and smiled. 'I should think so, Milly. Don't worry, we won't get into trouble, I'm sure of it.'

They walked up the lawn, moss-filled and un-nurtured, but recently cut, towards the cottage. 'I wonder if anyone lives here?' Lotte thought aloud. She peered through the windows into a dark, unused space.

'I don't like it, Mummy,' Milly said.

Lotte turned to her, and a thought that hadn't even been processed came right out of her mouth. She said: 'Don't you, darling? I think it's rather nice, and with a lick of paint and some cleaning up it could be wonderful, like camping out.'

Milly frowned. 'Are we going to live here, then?'

Lotte sighed. 'I don't know,' she answered. 'Let's have a good look round and see if there's anyone we might ask.' She led the children round the front of the cottage, to a small dark green front door, with peeling paint and a brass knocker, then down a muddy path to the front gate, which had a sign tacked on to it: 'Fishing lodge to rent.' There was a telephone number underneath. 'Blast,' Lotte said.

'Blast what?' Milly asked.

'I haven't got a pen,' Lotte said, 'and I want to write that telephone number down.'

'I've got one,' Milly said.

Lotte looked at her. 'You have?'

From inside the pocket of her coat, Milly pulled out a small red pencil. 'Here, Mummy.'

Lotte smiled. 'Thank you, Milly, what a helpful girl you are.' She wrote the number down on the back of an old receipt in her coat pocket and gave the pencil back to Milly. From where they were standing they could see Ludwell

132

Ponds in the distance, the water reflecting the colour of the sky.

Lotte took a deep breath. It was calm here, calm and private, the sort of place to think things through, to restore the soul. 'I'll ring this number when we get back,' she announced. 'It'll need some work, but we're not afraid of work, are we, Milly and Freddie?' Both children looked up at her with such innocence and trust that Lotte was suddenly sure this was the right thing to do. 'Course not,' she answered herself. And in celebration, they went back into the clearing found the spot with the best view and sat down to share out the bread that should have been for the ducks.

Lotte called the telephone number at lunchtime and spoke to a Lady Beatty at Bicester House. She was told that the fishing lodge was for rent, but that it needed work, and that Lady Beatty would be happy to have her estate man help with that. She asked Lotte to come up to Bicester House that afternoon to talk about it, if she was interested.

'I'll have my children with me,' she said. 'It might be a bit difficult to talk.'

'Oh, don't be silly,' Lady Beatty declared. 'What would we possibly want to say that couldn't be said in front of the children!'

'I didn't mean . . .' Lotte didn't bother to try and explain; Lady Beatty had rung off.

At three o'clock, with Milly and Freddie clean and presentable, Lotte arrived at Bicester House and pulled up to park in the sweeping drive. She wasn't sure where to put the car, not being used to visiting such grand properties, but hoped that smack bang in the middle of the drive wasn't too presumptuous. She climbed out, helped the children down and all three went up the steps to the

133

glossy black double front doors. There was no knocker, so Lotte yanked a bell pull twice, hard, and waited, seriously expecting the door to be opened by a butler in full livery.

'Hello, hello,' said a voice. 'Just coming, dear.' There was a scuffle, then a kick at the front door. 'This blasted door always gets stuck. If I've told Granger to fix it once I've told him a hundred times. Bugger! Bugger the thing. I can't do it!' There was the sound of more struggle. 'Come on round the back, will you? I can't get it open.'

'Round the back?' Lotte called. 'Which way?'

'Go to the right, follow the lawn along and that'll bring you down on to the kitchen side of the house. Sorry, dear! Can't be helped. Bloody door!'

'The right side,' Lotte muttered. She shifted Freddie on her hip and held on to Milly's hand, more for her own comfort than Milly's. They followed the lawn round the right side of the house and came down a slope into a kitchen courtyard at the side of the house. Lady Beatty, or so Lotte supposed, was there to meet them.

'Hello, dear, found it all right then? What little darlings. Hello, dearie, you're a poppet, aren't you?'

Lotte tried not to stare and nudged Milly to smile. Lady Beatty stood at five eleven, with a shock of long, curly grey hair pinned badly into some sort of topknot, from which it was escaping. She was wearing an ankle-length black linen skirt and a khaki linen smock, with three thick ropes of amber beads round her neck, and reefer sandals. Not at all Surrey, Lotte thought, then smiled.

'Right, well, a cup of tea, I think, and an ice lolly for the children. I'm sure they love ice lollies, I know I do. Come on, come on into the kitchen and we can talk about the lodge and dribble some sickly sugary goo all down our fronts, can't we, children?' She led the way into the house and, prodding Milly gently in the back, Lotte followed after.

'The lodge,' Lady Beatty said, having dispensed tea, cake, ice lollies and Ribena, 'is my special place, and I want to see someone in it. It's been empty for over a year now and I can't bear to see it that way. I don't advertise, though, can't bear that kind of thing; every Tom, Dick and Harry traipsing through one's property. Has to be someone local. Lovely chap had it before, his brother lived down here. He was something in the city, used it for fishing with his mates, but he went and got himself married and wifey didn't like the sport, so he gave it up. He's probably doing something ghastly and suburban like golf now. Poor sod. Anyway, Bertie had it done up for me years ago, over twenty years now, I should think, but I never get down there. Joints, you see, terrible they are, too much riding, and the cold doesn't like them at all, so I don't bother, haven't done for ages, and I'd like it rented. It's not so much the money; more a question of not letting the place go to waste. It's beautiful there, used it all the time when I was young, and then, when I had my troubles, it saved me, I'm sure of it. Beautiful, really, and quiet too, peaceful.' Lady Beatty poured Lotte another cup of tea. 'So when do you want it?'

'Well,' Lotte began, 'I think I'd like it right away, but I'd have to have a good look at it and have a chat with my mother first.'

'Is your mother local?'

'She's Meg Chandler, they live in Harman Court.'

'Oh, good lord. Dear Meg, such a darling, and so good with her hands! Ah, so you're Meg's girl. Wonderful! Charming couple, Meg and Leo, absolutely charming. Well, I don't think I'd want more than fifty pounds a week, dear, not with you being Meg's daughter. Plus your heating and gas, and so on. Or is that too much, yes, maybe a bit steep, how about forty a week? Would that do? Of course, my chap Granger can do it up for you, he's terribly good, young and very useful. I could get him to come down now and see it over with you, tell you what's what, so to speak. Would the children like another lolly?'

Lotte felt bamboozled. 'Well, yes, I mean no, no thank you, I think if they have another lolly they'll be bouncing off the ceiling tonight, but yes, could your chap Granger come down to the lodge with me now and we could see what there is to do? I think I'd be seriously interested at forty pounds a week, but I do have to let my mother know and I'd like to discuss it with Leo. Is that all right?'

'Absolutely fine, my dear,' said Lady Beatty. 'I'll page Granger now and get him to come up to the house.'

'Page him?' It all sounded very technical.

'Oh, we've all got them,' Lady Beatty said, lifting her smock to show her own pager looped on to a belt round her waist. 'I love paging Bertie when he's on the loo. 'Bout ten o'clock most mornings, and if he's in a ghastly mood and buggering us all about, then I page him just as he's got his bum warm.' She laughed heartily at her own joke. 'Wonderful things. Wouldn't be without mine.' She went to the phone, picked it up and punched in the pager code. 'Granger will be here in about fifteen minutes, depending on where he is on the estate.'

'How big is the estate?' Lotte asked.

'Six hundred acres,' Lady Beatty said. 'Been in Bertie's family for over a hundred years now. His grandfather bought it from the Chatten family, who'd had it for six generations. The Chatten son was hanged, you know, for murdering a servant girl in 1897. Family never recovered. Lady Chatten never wanted to set eyes on the place again, apparently; terrible shame really, she designed a lot of the gardens, had them all done. Great shame, terrible. Would you like to see the gardens?'

'Yes, gosh, I'd love to.' Lotte had warmed to Lady Beatty, or Lady Batty as she had mentally filed her. 'Milly, Freddie? Shall we go outside?' They all stood and followed Lady Beatty down a long corridor and back out into the kitchen courtyard.

'We'll start with the kitchen gardens,' Lady Beatty said. 'I've got two gardeners who help me, young Sam and old Sam.' They filed past row upon perfect straight row of vegetables in freshly dug soil; the fruit cage; the flower garden; and the greenhouse, Lady Beatty pointing everything out to Milly and Lotte trying to keep Freddie off the beds. They went through to the rose garden, not yet in bloom, and past that to the Italian garden, which looked back up the lawns towards the house. It was beautiful, well designed, cared for and loved. 'And here,' Lady Beatty said, 'is the young man who keeps all this in such perfect order. Afternoon, Granger.'

'Lady Beatty.'

Lotte smiled at a man of about forty, wearing jeans, sweatshirt, fleece waistcoat. He nodded in her direction but turned his attention immediately back to Lady Beatty.

'Mrs Graham, this is Granger. Granger, Mrs Graham is thinking of taking the lodge and I would like you to take her down there now and show her around, if that's all right.'

'I don't think I can, Lady Beatty, not right now.'

'Oh? I thought you had finished mending the fences. Lord Beatty told me that . . .'

'There's other things that need doing.'

Lotte could see from Granger's attitude that there was some sort of hidden agenda here.

137

'Nothing that can't wait,' Lady Beatty said, overruling any objections. 'Mrs Graham needs to get a good idea of the place and I need a good idea of what has to be done. I think this should be top priority, please, Granger.' She turned to Lotte. 'Why don't you go off now. If you drive Granger down then he can show you the entrance from the lane. It's rather hard to find otherwise.'

'If you're sure?' Lotte said. She wasn't at all. Granger had a face like a wet weekend and Lady Beatty had a look of determined authority in her eyes. 'I can leave it for another day or so if that would be more . . .'

'Not at all!' Lady Beatty snapped.

'Right,' Lotte said.

'We'll go through the house to the car and I can show you that bloody front door, Granger. It still won't budge. Perhaps when you've got it open we can leave it like that and you could fix it later on this afternoon?'

There was a grunt, and Lotte began to feel unnerved. They went through the house, elegantly scruffy, and into the hall. Granger tackled the front door, kicking it hard, putting his shoulder against it and pulling it tight towards him, then he turned the key in the lock and shoved it open. 'There's a knack,' he said.

'Well there shouldn't be,' Lady Beatty replied. 'I can't possibly go through all that palaver when I want to open the door for my guests.'

'Not many of those,' Granger muttered under his breath. Only Lotte heard him.

In the car, he was just as surly, and Lotte regretted the decision to see the lodge. He was surly, in fact, to the point of being rude, but typical of Lotte, she wasn't brave enough to tell him so. He misdirected her twice, so that she felt thoroughly confused by the time they arrived; and then, climbing out of the car to open the gate, walked on up the track to the lodge without closing the passenger door, so that she had to unstrap her safety belt and lean right across the passenger seat to reach the handle and slam it shut. She almost gave up on the lodge at that point.

Parked on the grass, she climbed out with Milly and left Freddie, who had fallen asleep in his car seat. Granger had opened up the cottage. 'Lots of damp,' he said, taking a heavy-duty torch out of his pocket. 'I think the pond has seeped into the foundations.'

Lotte entered the house. It didn't feel that damp, especially not considering it had been empty for a year. 'I think the electricity's off as well,' he said. 'Probably buggered by the damp.' Lotte tried a light switch; nothing happened. Granger kicked at some leaves that had got in under the door. 'Rats,' he said, 'they're a right pest round water.'

'Rats?' Milly asked, her face excited.

'Maybe,' Lotte answered, particularly unnerved.

Granger opened a couple of windows, and Lotte was surprised at how light the house was. It needed a good deal of cleaning, redecoration probably, some warmth, light, some cooking smells and some children, but it had a good feel. It could be habitable, it could even be homely.

'I think this could be all right with some work, don't you, Granger?'

Granger turned. He had never, Lotte noticed, looked her in the eye, and he didn't do so now either. He stared at the walls, then the floor. 'Might be,' he said. 'But did Lady Beatty mention the fishing rights?'

'No? What are they?'

'People come to fish the ponds,' he said. 'Several people own fishing rights and well, you never know when they're going to come or who they're going to bring with them. It's not safe, not for a woman on her own with children. It could be anyone wandering round the garden any time of the day or night, and it's mainly all blokes. I wouldn't like it, not for my kids.'

'Oh, I see.' That's that then, Lotte thought, I'm not having it. Her heart sank. Of course it was too good to be true; get real, Lotte, she told herself, there you are, out walking with the children and a lodge for rent just appears. Of course there's a drawback, of course it's going to be impossible. When, she asked herself, for the past six years, has anything in my life that I wanted ever seemed easy? 'Well thank you,' she said, 'but I really don't think, with the fishing rights, it's for us.' She took Milly's hand and they went back out of the front door.

'D'you want to see the bathroom,' Granger called, 'before you go?'

Lotte turned. 'No thank you.' She went to the car and climbed in. It had all seemed so fateful, so right, and Lotte had always been a great believer in what felt right. Fat lot of good it had done her. She started the engine and swung the car round in reverse to turn. She wasn't going to offer Granger a lift back; he'd been so bloody rude on the way here she just didn't think she could face it. He could walk. And from the look of his boots, that was what he liked doing anyway.

Annie Taylor came down the stairs at the end of her shift and headed out of the nick. It was late afternoon, she'd been there since seven thirty and she was sick of the place. She had had adjustment periods before, but this had to be the worst. It was as if everything and everyone was conspiring against her. Her new direct line didn't work and her calls kept going through to other desks; her PC had crashed; someone had knocked into her in the canteen at lunch and spilt coffee all down her shirt; and yet again, for drinks after work, she was persona non grata. She slung her bag on to her shoulder and punched the code into the security pad. As she walked into reception, she saw the woman from yesterday, Jill Hooper, talking to the desk sergeant, and looked in the opposite direction to try and get by unseen. She shouldn't have done; it invited fate, and Jill Hooper turned just as she went by.

'DI Taylor?'

Annie stopped. 'Yes, hello. How did you get on with the officers this afternoon? I'm expecting a report on my desk tomorrow morning.'

'That's just it,' Jill said. 'I was explaining to the duty sergeant just now that no one turned up.'

'I'm sorry?'

'So am I, DI Taylor. I arranged for Professor Meredith to be around and for two of Claire's friends to stay in hall and miss their lectures, and I even asked Magda, one of the cleaners, to wait by the phone at home in case you needed to speak to her. This really is very poor, we have all been inconvenienced.'

Annie looked at the duty sergeant. 'But I requested that two officers go up to the university this afternoon. Have they not gone, Sergeant?'

The sergeant looked through his book. 'We couldn't spare anyone, I'm afraid, ma'am. I did ask DS Coulter before he went off this morning and he said that as it was a routine missing persons case then it could probably wait.'

'Oh did he?' Annie's lips pursed in anger. 'The elusive DS Coulter, eh? The only member of my team I haven't met yet, and who seems to have some sort of authority over

141

everyone in this nick, including me!' She stopped there, because she knew that if she said any more she would embarrass herself. This DS Coulter seemed to think that the job of DI was his, if not in title then certainly in terms of loyalty and influence. 'Well, I think that my instructions overrule DS Coulter's – at least they certainly do in any other division of the police force – and if I have requested that two officers go up to the university, Sergeant, then that is what they should do. Unless, of course, there is a major emergency and we are understaffed. Is that understood?'

'Yes, ma'am.'

'And while we're on the subject, I should like to see DS Coulter as soon as he can spare me the time. Perhaps you could leave a note to that effect in the book, Sergeant?'

'I don't need to, ma'am.'

Annie's temper was about to boil. 'I beg your pardon?'

'He's here, he came in ten minutes ago. You can see him now if you want to.'

'I see.'

Annie turned away. For a split second there she thought she had seen the faintest trace of a smile on the sergeant's face. I am being paranoid, she told herself. 'I am very sorry for this mistake, Miss Hooper,' she said. 'I will ensure that two officers are up at the university tomorrow morning, even if I have to escort them up there myself.'

'Thank you.'

As Jill Hooper turned to go, Annie went back into the nick. She marched up the stairs and into CID. 'DS Coulter?'

A man stood up. He was taller than her, interesting-looking, well made. Annie was surprised; she blinked twice, but continued to look at him. He smiled, a crooked, sexy smile – and even in the midst of her anger, Annie acknowledged it was a sexy smile – but it was also condescending.

It was obvious to her then that the surprise was all hers. DS Coulter knew who she was; he knew who he'd asked for a drink on Saturday night, and his smile told her as much.

'I'm DI Taylor, and I am your senior officer in CID,' she said.

The smile vanished. He looked at her. 'Boss.'

'When I give an instruction to one of my officers, I expect it to be carried out. Is that understood?'

She thought, but she wasn't entirely sure because she wasn't looking directly at him, that he had exchanged a look with one of the other officers, an insolent, arrogant look, and it made her furious. It suddenly felt as if the whole place was against her. 'If you see fit to change my instructions again without consulting me,' she said, 'then I will make sure that you are disciplined. There was no excuse for today's unprofessional behaviour; you embarrassed yourself as much as me, and you embarrassed the police force. I am serious about my job, DS Coulter, and I am here to stay. I won this promotion and I will do the job properly, with or without you.'

She turned heel and walked out. In the corridor outside, she leant against the wall and took a deep breath. Annie Taylor was fierce, but not nearly as fierce as she made out.

Lotte put Milly to bed, kissed Freddie, who was already asleep, and went downstairs to make herself some supper. In the kitchen she sat at the table, the letter from Gordon's lawyers in front of her, and put her head in her hands. She hadn't called Roper; she couldn't face it. He hardly filled her with confidence, and in the face of such opposition she was certain that he would be blown away. She didn't doubt Gordon's ability to win, to drag her through the divorce courts and leave her with nothing. He was a competitive man, he liked to control, to have power; he was a bully and he was damn good at it. Of course he would have hired a top team, she had been naive to think he'd do anything else. But for some reason – perhaps in the light of his terrible deceit, or because of all the years he'd run her down and used her for everything he could take – she'd thought he would be reasonable about the divorce. She'd thought that his background stood for something – Lord knows he'd gone on about it often enough: middle class, public school, a system that teaches honour, he'd said, a knowledge of duty. Did he really expect her to live on a hundred pounds a month, plus her own meagre earnings, and to buy somewhere for the children to live with a lump sum of twenty-five thousand pounds? Was it all down to just getting the better of her, winning? She squeezed her eyes shut tight to try and stop the tears, but they came anyway and splashed on to the pine table, leaving small stains on the pale wood.

'Mummy?'

She turned, and there was no hiding it from Milly.

'Mummy, please don't cry,' Milly said. 'I wish I could make it better.'

Lotte held out her arms and Milly came into her embrace. 'You can, darling, with one of your special hugs.' She held her breath and forced the tears back while Milly clung on to her neck and kissed her face with those warm, soft, damp kisses that children give; the best kisses in the world. 'You must go up to bed now,' Lotte said eventually. 'Come on, I'll take you up and tuck you in all over again.'

They rose and climbed the stairs together. Lotte tucked her daughter into bed and worried about life for her with no father. 'Goodnight, Milly,' she whispered. 'Sleep tight.'

'And make sure those head lice don't bite,' Milly added.

And despite everything, Lotte had to smile.

Chapter 12

Jill Hooper saw the police car draw up outside the hall of residence, and went out to meet the officers, one a WPC. She showed them up to Claire's room – which she had now locked – and let them in. The air in there was stale, rancid.

'D'you want me to hang around and answer any questions?' she asked.

'No thank you. Where can we contact you if we need to?'

'I've got a flat on the ground floor. I'll be in all morning. D'you want me to get hold of any of Claire's friends for you?'

One of the officers walked across to the window and opened it. He took out his notebook. 'We need to speak to Sarah and Jen. Can you organize that?'

'No problem.' Jill looked round Claire's room. A layer of dust had settled on the floor and the bed, half made, looked pitiful. She said: 'I'll get them both to come here in, what, half an hour?'

'Yes, thanks.'

Still she didn't move. She didn't want to leave them alone to rifle through Claire's things, it didn't seem right.

'Was there anything else?' the PC asked.

'No, I'll come up with the girls in half an hour,' she said, then she walked away and left them to it.

Twenty minutes later, earlier than she had arranged, she

took Sarah and Jen up to the second floor. The officers were just finishing.

'Was Claire a good student?' the WPC asked Jill.

'Yes. Bright, very able. She certainly had good grades, and Professor Meredith seemed to rate her.'

'Professor Meredith? Was he her tutor?'

'Yes.'

The officers exchanged a look, and the WPC addressed the girls. 'Has Claire ever mentioned him to either of you two? Has she ever suggested any kind of relationship with him?'

Jen rolled her eyes. 'She was always bragging that he had a bit of a thing for her. It was bizarre! I mean, Claire's attractive enough, but she's no stunner, and he's gorgeous. He could have any student on the campus if he wanted to, but he's not interested. He's got a girlfriend and she's lovely. We met her at Christmas, he gave a dinner for his tutorial group.'

'Was Claire there?'

The girls looked at each other. 'No, no, she wasn't. She said she didn't want to go.'

'Did either of you think she might have been depressed in the past month, the past couple of weeks? Has she said anything odd?'

They both shrugged.

'And you don't think there was anything in this Professor Meredith thing? Did you ever see them together?'

'No.'

'Did she have any other friends? Close friends, relationships that you know about that might have turned sour?'

'No.'

Sarah glanced at Jill, then said: 'She was pretty odd, actually, she rarely spoke to us, she didn't seem to connect very

146

well with anyone. She went to tutorials, did her work, always came first, lied about Professor Meredith, and that was it. I don't think she's disappeared or run off; I mean, it's not like she was always partying and might have taken off with a crowd for a binge or something.'

'I see.' The PC turned to Jill. 'Does Professor Meredith have an office here on campus?'

'Yes, I'll take you across if you like.'

'And where is the counselling practice? I gather Claire was having counselling.'

'So she said,' Jen remarked, and shrugged.

'I'll point it out to you as we pass it. I think she was seeing someone called Barbara Kimble. You can check that there.'

'Right.'

They walked out of Claire's room and Jill locked it up after them, then she smiled at Sarah and Jen. 'Thanks, you two,' she said. 'I'll let you know if you're needed again.' They both nodded and walked away. 'That's the problem with a loner,' Jill said to the WPC, 'and I think Claire was definitely a loner. No one seems to have noticed that she wasn't here until Monday.'

Charles was waiting for Jill when she arrived with the police at ten. She had e-mailed him the previous night and told him they would be there that morning. He didn't know quite what he could add to their investigation, and it unnerved him. He didn't like interviews at the best of times. Jill showed the officers to his room, then left him. She seemed edgy, eager to be away.

'Professor Meredith, how well do you know Claire Thompson?' the PC asked.

'Not that well, I'm afraid. She's one of my first-year

147

students and we haven't had the chance to get very well acquainted yet.'

'When was the last time you saw her?'

'I saw her last Tuesday, over a week ago now. She came to a tutorial, but there's been a flu epidemic on campus recently and everyone else was ill. I cancelled the tutorial and she left. That was the last time we spoke.'

'Did she seem well?'

Charles frowned. 'I suppose so. She looked all right. Why?'

'Professor Meredith, this is rather a delicate question, and I'm sorry to have to ask you this, but were you having a relationship with Claire Thompson?'

'A relationship? What d'you mean, a relationship?' He stared at the officers for a few moments, then said: 'Are you asking if we were having an affair?'

'Yes.'

'Good lord, no! She was my student, for God's sake, and I am happily . . .' He stopped and took a breath. 'I am in a committed relationship, Constable, and I do not have affairs with my students. Whatever gave you that idea?'

'She did.'

Charles blinked. 'She did?' He took a step back behind his desk. 'How? She's supposed to have gone missing.'

The WPC took over. She said: 'We had a look at her diary, and she has made numerous entries referring to you and to a relationship, a sexual relationship, that you were having.'

Charles shook his head. His mind was reeling. 'I don't believe this,' he exclaimed. 'I hardly ever spoke to the girl, I know nothing about her except that she's one of my students – the brightest, possibly – and that she delivers good work always on time. An affair? That's utterly ridiculous!'

'I see. So the entries in her diary are wrong?'

'Of course they're bloody wrong!' Charles burst out. 'For God's sake, do I have to spell it out for you? I hardly know Claire Thompson, let alone have any kind of feeling for her!' He took a deep breath and ran his hands through his hair. 'Look, I'm sorry, but this is a bit of a shock. It's not nice to think of one's students in trouble, however little you know them personally, and to be confronted with the accusation that I was having an affair with an eighteen-year-old girl who has gone missing is frankly a bit bloody much.'

The PC, who had been making notes, said: 'Of course. We're sorry to have upset you, Professor Meredith, but we have to make inquiries and we have to investigate everything we uncover.'

'Yes, I see that.'

'Well, thank you for your time, Professor.'

'Is that it?'

'Is there anything else that you want to add?'

'No, not at all.'

'Well, that's it then.'

The two officers walked out of the office and Charles saw them to the stairs. 'If you need to ask me any more questions,' he said, 'you can get me here at the university.'

'Right, thank you, sir.'

When they had left, Charles went back to his office. He sat down at his desk and dropped his head in his hands. What the hell was going wrong with his life? Two weeks ago he had been on top of things – not happy necessarily, but in control – and now his life was spiralling dangerously towards chaos. He picked up the phone to call Mia – a knee-jerk reaction – held the receiver for a few moments, then changed his mind and replaced it. They were no longer living together, he no longer had any right to call her for

149

advice or for reassurance when things went awry. He had lied to the police: he was not in a committed relationship, he was in a relationship that had broken down. So where did that leave him? He bit on his fingernail and stared out of the window. A bit bloody vulnerable, that was where. Charles was a highly intelligent man, and it didn't take him long to work out the implication of a failed relationship added to the fact that he had been accused in Claire's diary of having an affair with her. On top of which, on the night that Claire had gone missing, he had been in London with no witness to that effect. He was more than vulnerable; if he didn't get a handle on this pretty quickly, he could be in some serious shit.

Lotte had the house immaculate when Meg and Leo returned from Vienna. She had put two full-length Disney videos on and let the children wallow in schmaltz while she cleaned like a demon. Meg's daily had only been on Monday; she'd be back again on Friday and the house was far from dirty, but it made Lotte feel better to know that she had made a supreme effort. It compensated for the guilt she felt at staying there, at not being able to get on her feet yet, at having two very young children in a house that didn't cater for them. She had removed all the sticky jam stains off the cream carpets, had managed to scrub the felt pen off the work surface in the kitchen, and she had checked the conservatory for any signs that the plants had been disturbed.

She met Meg and Leo in the hall; the coffee was on, she had some muffins – not home-made – warming in the oven and her face gave away nothing of the worry and stress of preparing the house for this homecoming. She smiled, chatted, let the children dance in the hall and open the chocolate that Meg had bought them; then the phone rang.

Leo answered it, and came back into the hall with a serious expression.

'Lotte, it's for you,' he said.

Lotte was surprised. Then she read his face and said: 'Oh.'

'Take it in my study, you'll have more privacy there.'

'Come on,' Meg said brightly to the children. 'Let's go into the kitchen and find those muffins Mummy's made, shall we?'

'She didn't make them,' Milly said. 'We bought them at the shop.'

Lotte walked towards Leo's study. She perched on the edge of the desk, took up the phone and said: 'Hello, Gordon.'

'Lotte.'

'How are you?' What was she doing, asking him how he was?

'Fine. I'm in the States. Did you get the letter from my solicitors?'

'Yes, I did.' She should have denied it, given herself more time.

'Have you spoken to your solicitor yet?'

'No, erm, not yet, I . . .'

'Well you need to. If you want a divorce, then let's bloody well get on with it. I see no point in having your dead weight round my neck for months on end.'

Lotte swallowed. No one could be bullied for any length of time and just forget it, bounce back as if it had never happened. She swallowed down the big lump that rose in her throat, and the tiny portion of self-esteem she had managed to revive last week, that she had been nurturing and keeping close to her heart, just drained away. She said: 'My dead weight?'

'Yes, that's what you are, Lotte; you've always been a dead weight.'

Lotte held on to the edge of the desk, any perception of self shattered.

'If you insist on breaking up our marriage with this ridiculous accusation of an affair . . .'

'But you did have an affair, Gordon!' she burst out. 'You know you did, I know you did! Your affair broke up our marriage!'

'Marriage? Was there anything to break up?'

The words hit Lotte and she gasped. At that moment Milly crept into the room and came across to her.

'Mummy?'

'Not now, darling . . .' Lotte managed. She held her breath to try and regain some control.

'Lotte, if you insist on naming Eve in this divorce, if you insist on citing adultery, then I will make this extremely difficult for you . . .'

'Mummy?' Milly took a black marker pen out of the pen holder on Leo's desk. 'Mummy?'

Lotte put her hand over the receiver. 'Milly, please!' she suddenly snapped, close to tears. 'Go and see Granny!' She was on the brink of weeping and was holding herself together just long enough to get Milly out of the room and Gordon off the line. Milly walked away and Lotte said: 'Gordon, I don't want to talk about this now, I can't, I . . .'

Milly had begun to draw with the black marker pen on the wallpaper just by the study door.

'Don't be so pathetic, Lotte. We have to talk, we have to sort it out, we . . .'

'Milly! Stop that at once!' Lotte slammed the phone down and lunged across the room, snatching the pen out of Milly's

152

hand. 'What on earth do you think you're doing? You silly, silly girl!'

Seconds later Meg was in the room, Lotte had her hands up over her face and Milly was shouting: 'Stop it, Mummy! Stop crying! Stop it!' Meg took hold of her and lifted her up and away, and Lotte heard her screaming outside the door. She wept for several minutes, then wiped her face on the hem of her sweatshirt and went out into the hall. Leo was there.

'I am so sorry, Leo,' she said. 'I don't know what to say. When I get back on my feet I'll pay for the room to be redecorated, I'll . . .'

'You'll do no such thing, Lotte.' He came across to her and took her hands. 'She's four years old and she's upset that you're upset, and well . . .' He shrugged. 'If you can't do something really silly at four, then when can you? And if you never do anything really silly, then you never learn, do you?'

Lotte started to cry again and Leo said: 'I know a brilliant lawyer with a very good practice who does a lot of legal aid work. Shall I ring him?' He passed Lotte a handkerchief and she nodded. 'Right, I'll do it now.'

He walked off and she was left with his initialled linen hanky, which she thought was far too lovely to blow her nose on.

Annie Taylor had got in late that morning, to avoid meeting DS Coulter leaving work. He was due back on day shift in the next day or so, but the more breathing time she had the better. She was just about to start on a file when two uniformed officers came into CID. She stood up and went across to them.

'You looking for me?' she asked. 'I'm DI Taylor.'

153

'Yes. We've been down to the university this morning, ma'am, and had a good look round this Claire Thompson's room. We spoke to her tutor, the house warden, a couple of friends and her counsellor.'

'What did her counsellor have to say? Was she having problems?'

'No, not really. She was lonely, apparently, needed someone to talk to and told stories to boost her self-esteem. The counsellor, Barbara Kimble, wasn't prepared to go into details until we make a formal request to look at the records.'

'Right. Come on in. I need to make a few notes.' She led them over to her desk. 'Friends? What did they say?'

'Much the same, really. They didn't know of any close friends; she did her work, kept to herself. She apparently told people she was having an affair with her tutor and we found quite a lot of references to him in her diary, but her mates reckon that was a fabrication. He was pretty outraged at the idea and denied any relationship other than the student–tutor one.'

Annie chewed on a pen. 'Hmmm. So a girl disappears and no one reports her missing for nearly a week; in fact no one really notices that she's gone at all, except her cleaner. She doesn't seem to have any real problems, she's not depressed or suicidal. She has been making up stories about her tutor, claims she's having an affair with him, which he denies. Why did her friends think it was bullshit, by the way? Why couldn't they have been having an affair?'

'He's very good-looking, Charles Meredith, and according to one of the girls he could have had any of the students, so why pick Claire?'

'Have you got a photo?'

The WPC passed one across from Claire's university file. 'She's not unattractive. I mean, who's to say what makes two people hit it off? Could there have been any truth in Claire's story, d'you think?'

The WPC shook her head. 'I don't think so. Her friends are pretty sure, and mates usually have a pretty good idea about that sort of thing. Also, he was very shocked when we asked him about it.'

'So to continue, Claire is in counselling, but there doesn't appear to be any significant mental illness; she does her work, keeps herself to herself and gets on with it. On the night she goes missing she is drunk, she tells friends she is meeting her tutor for drinks and supper in town – which she didn't do because he was in London – and wanders into town alone. She never returns. Is there anything suspicious here, do you think?'

'No.' The PC was getting a bit pissed-off with this. He knew his procedure and this wasn't it. To deal with a missing person, you filled in the form, evaluated the case from the points scored, then logged it on to the central computer. This girl scored too low for any investigation, she was obviously a nutter, and nutters went walkabout all the time. What the hell was DI Taylor's problem?

'No? Nothing that you think might need looking at?'

'No.'

'OK. Thanks. If I need any more information I'll get back to you. Can you write your report and have it on my desk by this afternoon, please?'

'Yes, ma'am.'

Annie smiled at them both, but she didn't feel at all happy. She watched them walk off. So, this was it, her promotion, her lot. A CID team who were surly at best, obstructive at worst, and a uniformed force who had as much initiative as sheep. Could they seriously not see that there might be something amiss in this case? That things weren't adding up? Or was it that they couldn't be bothered? Had a memo gone round the nick saying: If DI Taylor asks, don't give? She took a breath and called Jill Hooper at the university. What was it her mother always said? If you want something done, do it yourself. Nice idea, but not exactly practical. Annie preferred: if you want something done, kick ass. And after this call, that was what she was going to do.

Charles got home late. He had played tennis with a friend at seven and had a meal in the bar at the club afterwards. When he got in there was a message on the answer phone from Mia:

'Charles, it's me. I rang to let you know that I'm OK and that I'm renting a cottage in Shorebridge. I've taken a three-month lease because I really feel that I need some time alone and some space to think things through. I hope you're well and that the book is going OK. I'll ring again another time. Take care.' There was nothing more.

He replayed the message, then dialled 1471 to try and find out her number, but the last call was from Jill Hooper, who had left a message on the answer phone too, telling him that DI Taylor from CID wanted to talk to her tomorrow about Claire, and asking if he wanted to come along. He called her back, but she must have been in bed, so he left a message saying that he didn't. Then he wandered into the kitchen, noticed how cold the house was and fiddled with the control panel on the boiler, turning the heating up. It was odd how only one person needed more warmth than two; the house seemed permanently cold.

He made himself a pot of tea, poured it, had a few sips then lost the taste for it. He went into the study and looked at his screen but didn't even bother to sit down and switch the system on. He was lonely; he missed Mia's physical presence, her voice, her being there with him. He longed to talk to her: he'd had a crappy day and he wanted to tell her about it. He went back to the phone and played the message a third time, but halfway through it he snatched up his keys and walked out of the house. In the car he slotted a tape into the stereo and headed in the direction of Shorebridge. He didn't give it any thought at all; he simply hit the road and drove.

Twenty minutes later, in Shorebridge town square, Charles parked up opposite the Somerfield supermarket and sat with the engine off. He watched the shelf stackers illuminated by the harsh fluorescent strip lighting inside the store, and wondered what the hell he was doing there. What did he expect to achieve, sitting in his car in the pay and display parking at eleven thirty at night? When he left the house he'd had some impulsive idea about finding out where Mia was living but that had evaporated as he drove until he found himself following the road round to the square and realizing that he'd made a mistake. Did he really want to know where Mia was? Didn't he need some space and time as well? He'd spent hours and hours of the last week thinking about a woman he hardly knew, fantasizing about her, wanting her more than he could remember wanting anyone ever before. What was all that, if it wasn't the need for time and space from Mia?

Charles suddenly felt foolish. Was this what obsession did to people, reduced them to impulsive, irrational decisions? Was he obsessive about this woman, or was it just the idea of the woman? He had been drunk; she might not be nearly as wonderful as his memory had recorded her. Alcohol changes perspectives. He closed his eyes and saw her face close to his, felt her mouth on his, her body, with its dark, exotic scent, pressed hard into his own. Then he remembered the number of the bar where they'd met, scribbled on a piece of paper and screwed up into a ball in the pocket of a pair of his trousers. How can I know what I want, he thought, unless I try to find out? He opened his eyes and started the engine, reversing quickly out of the parking bay. He would go home and find that piece of paper, and tomorrow he would ring the bar. Tomorrow he would find her, and then he'd know. Another impulsive, irrational decision? Charles was too confused to tell.

When Claire came to this time, she knew she had been drugged, but for how long she had no idea. Her head and body were heavy, weighted down almost, and her mouth was so dry that she could hardly swallow. She put out her hand and felt for the water bowl that he always left under the chair. She dragged it towards her, put her mouth down to the rim and drank. It tasted metallic, but she didn't care. She sat up when she'd had enough and gently pushed the bowl back safely under the chair. There was no light and she didn't want to risk knocking it over. She lay down on the sleeping bag again and pulled the blanket up to her chin. She was cold and her body longed to sink back into sleep. She closed her eyes.

Then she heard it. She sat up again immediately, suddenly frightened. She heard the keys, then the door opened and the intense beam of a flashlight cut the darkness. It swung up and round, then into her face. It blinded her and she cried out, bringing her hands up to protect herself.

'Get up,' he said.

She scrambled to her feet, but stood there unbalanced, her legs weak with fatigue and lack of use.

'You're moving. Come on.'

He lowered the beam of the flashlight to the ground and Claire followed it to the door. She stumbled twice, her legs burning with the effort of having to walk, her head heavy, muggy, drugged. When they reached the door she smelt the air and for the first time in days she began to cry.

'Where are you taking me? What do you want?'

'Shut it!' he snapped.

She couldn't. The sobs rose uncontrollably in her chest and she was too weak to fight them down.

'I'm sorry . . .' she cried, 'I'm sorry . . . I can't stop, I can't help it . . . I just want to know what you want, please . . . Please tell me what you want.'

He said nothing. He let her weep for several minutes, turned away from her as if it disgusted him. Then he said: 'Give me your hands.' She let him take them and tried to see his eyes. He wore a black balaclava with two eye slits and one for his mouth; she could see nothing else of his face. 'Pack it in!' he shouted suddenly. She jerked her face away. She had begun to shake.

'Who are you?' she whispered. 'Why me?'

He clicked the handcuffs over her wrists and held her hands for a moment, stroking the back of one of them with his thumb, tracing the pale blue veins. His touch was warm against her icy skin.

'I'm cold,' she said. It broke the moment. He dropped her hands, tied some rope to the handcuffs and wrapped it round his own wrist.

'Come on, we've got to walk.'

There was no moon, it was dark; but the blaze of electric light on the horizon meant that Claire could see sufficiently to make out where she had been. It was some sort of shed, like a watch for badgers or birds. It was low, just about her height, five foot eight or nine, and the corrugated iron of the roof sloped down to the ground and was covered with branches for camouflage. There was a door, and two windows, which had been boarded up. It looked desolate. It was desolate. She swallowed and turned away from the sight of it. Her mouth had loosened with saliva, but her throat still hurt.

They began to walk. Claire's legs hurt and the handcuffs chafed painfully. She stumbled every five or six paces, and each time she did so he pulled on the rope and the metal cut deeper into the sores on her wrists. It took a long time to cross the fields towards the light. As they got closer, she became more and more tired and fell more easily; twice, on her knees, she thought she would never get up again. But he yanked her to her feet and pulled her on. Her wrists were bleeding now, and the pain made her cry. The blood ran down her fingers, and when she put her hands up to wipe the tears and mucus off her face, she left streaks of blood in their place.

At the entrance to a field, she had to climb a gate, the effort of which made her whole body shake. She could see some houses to the left of the field, cottages, five or six of them. When she had dropped to the other side of the gate, she lay on the ground for a few moments, summoning the strength for what she knew she had to do. He gave the rope some slack so that he could unlock the boot of his car, which was backed into the entrance to the field, almost out of sight of the road. She watched him, his arm relaxed as he reached into his pocket for the keys with one hand, the other keeping hold of the flashlight, and as he lifted the hatch back she sprang, jumping up and running forward with all the force she could muster.

'Ahhh! Fuck . . .!' She had yanked his arm back so hard that it almost dislocated. She ran out towards the road and let out a scream, her lungs searing with pain as she did so. She drew breath and opened her mouth again, but she just wasn't quick enough. The sharp corner of the flashlight came down on to her shoulder with such force that it cut the flesh like a knife and the blow winded her. She fell to the ground, crippled with pain. She couldn't breathe.

She struggled there for thirty, maybe forty seconds, fighting for breath, then her lungs filled and she gulped the air down. He dragged her back towards the car, off the road, and she curled into a foetal position, lying there in the wet, muddy entrance to the field. Her shoulder had gone numb, but her other arm crept down her thigh to the pocket on her combats, and her fingers searched frantically for the Velcro. She located it, slipped her forefinger between the pads and opened the pocket. Inside was her purse. Despite the pain and the fear and the overwhelming sense of dread, hope surged through her, and with that hope came the last bit of strength that she had. She flicked her wrist and tossed the purse out on to the road, where it fell on to the grass verge. A few moments later, she passed out.

Chapter 13

Lotte slept in late, or rather, late for someone with two young children: until seven thirty. It had been a terrible night. Milly had thrown the worst tantrum she had ever thrown, and it had taken her a couple of hours to calm down. Meanwhile, Freddie had found a bumper box of Celebrations and had eaten his way through a good two thirds of it before he was discovered, covered in chocolate, in the corner of the sitting room. An hour later he had thrown the whole lot up.

As she rolled over in bed and listened for the customary sounds of her children, Lotte registered the quiet and was suddenly unnerved by it. She sat up in bed, waited a few moments, then went to check on them. Freddie was asleep in his cot, snoring gently; Milly had gone. Lotte turned and hurried to her room for her dressing gown, but when she got there, Milly was standing by her bed, waiting for her.

'Hello, darling. Did you sleep well?'

'Yes thank you, Mummy.'

'Would you like to snuggle into my bed for a story while Freddie is still asleep?'

Milly shook her head. She stood with her hands behind her back, angelic in her pink nightie, her hair unbrushed, and beamed at Lotte. 'I've got a surprise for you, to cheer you up,' she said. 'Get into bed and close your eyes, please, Mummy.'

'A surprise! How wonderful!' Milly's surprises usually consisted of perfect little unrecognizable drawings, or kisses planted firmly on the mouth while Lotte's eyes were closed. Lotte climbed into bed, pulled the covers up and closed her eyes. 'I'm ready,' she said.

'Here!' Milly declared.

Lotte opened her eyes. She gasped.

'I picked them myself, all for you . . .'

Lotte's hand flew to her mouth, and she held her breath. 'Oh my God . . .' she murmured.

Her daughter had cut all the blooms off Leo's rare orchid collection.

Lotte sat in the kitchen with the orchid flowers in front of her in three vases – there were too many to fit into one – and wondered if seven forty a.m. was too early for a brandy. She was waiting for Leo to come down, which he always did at seven forty-five exactly, every weekday morning, dressed and ready for work. She heard his footsteps across the hall, then the door handle turned and she braced herself. 'Leo,' she said, as he walked into the kitchen, 'I'm afraid . . .' She didn't have a chance to say any more. He had already looked past her to the vases of flowers.

'Oh my God . . .' He looked from the blooms to Lotte.

'Milly thought she was being kind, she wanted to give me some flowers and . . .' Lotte's voice trailed off. She stared at the ground. 'I am so, so sorry, Leo, I will replace every single one of the plants she has ruined, I promise, I . . .'

'You cannot replace my Paphiopedilum callosum. It is too rare.' His voice was clipped and high, as if he were on the verge of tears. 'I have had that orchid for twenty years and it has flowered only three times.' He walked across and took one of the orchids from the vase, holding it gently in his hands. 'Just three times . . .' he murmured. Then he turned and walked out of the room.

Lotte closed her eyes. She knew now that despite the state of it, despite the fact that fishermen wandered around the place at all hours of the day and night, and despite having little or no money to live on, she would be taking the lodge on Ludwell Ponds after all.

By nine thirty, Lotte had a clear plan in her mind. She asked Meg to keep an eye on the children – though Meg was barely speaking to her – and rang the bank.

'Good morning, I'd like a balance inquiry, please.' She gave her password and the number of her own personal account. There was three hundred pounds in there; the meagre earnings from her illustration.

'Can I have an inquiry for my joint savings account; it's held in mine and my husband's name.' Lotte held her breath. 'Eleven thousand pounds? Are you sure?' Why hadn't she ever checked that account? Eleven thousand pounds! She'd had no idea they had that much in there; more fool her, she'd never bothered to look before. Well, she was blowed if Gordon was going to keep it. Without hesitation she said: 'Do I need joint signatures to make a transfer? I don't? Good. Well, yes, then, I'd like to transfer eleven thousand pounds to my personal account. Today, please.'

She held her breath, expecting a problem, then smiled as the woman on the other end of the line told her that the transfer had gone through. It was so easy: God bless telephone banking! Then she did the same with the fifteen hundred pounds that sat in their joint current account. She was solvent; she had enough money to survive on until things were sorted. Gordon could jump up and down and threaten her – which he was almost certain to do – as much as he liked. Lotte was going to get her own life; she had to.

She went back into the kitchen and asked Meg if she could look after the children for a couple more hours.

'I really don't know,' Meg said. 'I am worried that Milly and Freddie aren't seeing enough of you, Lotte. I'm worried that they need more of your time and attention.'

Lotte was stung. 'Even with all the attention in the world, I don't think I could have stopped what happened this morning, Mummy, I really don't, although God knows I wish I could have. I've told Milly repeatedly about those plants in the conservatory, I've stopped her playing in there, I've emphasized how precious they are, but you know, I think that was all part of it. She was upset at me being so upset, and so she gave me the most precious present she could think of. I'm sorry, I really am, but I don't know how to make it better. She is four years old and I can't be cross at her gesture.'

'I know.' Meg sighed. 'I understand that, and Leo does too, but . . .' She shrugged. 'It's a bit like a death in the family.'

Suddenly Lotte smiled; she couldn't help herself. She had lived through losing a father who she adored, and this, this cutting of Leo's blooms, was exactly that: some cut orchids. It certainly wasn't like any death that Lotte had ever experienced. A bubble of laughter effervesced inside her, working its way up. She looked at Meg.

Meg's eyes relented, her face softened. With a wry smile she said: 'I shall probably have to wear black for at least a couple of months . . .'

That was it. Lotte burst out laughing. It wasn't that she thought Leo's misfortune funny, it was that it had to be put in its place, and the laughter did that. She laughed for

165

several minutes, the tears welling up and spilling over. When she had finally brought herself under control, she managed to say: 'I'm not laughing at Leo, I'm really not.'

Meg patted her arm. 'I know that. He will see the funny side too, in about five years' time.' She smiled. 'Why do you want me to have the children this morning?'

'I need some space,' Lotte said. 'I need some time to think things through.'

Meg frowned. 'Not good enough. Yes, you need to do some thinking, but you need to do some legwork too. I won't have the children just so you can go off and waste time. You need to work things through and get on with your life, you know that, don't you?'

'Yes, I know that. I have to meet someone, sort something out.'

'Meet someone?'

Lotte pulled her coat on and went to the back door for her boots.

'Who are you meeting?' Meg asked. Lotte carried her boots out into the hall to put them on by the front door. 'Lotte? I will not have you running off and getting involved with someone else and relying on them to get you out of this mess! You did it before and look . . .'

'Where that got me!' Lotte came back into the kitchen and kissed her mother on the top of her head. 'Trust me, Mummy,' she said. 'I have one little shred of confidence left and I am going to capitalize on that. It might work, it might not, but at least this time I am going to try.'

She was out of the door before Meg had a chance to reply.

The lodge at Ludwell Ponds looked dreary in the cloud-filtered grey light, and Lotte, coming up from the pond because she couldn't remember how to get there from the road, stood just clear of the trees to look at it with a heavy heart. This, she had decided, was where she would make her home, for the time being at least; this grey-stone, lichen-covered house, with its dark windows and empty feel was where she was going to bring her children. She pushed herself forward, up the sloping lawn, to the back porch and looked through the French doors into the small sitting room.

'That's OK,' she said aloud. She had a theory that saying things aloud made them more positive, more affirmative. 'It should clean up nicely; get a fire going, hang some curtains, it'll be fine, perfectly all right.' She wandered round to the front of the house and peered in through all the downstairs windows. The rooms were small, but there were enough of them; three bedrooms, she remembered, a kitchen, a sitting room, a boot room full of what had looked like fishing tackle, a bathroom. Here Lotte stopped. 'Oh dear,' she said. 'Oh dear me.' The bathroom was ancient, the bath was stained green and brown and it had a huge old chrome shower head suspended over it that looked as if it wasn't connected to anything at all, let alone a water pipe. 'It'll clean up,' she said loudly and brightly, but there wasn't anything more positive to add.

Half an hour later, she had walked home, fetched the car and was pulling into the drive of Bicester House. This time she parked confidently and walked right up to the front door, pulling the bell pull twice. There was a shout, the door was kicked once, then pulled, the handle was rattled, it was kicked a second time and finally opened. 'I've got the hang of it,' Lady Beatty called over her shoulder, 'but it's not what Granger told me to do at all! Ah, hello. Meg's daughter, isn't it?'

'Lotte Graham.'

'Yes, that's it, Lotte. Had a springer called Lotte once, beauty she was, like you, lovely colouring.'

'Oh,' said Lotte, having never been compared to a dog before. She hoped it was a compliment.

'Come on in. We'll go to my sitting room.'

Lotte followed Lady Beatty across the hall and through a door on the far right of it.

'Have a seat, dear. Would you like coffee?'

'Oh, no, I wouldn't want to put you to any trouble.'

'You're not, I'm not making it. I'll give Mrs Jacks a holler.' Lady Beatty went to the door, opened it and shouted: 'Two coffees, please, Jacks, when you've got a mo.' She closed the door again. 'So, what can I do for you, Mrs Graham?'

'I've come about the lodge.'

'The lodge?'

'Yes, at Ludwell Ponds. We spoke about it the other day?'

'That's right. Granger said you weren't interested. Shame, it's a good little cottage, it cleans up terribly well.'

'Well, I am interested. I've thought about it and I think it would be fine, very nice in fact.'

'Oh, I see! Well, that's splendid, I am pleased! When did you want it?'

'As soon as possible. Immediately, if I can have it.'

'Of course you can. It'll need some work, but I can page Granger and he'll get on to it right away. There's no furniture, of course, but we're stuffed to the gunnels with rubbish here, you can take some of it off my hands if you like. What'll you need?'

'I don't know exactly, but to start I suppose two beds, a sofa, a table, some curtains, some chairs, all the basics really.'

'Absolutely fine. Why don't we go upstairs and sort some things out now. I've got so many beds in this house, never

168

used them really. I don't like house parties, all those people stuck with each other for days on end in dreary weather, and Bertie always gets drunk and insults everyone. Never had many, really. Doubles or singles?'

'Sorry?'

'Beds. Doubles or singles?'

'Singles, I guess. One for me and one for Milly. I've got a cot for Freddie.'

'You can't have a single bed, my dear, not at your age, it's far too spinsterish. Besides, once you've shared a double you can never go back to a single. Bit like losing your virginity; once you've had the pleasure, you can't think of doing without it.'

Lotte blushed. She stood and followed Lady Beatty out of her sitting room, and was glad she was behind her.

'Jacks!' Lady Beatty shouted. 'We'll have our coffee up here, please!' As she climbed the staircase, she spoke over her shoulder to Lotte, not keeping her voice down at all. 'Mrs Jacks does for us,' she said. 'Deaf as a post. Wonderful sort, though, we love her to bits, wouldn't be without her.'

A large woman, older than Lady Beatty, appeared at the top of the stairs. 'Whaddid yasay, milady?' she asked, fiddling with her hearing aid.

'I said coffee up here, please, Jacks, for two!' Lady Beatty didn't exactly shout, but her voice was several decibels louder than was really necessary. Lotte saw Mrs Jacks flinch, then she tutted and carried on her way down the stairs.

'I hope you're not thirsty, it might be a couple of hours before we get the coffee,' Lady Beatty said, and they went on their way to look out the furniture for the lodge.

It was all very extraordinary, Lotte thought, as she drove back to Meg's house; it had been sorted out far quicker than she had expected, and now she was driving back to her mother's having paid a deposit on the lodge, chosen the most bizarre set of furniture, spoken to Granger about the bathroom and arranged to move in at the weekend. There was a great deal of work to be done on the lodge and she had offered to help with it, not because she felt obliged to, but more so that she could get a feel for the place and keep her mind off Gordon. It would mean she and the children were out of Meg and Leo's house, too, which could do nothing but improve the situation.

She parked the car in front of the house and climbed out. Leo was back early, but at least she had something positive to say to him. She went inside and straight into the kitchen.

'I've found somewhere to live,' she said to Meg. 'It's the fishing lodge down by Ludwell Ponds. Lady Beatty is renting it to me for forty pounds a week and . . .'

'The old cottage by the ponds?'

'Yes.' Lotte turned to Leo.

'But, Lotte, that place is virtually condemned. It's been empty and run-down for years. You can't take two children there.'

'What cottage, Leo? What are you talking about?'

Leo turned to Meg. 'That derelict building that overlooks the ponds, the one we've passed once or twice on walks.'

'Oh Lotte! You can't take the children there!'

'But it's all arranged. I've paid my deposit and . . .'

'And gone off again doing your own thing without taking any advice from anyone!' Meg was cross – it seemed to her that yet again Lotte hadn't thought things through. 'Really, Lotte! This is madness! How can you manage two children in a run-down ramshackle place next to a pond?'

'Lady Beatty is having it done up and furnished, and by

170

the time I move in on Friday it will be perfectly habitable. And I will manage two children next to a pond the same way I manage them anywhere else; with the utmost care and caution! I've had enough of Gordon telling me that I'm a bad mother without you doing it as well!' Lotte glared at her mother. She rarely spoke up for herself and her face was flushed with emotion as she did so.

Meg held up her hands in defeat. 'OK, if you're convinced, then so am I.'

Leo turned to her. 'What do you mean; if she's convinced, so are you? Have you seen that place, Meg? It's not fit for the rats, let alone two children!' Meg touched his arm. He looked at her and read her face, then turned back to Lotte. 'Are you sure Lady Beatty will do it up properly?'

'Granger is replacing the bathroom today, he's gone into Shorebridge to buy a shower unit and a new sink and loo. He will paint the place, woodwork and walls, and I will scrub the floors – they're all stone, so they should come clean. Lady Beatty has given me rugs for every room and furniture, not glamorous stuff, but perfectly all right. It will be warm, she has storage heaters for it, and it's got hot and cold running water. It has a small Rayburn for cooking on and she's looking for a second-hand electric cooker in case I can't cope with the Rayburn, and also she's giving me an old fridge from the pantry at Bicester House.' Lotte was near to tears. She had been so pleased with what she'd done and now it looked unthought-out and feeble. She waited for the criticism that was bound to follow.

'Well, I think you sound as if you've got it organized,' Leo said.

Lotte blinked. 'I do?'

'Yes, if it all comes off then you've got yourself a bargain, Lotte.'

'I have?'

'Looks like it.'

Lotte beamed suddenly. 'Great! I thought I'd take the children over there this afternoon and show them round. They can help slosh water all over the floors.'

'Good idea,' Meg said. 'Go and tell them now. They're playing in the garden.'

'Thanks,' Lotte replied, still smiling, 'I will.' She went out of the back door and Meg heard her calling to Milly.

'What in God's name was all that about, Meg?' Leo burst out. 'You do know that that place is a bloody wreck, don't you? I've ended up praising Lotte for making a bloody mistake!'

'You've ended up praising Lotte for thinking about something then taking some action, and don't swear, Leo, there's no need.' She smiled at him. 'It might not work out perfectly, but it will work; Lotte is determined and when she's determined nothing will stop her. Besides, she needs our support, not our criticism.'

'Then why don't we convert one of the outbuildings and let her live there?'

'Because she would never learn to stand on her own two feet then, would she?'

Leo shook his head. 'I don't understand all this psychobabble, Meg.'

'It's not psychobabble, it's simple human character. Lotte has always taken the easy route and very often it's ended in tears. With Gordon it ended in real heartache and it's not over yet. This isn't easy, Leo, she'll have to work hard to make it succeed, and that will do no end of good for her confidence.'

'And what if it fails? Will failing do no end of good for her confidence?'

172

'Yes, even failing, when you've worked bloody hard, is better than copping out.'

Leo suddenly smiled. 'OK, you win, you're right!' Meg smiled back; their easy camaraderie restored. 'And don't swear, Meg, there's no need.'

Annie Taylor had called a meeting; she wanted all the CID team there, everyone, even those on night shift. She was about to kick ass. She asked the two uniformed officers who had dealt with the case yesterday to attend, and earlier that morning she herself had taken a statement from Jill Hooper at the university to present to them. She got herself a coffee, counted heads and sat on the edge of her desk to begin.

'A missing persons case,' she said, 'on the surface reasonably ordinary. We get a report on Monday night that a student at the university, Claire Thompson, eighteen, hasn't been seen for just under a week. We follow procedure, she doesn't score very highly on our question sheet, the chances are, according to that form, that she's probably just taken off somewhere and not told anyone. Ordinary missing persons case – thousands of people go missing every year for no apparent reason. But her house warden isn't happy. She is convinced that Claire, a lonely girl with no friends, simply wouldn't do that sort of thing. Again, not out of the ordinary; how many shocked and stunned dependants are left every time someone walks away from their life? But I'm not happy either, I'm not at all sure that this case is ordinary and I'm not prepared to dismiss it as such. I'll tell you why.'

She took a sip of her coffee and looked round the room. DS Coulter was tapping his pen on his thigh and staring out of the window; she had the attention of about half the group. 'Claire took nothing with her. She took no clothes, no make-up or toiletries, she took no contraceptive pills. She took no coat, just a fleece waistcoat. She was last seen visibly drunk at a party at the university and told friends she was meeting her tutor for dinner. She wandered off into town and never came back. DS Coulter, tell me, does that sound odd to you?'

DS Coulter dragged his eyes away from the window and stared lazily at Annie. He continued to tap his pen against his thigh. 'Not particularly,' he replied.

'Why is that?'

'Because the girl was in counselling. She had a problem with reality, like, where am I? Who am I?' There was a wry smile from several members of the team. Annie was not amused, but she had all their attention now.

'I'm glad to see that you've read the file, DS Coulter. Did you know that Claire's parents have rung several times and are worried sick? They say Claire was a normal eighteen-year-old having a few problems settling away from home, but no more than that. The counsellor also said that there were no real psychiatric problems and that Claire suffered more from loneliness than anything else.'

'So this is a cry for help.' Coulter's tone was belligerent. 'She wants her friends to notice her.'

'Good point. Why didn't she leave some sort of clue, then? People who cry for help nearly always let you know what they're doing.'

'Maybe it went wrong.'

'Exactly. It could very well have been just a lonely wander into the wrong part of town that resulted in a rape and murder. Or maybe there was more to this relationship with the tutor than anyone thought.' Annie looked round the room.

'I doubt it,' Coulter said.

She turned back to him. 'Why's that?'

'Because WPC Hodges met him and she seems to think it's a load of bullshit. In a case like this, if you'll forgive me saying, ma'am, you need to take into account the responses of your other officers as well as your own opinions. One can get, how shall I put it? A bit too subjective?'

Annie's anger flared instantly. He had thrown down the gauntlet; she had to take it. 'Since when did responses or opinions have anything to do with proper policing, DS Coulter? What I think is worth bugger-all unless I can prove it. So the general opinion is that Professor Meredith is above having an affair with one of his students – rubbish! Maybe he is, maybe he isn't – it's up to us to find out. And if he isn't, what does that add to the case?'

'Not a lot.'

Annie looked across at Coulter. 'I'm sorry?'

'If he's having an affair with her, then surely that adds even more weight to the idea that she's gone off for a bit of time alone. What if he dumped her? What if she dumped him and needed to get away?'

'What if he strangled her during sex and threw her body in the canal? Don't make assumptions and think they'll do for the truth!' Annie was really riled now. DS Coulter was up for a fight and he wanted it public.

'But isn't all this based on an assumption, ma'am? The assumption – your assumption, if you don't mind me saying – that nice girls don't go missing? Nice middle-class girls at university don't run away from their lives and end up on the game in King's Cross.'

'No it is not! The fact that Claire is middle-class and at university has nothing to do with it!'

'What, you don't identify with her at all then?'

Annie knew his tactics; he wanted her to lose it, he was baiting her, just waiting for the explosion. She tensed her body and smiled. 'It has been a long time since I was eighteen and at university, DS Coulter. The only reason I am reviewing this case and that I want to take some action on it is because it doesn't add up. And when things don't add up I want to know why. I would feel exactly the same were it an eighteen-year-old boy who worked in McDonald's.'

DS Coulter shook his head and smirked. Some of the other officers looked at him, and Annie knew he'd got them on side. He wanted to make a fool of her. She swallowed down some more coffee. Let him bloody try.

'What I would like, please, is to try and find out more about Claire from her counsellor, so I've put in for an order to see her medical records. I'd like a couple of you to find out more about Professor Charles Meredith, and I'd like someone to make a visit to Claire's parents. All pretty low key, just to get some background and put this case where it belongs. I understand that it's not a high-priority case, but I want to try and introduce you to the way I work. If I think that something isn't right, then I want to know why; mostly there's a reason for it.'

'And when there isn't, it's a complete waste of police time. Haven't we got enough to investigate without making things up?' Coulter asked.

Annie turned to him one more time. 'If you are not happy with the way I work, DS Coulter,' she snapped, 'then speak to someone about it!' She glared at him but he simply stared back, still tapping his pen against his thigh, a faint smirk on his lips. Then he spoke.

'Actually, you know, that's not a bad idea. I think I might do it right now. I think taking a missing persons case this far is a waste of my time, and I know that several other officers in CID feel the same way. If you'll excuse me, DI

Taylor, I'll pop along and see the Super right now.'

Annie said nothing. She watched him stand, walk across the room and out of the door. She remained on the edge of the desk with her coffee beside her and let a small silence descend over the room. Then she said: 'If anyone else would like to make a complaint, then I suggest you go now so that we all know who you are.'

Two other officers stood up and left the room.

'Right,' she went on, 'let's put some names against some action, shall we?' She picked up her file and continued with the meeting as if the last ten minutes hadn't even happened.

But they had happened, and half an hour after the meeting the Super rang her and asked her to step into his office. As she gathered up her files, she saw Coulter watching her. This time he wasn't smiling, and Annie knew that round one had gone to her. Down the corridor, she knocked on the Super's office door and was told to go straight in.

'DI Taylor.'

'Afternoon, sir.'

'Seat?'

'No thanks.'

'I've had a complaint, from DS Coulter and two other DCs. There's some serious dissent about this missing persons case.'

'I know. I think it's more politics than anything else.'

'You do know what you're doing, don't you, DI Taylor? We do like to follow procedure in this division, regardless of what you've done elsewhere.'

'I understand that, sir. I don't waste time and I don't ask my team to perform unnecessary tasks. I think there's something criminal in this case and I want to make some preliminary investigations. That's all.'

'Right. Let me know how you get on. Give it a day or so, then drop it if nothing comes up. OK?'

'Yes, sir.' Annie turned and opened the door.

'DI Taylor?'

She glanced back.

'This job is teamwork, don't forget that, will you?'

'No, sir, thank you.' Putting me in my place, Annie thought, closing the door behind her; no room for stars, don't shine too brightly, Taylor, or you put everyone else in the shade.

She went back to her desk, grabbed her handbag and coat and left the office. She longed for a stiff drink and a bit of company, and for once she almost thought her mother was right about being alone. But only almost.

Peter and Alison Toke took their dogs for a walk at seven thirty every evening. They ate at seven then got out for some fresh air before they came back to do the washing-up and prepare for the following day. They were both teachers, and they had a grown-up daughter who was on her gap year between school and university, travelling the world with a backpack; and that was probably why they reacted as they did.

At seven twenty-five that night, they called Flossie and Grice, their two young golden retrievers. Peter had the leads and Alison took a plastic carrier from the bag tidy in the kitchen to make sure that they didn't leave any mess behind them. They left the house, a semi-rural three-bedroomed cottage on the outskirts of Shorebridge, and walked down the lane, letting the dogs loose. At the main road they put them both on the leads. They usually followed the main road for about half a mile, along past the row of Ditchling cottages, and turned right into the fields at the public footpath sign. Tonight was no different.

Alison tended to walk along the grass verge at the side of the road with one dog, and Peter on the road itself. When a car passed, they both stepped up on to the verge, and that was what they did now, to get out of the way of a passing lorry. Grice urinated on a bush after the lorry had gone, and Peter waited while Alison walked on. He saw Grice lower his haunches and called to Alison to wait up.

'You've got the bag, haven't you?'

'Right here,' she called. She made her way back and they both waited for Grice to finish.

'I don't know if I need to bother,' Peter said.

'Oh I would,' Alison countered. 'It's near the cottages and people walk along here. It's not nice, Peter. Here.' She handed him the bag and he bent to scoop the dog mess into it with his piece of card.

'Ali?' He was looking closely at something on the ground. 'Someone's dropped a purse here.'

'Well pick it up, then,' she said.

It was a silver nylon purse that had kept dry under the bushes, and half of it was covered in a dark red stain. 'Ali, look at this, will you?' Alison peered over his shoulder at the purse. 'You don't think this is blood, do you?' Peter said.

'It could be. Open it,' she told him.

He rifled through the receipts and notes. 'Twenty pounds in cash, several bank cards.' He pulled one out. 'Miss Claire Thompson,' he said. He pulled out the other cards; there was one for the university library. He handed the purse to Alison and she peered at the stain.

'You know, I think it could be blood.' She rubbed it with her finger. 'I don't like the look of this, Peter. What would a university student be doing this far out? There's not many

179

students round this area. I think we should take it to the police.'

Peter looked at her, and they both thought immediately of their own daughter, halfway round the world. They were acutely aware of the vulnerability of lone young women.

'D'you think something's happened to this Claire Thompson?'

'I don't know, but if it is blood, then maybe something has. Come on, put it in here and let's take it now.' She handed him a second clean carrier bag. 'Don't touch it any more, it might be important.'

'Ali, are you sure?'

'Of course I'm sure, Peter. Look, if it were our daughter you'd want someone to bother, even if it turned out to be irrelevant, wouldn't you?'

'Yes, I suppose I would.'

'Come on.' She pulled Flossie to heel and Peter stepped back down on to the road with Grice.

'Sorry, mate,' he said, 'no more walkies tonight, I'm afraid.'

They made their way back to the house, put the dogs in the car and went straight down to Shorebridge police station.

At the front desk, Peter handed the purse in and the duty sergeant filled in a form. 'The first thing we'll do,' he said, 'is call the university and see if Claire Thompson has reported it missing. I'm pretty sure that she will have; there's quite a bit of cash in here, and all her cards.'

'What about the blood?' Alison asked. 'Isn't that significant?'

The duty sergeant smiled; this lady had been reading too many crime novels. 'It might be blood, it might not be,' he said. There could be an entirely innocent explanation for it. I'll seal it in this plastic bag, though, just in case Forensics need it.'

'Right.'

'Will you let us know,' Peter said, 'if it's been restored to its owner?'

'Of course,' the duty sergeant replied. 'If you ring the station, sir, I'm sure whoever is on duty will pass that information on.' He sealed the plastic bag and looked at the two worried people in front of him. 'It'll be a simple case of a lost purse, I'm sure of it. Don't worry about it.'

'Right.' The Tokes turned away from the desk and left the station. They sat in the car for a few minutes in silence, both of them worried, despite what the duty sergeant had said.

'We've done all we can,' Peter said, starting the engine.

'I know.' Alison reached over and stroked Grice and Flossie in the back. 'I think I'll e-mail Lucy when we get home,' she said. 'She might pick it up at an Internet café in Bangkok.'

'Good idea,' Peter answered. 'Ask her to call us and let us know she's OK.'

'I will.' They smiled at each other, comforted by that thought, then Peter shifted into gear and they headed home. Meanwhile, the duty sergeant left the purse and its form on the desk, ready for the day shift in the morning. He had to admit, though, it did look like blood, and that worried him too.

Charles sat at his desk, his screen on, the telephone receiver in his hand. He had found the piece of paper where he'd written the number of the bar where he'd met the woman; it had been scrunched up into a ball in the pocket of his trousers. He had rung the bar and spoken to the manager, who was obviously busy and in no mood to help.

He'd asked: 'You wouldn't happen to know a woman

181

with shoulder-length chestnut hair, very attractive and slim, would you? She might be a regular.' As soon as he'd said it, Charles knew he'd phrased it wrongly. If you asked stupid questions you got stupid answers.

The manager had laughed. 'I know lots of women with brown shoulder-length hair, slim and attractive; they come in all the time, but no, no regulars of that description.'

'Of course. Look, what about the young chap who worked Tuesday last week? Would he know or remember her?'

'Look, mate,' the manager had said sharply, 'if you want to ask one of my staff questions, then come in and buy a drink and you can ask as many as you like. I can't help you now, sorry, mate, but I'm short-staffed and the place is heaving.'

Charles had rung off and sat at his desk staring at a blank screen. He had been there for over an hour now. He could jump in the car tomorrow night and drive up to Pimlico, but the odds of the same young man being on duty were slim, and even if he were, would he really remember Charles Meredith and his companion? Unlikely. 'Bugger,' he said. 'Bugger and shit and bugger!' He dialled Rob's number, the line connected and Rob answered straight away.

'Hi, Rob, it's me. I didn't really expect you to be there.'

'Charlie! Sorry I haven't rung, mate, things have been hectic since I got back from the States. How're you doing?'

'All right.'

'Only all right? What's up? You never ring me midweek after ten; there must be something wrong.'

Charles smiled. 'You know you're really quite perceptive for an insensitive bastard!'

Rob laughed. 'Whoa! Steady on, bro. You know what a sucker I am for compliments. I don't get that many, they're a novelty.'

Charles said: 'Rob, Mia's left me.'

'Shit!' Rob, who had been lounging on the sofa eating a bowl of cereal – his supper – and watching *Newsnight*, sat up and put the bowl down on the coffee table. 'What happened?'

'I don't know really. She wants a baby, I don't, she's got really hung up about it, she's been trying for one without telling me and I was angry, furious actually. It's all spiralled out of control and she's gone. She's renting a place in Shorebridge.'

'It's pretty permanent, then, if she's not just staying with friends.'

'I suppose so.'

Rob switched the TV off. 'So why no babies, Charlie? Isn't it what most couples do?'

Charles sighed. 'God, Rob, if I knew why, then it'd be a whole lot easier. I just don't feel ready, I can't see it somehow, I just can't get my head round it.'

'Is there someone else?'

Charles almost smiled. Here they were, the two brothers, one the serious academic, sensitive, thoughtful, insightful, and the other a city whiz-kid, fast car, temporary blonde, slick flat, and yet Rob had a handle on things that Charles would never get. How did he know? How could he sense that that was the problem?

'You've gone too quiet, Charlie. Who is she?'

'That's the whole fucking problem, Rob, I don't know!'

'What d'you mean, you don't know?' Rob couldn't believe this conversation. Usually he would call Charles late at night when one of the blondes had left him for another bloke – bigger bank balance, bigger dick – bemoaning his lot, getting a good talking-to about commitment and values. Charles was so sensible, so good, so big-brotherly.

'I met her in a bar, the bar up the road from you actually, the night I stayed at your place. I'd walked out on Mia because I was so angry at finding out that she'd been trying for a baby without telling me. I just upped and left. I dumped my stuff at your place and went out to get blasted, and I met this woman. She was amazing: long dark hair, and eyes that I could swim in, and she was so funny and wry, and vulnerable, broken in a way, struggling to make sense of things, and that made her even more attractive. We were pissed, really pissed, and we went back to your place. When I kissed her it was like, well, nothing I've ever felt before; it just felt like I was consumed with her. She was the most incredible woman I've ever met, I . . .'

'You were pissed,' Rob said.

'Yes, but it wasn't like that, Rob, honestly it wasn't!'

'So you slept with her and now you can't face Mia. You're guilty and taking it out on Mia.'

'No! I mean, yes, I'm guilty, I'm guilty because every time I look at Mia I know that she's so good and so kind and such a good partner for me, but I want this woman, this other woman. God, I can practically taste her and smell her every time I think about her.'

Rob stood and walked across to the window. He had never been in love. He had been in lust and shagged someone's brains out, been erect for twenty-four hours at a time, but he'd never been in love, never been consumed by someone. How could he advise? If that was how Charles felt, then bloody good luck to him. How often did that feeling come around? Once in a lifetime, and only if you were lucky. If not, it was shag and run, or get hitched because you were too old to do the shag-and-run thing any more and life alone was beginning to get boring. 'Charles,' he said, 'I don't know what to say. Are you sure you really feel like this and it's not just a rosy memory, an alcohol-fuelled memory?'

'I think so,' Charles replied. 'I just can't get her out of my head. We didn't sleep together, or rather we did, but nothing happened, she was asleep by the time I'd finished going through your system, remember? And she'd gone by the time I woke up, just disappeared. I didn't even get to know her name. I know nothing about her. Fuck, you know sometimes I wonder if I've imagined her.'

Rob watched a couple coming home, holding hands, walking across the gardens back to their flat. They were a unit, the two of them, standing together to face the world. Charles had had that with Mia, and now he wanted something else, something intangible. Something only a few people ever got to have.

'Forget it,' Rob suddenly said. 'Forget her, Charlie, and forget this whole thing! You had something good with Mia, something I envied. You were a couple, it worked. Don't chuck all that away on a one-night stand.'

'But it's not a one-night stand!'

'It is for her! Has she tried to contact you? She knows how to, so why hasn't she left a note here at the flat with her number on? She wants to forget it, that's why. Let it go, Charlie, please, just let it go!'

Charles had known Rob would say that, and he was glad of it. It was what he wanted to hear. Sense, reason, it calmed him. He said: 'D'you really think so?' And Rob, who didn't really think so, but reasoned that it was the only advice to give in this situation, answered: 'Yes. Let it go.'

So Charles hung up and ripped the piece of paper with the number of the bar into tiny pieces. It was the only thing to do; he had to let it go. He went into the latest chapter of his book on screen and read what he had written the other day. Let it go, he told himself, let it go. But he knew in his heart, as anyone who has ever loved knows, that there are some things that cannot be ignored, some things that we are simply unable to escape. And Charles, despite what he told himself, thought that this was one of them.

Chapter 14

It had been two months since their first night together, and Henry knew without a doubt that this was the most alive he had ever felt. He was twenty-one years old, and yet it seemed that he was seeing so many things in the world for the first time; everything looked different. He was in love, truly in love, the sort of love that defied the conventions of his time, a passionate, all-consuming love that he needed to express with his mind and his body. And this he did, in his diary and in his words to Daisy, in his desire to be with her constantly and in his physical longing for her. But she was capricious; she avoided him for days, then crept into his bed in the dead of night and gave herself to him completely. He never knew what she wanted or what she thought, he could never have enough of her. It was with this thought in mind, this yearning for her, that he went in search of her after the weekend; a weekend he had spent alone.

Daisy was in the morning room when he found her, dusting with the second parlourmaid, Ethel. He came in, looked at Ethel and said: 'Could you go and ask Mrs Blithe for some coffee, please, Ethel? It will save me ringing. I'll have it in the library.'

'Sir.' She curtsied and left, darting a look across at Daisy. Daisy continued to dust as if Henry wasn't even there.

'Daisy, what are you doing? I haven't seen you for days.' He faced her, but she wouldn't look at him. 'Daisy?' He put his hand over hers to stop her polishing. 'Daisy, I am going insane not seeing you. Speak to me. Why are you ignoring me?'

She moved her hand away from his and carried on with her task.

'I've been here all weekend waiting for you, and nothing, not even a word, have I had from you. What is the matter?'

Daisy stopped what she was doing. 'Nothing is the matter. I just need some time to myself, that's all.'

'Some time to yourself? Are you tiring of me? Is that it? You've had enough of me and want to discard me?' He looked at her. 'Oh Daisy, please say that isn't the case, please say it!'

Daisy sighed. 'Of course that isn't the case. I just need to think, I need to have some time away from you to think, that's all.'

'About what? What do you have to think about that I cannot be a party to? Tell me. What is it?'

Daisy shook her head. 'I cannot tell you, Henry, not yet anyway, not until I have it clear in my own head.'

'Come to me tonight, Daisy, please. Come to my room and I'll help with your thinking, I promise I will. We shan't go to bed, we shall just talk, get it clear, whatever it is that you need to have clear.' He took her hands in his own and looked at her, forcing her to return his gaze. 'Please?'

Daisy finally smiled. 'All right,' she said, 'if it means that much to you.'

'It means everything to me,' he said. He kissed her hands and hardly noticed that they smelt of polish. 'Until tonight then.'

When he'd left the room, Daisy sat down and put her head in her hands. A wave of nausea washed over her, the stench of the polish making it far worse. She retched twice into her hands, but there was nothing to bring up. Daisy was very careful and she had got the hang of it now. Most days she was sick until midday, so she ate nothing until lunch. That way, if she had to retch, only bile came up, and that, with a plant pot in sight, was easy enough to dispose of. Wiping her hands on a handkerchief she kept in the pocket of her apron, Daisy stood and went on with her polishing. Sickness or not, it had to be done; for Daisy there was no escape from the grinding toil.

Downstairs, just after her mid-morning break, Daisy went to the toilet, praying that she would see blood. There was nothing. She fastened her underclothes and went to wash. Ethel went in after her. When she came out she said: 'It ain't right, you know, Daisy, all this malarking about. You'll get yaself inta trouble, mark my words, and then you'll be sorry.'

Daisy dried her hands on a towel left under the washstand. 'I don't know what you mean,' she said.

'Yes you do. It's obvious, Daisy, and I ain't the only one who's noticed eiver. You gotta stop it or you're gonna end up on the slag heap, believe me. I seen it 'appen befores.'

Daisy hated the way the downstairs staff spoke, rough and incomprehensible. When she answered Ethel she did so in the sort of voice she always used with Henry: 'I am not doing anything that I am ashamed of and I will not get myself into trouble. Quite the contrary, actually. I will make something of my life, Ethel, just you wait and see.'

Ethel snorted. She dried her hands and said: 'You're a fool, Daisy Burrows, that's what you are. You've got above yaself, you . . .' She broke off suddenly as the housekeeper came into the cloakroom.

'Ethel, you are needed in the kitchen,' Mrs Blithe said. 'Get on now, please.' Ethel nodded and silently left the room, and Daisy went to scurry out after her, but the housekeeper stopped her. 'Daisy, you don't look very well. Is there anything the matter?'

'No, I'm fine, thank you, ma'am,' Daisy answered.

'It's just that, in a household this size, nothing goes unnoticed, Daisy. I have heard reports that you are not yourself.'

'Thank you, but I am quite well.'

'Good, I'm glad to hear it. You should remember, Daisy, that

189

there are eyes and ears everywhere at Bicester House; really, a person is not alone for a single moment. People talk, and talk leads to trouble.'

Daisy looked up. The message was clear, even though nothing concrete had been said. *'I will remember that,'* she replied.

'Good. Then I won't need to speak to you again, will I? You understand me perfectly, I think, Daisy. You are a bright girl, you have a good future in service; you may even make a house-keeper one day.'

'Thank you, ma'am.'

'We'll get on, shall we?'

'Yes, ma'am.'

Daisy left the servants' cloakroom and made her way along to the kitchen. All the way there she felt sick, but she could feel Mrs Blithe's eyes on her, and so she held herself tall and collected her cleaning things for her next duty. She made it upstairs, into the dining room, set out the dusters and polish on the sideboard and was then sick into the large potted aspidistra.

The night-times were difficult for Daisy, she knew the risks she took in going to Henry's room, but she took them all the same. Love and risk go hand in hand. She would wait most nights until she heard Ethel and the other housemaid fall asleep, gently snoring in the beds either side of her, then she would dress, arrange her hair and make her way down from the attic to the first floor of the house and along to Henry's room. So far, she had never been caught, but there had been one occasion when the butler was touring the house before bed and she had had to hide in the linen cupboard for fear of being discovered out of bed and on the wrong floor.

Tonight she had had to wait until after one a.m. to get down the stairs, and when she did, it was pitch dark and she had to feel her way along the wall, guided only by the thin wedge of pale light that came out from under Henry's door. She was frightened; she was also tired, worn out from the work of the day, and once or twice, when she missed her footing, if she hadn't been so far along the corridor she would have turned back and given up. But she made it and knocked gently on the door, before letting herself in. Henry was reading by gaslight when she entered. He saw her, put his book down and came to her immediately. He took her in his arms and held her for several minutes, loving every curve and line of her body. Then he released her and they sat down on the small two-seater sofa by the fire.

'You look pale, my love,' he said, and Daisy smiled to be so much cherished. 'Are you feeling unwell?'

Daisy looked away. 'No, I am fine,' she answered, turning back, 'but I . . .' She broke off. She didn't want to tell him now, not straight away; she needed him to love her first, for her to have the advantage. 'But I miss you and I want you to love me. I am sorry that I have been absent; it has been too long since I was last in your arms, being surrounded by your love.'

Henry touched her hair. He unfastened it and tugged it gently down over her shoulders, wrapping his hands in it. He pulled her face to his and kissed her. 'Will you come into my bed, Daisy?' he whispered. She nodded and they rose together, walking across to the bed. Daisy unbuttoned her blouse and slipped it off her shoulders, and Henry put his mouth to her pale soft skin. Behind her back he unlaced her corset, releasing her body in all its fecund beauty. She lay down and he rolled the stockings down her thighs and kissed the softest skin on her body, making her shiver in anticipation. They were ready for each and gave themselves up to a love that was so natural, so intense and so scorned by the society in which they lived.

Afterwards, Henry held her and told her truthfully that he loved her more than he loved life itself. She believed him; she was young, she had no reason not to.

Chapter 15

It was early Friday morning, and having left the children with Meg for the day, Lotte was in the car on her way back to the house she had once shared with Gordon. She had spoken last night to the lawyer Leo had recommended and was following his advice. It had seemed good at the time, inspired even, what with Gordon still in the States and the house empty, but now she was nervous, nervous as hell actually, even though she was determined to see it through. She would be there by nine, and with the seats down in the back of the Land Rover, she had a massive boot to fill. If she worked quickly she'd be home by lunchtime. It couldn't take more than a few hours to strip a house, could it?

Pulling up in the drive of the house, she yanked on the hand brake, turned the engine off and climbed straight out. She did not sit and look up at the house; she didn't want to be reminded of what she was leaving behind after today. She unlocked the front door, momentarily surprised that Gordon hadn't changed the locks – she had been half expecting that – turned off the alarm and walked upstairs. In the bathroom she pulled down the hatch to the loft and the ladder, climbed up it and took down the suitcases, four in all, along with five soft canvas bags that she'd had since university. She replaced the loft hatch and started on the master bedroom.

First into the bottom of the case went the silver photo frames, three of them, then the pictures off the walls, all hers, bought at various points in her life, the carriage clock beside her bed, her grandmother's, the silver brushes and all her jewellery, none of it vastly expensive, but important all the same. Whoever got Gordon next certainly wasn't having Lotte's trinkets. Then she cleared the wardrobe and the chest of drawers, taking every single item of clothing in that room that she possessed. Some of it she hadn't worn for years, but it was the psychology of it that mattered. Clear him out, the lawyer had told her, make it look as if you've taken everything, but in fact take only what's yours. She removed all the ornaments and her toiletries, including the candles she used in the bath, and having filled two suit-cases and one soft bag, moved on to her studio and the children's bedrooms.

An hour later she had finished upstairs and was amazed at how much of her own stuff had filled the house. She had been beholden to Gordon for most of their married life, made to feel grateful for every penny he spent, and yet she could see now that she had practically furnished this home herself. Downstairs the fun really started. She took all her kitchen equipment, which she loaded into several cardboard boxes from the garage, after emptying them of Gordon's wine. She took the dinner service Meg and Leo had given her, she took the best wine glasses, again her grandmother's, and a selection of nice teas that Gordon never drank. She emptied the cupboards of the food that he would never cook and that the children ate, and all the bottles, opened and unopened, of squash. In the sitting room she took three nice pieces of furniture: the Victorian sewing table she'd inherited, a sofa table, Georgian, mahogany inlaid with cherry wood – a birthday present from Gordon – and a French antique mirror that she had bought. She loaded the car slowly and carefully, using the children's duvets and her own – duck down, a present from her father when she had moved into her first digs – to protect things.

Next she went to the study, just to have a snoop. There was nothing in there that she wanted or needed to take; it was Gordon's room, and because of that it was pretty bare already. She flicked through a couple of files on the desk, saw a list of names for a forthcoming meeting and spotted the name Eve Francis. It made her start, just the sight of it, but as she looked at the list something occurred to her that she hadn't thought of before. Eve Francis worked for Gordon, of course she did. And why was he so worried about citing her as a co-respondent in his divorce? Perhaps in working for Gordon she had risen to a senior level a bit quicker than she should have done. Perhaps if she was named in his divorce it might throw Gordon's judgement into question. Perhaps – and knowing the senior partners in his law firm as she did, this was more likely than perhaps – promoting a woman you were having an affair with, no matter how much she deserved it, was considered unprofessional, immoral and even – now Lotte's mind started to somersault – a sackable offence. She put the file in her handbag, then she changed her mind and took out the top piece of paper, with the list of colleagues, and copied it on Gordon's printer. She replaced everything as she'd found it. Take only what's yours, the lawyer had said; this she had done.

By twelve thirty she had finally finished. She took a walk around the house, staggered at how empty it looked, and left, switching on the alarm and locking the door behind her. As she drove off she looked forward, not back; she didn't even glance in the rear-view mirror. What's the point? she thought; it is no longer my home, and if Gordon does get it, then good luck to him. Because apart from beds, a table and chairs and a couple of sofas, there wasn't much left in it.

The duty sergeant at Shorebridge station took a sip of his tea and started to work through the in-tray on the desk. On the top of the pile was a query regarding a lost purse. He picked it up, glanced at the attached form and reached for the directory. He found the number for the university, dialled and spoke to the switchboard. They put him through to information, and there Claire Thompson was searched for on the system. He was then given the name and number of her house warden and hung up.

'You all right, Jim?' a colleague asked as he passed the desk.

'Procedure,' he answered, 'that's all we get nowadays. No one seems to have any answers, they always pass you on to someone else.' He dialled Jill Hooper's number, heard an answer phone connect and prepared himself to leave a message. He hated answer phones – they put people under such pressure. If you hadn't got one and someone phoned when you were out, then they called later, when you were in. If you had one, then the first thing you had to do every day when you walked in the door was return all your bloody messages. Extra pressure, plus you got to foot the bill for someone else's call. He smiled, heard the beep and said: 'Good morning, this is Sergeant Healey from Shorebridge police station here. I am ringing about a lost purse that we've had handed in belonging to one of your students, a Miss Claire Thompson. I wonder if you could call me . . .'

The phone was picked up and Jill Hooper said: 'Hello?

Sorry, Sergeant, I was working and I leave my answer phone on so I'm not disturbed. Claire Thompson, did you say?'

'Yes, I've got her purse here. Can she come and collect it?'

There was a moment of silence, then Jill said: 'I think you should phone the city police and talk to DI Taylor, Sergeant. Claire Thompson went missing over a week ago.'

Sergeant Healey looked at the purse in the clear plastic bag. 'I'll do that right away,' he said. He hung up and called the city station, and was put through to DI Taylor. He told her about the purse and assured her that he would have it sent over immediately.

Annie Taylor put the phone down on the sergeant from Shorebridge and felt the stress levels of her body suddenly surge. It was a rush of adrenaline, and even though she was used to it, even though it went with the job, she still felt sick when it happened. She had been right: something had happened to Claire Thompson, and even though the purse wasn't a body, it was a bad omen. She looked across the room and said: 'I need to call a policy meeting in an hour. Claire Thompson's purse has been found in Shorebridge, thrown into the hedgerow.'

There was a murmur throughout the room. DS Coulter didn't look up. 'That's seventeen miles from where she was last seen, and . . .' she stood up, ready to go and see the Super, 'it looks as if it might be covered in blood.'

An hour later Annie had assigned DS Steve Brown, along with DC Carol Pinto and DC Allen Gorden, to the case, and had called a meeting of these three over coffee in one of the interview rooms.

'OK,' she began, 'Sheila is minuting this meeting and I want a policy document started as of now. We have to be exact with our procedure and I want all of you to remember that.' She took a sip of her coffee and Carol Pinto lit up a cigarette. 'Right,' Annie went on, 'let's run through a list of where our line of inquiry should be going. Firstly, the purse needs to be sent off for DNA tests, and along those lines we need to know Claire's blood group in order to match it to the purse. So we need to chase up the medical records I requested. Carol, if you could do that, and while you're there, I would like more from this counsellor, so can we get access to her records as well? I really think we need to know what Claire was saying to this Barbara Kimble, OK?'

DC Pinto nodded and made some notes.

'Claire's room needs another search. Allen, could you do that, please? I'd like you to try and find any letters, any notes, and I'd like to see this diary. Let me know exactly what you find, OK? Steve, if you could contact Claire's parents and inform them of our inquiry, and arrange for them to have blood samples taken, and I'd also like you to have another word with Charles Meredith, please. Subtle, though, OK?' She smiled. 'You do know what subtle means, don't you?'

Annie finished her coffee. 'OK, that's it for now. Can we meet again at the end of the day for an update, and in the meantime, if there's anything relevant then get back to me right away. I have asked the Super for a ground search of the area, effective as soon as he's got the capacity, probably tonight or tomorrow morning, and meanwhile, I'm going to talk to Jill Hooper again and to interview Claire's friends.' She glanced at her watch. 'We'll touch base at five?'

There was a general agreement. 'Good,' Annie said. 'Let's get on.' As she left the room, she felt that for the first time since she had arrived in the job, she might just have a few of them on her side.

* * *

Lotte pulled up at the lodge and saw Granger standing outside in the sunshine having a smoke. She waved, but he looked suddenly embarrassed, dropped the cigarette on the ground and put it out with the heel of his shoe. Climbing out, she took a walk around the outside of the cottage, which was already looking better, with clean windows and woodwork, then she went inside and along to the bathroom. Granger had just started fitting the new WC into place.

'This looks fantastic,' Lotte said. 'New bath, sink and toilet! It's amazing what a difference it makes.'

Granger didn't reply; he had his head bent over the pipes. 'Will you put some tiles up?' Lotte asked. 'Around the edge of the bath and sink?'

'I've got a tiler to do that. He's coming this afternoon, that's why I need to get on.'

'Oh, I see. Sorry.' She walked out and saw that Granger had also washed down the woodwork inside the house, ready for painting. She peered into the sitting room, hugely improved with two coats of white paint, then the kitchen, still bare and forlorn. There were rows of shelves and a melamine work surface – very seventies – with cupboards underneath which had once obviously been fronted with material threaded on to a wire. It all needed a jolly good wash and scrub.

Lotte went out to the car and took her plastic box off the front seat. She carried it inside and placed it on the floor. She had stopped off at B & Q on the way back from stripping the house and loaded up with an assortment of heavy-duty cleaning products and a plastic lidded box to keep them in. She took the huge denim apron, neatly folded, off the top of the box, put it on and removed the first product: ant powder. 'Shame,' she said aloud as she knelt on the floor and began to puff the noxious white powder all along the edge of the room. 'It's not as if you eat much, even in your thousands.' Then she set about cleaning, with an energy and determination she hadn't felt for years.

She was just finishing the floor when she glanced up at the window. She had no idea what made her do it, except that she was brushing a strand of hair off her face that was annoying her, and to do so she pulled her face up to toss her hair back over her shoulders. As she did it she caught sight of the window and of Granger, motionless, staring right at her. She started, then waved to try and cover her sudden fright. He made no gesture in return, simply turned and walked away. Lotte stood and went outside. She found Granger smoking in the garden.

'Did you want something?'

He shrugged.

'I thought you might have wanted something.'

'Nah.' He flicked the lighted stub into the bushes and went inside. For a moment Lotte was tempted to go after him, ask him what he was doing staring at her like that, but she knew she didn't have the nerve. It was nothing, she told herself, just idle curiosity; only she folded her arms around her body and experienced a certain wariness that she hadn't felt before. Then there was a cry from the bottom of the garden and she saw Lady Beatty striding up the lawn towards her, an armful of white spring cherry blossom and a huge blue porcelain vase clutched to her bosom. Granger was forgotten.

'Hello! How's it all going?' She reached Lotte and stood the vase on the ground, stuffing the blossom into it. 'My God, you look pooped! I hope you're not wearing yourself out! Is Granger doing as he's told?'

'No, I'm fine, I've just finished cleaning the kitchen, and

199

yes, Granger is doing the bathroom and seems to be getting on very well.'

'Splendid! Thought the blossom would cheer the old place up a bit! Lovely day, isn't it?'

Lotte smiled. 'Yes it is, and the blossom is lovely, thank you.'

'Not at all. Is Granger around? Can I have a word?'

'He's inside,' Lotte said. Lady Beatty nodded, then disappeared into the cottage.

She reappeared a couple of minutes later. 'Just needed to remind him about the cubs. They've got a badger watch at the hide Bertie's got on the estate.'

'How lovely.'

'D'you think so? Sounds perfectly ghastly to me, stuck in an old tin hut in the middle of nowhere in the dead of night. God! Deathly dull! Give me a round of bridge by the fire and half a bottle of gin any day!'

Lotte laughed. 'Would you like to have a tour of the cottage? It's looking really quite good, or rather it will do when the kitchen is more complete and the bathroom's in.'

'Love to. All the stuff's arriving this evening. Bertie hired a van, mad about that sort of thing he is, vans and trucks, used to adore the lorry for the horses! Anyway, Granger's going to load and unload and Bertie's going to flog the stuff over. It'll be different again by the morning.'

Lotte led the way inside and Lady Beatty made reassuring noises. It took less than five minutes before they were outside again on the terrace, looking at the ponds beyond the trees. 'It's very peaceful,' Lotte remarked. 'Calming. I think it will do me the world of good living here. It has a great sense of space.'

Lady Beatty said nothing. There was a comfortable silence, then suddenly she said: 'There *is* something restorative about this place, something good. It has, what's that expression? Karma, that's it. It has a good karma.'

'Yes, yes, it does.'

'It has quite a history, this place. It was used by Henry Chatten's lover, you know; she came here to have their baby.'

'Henry Chatten?' Lotte turned to her. 'Who's he?'

'His family used to own Bicester House. He was hanged in 1897 for the murder of his lover, a servant girl, Daisy Burrows. They never found the body, but they convicted and hanged him all the same. Terrible. The family never got over it, sold the estate right away, then Bertie's family bought it just after the First World War. Daisy Burrows lived here for her confinement. When I used to come here, when I needed the lodge, I used to wonder if I couldn't hear her crying sometimes in the dead of night. Strange. I found it comforting, in an odd way; it made me realize that other people suffered too.'

Lady Beatty's voice had changed, and Lotte glanced side-long at her to check she was all right. There was another silence, then she said: 'We tried for years, Bertie and I, to have a baby, you see. Eight years in all. We met late on, I was thirty-seven when we married, and it took eight years. I was pregnant with twins and I fell down the stairs. I lost them and I came here, to . . . to try and regain my sanity.' She glanced behind her at the lodge. 'Bertie did it up for me. It saved me, I'm sure of it; odd really, I've no idea why, but some places are like that, aren't they? They have an aura, a good feeling about them.' She suddenly laughed. 'Good God, listen to me! I'm waffling on about things in the past, I sound like an old lady!' She looked at Lotte. 'Of course I am an old lady, but I don't feel like one. I suppose it's like that for most people; what's happening on the outside bears no relation whatsoever to what's happening on the inside.'

She moved off the terrace and said: 'I must go. I must stop gassing and get on. I'll be here in the morning arranging things, so why don't you come early and tell me where you want everything.'

'Thanks,' Lotte replied, 'I'll do that.'

'Good!' Lady Beatty smiled, and Lotte caught a glimpse of the woman she must have been at thirty-seven. 'Cheerio!' Lady Beatty called. 'See you tomorrow!' She strode off down the garden and disappeared through the gap in the trees.

Lotte stood there for ages, staring at the ponds, wondering if she'd catch sight of Lady Beatty on the footpath that circumnavigated them, but she didn't. She turned to go back inside and saw Granger, five or six paces away, staring right at her again. 'Yes?' she snapped. 'Did you want something?' This time he had to answer.

'I wondered if you wanted a look round,' he said. 'I can show you where and where not to go, specially with the kiddies. There's a lot of marsh land and some traps here; it's best to be told and not go wandering off on your own.'

'Oh, right.' Lotte glanced at her watch, embarrassed by her attitude. She was too quick to judge. She didn't really have time but she felt obliged, so she said: 'I have to get home by three. Will it take long?'

'As long as you like. There's sixty acres here, but round the lodge, 'bout half an hour.'

'Sixty acres? Really? Do all those woods belong to the estate, then?'

'Yeah. And the ponds.'

'Goodness.' Lotte smiled at him. 'Thanks, then, I'd love a quick tour. Can we start now?'

'All right. The tiler said he'd be here 'bout four, after he's knocked off his other job. Come on.'

Granger turned immediately and cut across the grass into the woodland. Lotte hurried to catch him up. He took her through the woodland, following no path, until, about a mile and a half from the lodge, he stopped. Lotte was puffed and stood to catch her breath.

'Can you find your way back?' Granger asked.

Lotte frowned. 'Sorry?'

'I said, can you find your own way back?'

This wasn't funny. She glared at him and said: 'Are you seriously expecting me to find my way back to the lodge without a map or a compass?'

'How often would you wander out with a map or a compass?'

Lotte held on to her temper, but only just. 'What the hell does this have to do with showing me round the woods and ponds?'

'Everything,' Granger replied. 'You've got no idea how to get back, and nor should you, because you don't know the woods or the lie of the land round here. Even with a map you'd be hard pushed to do it, 'cause there's no distinguishing geographical features. You'd be lost, wouldn't you? And with two kiddies in tow you could be in serious trouble at night, in the winter.'

Lotte narrowed her eyes. 'So this is your way of illustrating how difficult it is to find my way round here, right?'

'Right.'

'I see.' She was about to explode, but thought of the bathroom that needed tiling and the rest of the lodge that needed painting. 'Fine,' she said tensely. 'Thank you for showing me.'

'Yeah, well, as I said, there's bog land all over the place

203

here, 'cause of the ponds and the underground streams that feed them, and there's traps that we put down for the foxes, so if you want to go out wandering, then let me take you or follow the public footpaths.' He looked at her. 'All right?'

Lotte was annoyed; she was not a child and didn't need instruction like one. All he need do was tell her to keep out of the woodland and she would have done it. 'Yes, fine,' she said. 'Thanks.'

Granger walked off without another word and Lotte went after him. It pained her to have to tail him, but she'd taken his warning; she wasn't a fool. They made it back to the lodge in twenty minutes, and at the door she said: 'I'll let you get on with the bathroom then.' She didn't want to even go in and collect her cleaning things. Granger unnerved her and she wanted to put some distance between them. 'I'll get off home now and pop back later to see how things are going.'

'There's no need.'

'No, possibly not, but I'll come anyway. I'm going to bring the children.'

He turned and looked at her.

'If that's OK?' she added sharply, making her point.

He shrugged and walked into the lodge. Lotte turned towards her car. I will not let myself be bullied by Granger, she told herself, but as she walked up to the Land Rover, she felt his eyes on her back and shuddered. To escape the mantle of victim took more courage than Lotte thought she had, but she knew that from somewhere, and somehow, she was going to have to find it.

DS Steve Brown pulled up outside the humanities building at the university and parked his car, letting his head drop back against the head rest on his seat and rubbing his hands wearily over his face. It had been a hell of a day already. He'd had to drive two hundred miles to talk to Claire Thompson's parents, with a WPC who made mindless chit-chat all the way there and who was useless when it came to comforting and reassuring two very distressed people, and now he had to talk to Professor Meredith with 'subtlety', whatever that meant. He could well and truly do without this. Meredith was almost certain to be a clever dick who'd use the sort of words Brown didn't understand in order to assert his superiority, and as he climbed out of his car, DS Brown had decided already that he didn't like him.

He went inside, spoke to reception and was directed upstairs to the first floor and the history department. He found the admin office and gave his name. The department secretary looked surprised, then flustered, and finally, after twittering for a few moments, he was asked to wait while she went to interrupt Professor Meredith's tutorial. As he waited, he glanced over some papers on the desk, stuff he had no idea about – some French-Russian War – then turned as Professor Meredith came into the room.

'DS Brown? I'm Charles Meredith.'

They shook hands and DS Brown had to immediately reassess. Meredith was younger than he'd imagined, more normal-looking, not at all academic – by which Brown meant stained green cardigans, dotted with dandruff, glasses, baggy corduroy trousers, sandals, little or no hair and a grey tinge to the skin. Meredith looked positively athletic, fitter than Brown, slightly tanned, well dressed and approachable. 'Can you give me ten minutes, please, Detective Sergeant? I have to finish a tutorial.'

'Yes, sure.'

'Good. I'll get Marian to make you some tea or coffee.' Charles smiled, although his stomach had seized up at the sight of the police. 'Come down to my office at four, will you? I'll be finished by then.'

Brown nodded and Meredith disappeared.

'Not what you expected, Sergeant?' Marian asked, coming into the office. 'Not your usual academic type? Tea or coffee?'

'It's Detective Sergeant, CID,' he answered. 'And a cup of tea would be lovely.'

At four o'clock, Brown walked down to Meredith's office. He found the door open. He knocked, then stepped inside. Meredith glanced up. He looked as if he were deep in concentration, but Brown reckoned that was a ruse. Meredith was worried. He had that edge about him that people got when they were uneasy; it was a rawness, something almost unnoticeable, except to the trained eye. And Brown had a trained eye; he'd been in CID for seven years now and was on his way up. Not the way that Coulter did it, though, aggressively, pushing and pushing. No, DS Brown was a hard worker and a good policeman, quiet, a backgrounder, but backgrounders got to the foreground with patience, working their way forward, slowly but surely, biding their time.

'Thanks for waiting,' Charles said. 'Please, come on in and take a seat.'

DS Brown did so. Charles watched him, watched his body language and knew that this man was here to interview him. He also sensed that Brown didn't like him. He smiled and said: 'You're here to interview me about Claire, aren't you?' Attack was the best form of defence.

'Yes, more or less.'

'More or less? Is there anything else?'

'I don't know until I start asking questions,' Brown said. 'That's the skill of the job.'

'Of course it is. Please fire away.'

'Well firstly, let me ask you how well you know Claire.'

'She's a first-year student in my history group. She's quiet, does her work well, hardly asks any questions in tutorials, just seems self-contained and studious.'

'Do you ever see her out of her timetabled hours?'

'No, never.'

Emphatic answer, Brown thought; too emphatic perhaps?

'In fact I always have a small dinner for my first-year tutorial groups at Christmas, so that they can get to know each other and me; it sort of breaks the ice. I had one this year, or rather last, at the end of the Michaelmas term, but Claire didn't come.'

'Why not?'

Charles swallowed. Somehow this questioning wasn't what he'd expected. It was sharper, less giving. Brown had an agenda and Charles hadn't anticipated that.

'I don't know. I just accepted her refusal, I assumed she was busy.'

'I see.'

Charles was waiting; he assumed Brown was going to ask what the other two had asked, about having an affair. He braced himself.

'When was the last time you saw Claire Thompson?'

'Tuesday the second of May. She came here, to my office, for a tutorial, but I cancelled it; she was the only one to turn up and I didn't think there was much point.'

'Did she seem all right then?'

'All right? How d'you mean?'

'She wasn't upset in any way? She didn't seem unusually low, depressed?'

Charles frowned. If he was honest he'd have to admit that he hadn't paid Claire the slightest bit of attention, but

207

that didn't look very good, so he said: 'No, I don't think so.'

Brown noted the hesitation; was he holding something back? He made a note of it. 'Are you sure?' he asked.

'Yes, I'm sure,' Charles replied. He didn't like having his answers doubted.

'And were you at all worried when she didn't turn up at the following session?'

'No, not as such. I'm a tutor, not a keeper. What my students do is largely up to them, and that includes the work. You can't make young people of eighteen and over do exactly as you want; this isn't a school, Detective Sergeant. I asked after her and no one knew where she was, so I got on with the tutorial and expected to see her the next time.'

'And when you didn't?'

'Jill Hooper had already reported her missing by the time of my next tutorial, so it didn't arise.'

'Were you surprised by your colleague's action?'

'Surprised? No, why should I have been?'

'So you suspected something might have happened to Claire?'

Charles stopped and took a deep breath. This man was leading him and he didn't like it.

'No, I did not suspect anything might have happened to Claire; one does not go around thinking the worst every time a student doesn't turn up for a tutorial, but I wasn't surprised by Jill Hooper's action. She is an extremely caring professional and she exercises a great deal of thought about every action she takes regarding her students. If she was worried about Claire, then no, it doesn't surprise me that she took the appropriate action. Does that clarify things for you, Detective Sergeant?'

Brown nodded and made a note. He was getting Meredith rattled and it might be time to leave it.

'One last question, if I may, sir? A slightly personal one.'

'Of course, I've got nothing to hide.' As soon as he'd said it Charles regretted it. It was stating the obvious and there was nothing more suspicious than that.

'Are you in a relationship, sir?'

'I . . .' Charles stopped. 'I have been living with a woman called Mia Langley for three years, but recently, due to irreconcilable differences, we have separated, temporarily. It was her decision and she is living in Shorebridge.'

Brown made a note of Shorebridge. Was that relevant? he wondered. He stood to leave. 'Thank you for your time, Professor Meredith.'

'No problem.' They shook hands and Brown left the office. Charles sat down at his desk, far more unnerved by the experience than he'd expected to be. So this was being interviewed by the police, he thought, stage one. He dropped his head in his hands; he couldn't even begin to think what stage two was going to be like. His phone rang and he picked it up. It was Leo Chandler.

'Hello, Leo. How are you?'

'Fine, Charlie, thanks. You?'

'Just about surviving. I've had the police here just now, not a pleasant experience, I can tell you.'

'No, I shouldn't imagine it is. Listen, Charles, you couldn't pop by the house this evening, could you, for a quick drink and a chat, about sixish?'

Charles smiled. 'Yes, sure. Actually, I'd like that. I could do with a chat. See you later.' He hung up and reached for a file of papers that needed marking. He opened it and began on the first paper.

*   *   *

At Harman Court, Leo Chandler put the phone down and went to find Meg. 'Did you get hold of him?' she asked.

'He's coming over around sixish.'

'Poor Charles,' Meg said.

Leo shrugged. 'It's the best thing,' he replied. 'For the moment.'

She patted his arm. 'Of course it is, Leo. I can't imagine you advising anything else.' —

Claire sat, her wrists tied, her legs bound to a chair. She had been asleep. Exhaustion had finally consumed her and she had drifted for hours in and out of consciousness. But now she was awake and waiting. Every muscle fibre in her body ached, a slow, decaying ache that ate away at her, but she would not give in to it. From somewhere deep inside her she prayed she would find the strength not to give in to any of it. She was hungry and thirsty and it was getting dark. She knew he'd come soon, he always came just after dark, his face covered with a balaclava, the beam of his torch lighting up her damp, rotting cell. She heard him each time long before she saw him, and she could smell him too. It was peculiar that, peculiar and marvellous and it filled her with awe, that because of the dark and her inability to see, her other senses compensated. She could hear a rat now, from across the room, and even if the rain was drumming on the roof of the building, she could hear it and she knew to keep absolutely still, to hardly breathe until it went away. She knew she was near water; she could smell it, and she could smell the time of day by it as well. In the early morning it smelt sweet and damp; it filled the air as it settled in a mist over everything. By midday, if it was dry and fair, the water gave off the scent of its reeds and rushes, the sap of leaves in the sun. By early evening she could smell the insects. The water had seeped away from the bank and the odour of the mud exposed was heavy and rancid. And she heard voices too, voices across the water, voices so faint that at first she wasn't sure if they were just an echo of her own cries. But as she became more perceptive, as her sense of hearing grew, she knew they were real. They were real and they weren't far away. They gave her hope, and with hope her fear was manageable.

He came as dusk fell, just as she'd expected. She heard him from some way away, heard the soft snap and crack of woodland underfoot, and she braced herself. The door opened and she could smell engine oil and white spirit. The beam of his torch lit up her watery prison and she gasped as she saw a dead rat in the corner of the hut.

'I brought you some blankets,' he said. 'You said you was cold.'

'I am.' She tried to move round to see him better, but the ties were too tight and a pain shot through her arm where he'd hit her. She swallowed back the urge to cry. I will not die here, she thought, I will survive this. She stared at his shape in the semi-darkness as he unpacked her food: some sandwiches and a thermos of soup. Why was he keeping her alive like this?

'I got you these.' He came across to her and held out his hand; his dirty, gnarled fingers disgusted her. 'You said your arm hurt. Here, take them. Open your mouth.'

'What are they?'

'Pain killers.'

'How do I know that? How do I know they're not poison?'

He looked at her for a moment, then dropped them on the floor. 'Forget it.'

'No, wait, please, please, I'll take them, my arm does hurt . . .'

He crushed them with the heel of his boot. 'Too late.'

Claire looked away. The urge to cry was so strong now that she had to tense her whole body to stop herself from breaking down. Suddenly he knelt in front of her and unlocked the handcuffs. She stared for a moment down at her wrists, at the bloody, open sores on them, and then brought her hands up to her face. 'Why am I here?' she whispered. 'Please, tell me what you want . . .' She began to cry. 'Please, please, just tell me what you want. I don't understand, I'm so frightened, I . . .' She dropped her hands away and looked at him. 'Please, let me go . . .'

He turned away. 'I can't.'

'Why not? Why can't you?' Her voice rose. 'You don't want to hurt me, do you? You don't want to kill me, I know you don't. You can let me go, you can do it. All you have to do is untie me and I'll walk away and I'll never tell anyone about this, never, I swear to you . . .' She was weeping openly now, her face crumpled with pain. 'Please, please let me go . . .'

'Shut up!' he shouted suddenly, spinning round. 'For fuck's sake shut up! I can't hear myself think! You've got me all confused!' He raised his arm to strike her and she cowered back. 'Can't you see it? I need you here. I can't let you go, I just can't!' He dropped his arm down and walked away back into the shadow. 'I want you here,' he said quietly. 'I need you to be here for me . . .'

Claire closed her eyes. All this, all this violence and pain, all her own fantasy and lies, it was all the same thing. Loneliness. Need. It was all so pathetic, but so critical. To be needed, wanted, liked. 'I can be your friend,' she murmured. 'You don't have to make me . . .' She wiped her face on her sleeve. 'You can't make people be your friends.'

He didn't answer her. He brought her food over to her and placed it by her feet.

'Eat,' he said. 'I'll come back in ten minutes to put your handcuffs on again. I'll be outside.'

As he straightened, she caught his arm. 'Please,' she said, 'Please help me . . .' He stared at her hand for several moments; Claire held her breath. He seemed almost to be in pain. 'Please,' she whispered. He dropped her hand and moved away from her suddenly, as if she repulsed him. He left her alone, and knowing she would die if she didn't, Claire began to eat.

Lotte had fed the children and cleared up when Meg came into the kitchen. She had changed out of her gardening clothes and Lotte said: 'Going somewhere nice?'

Meg smiled. 'We've got a colleague of Leo's coming round for a drink.'

'Good, I'm glad I'm out of the way then.'

'You are?'

'Yes, I'm taking the children to the lodge to show them where we're moving to tomorrow. The bathroom should be in by now and it's looking quite good.'

Meg frowned. 'Quite good? Does that mean habitable for two children?'

'I think so.'

'You don't have to go tomorrow, Lotte, you could wait until it's completely ready, or until summer, when it's at least warm.'

Lotte shook her head. 'I have to go now, I have to be independent, you know I do.'

Meg came over and kissed the top of her head. 'Yes, I know you do.'

Lotte stood, helped Freddie out of his high chair and let

Milly down from the table. 'Come on,' she said. 'We're going out in the car.'

'The car?' Milly repeated. 'Why?'

'Surprise,' Lotte said.

Milly jumped around the kitchen. 'Surprise, surprise surprise!' she cried.

Lotte, with Freddie on one hip, took Milly's hand and said: 'Say goodbye to Granny and we'll be back in a little while.'

'Bye, Granny! We'll be back in a little while!'

Lotte ushered them both out of the kitchen, into the hall, where she put on their shoes and let them run out on to the drive. 'Car!' she called. 'Now!' She chased after Freddie, loaded him in and called to Milly again. Meg came to the door to wave them off. She watched Lotte reverse and go off down the drive.

Meg went inside and was about to close the front door when she heard a screech of tyres, then a horn, and moments later Charles Meredith turned into the drive. He parked and climbed out. 'Christ, I just missed some woman in dark glasses up the road there. She pulled out into the main road just as I was coming along. I missed her by inches. I didn't get a look at her face, or her number plate; if I had I might report her. Bloody idiot!'

Meg flushed. She was sure that that had been Lotte, but she wasn't going to admit it. It would be far too embarrassing for Charles. 'Come on in and have a drink,' she said. 'You look as if you need one.' As she led the way inside, she almost added: 'Actually, so do I.'

Leo was reading in his study when Meg called out that Charles had arrived. He came out, folding the paper. 'Charles, good to see you. Come on into the sitting room.

What would you like to drink? Meg, can you do the honours?'

'I'll have a whisky, please, just ice.'

'I'll have the same, darling.' Leo smiled, but Meg caught the tension in his eyes.

'I'll bring them through,' she said, and went into the kitchen.

Charles followed Leo into the sitting room and wondered why this formality; the Chandlers were usually very relaxed.

'Charles, I spoke to the Vice-Chancellor this afternoon and he asked me to have a word with you. I'm sure you already know that the police have been up at the university today asking all sorts of questions. They've found Claire Thompson's purse, seventeen miles away, in Shorebridge, and this is fast becoming a full-scale investigation.'

'They found her purse in Shorebridge? Is that significant?'

'It would seem so. They spent a good deal of time this afternoon with Barbara Kimble, one of the counsellors from the university practice.' Leo hoped this would alert Charles to what he was about to say. It didn't.

'Did they? They spent quite a bit of time with me as well. This whole incident is thoroughly upsetting. Poor girl, I hope to God nothing awful has happened to her.'

Meg came in with the drinks, but instead of joining them, she handed a glass to Charles and one to Leo, then left the room. Charles sensed bad news.

'Look, Charles, there isn't any easy way of saying this, but Barbara Kimble had to tell them that Claire was making allegations involving you.'

Charles froze. 'Involving me? What sort of allegations?'

Leo was hating every moment of this. 'I don't know the details, but there's a lot of gossip going round and it's all pretty unhealthy. The vice-chancellor asked me to suggest to you that it might be helpful if you took a few weeks' leave, fully paid, of course, and not affecting your holiday entitlement.'

'Leave? But that makes it look as if I've done something wrong! I cannot believe that Claire Thompson was making allegations against me, Leo! I hardly knew her. What the hell has she been saying?' Charles was very upset. 'I mean, I knew about her diary, the police told me that, and well, frankly I've been trying to dismiss it as teenage fantasy, but if she's been making accusations of the same nature to colleagues of mine, then where the hell does that leave me? It's my word against that of a dead girl.'

'Dead girl? She's missing, Charles, not dead!'

'Of course not, I didn't mean anything by that, I just meant . . . Oh, forget it!' He drank his whisky down in one and went towards the door.

'Charles, please stay and discuss this.'

He turned. 'There's nothing to discuss, Leo. I have been given a temporary suspension, a missing girl has made all sorts of false accusations about me that I cannot disprove, my colleagues doubt me and the police obviously have me down as a suspect in her abduction. Great! Fucking great! What more is there to say?' He walked out of the room, across the hall and out of the house.

Leo heard him drive off and went to find Meg.

'How did it go?' she asked.

'Terrible,' he replied. 'Worse than I expected. I don't think I handled it at all well and Charles certainly didn't take it well.'

Meg shook her head. 'Poor Charles,' she said.

'Poor girl,' Leo added. 'I wonder what the hell could have happened to her.'

Meg thought about her own daughter and granddaughter and shivered. They both fell silent.

Charles drove to Mia's office. He parked outside, next to her car, and went up. The receptionist had already gone, so he knocked on the glass door and Mia herself came to see who it was. She hesitated for a moment when she saw him, then unlocked the door and let him in.

He stood there for a few moments, unable to speak, and she said: 'You look terrible, Charles. What's happened?'

He hung his head. 'Loads of stuff. All of it crap. I won't bore you with it.'

'Come into my office,' she said. 'Come and sit down.'

In her office he accepted a glass of water. She could smell the whisky fumes on his breath and wondered if he was drunk.

'I don't know what's happened in my life, Mia,' he began. 'It seems that everything has gone wrong and I don't know how to get it right again.'

She sat on the edge of the desk and watched him.

'Rob told me to get you back; he said that we're a couple, and we were, you know, we had it right, didn't we?'

'Up to a point,' she said, 'yes, we did.'

'Up to what point?'

'To the point of the future. There we disagreed and had to split.'

'Did we have to split? Couldn't we have worked it out?'

She shrugged. 'I don't know. How do you work out one partner wanting a baby and the other not? There isn't a compromise, is there? One of you has to back down, and I can't. It's what I want, what I long for, and I can't commit myself to someone who doesn't want it too.'

'I never said I didn't want children, I just said I wasn't ready.'

She smiled sadly. 'It doesn't matter what you said, it's how you feel. You don't want children with me, do you, Charles? It's not that you're not ready, it's that I'm not right.'

'But you are right! Rob said as much the other night. We fitted together, didn't we?'

Mia sighed. 'Yes, I suppose we did.'

'We had a good relationship, a good partnership, didn't we?'

'Yes, but . . .' She stopped and shook her head. 'Charles, I don't know where this is going.'

'Nor do I. I've never known and I know even less now. Do you still love me?'

She looked down at her hands, long, elegant hands, the fingers locked together to stop them from shaking. 'Yes,' she said, 'I still love you.'

He felt suddenly very relieved. If he could get Mia back, then maybe he could get some balance back too. What was love, if it sent the world into chaos? He stood and went across to her, taking her hands and holding them, taking the strength her belief in him gave. 'Don't give up on me, Mia,' he said. 'Please.' Then he released her and left the office.

For a long time she sat there, while the light grew dim and the street outside silent. Charles loved her, she knew that, but not with the passion with which she loved him. And what kind of love, she thought, was simply comfort and convenience? Was it enough? And was she prepared to take it for the sake of a baby?

Chapter 16

Henry had been gone for nearly two weeks, and Daisy mourned him. She had lost weight; when she ate, food stuck in her throat and she had given up trying to force it down. She hardly slept and her work suffered for it. She was fatigued, she had dark circles under her eyes and her mind was addled; she could think of nothing but Henry and what was growing inside her body. She was slow, she missed things, dirt and dust, and she had been warned again by Mrs Blithe to mind herself. She was frightened and alone. Henry, she thought, had abandoned her.

She was cleaning the silver in the dining room when Maekins, the butler, came into the room. She glanced up, then gave a small bow and kept her eyes lowered. She thought he would tour the room as he always did, check everything was all right and then oversee her work for a few minutes. She scrubbed a little harder and wished him gone. He was a big man and he unnerved her with his sheer physical presence. She finished brushing and took up a rag to buff the platter to a shine. Maekins came over and stood in front of her, looking at the pieces she had already done. She polished frantically, averting her eyes, then suddenly his hand came down on her own and her polishing was curtailed. She stared at it, a big hand, smooth, unlike her own, with dark hairs that covered the wrist. It revolted her.

'You have been looking tired recently, Daisy, and yet you haven't been getting those late nights that you used to.' Daisy caught her breath. 'And you've lost weight, you've not the figure

219

that you used to have, but your breasts still swell as they should, don't they, Daisy?' She started and a wave of panic washed over her. He moved his hand very gently over hers in a small circular movement. 'Indeed, with your smaller waist, your breasts seem even more appealing than they ever did.'

Daisy jerked her hand away and glared at him. He smiled slowly. 'Don't tell me you're shocked, Daisy, not with what you get up to after hours. There are some . . .' he picked up a piece of silver and held it carefully, inspecting every inch of it, 'who would be very partial to your favours, Daisy, some who might be able to show you an even better time than you are used to.' He put the small silver jug down. 'You should think about it.'

She looked at him. 'Never,' she said.

'Because your skills as a housemaid are slipping,' he went on, as if she'd never spoken. 'And if the master's favour has cooled, then you might need to find favour elsewhere – or find employment elsewhere.' Daisy dug her hands into the pocket of her apron, the feel of his hand on her skin revolting her. 'We'll give it a month, shall we?' The door opened and Ethel and Evie came in. Maekins turned, glanced at the two maids and walked directly past them to the door. 'A month, Miss Burrows,' he repeated, then he left.

Daisy put her hands up to her face. Ethel and Evie exchanged glances. Daisy's hands, rough and chapped, were shaking uncontrollably.

After luncheon had been served, Henry wandered outside from the drawing room – the domain of the men – on to the sloping lawn of the Testrys' Brighton villa. He put his face up to the sunshine and stood for a few moments enjoying the warmth. When he opened his eyes he saw his mother on a wicker sofa at the bottom of the garden, chatting to Mrs Testry. He was about to turn away, but she spied him and waved. He waved back and she motioned for him to join them. Silently he cursed and walked down towards the ladies.

'Have you given up on politics and business, Henry?' his mother asked.

'It's all very interesting but I have been lured outside by the sunshine. There is nothing more glorious than England in the sunshine.'

'I quite agree,' said Mrs Testry. 'In fact there is nothing more glorious than being beside the English sea in the sunshine, wouldn't you agree, Isabella?'

Isabella Testry turned her head from the view and smiled at Henry. She had made a point over the past two weeks of not speaking to Henry unless she was asked to do so. She knew what her mother was up to and she would conform only to a certain extent. Henry had got it wrong about Isabella; she was nice, but she was far from dull. 'I think it is glorious here in any weather. I love the seaside.'

Henry smiled back, but not with any sincerity. Personally, he found it rather dull, artificial enjoyment, and he longed to get back to Bicester House. 'Why don't you young ones take a stroll along the prom?' Mrs Testry said, 'It would be far nicer than sitting here listening to the ladies gossip.'

'Especially in such sunshine,' Lady Chatten added.

Henry looked at Isabella, who was still smiling, and said: 'Why not? Isabella, would you care to take a walk with me?'

'I should love to, Henry, thank you.' She stood and he threw a glance at his mother, warning her not to try this again. He offered his arm and Isabella took it, positioning her parasol so that the sun was off her face. 'We'll see you later, Mama,' he said. 'Mrs Testry.'

'Goodbye. Enjoy yourselves.'

Isabella and Henry walked up the lawn to the house and Lady

Chatten leant in to Mrs Testry. 'Henry looks very relaxed, wouldn't you say?'

'Yes, better than when he arrived.'

Lady Chatten smiled. 'And I wonder why that should be?'

Mrs Testry smiled back. This was going far better than she could ever have imagined. Lady Chatten was more than keen for a match; indeed, at times, Mrs Testry didn't wonder if she seemed a bit, well, desperate. 'Isabella is certainly fond,' she said. 'I think she would be most open to suggestions.'

Lady Chatten watched Henry and Isabella disappear into the house. 'Wonderful,' she murmured, adding silently: 'And how convenient.' She sighed and turned back to Mrs Testry. Beggars can't be choosers; it was as simple as that.

As they walked along the promenade, Isabella nodded frequently to her Brighton acquaintances, and Henry, despite his languor, was flattered to be with her. They walked for some time, making small talk, very pleasantly really, then they stopped and leant on the railings to look out at the blue horizon and enjoy the fresh sea breeze. 'I am afraid Henry,' she began, not looking at him, 'that some people are pushing us towards a conclusion.' She took a breath. 'And I am afraid that it might be a conclusion that you do not want.'

Henry kept his gaze towards the sea and said nothing; he did not know what to say.

'I think that perhaps you are sad, Henry.'

He smiled wryly. 'How very observant you are, Isabella.'

'Am I?' He turned to look at her now and thought how lovely she was, with the pink of her parasol reflected on to her skin.

'Yes, you are.'

'Thank you for your concern, but I am fine. And . . .' he shrugged, 'I have no thoughts on any conclusions.'

She smiled. 'Then I am in with a chance.'

He smiled back. 'You flatter me, Isabella.'

'I don't mean to.' She placed her hand on his arm, very briefly, then glanced back at the sea. 'I have grown fond of you, Henry, although that wasn't my plan at all.'

Henry stared at where she had placed her hand, her delicate, gloved hand, then his gaze went to the long silk-wrapped fingers that now curled over the railing. Everything about her was refined: her manners, her voice, he neat figure encased in pale pink silk, her elegant hands and the smile that was more knowing than he had originally thought. She would make a good companion, a good wife. 'What was your plan?' he asked.

'To spite my mother. She is the most frightful snob and I will not marry just anyone simply for money.'

'I am glad to hear it.'

'Although of course you have money as well!'

Suddenly Henry laughed. 'You have a sense of humour, Isabella.'

She smiled, pleased at having entertained him. 'With my mother I need one.'

Henry offered her his arm. All this time, staring at the sea and talking to Isabella, an idea had been taking shape in the back of his mind, and now he realized it was fully formed. 'Shall we walk on?' he asked.

'That would be lovely.' She took his arm and they set off again. 'That's better,' she said, a few minutes later.

'What is?'

'You. You don't look nearly as sad.'

'I don't feel nearly as sad,' he answered. It was true, his spirits had lifted. 'And I have you to thank for that.'

'Me? What have I done?'

You have given me a way out, he thought, given me a solution; but he simply said: 'Far more than you imagine, Isabella Testry.'

'Good, I'm glad.'

Henry looked at her and patted the hand that was on his arm. 'So am I,' he said. 'So am I.'

Later that day, after Henry had dressed for dinner, he went to his mother's room, knocked and was told to enter. She was in evening dress and was having her hair arranged.

'Mama, may we talk privately for a few moments?'

Lady Chatten glanced at him in the mirror. 'Peters is just finishing my hair, Henry, can I see you downstairs in the drawing room?'

'May I wait, Mama?'

She sighed, then smiled indulgently, and he took a seat, watching Peters as she coiled and pinned his mother's auburn hair. When it was finished, Lady Chatten said: 'Thank you, Peters. Henry? Will you help me choose my jewels for tonight? We are dining with the Atkinses and Lady Atkins has such a wonderful collection I don't know what to put on to compete.'

Henry came across and took up the first leather box from the pile. It was diamonds and rubies. 'Too showy,' he said, closing it and moving on to the next. He worked his way through four boxes until he came to the pearls. 'Perfect,' he said. 'They will show off the black silk beautifully.' He removed a three-string choker with a diamond clasp and fastened it round his mother's neck. She took the earrings and put them on herself, all the time staring at him in the mirror.

'So?' she asked, once she had finished. 'What was it you wanted to say to me in private?' She turned on her dressing table stool and faced him.

'I am going to ask Father tonight for his permission to ask Isabella Testry to be my wife.'

Lady Chatten stared at him for a few moments, then at last she smiled. 'Henry, I am delighted,' she said. 'Come here.' He *came across to her and she kissed him. He was unusually tense. She pulled back and said: 'And?'*

Henry swallowed. 'I would like you to speak to Father to ask him to increase my allowance to five thousand a year.'

'Five thousand?' She shook her head. 'Henry, that's ridiculous! What could you possibly want with five thousand a year?'

'I will be married, remember.'

'But still! You will have the house in London, which your father will maintain; you will have a wing at Bicester. Why five thousand?'

Henry looked away. He had never been able to lie well, and it showed now. Lady Chatten eyed him, then said: 'What is it, Henry?'

'I want to be able to look after Daisy,' he said. 'If I have five thousand a year and the house in London, then I can set her up in a flat near by and look after her and my son.'

'Your son?' Lady Chatten forced down the sudden anger that rose in her chest. She did not want to fight with Henry; this situation was far too precarious to fight about. As calmly as she could, she said: 'You do not know that Daisy is carrying a boy, Henry; it might be a daughter.'

'Then I will care for Daisy and my daughter. I will do it, Mama, I will see this through.'

'Henry, this is not right,' Lady Chatten said. 'You cannot ask a young woman to marry you knowing all the time that you have a mistress and an illegitimate child whom you have no intention of renouncing. It would be a terrible lie and I will not allow you to live your life as a lie!'

'Then I will do as I told you when I first arrived. I will marry Daisy and we will take our chance in life!'

Lady Chatten stood up abruptly and walked to the window. 'How can you do this to me, Henry? How can you hurt me so?'

Henry came across to her. 'Mama, it doesn't have to be like this, I don't have to hurt anyone. I would keep it secret, my life with Daisy would be known only to me and you, but after today we would never speak of it again. Isabella is fond of me, she is doing as her mother wants and I am a catch for her. She will make a good wife, she is what you want, and if she never knows about Daisy then what difference will it make to our marriage?'

'It will be a false marriage, Henry, it will be a sham!' Lady Chatten cried. 'You must see that!'

'And yours isn't? Tell me what marriage is honest and true? You have never loved my father, I can see it, I have always seen it in your eyes. You love me, I am the one who makes you happy, and if that isn't a lie, then I don't know what is!'

Suddenly Lady Chatten slapped him, bringing her hand up and hitting him hard across the face. He stumbled back. 'Don't you ever speak to me like that again! Ever!' She turned her back on him and he rubbed his face.

'I am sorry, Mama, truly I am, but you have to understand how I feel about this. I have promised Daisy that I will look after her, and I will never break that promise. If you ask Papa to increase my allowance, then he will do it, you can persuade him, and I will marry Isabella Testry. We will be happy and so will you. There will be no scandal, no one will ever suspect, and I will fulfil my promise to the woman I love.'

'But she is a servant, Henry! This woman you love is a servant! She is not and can never be worthy of you!'

'That is nonsense and you know it, Mama! Why isn't she worthy of me? Because I have money and a title? Because I am from another class, a class who would think nothing of abandoning a woman with a child, of letting them end up in the workhouse, for nothing but snobbery? I think it is I who is not worthy of her, of her honesty and love.'

Lady Chatten put her hands up to her face.

'Mama, please! Please don't cry, please help me. Please understand me.'

She dropped her hands away and Henry saw the raw pain on her face. 'I understand you, Henry, I understand you better than you will ever know.' There was a long, painful silence, then she took a breath and came back into the centre of the room. 'I will speak to your father,' she said. 'I suggest that this girl spends her confinement in the lodge, then you can arrange things once the baby is born.'

Henry reached out for her hand, but she withdrew it. 'After tonight, Henry, I do not ever want to speak of this subject again. I will arrange for Mrs Blithe to dismiss this girl and you can move her into the lodge. No one must ever know of what becomes of her, and I never want to hear her name. Ever. Is that clear?'

Henry bowed his head. 'Yes, Mama,' he said.

'Good.' Lady Chatten went to her dressing table and sat down in front of the mirror to pin an ornament into her hair. 'I will see you in the drawing room for cocktails at eight,' she said.

Henry moved towards the door. He wanted to say something, anything to break down this barrier that had suddenly sprung up between them. 'Mama, I . . .'

Lady Chatten held up her hands to silence him. He nodded and left the room. When he had gone, she stared at her reflection in the mirror and wished that she'd had Henry's courage twenty-five years ago; that way she might have had a chance at some of his happiness.

Henry left Brighton the following morning, after asking Isabella Testry to become his wife. He would go to Bicester House first, then up to London to speak to Isabella's father. Isabella had agreed to become engaged with her father's blessing; Henry had just to ask for it.

He arrived at Brierly station by train at midday and went

straight to Bicester. It was Thursday, Daisy's afternoon off, so he rang for Mrs Blithe and asked for luncheon to be served in the dining room, confident that Daisy would be sent to set it up. She came with a tray to lay the table and he took it, closing the door behind her. She turned away from him, walking across to the window. 'I thought you had left me,' she said numbly. She stared out, her arms folded defensively across her body.

'I could never leave you, Daisy, never,' he replied.

A sob escaped her and she bit her hand to keep control. He stood across the room from her and said: 'I have made a promise and I will keep it.' She wiped her face on the back of her hand and he went to her then, to hold her. 'This afternoon I want to show you something. Can you meet me at the gate to the woodland?'

She nodded.

'In an hour?'

'I'm not off duty until two thirty.'

'At quarter to three, then?'

'Yes, fine.'

He kissed her hands.

'I must set up, for your lunch.'

'Of course.' He let her go and watched her for a few moments as she laid the silver neatly on the dining table. The gulf between master and servant never crossed his mind; his great gift was to see past it – it was also his great downfall.

At two forty-five Henry waited for Daisy by the gate. She was late and it worried him. At three he saw her running across the field and ran towards her, catching her up in the middle and holding her close. 'God, I've missed you so much,' he cried, then he kissed her and instantly felt the intensity of her sexuality. He led her on to the woods, her hand in his, telling her that what he was about to show her was just the beginning, the start of

228

their future together. They took the path by Ludwell Ponds, a place so significant to both of them that they fell silent, remembering. Then Henry stopped at a small bar gate in a yew hedge and opened it. He let Daisy go first and stepped after her, through a clearing in the trees and on to the lawns of the fishing lodge. She stopped and turned to him questioningly, and he said: 'My mother has agreed to my plans and she wants you to use the lodge for your confinement. I will have it made more comfortable for you, more feminine, and take care of everything you and the baby might need. Then, once you are ready, once I am married, I will find you a small house in London, something in a good area, something . . .' He broke off as she stared at him aghast.

'Married?' she uttered. 'I don't understand, I thought . . .' Her voice failed her.

Henry said quietly: 'I am engaged to be married. It was the only way, Daisy, the only way I could get us enough money to live on! I don't love her, of course I don't, and it will never be anything like we've got, but I had to do it, there was no other way. If I marry Isabella then my father will increase my allowance and we can . . .'

'Isabella?'

He took her hands. 'Isabella Testry. She's an ordinary girl whose mother wants her to marry money. It's nothing, Daisy, nothing at all! It is just an agreement!'

'But I thought you were going to marry me!' Daisy stood and looked at him, and for the first time she saw how hopeless it all was, how hopeless it had always been. Why had she let it come this far? How could she have deceived herself so? 'You said you would marry me!'

'No, I promised to look after you, and that is what I will do! You will never want for anything, Daisy, nor will our child. I can see you and love you just the same and . . .'

229

'You will be married!' Daisy cried. 'You will be married and sharing your life with another woman, and I will be what? Your mistress!' She jerked her hands away and turned from him.

'What else did you expect?'

'I expected you to act with honour! You have condemned me to a life of sin, our child to a life as a bastard. If you will not acknowledge me, then . . .' She turned and ran, picking up her skirts, and disappeared into the woodland that bordered the lodge.

'Daisy!' Henry called. 'Daisy, come back!' He set off after her, but lost sight of her amongst the trees. 'Daisy!' he shouted. 'Daisy, for God's sake come back!' He stopped and listened hard. Maybe she had run out towards the road. He heard nothing, then suddenly a scream pierced the silence. 'Daisy!' He ran, not knowing if it was the right direction. 'Daisy?' he called again. 'Daisy!'

He found her minutes later, lying on the ground. She had fallen, caught her foot on the edge of something and lost her balance. Her ankle was beginning to swell and she was crying.

'My God! Daisy, you fool, you could have damaged yourself and the baby!' He helped her to sit up. 'Is it broken?'

'No, I don't think so. I can move it and my toes.'

'What in God's name happened?'

'I caught my foot, there.' She pointed to a brick edge. Henry stood and went over to it. 'Dear God!' He ripped at the grass. 'Daisy, you could have been killed! This is a well, an unused well!' He looked at her. 'You could have fallen down it, you could have broken your leg! My God, Daisy, that was so irresponsible!' He was angry, at her and at himself. This was not what he had planned, this pain and guilt was not what he wanted. He went back to her and knelt over her foot. The ankle was badly swollen now. 'Can you walk, do you think?'

She nodded. 'I'll have to.'

'No, I can carry you if you can't walk.'

'Don't be ridiculous, Henry!' she snapped. 'You are the one

so concerned with opinion; what would it look like?'

'It would look like I tell it!' he snapped back, then he turned away and took a deep breath. 'Daisy, we have to stop this, please! We cannot let anything come between us.'

'Not even a wife?'

He looked down. 'Isabella will not alter the way I feel about you; nothing and no one could ever do that. If I am to look after you, Daisy, and that is all I want in the world, then I have to marry Isabella, I have to rise above any suggestion of scandal. I cannot let my feelings for you ruin your life or mine.'

'But my life is already ruined,' Daisy said. 'I am carrying your child and you will not make an honest woman of me. My life is over, Henry.'

'No! Don't say that, Daisy! I will not let you say things like that!'

She shrugged and bent over her foot.

'Daisy, I mean it! You must not talk like this!' He caught her shoulders and made her look at him. 'We do have a future, I promise you!' He stared hard at her and willed her to believe him. 'Trust me,' he implored. 'Do as I ask, take the lodge, move in here and let me look after you. Please, trust me!'

There was a silence, then finally she glanced away and nodded. Of course she would do as he asked, take the lodge, let him look after her; what other choice did she have? But trust him? Something inside Daisy had slipped in that past hour; and in her fall something inside her had broken. Perhaps it was her belief in Henry, perhaps her will, maybe it was even her love. They did not have a future, she knew that, no matter how many promises he made. They had no future and he would never acknowledge their past. So where did that leave her?

He helped her to her feet and she leant on him for support. It left her, she thought, where so many people who love are left: vulnerable, alone, like a poppy in the wind.

Chapter 17

Lotte left for the lodge very early on the morning after Lord and Lady Beatty had delivered the furniture. She wanted an hour or so to herself to get a feel of the place before Meg and Leo brought the children up, ready to move in. She drove along the lane and turned into the opening for the lodge, stopping just inside the gates, right at the end of the small muddy drive. She climbed out of the car and looked up towards the small flint, brick and tile-hung cottage, feeling, for the first time in a very long while, a sense of personal satisfaction. This was hers, this was something she had gone out and achieved on her own, a house to rent, a home. This was her small piece of life, her independence, and even though it scared her, she was going to make it work.

Lotte had never been very good at self-analysis, she had all her life just done what was easiest and thought little about why or how. Now she was thinking hard, she was making a choice that involved nothing easy, but for the first time she knew exactly why. Lotte knew that if she was going to make something of her life – and this she must do, for Milly and Freddie – then she had to be her own person, make her own choices and carry the responsibility of those choices. All the time she had been married to Gordon, all the years of emotional and mental bullying, he had absolved her from any responsibility. She did as she was told and then she blamed him – though never openly – when it was wrong. Now she had no one to blame but herself. Terrifying, but liberating.

She wandered up to the house, said good morning to it and let herself in. True to her word, Lady Beatty had delivered everything she had promised. It was all piled high in the small sitting room, except for the rugs, which she had strewn across the floor, making the house look instantly a home. Lotte walked round the pile, identifying several pieces she had chosen, along with a great deal more she didn't remember at all. She smiled, from pure pleasure, and went into the kitchen. Here Lady Beatty had installed a cooker, old, probably early eighties, but clean, electric, and – she turned one of the rings on – all in good working order. There was a mini fridge, the sort hotels used for mini bars; a toaster, one of the huge catering kind, which took eight slices; and in the centre a sixties melamine table, marble effect, with four wooden chairs. Lady Beatty had placed her vase of spring blossom on it.

Lotte went outside, leaving the back door open to air the kitchen. She stood on the small terrace and wondered if Leo and Meg would lend her some garden furniture. She listened to the sounds of the wood and the water, the air alive with them, and felt the first rays of sunshine breaking through the clouds onto her face. She thought of Gordon, of all that love gone bad; then she thought of Milly and Freddie and knew that something wonderful had come out of it, no matter how much it hurt now. She had turned to go back to her car and start unloading when she stopped, listened hard again and heard something strange. It was a cry. A cry so faint that she almost missed it, a high-pitched woman's cry, and Lotte wrapped her arms around her body and shivered in the spring air. Silent voices. Voices that remind us that we are not alone, that everyone everywhere has suffered something.

Phil Granger was washing his paint brushes on the few square feet of dirty paving slabs outside the cottage he shared with his mother when he heard the back door open. He swore under his breath; he was usually gone before the old slag was up.

'You not left yet, Phil?' she sneered. 'Late today. Her ladyship'll have you.'

He ignored her and continued to rinse the brush under the running water of the outside tap.

'What's that you're doing?' She came closer and stood over him. He could see her ankles, swollen and blue, and her feet, dirty, the skin dry and cracked. She had stuffed them into flip-flops and her toe nails were ragged and filthy. 'I heard there was fresh totty up there. No wonder you're late, boy, you've been laying awake at night fantasizing, haven't you? Eh?' She prodded him in the back and he could smell her, that rancid, unwashed smell. She started to laugh. 'My Phil, the impotent cretin, can't get up in the morning for wanking over some married totty up at the lodge!'

'Shut it!' he snapped, but she laughed again and he wanted to smash her feet in with the end of the paint brush.

'Oh that's got you riled, has it, Phil? Eh? Like that totty up there, does you?'

He gritted his teeth and continued to wash, moving on to the last brush. He'd be finished in a few minutes, then he could leave.

'God, you're pathetic, you are, call yourself a man?' Her voice was malicious, sneering and cruel. 'Sitting there, wash wash wash, like a woman!' She kicked the bucket that held his brushes and sent them clattering over the paving slabs. Phil held the brush he was cleaning so tightly that his hands hurt. 'Fuck off up there! Go on! I can't bear the sight of you, you impotent little runt!' She turned and shuffled inside, locking the back door behind her.

He stayed where he was for several minutes, the cold water tap running over his hands, numbing all feeling in them. He hated her, he hated her and he loved her, and he wanted to give himself to her, but she wouldn't let him, she had never let him, never. Finally he stood and turned the tap off, shaking the water out of the brush and collecting up the others, putting them back in the bucket. He carried the bucket to his car and put it in the boot. As he slammed the boot shut and went round to the driver's side to climb in, he caught sight of himself in the wing mirror. He hadn't even registered the fact that he was crying.

Gordon had caught the overnight flight from New York to Heathrow and was on his way home to shower and change before he called in at the office to collect his post and check on the week's business. Weekend or not, he had been out of the office for several days and needed to catch up. He had several calls to make as well, the first being to the locksmith in order to arrange for them to come and change the locks on the house. He would tell Lotte that it was because she was so dopey with keys; a safety measure, nothing more. In truth it was just another acrimonious side to his divorce.

Gordon was very bitter; he had never thought that Lotte would leave him, he was angry and humiliated. He'd had to tell the other partners at the firm, knowing it would come out sooner or later, but the news had been greeted coolly, as no one brought in as much revenue when their personal life was in turmoil. He hated not having Lotte

235

there; he had relied on her enormously, and now the expense of laundry, commercial cleaners and eating out was starting to make inroads into his income. Of course he liked the peace and quiet, not having to talk to Lotte or the children, or to suffer the children's constant noise and mess, but in retrospect, that was a small price to pay for all the domestic comfort she'd given him.

He finally pulled up into the drive of his house and climbed out of the car. He stretched, collected his suit and overnight bags off the back seat and went into the house. He switched off the alarm and put his keys in the china dish on the hall table, then stopped. The framed botanical print that Lotte had done for *House and Gardens* had gone from over the hall table. All that was left was an ugly hook in the wall. Gordon rushed into the sitting room. The TV and stereo were still there, but all the ornaments and pictures had gone, along with several pieces of furniture. His heart started to pound. He was thinking: Oh Christ, a bloody insurance claim and no Lotte to deal with it. He went upstairs and into his bedroom. Yup, someone had cleared them out, there was virtually nothing left. Then he opened the cupboard and saw that all Lotte's clothes had gone. Suddenly it dawned on him. He sat down on the bed, a bed missing a duvet and two of the four pillows, and smacked his fist against the palm of his hand. The bitch! The fucking bitch! He got up and walked into the children's bedrooms – nothing left; then into the bathroom and saw that only his own measly toiletries stood alone and pathetic-looking on the shelf.

Downstairs he took a piece of paper from his study, then went round the house and started to make a note of everything missing. Finally he went into the kitchen to make himself a cup of herbal tea, something that Eve was trying to get him into. He reached into the cupboard for the tea bags and saw it was empty; she had even taken the food and drink out of his mouth!

He picked up the phone and dialled Meg's house.

'Meg, it's Gordon.'

Meg braced herself. He might have brow-beaten her daughter for several years, but he was not going to get the better of her. 'Hello, Gordon,' she said calmly.

'I want to speak to Lotte,' he said.

Meg took a deep breath. Keep cool, she told herself, just keep cool. 'I'm afraid she isn't here.'

'Then tell her I want to speak to her when she gets in.' He went to hang up and Meg said: 'I can't do that, Gordon, she doesn't live here.'

Gordon stopped. 'Come off it, Meg,' he said. 'She was there when I rang last week. Where else would she go?'

'She has rented herself a little house, Gordon, that's where.'

His immediate reaction was fury. How dare she? Rent a house with his money! 'A house? Where?' he demanded.

'She asked me not to say, not until she's spoken to her lawyer,' Meg replied. She had the upper hand; Gordon was angry and she was calm, so calm in fact that she was even beginning to enjoy this.

'Until she's spoken to her lawyer? What, some two-bit operation who can't even serve a decent separation notice? What's his name, Groper, isn't it?'

'It was Mr Roper, but Leo has recommended someone else. I don't recall his name, but Leo says he is first class, and he's legal aid, of course. He specializes in this sort of case.'

'What sort of case?' Gordon snapped. 'What the hell is that supposed to mean?'

'He specializes in getting a fair financial settlement, that's all I meant.'

'Don't give me that crap, Meg. Come on, spit it out, what the hell did you mean by that comment?'

He was cruising for a fight, but Meg wasn't retaliating. 'I meant nothing,' she said. 'Look, Gordon, I have to go, Leo is calling me. I'll tell Lotte you called when I next see her.' That would be in about half an hour of course, but Meg wasn't going to tell him that. 'Good . . .' She stopped; Gordon had already hung up.

In the kitchen of the house he had once shared with Lotte, Gordon paced the floor. He had hung up from Meg and dialled the bank manager to put a stop on all their joint accounts, but instead had been told that all shared monies had been transferred to Mrs Graham's personal account. He was livid, so livid in fact that he threatened to sue the bank – a threat he couldn't possibly carry out, owing to the fact, as the voice on the end of the phone pointed out, that the account was held in joint names and either party could transfer money. He had slammed the phone down on the voice after that, but not before calling her several rude names. If he had seriously never thought that Lotte would leave him, then he had certainly never imagined in his wildest dreams that she would have the nerve to ring the bank and transfer his money into her account. Good God, she'd never taken the slightest bit of interest in anything financial, didn't even know the password to their account as far as he knew. That was women for you, he thought bitterly, they had no honour. The fact that he had been planning to do exactly the same thing passed him by.

He went upstairs for his shower, hoping that a long, warm soak under torrents of gushing hot water would relax him. He turned the shower on to warm up, took a towel out of the airing cupboard and stripped off his tired, slept-in clothes. He opened the door to the shower cubicle and stepped under the water.

'Ahhhhh, SHIT, FUCKSHIT!' He dived out and hopped round the bathroom, grabbing at his towel, his whole body pulsating with shock. Finally he collapsed shivering on to the edge of the bath. He had been away for three days and had turned the heating off while he was gone. Consequently, every drop of water in the house was freezing cold.

Meg and Leo strapped the children into the car with far more efficiency than Lotte ever did – no fuss, and certainly no moaning – then climbed in themselves. Meg glanced round, smiled at the two angelic faces and thought it really very unfair. Granny got them just a few hours a day and they were always charming. Lotte had them the rest of the time and they gave her merry hell.

'Right then,' she said, 'you've got your teddies, so let's go.'

As they drove off, Milly said: 'Will I like it, Granny? The new house.'

'Of course you'll like it,' Meg replied. 'It'll be . . .' She stopped and searched for the right word, then looked to Leo for help.

'It'll be an adventure,' Leo finished for her. 'The biggest adventure you've ever had!'

'Will it?' Milly said excitedly. 'Will it really?'

'Absolutely!' both Leo and Meg said at the same time. If it was nothing else, it would certainly be that.

Ten minutes later they were at the lodge. Meg was relieved it was only ten minutes. If Lotte had problems, then at least she was down the road, and pulling into the muddy track that ran up to the cottage, Meg reckoned that it was more than an 'if'. They helped the children out and walked up to the house, Meg silently shocked at how basic it was. This was no country idyll; it was a rough-and-ready brick and flint house that looked part derelict. Despite Lotte's enthusiasm about washed woodwork and new paint, it still had a deeply dilapidated air. The front garden was choked with weeds and the path overhung with nettles, which Leo held back with the sleeve of his jumper over his hand so they didn't sting the children's legs.

The front door was open. Meg peered in. The house smelt damp, old and uncared for, and it made her shudder. She glanced at Leo, who shook his head. Lotte appeared moments later, her face alight with a smile. She looked, Meg thought, despite all this mess, radiant.

'Hello, my darlings!' She scooped both Milly and Freddie up into a hug and carried them inside. 'This is your new home!'

'Pooh, Mummy,' Milly said. 'It's stinky!'

'Stinky!' Freddie repeated.

'Well it won't be by tonight, that's just the paint and all the cleaning. Tonight it will smell of hot sausages and chips and bubble bath and warm beds with hot-water bottles in. Come on, let me show you round!' Lotte grinned over her shoulder at Meg and Leo. 'You too!' she called. 'And you can stop looking so disapproving, Mum, I'm staying and that's all there is to it!'

Leo took Meg's hand and led her into the house. It's Lotte's life, Meg thought, and she's determined to make it work. So what was a bit of damp and mould, cold floors and ants, nettles as high as a man and a pond at the end of the garden that two young children could drown in? She sighed and let Lotte prattle on about how lovely it all was. Had her daughter finally lost it? She would never survive this; never.

Lotte finished the tour in the children's bedroom. It had two single beds with their own duvets on and two huge boxes filled with all their toys. She had put their pictures up on the walls – they covered the stains – and a rug on the floor. In an old pine chest she had arranged all their clothes and on top of it she had piled their books, next to Milly's ballerina bedside lamp. There was a storage heater that looked clean if a bit rusty and a teddy hot-water bottle on the end of each bed. It wasn't home, but it was a bloody good try at it, and Meg, despite what she felt, despite her doubts and her fears for Lotte, had to admire her daughter. Perhaps she would survive it after all.

Annie Taylor finished writing up her notes and stood. 'Steve?' she called across the open-plan office. 'Case review, please, five minutes.' She was tired; it had been a long day, started early and likely to be finished late, and it was a Saturday. There was something about working weekends that made the day seem harder. She stretched and rubbed her lower back where it ached from sitting so long, and walked out of the room to the coffee machine. By now, day two of a high-level investigation, she knew how everyone took their coffee and found a drinks holder beside the machine to carry the drinks. Actually she usually knew by the end of the first meeting; it was one of the mind games she liked to play, testing her memory, and it always amazed her what a difference it made to people to think that she bothered to remember how they took their tea or coffee. She pressed the relevant buttons on the machine and waited for the first drink. It was foul stuff but it was free, and

Annie, even though she tried hard to cut down, drank gallons of it.

She took the drinks holder back to her desk where the team were assembled, waiting for her.

'Steve,' she said to DS Brown, handing a cup across, 'black no sugar. Carol, white no sugar, and Allen, white with sugar. Horrid, can't think how you can drink it like that!' She took a sip of her own, straight black, and said: 'OK, where are we? Steve?'

'I spoke to Meredith last night and I'm not convinced about him. Everyone says he's above an affair, but he looked like a regular bloke to me, and most regular blokes aren't above having an affair.'

'Thanks for the vote of confidence in the male species, Steve. Why not convinced?'

'He looked edgy, he hesitated a great deal, he was very emphatic with certain answers. And – this is relevant, I think – his relationship is over, and she's living somewhere else, renting a house in Shorebridge.'

'Shorebridge? Is that a coincidence, d'you think? Could you interview the girlfriend tomorrow and get her side of things? Ask her where she was a week last Tuesday, find out as much as you can from her about Meredith, and while you're there, make sure you get her full measure as well. If he was having an affair, she might have known about it and been very angry and upset. Also, check when she moved into the place in Shorebridge, have a look at her rent agreement. OK?' Annie thought for a moment. 'Let's keep things very informal for now, OK? Carol, what did you come up with yesterday with the Kimble woman?'

'She talked about Claire, but not in a great deal of depth. We've seen the medical records but they don't say enough. She said that Claire had been coming to counselling for about six weeks, since the beginning of term, and that she would describe Claire as a normal girl, lonely, with mild depression caused fundamentally by her shyness and inability to make friends easily. She was also suffering from a mild obsession with a member of her teaching team. Obviously, that was Meredith. Kimble said she had always felt that Claire was deluding herself when she talked about this particular member of the team, as he was in a happy relationship, was very popular and inaccessible. He was, she says, a typical target for an obsession. Only now she's wondering if there might not have been something in the stories, although she didn't say what stories. She knew about the split with the girlfriend but didn't know why, and of course is wondering if it's connected to Claire.'

'Good work, Carol. Let's go for medical access to her records on Monday – if it is true that they were having an affair, then it might give us a clue to Meredith's behaviour. I'll leave that one with you. I'd also like you to chase up forensic. We won't get it any quicker but it makes me feel better to know we're on their case. Claire's blood group?'

'No, not yet.'

'Monday then, no later. I want the information ready for when we get the DNA back. OK?'

Carol nodded. She took out her cigarettes but didn't light one; she knew DS Taylor didn't like it.

'Allen?'

'We carried out a thorough search of Claire's room and collected some samples for testing. It had definitely been left with the intention of returning, I'm sure of it. I had a good look through her files and work; she's a good student, mostly high B's and A's. I found a note in one of her files from Meredith. It says: "We need to talk about this" with his initials underneath. I don't know if it's relevant, or what it refers to; it might be an essay, but then it might be something else.'

'Good work,' Annie said. 'It might well be something else, it could easily refer to their affair. It's certainly worth noting. OK, as far as the area search has gone, there's been nothing yet, but they're still on it, and I'm seeing the Super as soon as we're finished here to ask him to step it up with house-to-house inquiries starting tomorrow. As far as this team is concerned, the next stage is: one, interview with Meredith's girlfriend, we can do that tomorrow, better on a Sunday, I think; two, chase up forensic after the weekend; three, find Claire's blood group; and four, access to medical records. I think I'd also like to bring Meredith in again by tomorrow night and formally interview him. Is that OK with everyone?'

There was a murmur of assent and Annie smiled. 'What a docile bunch you are!'

The meeting over, Annie reached for her bag. 'You've all got my mobile; I'm off home for a few hours R & R when I've seen the Super, so give me a ring if anything comes up. OK?'

'Yes, boss.'

She smiled and stood to leave. 'Thanks, everyone. Carol, you're on tomorrow, so am I; the rest of you, I'll call if we need you. Let's keep our fingers crossed for the house-to-house. OK, class dismissed.' She walked out of the office and moved on to the next stage of finding Claire Thompson.

It was Saturday, early evening, the sort of time that Charles and Mia would usually have a drink. They would open a bottle of wine, lay out some tapas, some Parma ham and olives, some garlic bread, and if it was warm, like it was now, they would sit in the garden and look over the papers, discussing what they'd read, exchanging quotes, drinking and eating. In winter they'd light a fire and drink red wine, sitting on the floor in front of the flames.

Tonight, Charles sat at his desk and looked at what he had written on screen. It was good, it was unfolding, like the plot of a good novel. He was pleased and he wished he had someone to share that pleasure with. He wished he had the *right* someone to share that pleasure with. He knew that he had to get his life in balance, he knew that he missed Mia, but did he only miss her because she represented everything that was calm and ordered? Was he just clutching at straws? He knew he missed *that* woman too. He knew he longed for her in a way that he had no control over. He should do what Rob had told him to do, just forget it, forget her. Mia still loved him and he loved her, in his own way. So why all this? Why the constant questions and doubts? Why couldn't he get her out of his mind, resolve the situation? God, if only it was as clear for him as it had been for Henry Chatten; if only Charles knew the true nature of love. He smiled to himself and switched off his screen. And if he did, he wondered, would he be able to face up to it?

He stood, put his notes in order for the morning and left his study. He ambled into the garden for a few moments and listened to the birdsong. It was too nice an evening to stay inside; he needed a walk, he needed to unwind. He went back to his study and took the OS map of the area of Ludwell Ponds off his desk, a map he gazed at endlessly, trying to get a feel for where he was writing about. Nothing like the real thing, he told himself, making a spur-of-the-moment decision, and he grabbed a jacket and left the house. Normally so cautious, Charles thought he had a right to act rashly now and then. He climbed into his car and spread the map out on the passenger seat. He would go to

Ludwell Ponds, visit the lodge and get a sense of the place. He would stand where Henry and Daisy had stood and would try and imagine what it must have been like to sacrifice everything for love.

Charles parked his car in a public parking bay and decided to walk through the woodland to Ludwell Ponds and try to find the lodge that way. He wanted to come across it by chance almost, and see it as Daisy would have first seen it. He took the woodland path, walked around the ponds, sensing a place untouched, and came to the gate in the hedge and the back entrance to the lodge. He opened the gate, went through a gap in the trees and out on to the lawn of the house. The low, small cottage was inhabited and he was surprised; he could see toys on the grass and the woodwork freshly painted. He could smell the last of a bonfire and it deprived him of the isolation of the place. This wasn't how Daisy would have first seen it, and Charles prickled at not getting what he wanted. This wasn't going to help at all, this was a place completely different to the place Daisy Burrows had known in her loneliness and pain. He walked quickly up the grass towards the back terrace of the little cottage, shielding his eyes from the glare of the late evening sun, low in the sky.

He could see a woman there, sitting, her head bent in concentration over something. Her long auburn hair shone in the fading sunlight, her face was composed and serene, and yet she had a vulnerability about her that Charles thought he could almost feel, despite the distance between them. He was about to turn back when she glanced up and saw him. He stopped. For the first time in his life Charles felt a moment in time stand still, a moment suspended out of his life that he could see quite clearly above himself, like

246

an out-of-body experience. It was ridiculous, he didn't believe in all that sort of crap; he had struggled with the concept of falling in love with someone in just one night, but it had happened and now, right now, in this moment, it happened again. He moved towards her and she stood up, her face ashen, shocked.

'It is you, isn't it?' he asked.

She looked down at the ground and he couldn't see her eyes, slanted eyes of the oddest brown colour with flecks of blue, eyes he had dreamed of for ten long nights. Finally she nodded.

'The woman from London, the woman I . . .' He broke off and stared at her. Ripped jeans, a T-shirt, too small, with a tomato stain right in the centre of it, dirty hair, tied up and knotted at the back, wild, unruly hair, and bites, three big red itchy bites on her face. She put her hand up to brush her hair off her face and he loved her. He had no idea how or why, but he did; he ached to take her hand in his and put it to his mouth.

'You ran out,' he said. 'I tried to find you, I rang the bar.'

Lotte looked up. 'I'm sorry, I had to get home, I shouldn't have stayed anyway.'

'But you did.'

'Yes, I did.' Lotte had stayed, and she had remembered the touch of his mouth on her skin every day since. He was the one, he was the reason she had left Gordon, started again. He had shown her in one night, in one drunken, passionate embrace, that she was still a woman, a sexy, attractive, desirable woman, and it had given her the courage that she needed. It had made her realize that there was more to life, and that she was entitled to it.

'Do you live here?'

'Yes. I've just moved in. I left my husband after we . . .

I mean, after I met you, and I'm renting this, for now.' She didn't need to tell him about Gordon; why was she telling him that?

Charles felt suddenly euphoric. He felt suddenly stupidly, insanely happy. He smiled, and his smile was from his heart and in his eyes. Lotte smiled back. Her stomach flipped over and made her catch her breath, and she smiled with her whole self.

'This is bizarre,' Charles said, standing there, grinning inanely. 'Totally bizarre. I'm writing a book about this place, about Daisy Burrows and Henry Chatten. She stayed here. I came to get a feel for it, I came to see if I could feel what they felt, Henry and Daisy.' He shook his head, still grinning. 'I can feel it, I do feel it.'

Lotte laughed. 'Hardly!'

'No, I do!' Charles moved closer to her, wanting to touch her. 'How did you end up here, from London?'

'Not from London, I'm not from London.'

'Oh, I thought . . .'

'No, I escaped up to London for the night, to try and think things through. I stayed in Leo's flat in Dolphin Square.'

'Not Leo Chandler?'

'Yes.'

Charles shook his head. 'Spooky. I don't believe all this! I'm a professor at the university; I know Leo. He has the flat next door to my brother in Dolphin Square.'

Lotte raised an eyebrow. 'So that's it.'

'Yes, that's it.'

'Fortuitous.'

Charles took her hand. 'Incredible.' He turned it over and stared at her long, thin fingers. Gently Lotte eased her hand back. He looked at her. 'So, where do we go from here?' he asked.

Lotte blinked. 'What do you mean?'

'I mean, I've been looking for you ever since we met, and now that I've found you, what next? There's so much we need to learn about each other, so much to talk about, to say.' He smiled. 'I can hardly believe this is happening. I've dreamed about you every night since we met, I've had you in my head, you've filled my senses . . .' He stopped. 'What's the matter?'

Lotte had hung her head and was twisting her fingers together nervously. She could see his attraction, he had been the impetus for her finally standing up to Gordon, but she thought: I cannot be taken over like this, I cannot be swept away. I am not ready for this, I have to be independent. She said: 'This is too much.' She didn't look at him. 'I'm sorry, but this is all too much for me. I don't know you, I don't even know your name, I can't . . .'

'Charles, Charles Meredith.'

'I can't get involved. I'm sure you mean well, but I . . .'

'Mean well? Look, you don't understand . . .'

Lotte faced him. 'Yes, I do understand. I do not want to get involved with you. I'm sorry, I'm sorry for all these things that you think you feel, but I do not feel the same and I do not . . .' She paused and took a breath, her courage rising as she spoke. 'I do not want to have anything to do with you.'

Charles stared at her. He saw the flecks of blue in her eyes, he saw her fire and her vulnerability, and his heart ached. So this was love. All that he had thought and felt had come to this. 'Is it just now that you don't want to have anything to do with me, or is it never?'

Lotte swallowed. She was drawn to him and she had to take a step back, to put some distance between them, both physically and emotionally. 'I don't know,' she answered truthfully. 'I'm getting divorced, my life's a mess, I need . . .' She shrugged. 'I need to find out who I am, what I am capable of.'

'Can I come back and see you?'

Lotte hesitated. There was hope then, Charles thought. Was this how unrequited lovers went on and on, on the tiniest shred of hope?

'No, I don't think so,' she said.

Charles turned away. He stood for some time looking at the ponds beyond the garden, at the setting sun reflected in the water. I am in love with her, he thought, and she is not in love with me. How could he have made the assumption that his love would be reciprocated? How could he have been so blind? Then he thought of Mia, he thought of her yearning for a child, of her total love for him and thus her pain. He felt suddenly humbled and he wondered if this were the true nature of love, to go on loving when there was no point, when there was nothing to be gained. He looked back for a moment at the woman. He wanted to ask her name, but that would only make it worse. 'Goodbye,' he said, and he walked away.

Lotte watched him go and knew that his leaving was her own small personal triumph. A short time ago she would have let him rescue her. She would have surrendered herself up to this feeling she had, this attraction – no, more than that: this longing for him, and she would have let him save her from herself. But she *had* emerged independent today, she had asserted her own will, she was a new person. And although it felt good, as she watched Charles Meredith walk away, she knew that it only felt half as good as it should have.

Chapter 18

There was a great deal of activity downstairs the morning of the Friday after the Chattens returned to Bicester House. They were having a house party, a few close family friends: Henry's godparents, Lady Chatten's sister and her family, and Mr and Mrs Lawrence Testry with their daughter Isabella, who had that week become unofficially engaged to Henry. The house was a buzz of excitement. Cook had been preparing since Tuesday, but was having difficulty keeping everything cool because the weather had suddenly turned hot. The house had been cleaned from top to bottom and was now being thoroughly aired, all the main windows and doors open to let the warm, stuffy air out and the cool south-easterly breeze in. The gardens had been clipped, trimmed, weeded and preened, with the best of the flowers displayed all over the house, and the head gardener was delighted that it was June and not October because at least he had some wonderful asparagus and gooseberries to offer up to the guests instead of parsnips and swede.

Daisy worked as tirelessly as the others, her ankle strapped up, waiting every day for the notice of dismissal that Henry had promised. She wanted to leave, she had begun to hate the downstairs, the girls with their coarse accents and manners, their inane gossip and stupid reverence for the family. Daisy knew better, she knew that the Chattens were just like everyone else in this world, opportunistic, snobbish, dishonest; she suspected that they knew of her situation but chose to ignore it, and for *that she had no reverence for them, no respect or liking, she had nothing but bitterness, and it was a bitterness that was slowly engulfing her.*

At eleven thirty, with most of the staff having been up since six, Mrs Blithe called them all downstairs for coffee and cake, a rare treat, and spoke to them about their duties for the weekend ahead. 'Most of the guests,' she began, 'will be arriving throughout the afternoon, so I want everyone to keep neat and tidy about their persons and the housemaids to take great care not to be seen around the house. All of the bedrooms are ready, and most of our preparations this afternoon will be for this evening. However, five guests will be arriving for luncheon . . .'

'That'll be his lordship's lady friend,' Evie whispered to Ethel so that Daisy could overhear. Daisy ignored it.

'So I will need Ethel, Evie and Daisy,' Mrs Blithe went on, 'to be on duty in the dining room and to help clear the table at luncheon. Please make sure that you are in your best uniforms by midday. Everyone else, keep a pleasant and cheerful demeanour at all times and let us show our guests and Lady Chatten how well we manage Bicester.' She smiled, and Daisy resented her superiority. 'As soon as you have finished your coffee, please get on.'

Daisy didn't bother to drink hers; she left it and began to make her way up the stairs to continue setting the table in the dining room. She heard a furtive giggle as she left, Ethel and Evie's private joke, and made her way along the side passage to the back stairs. She was halfway along it when the door to the butler's study opened and Maekins came out. She stopped and shrank back against the wall. He turned, saw her and smiled. 'What a remarkable coincidence, Miss Burrows, and alone too. Why don't you come into my study for a few moments; we could have a nice little chat.'

Daisy dropped a small curtsy and said: 'I must finish my

252

work, Mr Maekins, I've got a great deal to do for this weekend
and . . .'

'Of course you have, how very conscientious of you, Daisy.
Well done. It should be quite an occasion. Apparently Miss Testry
is a beauty. I saw her portrait in one of the society magazines,
and I have to say that I think our Mr Henry has done very well
for himself, very well indeed.' Maekins moved a step closer. 'So
well, in fact, that I shouldn't think he'll be wanting for anything
else, would you?'

Daisy winced and turned her face away, but Maekins took
her wrist and pressed her hand against his chest. His own fingers
were hot and damp and they smelt of carbolic soap. Daisy stood
very still. She averted her face and held her breath, not daring
to move an inch. Moments later he dropped her hand and said:
'Two weeks left, Daisy. Remember? I'm a patient man but I won't
wait for ever.' He moved past her then, his body indecently close,
and walked away into the kitchen.

Daisy pressed herself back against the cold wall and turned
her burning cheek to the plaster. She would not cry. She had
suffered enough in her life, she would not suffer this; she would
do whatever it took to escape it. Moving off, she was unsteady
on her feet for a few moments, dizzy with fear and loathing,
but she held herself tall and walked on. Daisy was not going to
go under; she would make sure that Henry saw to that.

The drawing room at Bicester looked splendid, the paintings,
furniture and objets d'art stunning in the sunlight that streamed
in through the windows, and Mrs Testry noted it all. She was
impressed. Not that she would have let the sunlight stream in, of
course, if Bicester were hers – and that was certainly something
she would have to speak to Isabella about when the occasion
arose. There was no point in having expensive things if they were
going to be spoilt in the heat of the midday sun. She took her

seat, and Lady Chatten came to sit next to her as the bags were unpacked from the carriage and taken upstairs. Lawrence was in the hallway with Sir Lionel, a boorish and domineering man, Mrs Testry thought, saved only, in her mind, by his wealth and title; and Isabella stood at the window with Henry, who was pointing out the landscaped park. She, at least, Mrs Testry thought, was animated. In fact she had looked radiant for two weeks now, radiant and even happy. Although Mrs Testry wouldn't know quite what happiness was; she didn't aspire to any such romantic notions. This was a good match, albeit a trifle sudden, and Henry, though a bit weak-looking – sensitive, Isabella had said, whatever that was – seemed sensible enough. Mrs Testry didn't particularly like him, but then she didn't particularly like anyone, except a few of the elite who moved in the royal circle, and then only because of their influence, nothing more.

'How was your journey?' Lady Chatten asked.

Mrs Testry turned to her. 'Oh, it was passable. I never enjoy journeys, they are tedium itself.'

'Oh, I love them,' Lady Chatten said. 'I always take a book and a picnic and I do so love to watch the countryside roll by outside the carriage. I always think of them as an adventure. I suppose it's childish in a way, but I get terribly excited when we go away.'

'Yes.'

Lady Chatten waited for more, but that was obviously all Mrs Testry was prepared to say on the subject of journeys.

'How many do you have for the weekend, Lady Chatten?' Mrs Testry asked.

Lady Chatten thought for a moment, then smiled. 'D'you know, I'm not quite certain! I think we have around eleven guests, but then I can't remember if Henry's godmother, Maud Staughton, said she was bringing her nephew or not, and I think the Grant-Tylers are coming but I'm not sure.'

'You're not sure?'

Lady Chatten suddenly flushed. Of course, it sounded ridiculous now, but Mrs Blithe didn't seem to mind. She said: 'We can sometimes be a bit chaotic here, Mrs Testry. I have a wonderful housekeeper and she seems to take it all in her stride.'

Well, Isabella won't, thought Mrs Testry, and nor, for that matter, shall I.

Isabella turned at that point and came across to them. 'Henry has been showing me the park,' she said. 'He suggested we take a walk before the other guests arrive. Would that be convenient, Lady Chatten?'

'Of course, my dear, you must seize the moment when you can. Henry?'

Henry turned.

'Be sure to show Isabella the rose garden, won't you? It's my pride and joy, Isabella, all my own work.'

'I look forward to seeing it then.'

Henry came across and offered his arm. 'Shall we go?' He wanted to be out of that room. It was hot and stuffy and Mrs Testry was suffocating him with her personality.

They left the drawing room and made their way across the entrance hall, past Sir Lionel and Lawrence Testry, down the front steps of the house.

'I am so glad to be out in the fresh air,' Isabella said. 'My mother was beginning to suffocate me.'

He turned to her. How extraordinary. It was exactly what he had been thinking, though of course he would never say as much.

'She could hardly concentrate on what Lady Chatten was saying because she was mentally calculating how much everything in that room was worth.'

Suddenly Henry laughed. 'Isabella, you are wicked! It is not ladylike to talk about your mother in such a way!'

'Well, it's true, ladylike or not. Besides which, young ladies need to be ladies only until they are engaged, and then they can be who they really are.'

He turned to her on the bottom step and looked at her face. She was laughing up at him and her eyes were warm with affection. 'And who are you, Isabella Testry?'

She reached up on to her toes and kissed his mouth. It was very brief, barely a touch of her lips, but it surprised and excited him. 'You have a lifetime to find out,' she said. And she took his arm, her hand resting affectionately over his so that they could walk together, as a couple, off towards the parkland of the Bicester estate.

From the window of the blue bedroom, made up for Miss Isabella Testry, Daisy saw every moment of Henry's exchange with his fiancée, and her heart burned in her chest. It felt as if someone had put their hand round it and squeezed it, and for several minutes she could hardly breathe, holding on to the window ledge for support. When finally the tightness eased and her body began to relinquish the terrible pain that consumed it, she stood straight and took a deep breath. She ran her hands over her face and turned back into the room. Then she went to the bedside table and lifted the glass off the water decanter. She spat into the water and replaced the glass, then she left the room and began work on her next task.

Before luncheon Sir Lionel called Maekins and asked him to serve champagne, the vintage Bollinger, in the drawing room. He went down to the cellar where he already had a case on ice and brought up three bottles. On the way back he saw Daisy.

'Champagne,' he said, 'for upstairs. To toast the happy couple. Very nice too, best we've got.' He smiled and carried on his way. Daisy felt as if he'd cut her down. She followed him into the kitchen and watched him place the champagne on a silver tray.

256

He had the glasses lined up ready, long-stemmed, cut glass with a delicate wide rim, glinting every time they caught the light. Daisy imagined herself holding a stem, fingering it, cool to the touch, droplets of condensation on the bowl of the glass from the ice-cold champagne. She had never tasted champagne, never even seen it, but she could imagine it; she imagined it the colour of pale honey and tasting sweet, cold and sweet. Maekins finished laying the glasses out and placed a bottle in the centre, then put the other two in a silver ice bucket which one of the boys was filling with ice. He looked across at Daisy and winked. He knew how she felt and he thought it brought him closer to what he wanted. 'Why don't you bring the ice bucket up, Daisy?'

'That's a job for one of the male staff, ain't it, Mr Maekins?' she said.

'I think you can do it, just this once,' he replied.

Daisy glanced across at the boy who was filling the bucket, but he kept his head down and avoided her eye. She crossed and took the bucket in her arms. It was heavy, cold and wet, and it marked the pristine whiteness of her apron.

'Follow me, Daisy.' Maekins went out of the kitchen, along the passage and up the back stairs. When he got to the top he stopped and took his handkerchief out to wipe the sweat off his face. Daisy found it repulsive. She waited, sweating as well in the unexpected June heat, then followed him to the door of the drawing room. He knocked, was told to enter and walked in, leaving the door open for Daisy. She followed him and he nodded at the sideboard, where she was to place the bucket. As she did so, she glanced down at the dark stain it had left across her chest and turned, embarrassed, to hurry out of the room. At that moment she heard laughter, spontaneous, genuine laughter, the sort of sound that comes from deep amusement and contentment and happiness. She glanced up and saw Isabella Testry. Henry had said something amusing and Isabella had laughed at it. She was looking at him, her pale face alight with amusement and love, her pale hair framing her face so perfectly that Daisy caught her breath. Isabella was beautiful, but Daisy could have forgiven her that were it not for the fact that Isabella was also in love.

Daisy turned. She spun round so fast that she knocked the aspidistra pot and it toppled precariously for a few moments, threatening to fall off the sideboard and smash on the floor. Everyone looked up. Daisy ran out of the room. Mrs Testry tutted, throwing a disapproving glance at Lady Chatten, who glared at Henry. Henry said: 'I should see if something is wrong, Mother,' and left the room, closing the door behind him.

Once in the hall, he ran across it to the door to the back stairs. Flinging it open, he caught Daisy as she ran down the steps and pulled her back. She was crying, running blindly, and he seized her, pressing her into his body so hard that the force of it shocked them both.

'Daisy, I . . .' He didn't finish. She brought her hand up and hit him in the face, hard, right across the nose. 'Christ! I . . .' As he put his hand up to stem the blood, she went to run off, but he kept hold of her, grabbing her shoulder and yanking her round to face him. 'Christ, Daisy! What the hell was that for?'

'I hate you!' she cried. 'I hate you and your family and everything about you!'

'Stop it, Daisy, stop it! Take hold of yourself; you're hysterical! STOP IT!' He shook her, holding her shoulders in a vice-like grip.

'I'll tell her,' Daisy threatened. 'I'll tell Isabella Testry everything. I'll ruin you, Henry, ruin everything for you!'

'You will ruin nothing, Daisy, believe me!' His voice had hardened. The blood from his nose dripped down over his lip on to the collar of his shirt, but he did nothing to stop it, keeping his grip firm on her shoulders. 'If you tell Isabella anything then you will feel the full force of my fury.'

'But you have ruined my life!' Daisy cried.

'This is nothing to how it will be ruined if you do something stupid!' he hissed. 'Stop this now, Daisy, stop it and think hard.'

He held on to her until she had stopped crying and calmed. He wiped her tears away with his hand and she reached up and touched his blood with her finger. Suddenly he released her and dug in his pocket for his handkerchief. 'Christ, that was one hell of a blow!' He held the white linen up against his nose and it absorbed the blood, a bright red stain spreading quickly across it. 'I must go,' he said, 'or they'll wonder what has happened. Come to me, come tonight.'

She said nothing but turned on the dark stairwell to go. Henry stroked the back of her head and caught a strand of her heavy auburn hair in his hand. 'Daisy, I love you . . .' he whispered, but the silken hair slipped through his fingers and she had gone before he could say it loud enough for her to hear. He too turned and walked up the few steps to the top. He closed the door to the back stairs and started across the hall. Behind him, Maekins emerged from the shadow of the main staircase, and Henry caught a glimpse of the butler in the huge Louis XIV gilt mirror that hung along one side of the hall. He turned, but Maekins had disappeared. 'Bugger,' Henry murmured. Mrs Blithe had been right: nothing much went unnoticed or unheard at Bicester.

As Henry walked into the drawing room with a bloody handkerchief to his nose, Isabella jumped up and his mother let out a gasp. 'What the heck have you been doing, boy?' Sir Lionel demanded.

'I was so busy trying to see if that servant girl was all right that I walked straight into the door. Stupid mistake. I've taken quite a bang on the nose!' He dropped the handkerchief and smiled.

'Oh, Henry, for goodness' sake! I do wish you'd be more careful!' Lady Chatten was smiling as she said this, making light of the situation. She had a shrewd idea of what had really happened and needed to cover any hint of that. 'Do go and change before lunch!'

'Not before we've had a bally drink, Madeleine! We're all gasping!'

'Oh, Lionel, you are so forthright!' Dehlia Heaton said. 'But correct!' They all laughed, and at that point Maekins reappeared to serve the champagne. He handed round the glasses and Isabella came to stand with Henry at the fireplace.

'I should like to propose a toast,' Sir Lionel announced, when everyone had a glass, 'a private toast, here among family and future family.' Mrs Testry nodded and smiled and Lady Chatten wondered how on earth they were going to be able to tolerate her. 'To my son Henry and his fiancée, Isabella. Congratulations!'

Everyone stood and raised their glasses to Henry and Isabella. Henry, Lady Chatten noticed, dropped his head down for a few moments, and she could almost feel his pain.

'Congratulations,' they all said at once. Henry drank his champagne and took Isabella's hand in the dazzling, opulent drawing room of Bicester House.

And downstairs, in the dark, damp passage behind the scullery, Daisy stood alone and held on to the wall for support as her baby kicked out against the wall of her uterus for the very first time. It was the tiniest fluttering movement, like a trapped butterfly inside her.

Chapter 19

Claire was cold. She shivered uncontrollably all the time, her body was exhausted with it. She had a fever, she knew that, she was dizzy and weak, bitten by mosquitoes all over her body, and the bites itched, burning with the poison under her skin. She was no longer tied to the chair, she was free to move around, but she had little energy to do so. She was in some sort of hut. It had no windows, just a door, bolted from the outside. If she'd had the strength she would have tried the door, kicked it down, but she could hardly raise herself off the mat on the floor, and lay huddled under blankets for hours on end. He came every night, bringing food, and emptied the bowl she used as a toilet. The smell of the reeds permeated everywhere, and she imagined them as long, twisted fingers that would come in the night, curling round her body and dragging her down to her death. She heard the rats at night, lots of them now; she felt them scurry around her and she wondered if they would eat her when she was dead. She told herself all the time that she wouldn't die, that someone would find her, that he wanted her alive and that she had more strength than he had bargained for, but she wept intermittently when reality took hold and she realized that in all probability this damp, dark place would be her watery grave.

She recited Shelley, it was the only poetry she could recall, and she said the Lord's Prayer, over and over, having remembered it, a secret sliver of religious knowledge hidden deep in her mind, stored up from her childhood. She wanted her mother, she longed for her mother, and she cried out for her in the dark, silent hours before the water came alive with the dawn. No one heard her, but still she cried out, a silent voice echoing in the wet wilderness.

Mia was about to leave to meet her friend Helen when two police officers arrived at her rented cottage in Shorebridge. She looked surprised and worried, but checked the ID, then let them into the hall.

'What can I do for you?' she asked.

'We wanted to ask you a few questions about your relationship with Charles Meredith. Would that be all right?'

She chewed on her fingernail for a few moments while she made up her mind. 'Will it take long? I have to meet a friend, we're going riding.'

'It might take a while. It's important,' DC Pinto said.

'Hang on, I'll ring her.' She went to the phone in the kitchen and dialled her friend. 'Helen, it's me,' she said. 'Something's come up and I won't make riding. Shall I still meet you in the pub for lunch? OK, see you then.' She hung up. 'It's a group hack, so she didn't mind too much.'

'Sorry.'

Mia shrugged. 'Come on in, I'll make some coffee.'

'Thanks.' Carol Pinto had brought a uniformed officer with her; often it gave the situation more gravity.

'How d'you take it?'

'White no sugar, thanks. And PC Hale has the same.'

Mia made the coffee. 'It's just instant, I'm afraid.'

Her voice was flat, Carol Pinto noticed, depressed almost. 'Instant is fine, thanks. I prefer it actually.' Mia handed them their coffees and picked up her own. She sat down at the kitchen table and Carol moved across, pulling a chair out to sit opposite her. She took out her notebook and Mia tensed. 'Sorry,' she said, 'I know it looks formal, but it helps my memory.'

Mia took a sip of coffee and looked away.

'Ms Langley, can you confirm that you have recently been living with Charles Meredith?'

'Yes, I can confirm that. I moved out just under a week ago. A week tomorrow, actually. We've been together three years.'

'When did you take this cottage?'

'I rang the letting agent in Shorebridge on Monday morning, looked at this Monday afternoon and took it on Tuesday. It's not the most exclusive property, as you can see. It had been on the market for ages.'

I'm not surprised, Carol thought. It was a grubby place, well used, with no charm. It needed someone with a lot of money to come in and do it up.

'So you moved out on Monday and stayed with a friend? Can we confirm that with your friend?'

'Yes. Helen Trant. I just rang her, I'm sure she'll confirm it. I wasn't anywhere else.'

'And what about a week last Tuesday, the second of May? Can you tell us what you were doing then?'

'Is this all to do with that missing student?'

Carol nodded. 'We're investigating the disappearance of Claire Thompson,' she said.

'And you think Charles is involved?'

'We couldn't possibly say at this stage,' Carol replied. 'Could you answer my question please, Ms Langley?'

Mia shook her head. She didn't answer, but looked away. A few moments later she took a crumpled tissue out of the sleeve of her cardigan and blew her nose. When she turned back, Carol saw that she had probably done a good deal of weeping in the past week. 'I was at home on that Tuesday, the home I shared with Charles. We had a row. I was disappointed, upset actually, because I thought I might be pregnant and I wasn't. My period came that afternoon and I went to bed in the afternoon with a bad pain. When I woke up, Charles accused me of trying for a baby without his consent and flew out of the house in a rage.'

'In a rage? What sort of rage? Was he shouting? Violent?'

'No, nothing like that. He was angry, though, and upset. He felt I'd deceived him. We had a row about starting a family, the usual sort of thing: he doesn't want to, I do. Then he left. Just upped and left.'

'Did he tell you where he was going?'

'No.'

'And did he call you to let you know where he was?'

'No. He came home early the following morning and said that he'd slept at his brother's place.'

'Do you believe him?'

She shrugged. 'To be honest, I don't know. I have wondered recently if there might be someone else. He hasn't felt very committed to me for some time now, but then it might just be the book. He's trying to write a book and he's been struggling with it. You could check with Rob.' Mia stood and took her address book from by the telephone. 'I've got his address and telephone number here.' She read it out and Carol wrote it down. '*Do* you think Charles had something to do with this student's disappearance?'

Carol stood up. 'I'm really not able to say, Ms Langley, I'm sorry. Do you have a copy of your rent agreement, by the way, just to verify your dates?'

'Yes, of course I do, I'm a lawyer.' She went to a drawer

in the kitchen and took out a file. In it was the tenancy agreement for her cottage. 'Take it if you want,' she said. 'I've got a couple of copies. Occupational hazard, copying legal documents. I can't help myself.' She shrugged, and again Carol noted her sadness. Was there more to it?

'Thanks, I will.' Carol put the document in her bag and drained her coffee cup. 'Thank you for the coffee. I don't think there's anything else we need to ask you at this stage.'

'At this stage,' Mia repeated blankly. She followed DC Pinto and the constable to the front door, opened it for them and watched them climb into their car and drive off. Then she turned and went back into the kitchen to finish her coffee.

Gordon had been trying to get hold of his lawyer since he'd arrived home yesterday, and the first thing he did when he got up on Sunday morning was to ring again and leave another message on his lawyer's voicemail. Lotte was not going to get away with this, no matter how much legal clout it took. Then he looked in the fridge – empty – and decided on breakfast at the club after members' morning. He went to find his tennis kit. It was dirty. He hadn't done any washing since last week, and two sets of shorts and shirts lay in a sweaty mound in the laundry basket, his socks giving off a terrible pong. He put the lid back on it immediately and went to the cupboard. Of course, there was very little in there. He had sent the week before last's shirts to the laundry on Wednesday but had forgotten to pick them up yesterday and was down to three that he didn't particularly like. He had no clean tennis gear, five pairs of boxer shorts that he found uncomfortable and never wore, some weekend clothes, and his suits, two of which he should have taken to the dry cleaner's but had forgotten about in his haste to pack for the States. Then there was his bag, which he hadn't unpacked yet; three shirts, gym kit, underwear and socks, all dirty and all probably smelling a bit evil by now.

Gordon sat down on the top stair and wondered how it had come to this. Lotte had been gone a week and it was all falling apart. She didn't run his life, so what had happened? And it wasn't just the laundry. He'd had to eat out last Sunday, then Monday and Tuesday. The rest of the week had been on expenses in the States, but there had been a curry last night, and now breakfast and probably lunch at the club. It was all starting to add up. Plus he'd had to hire some contract cleaners to come in and do the place over while he was away, as the bathroom had looked as if a bomb had gone off in there and Lotte had literally just walked out of the house last Saturday night without tidying anything at all before she left. How much more was he going to have to spend? As for Eve, well, she hadn't set foot inside the place, wouldn't even consider coming over to cook for him last night. She'd said: 'I'm very good in bed, Gordon, and very bad in the kitchen.' That was it! No more explanation, and no amount of talk about home-cooked food could persuade her that eating out wasn't the way to go.

Gordon dropped his head in his hands. Of course Lotte's cooking wasn't anything out of the ordinary, but at least it was cooking. He had never, in five years, had a duff meal. And he'd certainly never been short of clean clothes. Still in his dressing gown, Gordon went back down to the kitchen and picked up the phone. There was nothing else for it, he thought; he would have to take Lotte back. In his arrogance he assumed that there would be no question of her not wanting to come. Of course there would have to be changes; she'd have a huge amount of making-up to do, and he wouldn't be able to trust her, certainly not with money, not for a long while. He dialled Meg's number and Leo picked up the phone.

'Hello, Leo, it's Gordon. I'm calling for Lotte's address.' Gordon drummed his fingers on the desk top. 'But it's not a question of whether Lotte would want me to have it, I'm afraid, Leo, my solicitors need it . . . No, I'm sorry, I won't go through you and Meg, I need to see Lotte and I need her address. Legally, of course, I'm entitled to it.' Legal bluff always worked. It might not always be true, but it always worked. 'You do realize that, don't you?' He waited while Leo blundered on a bit more, then smiled as he got what he wanted. Leo gave him the address, Gordon thanked him, then hung up.

Perhaps he'd take a drive down there, go and see the children, take Lotte some flowers. He put the kettle on before he remembered there was no tea, so left it to boil unnecessarily and went to dress. A day off in the week should do it, a trip down to see Meg and Leo, then over to Lotte and a good long chat, clear up all the misunderstandings. He could even go today; at least he'd have the house back in order by the end of the week if he went now. Gordon stopped mid-stairs and thought about it. No, not today, today was members' tennis morning, and in all the time he'd been a member of the club, over ten years now, he'd never missed a members' tennis morning.

Annie Taylor hated Sundays in the office, especially warm sunny Sundays. The only saving grace today was that work had got her off Sunday lunch with her parents and yet another suitable man from the golf club her mother would have dragged over for her approval.

She was thinking about how unfortunate it was to be single and like it, especially with a mother like hers, when Carol Pinto came into the office.

'Morning, boss. I've just been to see Mia Langley.'

'You have? Well done, Carol. That was early.'

'She was on her way out for riding; she cancelled it.'

'And?' Annie pulled a chair over to her desk so that Carol could sit down.

'Well,' Carol opened her notebook, 'first, she's upset about the break-up. She wants kids, he doesn't – it's crunch time.'

'Any reason for him not wanting kids?'

'No, she wasn't forthcoming and I didn't pry. She did say that she had been wondering recently how committed Meredith was to the relationship and if he had someone else.'

'Interesting.'

'Yes. She wasn't convinced, though, it was more of an afterthought, I reckon. There was no fire there. If she seriously suspected, she'd be very angry.'

'Hell hath no fury like a woman's wrath and all that. So you don't think she's connected, then? When did she take the cottage in Shorebridge?'

'Tuesday the ninth of May. She signed the lease Monday afternoon and moved in on Tuesday.'

'That puts her in the frame for the purse, then, doesn't it? At first glance Forensics said that the purse hadn't been out for very long, maybe a day or two at the most. It wasn't wet, remember, and it rained over the weekend, but it hasn't rained this week. My guess is that the purse was dropped Tuesday the ninth or Wednesday the tenth, so that does put Langley in the frame. She was in the right place at the right time. What about her alibi for the night Claire disappeared?'

'She was home alone. She and Meredith had a row, he stormed out. She doesn't have any witnesses, it's just her word for it.'

'What was the row about?'

'He found out she'd been trying for a baby behind his back and was furious. He left in a huff.'

'It wasn't about Claire?'

Carol shook her head. 'I don't think so. Mia Langley is depressed and weepy, but I don't think she's murderous.'

'But you're not convinced?'

'No, not yet.'

'OK, we'll leave it there until we've checked her alibi. The other interesting thing about this, of course, is that Meredith stormed out, and came back at what time?'

'He didn't come back until the following morning. Early, she said, but he didn't ring to tell her where he was, just said he'd been at his brother's. I've got the brother's name and address, I can check that today.'

'Good work, Carol. This is very interesting indeed. They row, he storms out, angry and upset, he doesn't come back until the morning. Get on to the brother. Where does he live?'

'Pimlico.'

'OK, get up to Pimlico, tell him you're coming and interview him face to face. I am going to ring Meredith and get him in this afternoon. I'll call DS Brown and ask him to come in on the interview with me. Primary objective now is to find out where Charles Meredith was on the night Claire disappeared. OK?'

Carol stood to go back to her desk to call Meredith's brother. 'OK,' she replied. And despite what everyone said, she reckoned that DI Taylor was all right. She knew how to get things moving.

*   *   *

269

The lady at number fifteen Market Square, Shorebridge, had just returned from her holiday and was frankly a bit miffed to be woken up by police officers banging on her door on a Sunday afternoon. She had flown in from Miami the day before and was jet-lagged. She had been catching up on a bit of sleep on the sofa when they woke her. The dogs were barking fit to raise the dead and there was no way she was going to get any rest until she opened the door and showed them who was there. She went to the door with the three Yorkshire terriers, grumpy and unco-operative.

'Good afternoon, madam,' a WPC said. 'We are conducting a house-to-house inquiry to see if anyone might have heard anything or seen anything out of the ordinary last Tuesday, that's the ninth, or Wednesday the tenth, probably at night.'

'I wasn't here,' the lady snapped, above the yapping. 'I've been on holiday, I can't help you.' She went to shut the door, but the WPC said: 'What about the dogs?'

'What about them? I'm pretty certain they didn't see anything, and if they had they wouldn't be able to tell you, would they?'

'I meant, who looks after them while you're on holiday? Do they go to kennels?'

'What business is it of yours, young lady?'

'We're investigating the disappearance of an eighteen-year-old girl, and it's my business to find out any information that might help us find her,' the WPC said calmly and with more authority than she felt.

The lady sighed. 'I've got a sitter,' she said. 'It's my nephew. He sits while I'm away, feeds the dogs, makes a bloody mess of the place, and for that pleasure I give him eighty quid a week.'

'Was he here last week?'

'Unless he left the dogs alone, yes, he was!'

'Do you have his name and address so that we can contact him?'

The lady sighed again, even more theatrically this time. 'He lives in London,' she snapped. 'Hang on, I'll get his address.' She disappeared and the three dogs stood guard in the hall, growling pathetically. The lady reappeared with a scrap of paper and handed it over. 'Don't know that he'll remember anything,' she said. 'He's not the brightest.' Then she slammed the door shut without another word, the letter box rattling with the force of it.

The WPC walked across to the sergeant and told him what had happened. 'Give him a ring when you get back to the station,' he said. The WPC nodded, tucked the piece of paper into her notebook and continued with her inquiries.

Charles found the message on his answer phone when he came in from shopping. It was ludicrous, he thought, shopping on a Sunday, sad and pathetic, like he had no other life, but it had to be done. He unloaded his carriers from the car, dumped them in the kitchen, put away the frozen things – mainly ice cream – and pressed play on the machine. He heard DI Taylor's voice, left the rest of the shopping where it was and walked straight out of the house. He had been expecting this, and now it had happened he wanted it dealt with immediately. Twenty minutes later he was being shown into an interview room.

Annie came down the stairs and met DS Brown on her way to the interview room.

'Thanks for coming in, Steve, I didn't expect him to react so readily.'

271

They went into the interview room, where Charles was waiting. He had been given a cup of tea, but hadn't touched it. Annie said: 'Professor Meredith, I am Detective Inspector Taylor and this is Detective Sergeant Brown. Thank you for coming in so promptly. This is a voluntary but formal interview and I will have to caution you. I must stress that you are not here under arrest and that you are entitled to have a solicitor present if you so wish. You can also telephone someone of your choice at any time.'

Charles nodded. He had nothing to fear, he kept telling himself, he was not involved, but he was scared shitless.

'Charles Meredith, you do not have to say anything, but it may harm your defence if you do not mention when questioned something which you later rely on in court. Anything you do say may be given in evidence.' Annie smiled. 'That's the gruesome bit over with, now we can chat. Is your tea all right?'

'Actually it tastes like mud.'

Again Annie smiled. 'We somehow get used to it.' She wanted to keep him relaxed. So far they had a lot of suspicion but no evidence. She didn't want this to go even half a millimetre the wrong way. 'Professor Meredith, can you tell us where you were on Tuesday the second of May this year?'

'Yes. I worked all day at the university but my last tutorial was cancelled. Claire Thompson was the only person to turn up, all the rest had flu, so I sent her away and went home early. When I got home I discovered that Mia, my girlfriend, had left all the paraphernalia of conception lying around, an ovulation kit and charts, diary dates, that sort of thing, and that she had been trying for a baby without my knowledge. I was very angry; we had not discussed having a family and I am not sure that I want children. I felt she had deceived me, and after a row, I left the house. I went up to London to stay in my brother's flat. I needed some space.'

'Can anyone verify that?'

Charles swallowed and Annie watched him. He was thinking about what to put in and what to leave out.

'Yes, and no. Rob, my brother, called me at midnight. I answered the call, so I was there, but after that I was alone.' He just couldn't bring himself to mention her. It hurt too much even to think about her, let alone try to explain her to these people.

'Did you go out at all?'

'I went out for a drink.'

'Where to?'

Charles faltered for a moment, then said: 'I don't know. Some pub up the road. I had a couple of pints and that was it. I can't remember much about the place.'

Annie exchanged a glance with DS Brown.

'Not even the name?'

'No.'

'Where were you this Wednesday, the tenth?'

'I worked at the university and in the evening I played tennis with a friend, had a meal in the bar at the club afterwards, then went home. I got in around nine. You can check it with my friend.'

'Thanks, we will.' Annie made a note of Charles's friend's address and number as he recited it. 'Were you having a relationship with Claire Thompson, Professor Meredith?' she asked.

'No, I wasn't.'

'Have you ever had a relationship with Claire Thompson?'

'No, I haven't. Apart from the usual student–tutor relationship.'

'Have you ever taken her out for dinner, met her for a drink outside your teaching hours?'

'No, never.'

'Were you going to meet her for dinner on Tuesday the second?'

'No, that night happened exactly as I've explained it. I have never met Claire socially, she didn't even come to my first-year supper at Christmas. I barely know her.'

'Yet she writes about you in her diary. How do you explain that?'

Charles had begun to sweat. He reached into his pocket for his handkerchief and wiped his face. 'I can't,' he said honestly.

DS Brown said: 'There was a note from you in one of her files. It said: "We need to talk about this." Can you tell us what that refers to?'

Charles tried to think; his mind was blank. 'No, I can't. It must have referred to an essay, but I have no idea why. I wouldn't have written it unless it referred to a piece of work.'

'But you don't know which piece of work?' Annie pressed.

'No, I don't! I have over forty students in my tutorials, I mark hundreds and hundreds of essays a term. I simply cannot be expected to remember every one of them!'

'Of course not,' Annie said. 'Professor Meredith, would you mind telling us why you have recently split up with your girlfriend?'

'We have different ideas about what we want. She wants a baby, I am not ready for that yet.'

'How old are you, Professor Meredith?'

Charles frowned. 'I'm thirty-nine.'

'Too young to have children then?' Annie said it with a smile, but she was letting him know her doubts.

'It has nothing to do with age,' Charles said. 'It's a frame

274

of mind, a desire to take on that sort of responsibility. I don't have that desire.'

'Perhaps something else got in the way.'

'Meaning?'

'I don't know, you tell me.'

Charles ran his hands through his hair. 'Nothing else got in the way and certainly not Claire Thompson, if that's what you're implying.' He was angry – this was intrusive and aggressive.

There was a few minutes of silence, then Annie suddenly stood up. 'Professor Meredith, I think we've finished our questions.'

Charles was startled. 'You have?'

'Yes. There is one more thing. Could I ask you to let us take a sample of blood?'

'You can ask, but I'm sorry, you won't get it.'

'Why not?'

'Because I hate needles, that's why not, and if you think, after I've come here voluntarily to answer a barrage of questions, that I'm going to let some cack-handed police surgeon near my veins, then you're very much mistaken. I have been very co-operative and now, if you've finished, I should like to go home!'

Annie nodded. 'Of course,' she said.

She opened the door and Charles stood. He walked past her and out through the security door of the inner station, then down the steps out of the nick. As he reached his car and tried to put his keys in the lock, he realized that his hands were shaking so badly that he simply couldn't manage it.

Annie went back to her office with Steve Brown.

'So?' he asked.

'I think he's worried,' Annie said. 'He's on edge and he's hiding something. Let's find out what pubs are in the vicinity of Dolphin Square and then I'll contact Carol and ask her to pay them all a visit. She's up there now interviewing Meredith's brother. We might get something from it. Also contact Dolphin Square management and find out if they have any CCTV cameras around the place; we might get something from those as well. Our priority now I think is to find out where Meredith was on the night Claire disappeared. If . . .' Annie stopped as a WPC came into the office.

'Excuse me, DI Taylor, but I've just rung the number of a man who was dog-sitting in Shorebridge last Wednesday, and he says that he heard a scream at around ten last Wednesday. He was walking the dogs round the block when he heard it. He says he heard it twice, went in the direction he thought it came from, but couldn't see anything.'

Annie looked at DS Brown.

'Did he notice any cars? Anyone who looked out of place?'

'He didn't say.'

'OK. Have you got his address?'

'Yes, ma'am.' The WPC handed it over and DS Brown said: 'D'you think we should go up and interview him?'

Annie stood up. 'Yes, I do,' she replied. 'Steve, get on to the local nick and find out the pubs in the area, then speak to Carol and put her on to that once you've got a list. I'll get up to town now, interview this Pete Cullis bloke and we'll speak later on tonight. OK?'

'D'you think Meredith did it, boss?'

Annie shook her head. 'Let's get him clearly in the frame and then we'll start asking questions like that. OK?'

Steve nodded.

'Policy update meeting first thing tomorrow, eight a.m. OK?' She picked up her handbag. 'I'll get downstairs and see if I can get a car organized, plus a uniformed officer to accompany me. I'll pop back before I leave.' She walked to the door, then turned. 'You all right with this, Steve?'

He glanced up. That was the thing about working for a woman, the thing that he really liked: there was no macho shit. 'Yeah, sure,' he said. 'No problem, boss. Thanks for asking.'

Annie left the office. Twenty minutes later she was on her way up to Brixton in a squad car with two uniformed officers for company.

Chapter 20

Finally, Daisy was dismissed. Mrs Blithe came to her on the Monday after the weekend house party and asked her to come into the housekeeper's study for a few private words.

'I am afraid that I have bad news for you, Daisy,' she began. Daisy was impassive; it was what she had been waiting for. 'After this weekend, Lady Chatten has decided that we are currently overstaffed for the needs of Bicester House. She is very sorry, but the rule is last in, first out, and that has to be you, Daisy. I did try to argue your case, but her ladyship was very insistent that we really don't need three parlourmaids. She sees no opening for you anywhere else, I'm afraid. I'm sorry too, Daisy, I thought you might do well here.'

Daisy said nothing.

'You can stay on till the end of the week and then you have to go. You can have your Thursday afternoon off to look for something else if you'd like, but I can't let you have any more than that.'

Daisy nodded.

'Have you got anything to say, Daisy?'

'No, nothing.'

Mrs Blithe let out a sigh. Some girls were just too pretty for their own good. She'd seen this coming: undue interest from Mr Henry, disappearing on afternoons off, house gossip. Did these girls never learn? 'Well then, I'll sort your wages and let you have them Friday morning. Thank you, Daisy. You can get on now.'

Daisy nodded and left the study. She should have shown more respect, but she couldn't be bothered. She was moving on, not up as she'd hoped, but on. She went back to cleaning out the fire grate in the drawing room – the same fire grate that Henry and Isabella had stood in front of to receive the good wishes for their engagement.

On Thursday afternoon, Daisy met Henry at the entrance to the woods as she usually did, and they walked separately into the copse, where they immediately stopped and embraced. Henry kissed her passionately, taken with such longing and desire for her that he couldn't wait to touch her. He lifted her skirts and ran his hands over her thighs, dropping to his knees to kiss the soft damp skin at the top of her stockings. She shivered, but pushed him gently away. 'Not now,' she said. 'Please, not now.'

Henry stood. He took her hand and kissed it, pressing her palm to his mouth. 'Soon we will be able to love each other as much as we want.'

She looked at him. 'But not legally.'

Henry dropped her hand. 'Oh for God's sake, Daisy! Not all this again, please! I thought we had it settled!'

She saw his mood and knew her own vulnerability. She said: 'We do. I'm sorry, it's the baby, it makes me difficult.'

'You have always been difficult, Daisy, it's nothing to do with the baby. I never know where I am with you, which is why I love you so much.' He smiled, and grudgingly she smiled back.

'I've been dismissed,' she said. 'I am to leave on Friday.'

'I know. The lodge is almost ready. I have hired workmen and they should be finished in a week. They have put in proper plumbing, Daisy, so that you will have running water, hot and cold, and they are installing a range for you to cook on.'

He tilted her chin up so that she looked at him. 'Come on, Daisy, it will be exciting, like having a proper home, at least until we get settled in London. There are two bedrooms, one for us and a nursery for the baby, and a small sitting room for us to be comfortable in.' He smiled again. *'I am quite excited, you know.'*

'Of course,' she said. She wondered how much time he would spend in this proper home once he was married to the beautiful Isabella.

'I have arranged for you to stay in a rooming house in Shorebridge until the lodge is ready. It's about ten miles from here. I hope that is acceptable.'

'It is fine, Henry, everything is just fine. Thank you.' Of course she didn't mean that; nothing was fine, everything was far worse than she had imagined. *'Can we go and see the lodge today?'*

'Right now if you'd like. I gave the workmen the afternoon off so that we wouldn't be disturbed.'

So that we wouldn't be seen together, he should have said; she knew that was what he meant.

'Come on. It looks quite pretty in the sunshine.'

They took the route round Ludwell Ponds to the opening in the trees that bordered the lodge, and went through it on to the lawn. Henry took her hand and together they went up to the little house. True to his word, inside the lodge it was indeed like a proper home, and Daisy was pleased, despite her unhappiness. She wandered from room to room, as yet unfurnished, and could sense that this was somewhere, if things had been different, she might just have been happy. She turned, and Henry said: *'Do you like it?'*

'It will be fine,' she answered.

'Come back into the sitting room,' he said. *'I want to show you something.'* She followed him into the room at the back, with a long French window looking down towards the ponds, and watched as he took a roll of paper from the floor. *'I am having a new fireplace built,'* he said. *'For you. It is being carved right*

now, out of local stone, and I have designed this to go over the fire, underneath the mantel. Look.'

He held the paper up and Daisy saw a drawing of a fireplace. There was a crest in the centre of it, Latin words, bordered by flowers. She stepped closer and saw that the flowers were daisies. She smiled. 'Very romantic. Verbum Tuum Mea Veritas. What does that mean?'

'Well, you don't pronounce it like that, but it's Latin. It means "your word is my truth". I just thought that you should know that, that it should be carved in stone.'

Daisy stepped forward. 'My word is your truth?'

'Your word and your love is my truth.'

She moved close to him and placed her hands on his shoulders. She wanted to believe it; it was the most beautiful thing she had ever heard, and she so desperately wanted to believe it. Henry unbuttoned her shirt and slipped it off her shoulders. She closed her eyes as he put his mouth against the warm skin of her chest. *Your word is my truth*, she thought, *your word is my life and your word will be my death.*

Later, they lay naked on a rug in the centre of the room with no fireplace, and Henry rested his hand on the curve and swell of her belly. He had felt the baby kick and it humbled him, that he could have been part of this creation growing inside the woman he loved. He touched her flesh, hard with growth, and said: 'When I return, the baby will be almost born. You will be changed from a girl, Daisy, into a mother.'

He felt her tense under his hand.

'When you return from where? Where are you going?' She kept her voice as calm as she could, but his words racked her with fear.

'I have a date for my wedding,' he said, moving away from her and sitting up. 'My parents have agreed a date with the

Testrys, eight weeks from now, the end of August, the twenty-fifth, and I will be away for two months after that on my honeymoon.'

'Your honeymoon?' For some bizarre reason it had not occurred to Daisy that she would have to suffer this, this thought, this reality of her lover lying with another woman. For a moment she was so seized with jealousy that her whole body stopped. Then she caught her breath and jumped up, scrabbling around on the floor for her clothes. Of course she would have to suffer it; she had known in her heart, from the moment that she saw Isabella Testry, that Henry would lie with her and enjoy it, that it would not be a simple consummation of the marriage, but more, much more than that. She was a fool, she had tricked herself into not thinking about it, she had believed that it wouldn't matter, almost that it wouldn't happen, but it would, of course it would, and that thought made her insane with anger. She was fumbling with her clothes, pulling on her corset, her trembling fingers making a mess of the laces, when Henry stopped her.

'You have nothing to fear,' he said quietly.

Daisy stared at him. 'I have everything to fear,' she replied.

'No. Your word is my truth, you are my truth.'

'Henry, I have everything to fear,' she said again. 'I fear that you will not come back, that you will love Isabella as she loves you, that I will die from the pain of losing you.'

He stroked her hair, the hair that had once fallen wet over her naked breasts and made him realize that he had not been alive until that moment. 'You have nothing to fear,' he said again, 'I promise you.' Daisy did not argue further; it would have been pointless. Promises are easily made and easily broken, and one man's promise is another man's lie.

That night, her last night, Daisy packed her small bag in the attic room she shared with Ethel, and lay down on the bed to read. She was on duty again that evening at seven, and was leaving the following morning after breakfast. She was desperate for sleep – emotion, anger and despair had worn her out – but she knew if she closed her eyes she might sleep all night, and then it would be docked off her wages. She couldn't afford that. She opened the book and began the chapter, but had no inclination for the words. What did words mean anyway? They were empty, most of them, meaningless. She heard footsteps outside and called out to Ethel; she would be glad of the company, she needed some human contact. The door opened and Maekins came in. Daisy immediately sat up.

'Don't get up, Daisy,' he said. 'You look so comfortable there.' He stood in front of the door and Daisy saw his hands working behind his back.

'Mr Maekins, I don't think you should be up here, it's against the house rules and Mrs Blithe . . .'

'Mrs Blithe is down in her study, three floors away, chatting to Cook, and rules – well, Daisy, you should know about those, rules are made to be broken, aren't they?'

Daisy brought her knees up and hugged them to her, suddenly frightened. Maekins came towards the bed.

'If you come near me, I'll scream,' she said.

He smiled. 'Come now, let's not be melodramatic! You're surely not going to refuse me your favours, are you, Daisy? I mean, you give them to everyone else.'

Daisy pressed herself back against the wall. 'Please,' she said quietly, 'please leave me alone, Mr Maekins.'

Maekins shook his head. He had wanted Daisy from the first moment he saw her, had even entertained ideas of asking her to marry him at the outset. But that was before he knew about Chatten, that was when she was pure, unsullied. She wasn't that now; she was as black as sin and he wanted a bit of that sin. He stepped closer, unmoved by her obvious fear.

'Mr Maekins, please . . .'

Without warning, he lunged at her, but she rolled sideways and scrambled off the bed. She made a run for the door; he caught her within a few paces, overpowering her with his brute strength. He pulled her to the floor and covered her body with his own, pinning her arms back. She screamed and he hit her, hard across the face. She bit her lip, and the blood gushed into her mouth, its warm metallic taste making her retch. Maekins moved up her body, he knelt on her arms, crushing them with his weight, and with his free hand pulled at her skirts, ripping her underclothes.

Daisy began to cry. She writhed under him but it excited him, made him stronger. She felt his hand on her flesh and screamed again. He lifted it to hit her and she kicked out with all her might. Somehow her movement unbalanced him; there was a moment when he released her to get a better grip, and she seized that moment. She brought her knee up into his groin and closed her eyes. Seconds later it was over. Maekins had fallen to one side, curled up in pain.

Daisy struggled to her feet, her mouth bleeding, and staggered to the door. Maekins had locked it, and she fumbled with the key, her hands shaking uncontrollably. It turned, she pulled the door open and fell out of the room. She ran down the stairs, the key in her hand, Henry's words echoing in her head. 'You have nothing to fear,' he had said, and she knew he was wrong. She had everything to fear, there was no meaning any more, her world was slipping towards chaos, and because of that she feared the worst thing of all. She feared herself.

Chapter 21

It was early Sunday evening when Charles went to the university library up on campus. He couldn't stay at home, the silence was driving him crazy. He needed a book, not desperately, but it was a good excuse to get out and take a drive.

In the library he went straight to the history section and the Victorian period. He selected the book he wanted, an analysis of the Victorian criminal justice system, and took it to a desk. He sat, opened it and put his head down to read. He liked silence, but within a few minutes realized he wasn't going to get it. There was a murmur of chatter at the desk in the next section and it irritated him. He sighed loudly, twice, then coughed, but short of standing up, walking round the bookcases and reminding the culprits that this was a library, which he was loath to do, he wasn't going to silence them. He tried to read, but his brain kept picking up snatches of their conversation. He gave up, sat for a few minutes and listened. He heard his name and his heart stopped. Standing, he walked over to the bookcase and peered through the gap into the next section. He felt ridiculous, but couldn't help himself. A group of students sat with their files open, gossiping freely in hushed tones, despite the no-talking rule. Charles squatted down and took a book off the bottom shelf.

'Of course he was!' one of the girls in the group exclaimed.

'He's that sort. Reckons he's really hip and trendy, on your level, but all the time he's dying to get into your knickers.'

Charles gripped the book. Was this him, this hip and trendy saddo? He stayed where he was, compelled to listen.

'Well, Meredith might have been giving her one,' the boy next to her said, 'but d'you really reckon he could have bumped her off?'

'Who knows?' the girl replied. 'Everyone is capable of the most heinous acts in certain circumstances.'

'Come off it, Bridge! He's harmless, old Meredith! Just a bit of a laddo, nothing more. Anyway, Claire was barmy, you know that! She probably just got drunk and fell into the canal. I notice they're not dragging the canal bed.'

'Or maybe she was pushed!' They all sniggered.

Charles felt sick. This was sick, this whole conversation.

'We shouldn't talk about her like that,' one of the girls said. 'It's not right. We should all be thinking positively, sending her positive thought vibes.'

'Groan groan, Chiara!'

'Well, I'd heard that her diary was full of vivid descriptions of sex with Meredith,' the first girl, the sensationalist, said. 'And that he was into all sorts of stuff. Jen reckoned that Claire had threatened to expose him and he got nasty.'

Charles couldn't stand it any longer. He stood up and walked round to the group of students.

'I can assure you,' he said coldly, 'that Jen is absolutely and categorically wrong.' There was a stunned silence, and five shocked faces stared at him. 'I might remind you, as well, that talking about me in this way is slander, and I would have no compunction in suing if this sort of malicious gossip got out of hand.'

He turned and walked away. So intense was the embarrassment behind him that he could almost feel it. Christ, what a mess, he thought. So many people were doubting him that he was even beginning to doubt himself.

Mia was eating an omelette in front of the telly when Charles knocked on the door. She had left her address and number on his answer phone on Friday but she hadn't expected him to call round. She went to the door in tracksuit bottoms, a T-shirt and slippers, and wished immediately she saw him that she hadn't.

'Can I come in?'

She nodded, and he walked into the small cramped hall. 'Come into the lounge,' she said. He followed her into the colourless, scruffy front room with its brown dralon sofa and beige wood-chip walls. Her plate was on the floor with her dinner on, half eaten. He said: 'Sorry, you're eating. I'll come back.'

'No, honestly, it's fine,' she replied quickly. 'I'd had enough anyway.' She looked at him. 'Are you all right? You look ghastly.'

'I had a bit of a shock,' he said, 'at the university today. I heard some students gossiping about me; they think I killed Claire Thompson.'

Mia knew how important Charles's reputation was to him, but it irked her, it always had. He took himself far too seriously. 'People talk,' she said. 'It's just talk, it doesn't mean anything.'

He looked at her. 'Do you think I was involved?'

Mia looked away.

'Mia?'

'The police were here this morning,' she said. 'They asked me about my alibi for the Tuesday Claire Thompson disappeared. I had to tell them that I was alone and that you went off and didn't return until the morning. Where were you, Charles?'

'I told you, I was at Rob's!'

'All night?'

Charles stared at her. 'You don't believe me either, do you? You think that I'm capable of abducting one of my students. I don't believe it! Christ, how did all this happen? One minute I'm a respected professor, the next I'm suspected of murder!'

'Murder? They haven't found a body yet, Charles.'

Charles looked away. 'I can hear it in your voice,' he said, 'I can hear your doubt.' He faced her. 'What's the point, if even you don't believe me?'

She shrugged and he turned towards the door. 'Thanks,' he said. He opened the front door and was gone. Mia stood for quite some time staring at the empty space, then she picked up her plate and carried it into the kitchen. She didn't think about it again – the truth was too difficult to face.

Annie Taylor phoned Carol Pinto just as they reached Brixton. DS Brown had texted her a list of pubs and she needed to discuss them. She instructed Carol to leave the pubs and bars – three of them – nearest to Dolphin Square until she reached Pimlico, in about an hour.

'I'll do them with you,' she explained. She finished the call as they pulled up outside Pete Cullis's flat.

'I think one of you had better stay in the car,' Annie said, looking out at the street. 'Nice neighbourhood!' She climbed out and went up to the block of housing association flats, ringing the bell for number five. Cullis answered, pressed the door release and Annie and the PC went on up.

'Hi, Mr Peter Cullis?'

'That's right.'

'I'm DI Taylor, CID, and this is PC Warren. We've come to follow up a call made to you earlier this afternoon. We are making inquiries into the disappearance of an eighteen-year-old student.'

'Yeah, sure. Come in.'

Cullis glanced out nervously into the hallway as they went in, and Annie wondered what he had to hide.

'OK, just to confirm, Mr Cullis, you were dog-sitting for a lady in Shorebridge last week, is that right?'

'Yes. My aunt, Mrs Doris Pritchet, and the three hounds from hell. Little rats they are, always at your ankles. I was there for two weeks.'

'And when one of our officers called you earlier this afternoon, you said you remember hearing a scream one night last week. Is that right?'

'Yes. It was Wednesday night.'

'Are you sure?'

'Yeah, definitely. I called a mate because I was bored out of my brain, told him nothing ever happened down there, then when I took the dogs out for their bedtime piss I heard this scream. Twice. It was a woman and it ended suddenly, like she'd been shut up. I called my mate when I got in and told him all about it. You can check Doris's phone bill, there'll be a call to Newcastle, that's where he lives, but I'm sure it was Wednesday because Tuesday I was down the pub in the square.'

'What time did you hear the scream?'

'About half eleven. I always take them out at that time, then the little buggers don't wake me up too early in the morning.'

Annie made a few notes. 'Do you remember anything else about that evening? Did you see anything else that might help us with our inquiries?'

'Yeah, I've been thinking about that since you rang. When I called Mick, that's my mate in Newcastle, he said had I had a look around and checked that it wasn't some girl being raped or something, and I felt guilty then, so I did wander out and have a look round the square. I couldn't see anything, but there was a car parked in the square with a bloke in it. He was just sitting there. I walked past the car a couple of times and had a bit of a look in the back, and then I went in to get a pencil to write down the registration number. By the time I went out again he'd driven off.'

'Can you remember what sort of car it was?'

'It was blue, a saloon, maybe a Rover or a Ford, something like that. I wasn't too sure because I'm dyslexic and I find it hard to read things, but it wasn't flash, not like a Merc or a BMW. I'd have recognized the badge.'

'OK, so it was a blue saloon, Rover or Ford. Was it light or dark blue?'

'Dark blue, navy blue, but it wasn't new, I'd have noticed if it was new. I like new cars.'

'How long was it there, d'you think? Was it there before the scream, for example?'

'No. Only after I rang Mick. I didn't notice it before.'

'OK. Well I think that's about as much as we need for now. Thank you, Mr Cullis, you've been very helpful.'

Cullis nodded. 'So what's happened to her then? This student? D'you think she's been murdered?'

'We can't say at this point; all we are investigating is her disappearance.' Annie took a glance round the flat: scruffy, grubby, uncared for. 'If you can remember anything else, perhaps you'd be kind enough to ring me. It's DI Taylor, here's my direct line.' Annie handed him a piece of paper, PC Warren opened the door, and he and Annie left. As they went down the stairs she said: 'Could you get on the radio to the nick and ask them to run a check on Meredith's car, find out the make, colour and registration, please?'

He nodded. Outside the flats, Annie rang DS Brown. 'Have you checked with Meredith's friend about the game of tennis on Wednesday?'

'Yes, it's as he said.'

'What time did he leave the club, did the friend say?'

'Nine. They played tennis at seven for an hour, had a meal, and he left the club about nine. It's a ten-minute drive from the club to Meredith's house.'

'Can you go round and check the neighbours, please, Steve, to see if anyone remembers him going out again that night? Check two houses to the right and left of Meredith and the house opposite. Give me a ring when you've got some answers.' She pressed end and went over to the car.

'Professor Meredith owns a Renault Megane saloon, boss, dark blue,' PC Warren said. He read out the registration number.

'Great, that puts him closer to being in Shorebridge the night the purse was dropped. Right, let's get back up to Cullis and take a statement from him about what he saw and when.' She waited for PC Warren to climb out of the car, and they made their way back to the flats.

An hour later, Annie met Carol Pinto in Dolphin Square.

'How d'you get on with Rob Meredith?'

'He confirmed that Meredith was there, he showed me the entry on his system and his phone bill to show the call made from his mobile. He talked a bit about Meredith's relationship with Mia Langley, said he'd always felt it was watertight and was shocked that they had split up. He didn't reckon the split would last, thought they'd be back together by the end of the year, at the latest. He talked a bit about Meredith, said how honest he was, how passive, unviolent. Said he didn't even like rows and thought him incapable of an affair. That's about it really. I made some more detailed notes but nothing special. D'you want to me to run through them now?'

'No, save it for later. Good work, Carol.'

They made their way to the first pub, the nearest, and went inside. It was just opening.

'Hi,' Annie said, as the barman looked up. 'I'm DI Taylor and this is DC Pinto. We're looking for the manager.'

'That's me.' He didn't look particularly pleased at having to reveal that information. 'What d'you want?'

'Can we have a few words?'

He carried on drying the glasses. 'Fire away,' he said.

'Can you tell me who was working on Tuesday the second of May? That's a week last Tuesday.'

'Not off hand, no.'

'Can you look it up for us? You must have some kind of staff rota.'

'Hang on.' He went into the back and returned with a diary. 'I was on, along with Debbie. Just the two of us.'

'Was it busy?'

'Nah, it's never busy early on in the week.'

'Do you remember a man, mid-thirties, well dressed, good-looking. He may have been with a much younger girl, or on his own.'

The barman looked blank. 'Sorry,' he said, shaking his head. 'I couldn't possibly remember that far back, not unless you've got a photo. We get loads of people pass through here every week, specially coming into the tourist season.'

Carol Pinto took a university brochure out of her handbag.

'This is him,' she said. Annie was surprised.

The manager shook his head. 'Sorry, don't remember him.'

'Would Debbie?' DC Pinto asked. 'He's pretty attractive, stands out from the crowd.'

'You can ask her, her shift starts in half an hour.'

'OK, we'll come back,' Annie said. 'Tell her to expect us, please.' They left the pub and Annie said: 'Good thinking, Carol, I'm impressed.'

Carol handed the brochure over. 'Steve picked it up when he was at the university. It's the history department prospectus. Nice photo of Meredith.' Annie took a look. There was a shot of Charles Meredith at the front of a lecture theatre. He photographed well.

'Well done,' Annie said. Carol smiled. 'Actually, it's a fluke. I picked it up this morning with the intention of reading a bit more about the history department, background stuff, and shoved it in my bag for later. I only opened it while I was waiting for you and spotted the picture. It was a stroke of luck, really.'

'You make your own luck, Carol,' Annie replied.

They carried on to the next pub, but got the same response as the previous one. 'There's a bar on the corner,' Carol said, 'but it's a cocktail bar, not a pub. Didn't Meredith say he went to the pub?'

'Yes, but let's give it a try anyway.' Annie never left anything uncovered.

They knocked on the door; the barman was just setting up. He came across and pointed at his watch. 'We open at seven,' he shouted. Annie held up her ID card and he immediately opened the door.

'Anything wrong?'

'No, but we'd like to ask you a couple of questions,' she

replied. They went in and the barman said: 'Can you wait until the manager comes in? He's here around eight. It's just that I'm only the hired help and I'd prefer it if you spoke to him.'

'We can come back,' Annie said. 'But can you tell us who was working Tuesday the second of this month?'

'It would have been me, I work Tuesdays, Thursdays and Sundays.'

'OK, then we don't have to wait for the manager. Have you ever seen this man in the bar?'

Carol held out the prospectus and the barman looked at the picture. It took him quite some time before he answered. 'Yup, I think so,' he said, 'I think he was here a couple of weeks ago.'

'On the Tuesday?'

'Yes, probably.'

'Are you sure it was Tuesday? It's important.'

'I'm pretty certain it was Tuesday. The bar was empty, and usually on a Thursday it's full to capacity. I wouldn't have remembered him if it had been a Thursday.'

'Was he alone?'

The barman shook his head. 'No, he was with a woman.'

'Can you describe her?' Annie felt the adrenaline suddenly fire up her body.

'Attractive, shoulder-length brown hair. I don't really remember, to be honest. She was pretty drunk, I do remember that, and he had to help her walk out of the place.'

'Was she younger than him, do you think?'

'I'd have said so, yes.'

Annie looked at Carol. 'Excuse us for a few moments,' she said to the barman. He nodded and disappeared round behind the bar. 'Is this kosher, d'you think? Or is he making it up?'

'He seems quite certain,' Carol answered. 'And if the

woman was plastered, that would have made them stick in his mind.'

'Hmm. I'm not sure, he must see loads of drunk women in the course of a couple of weeks. Was the woman Claire, I wonder?'

'Who else? She was drunk when she left campus, wasn't she?' Carol asked.

Annie nodded. 'We need a photo of Claire and we need this young man's statement. I'll get on to the nick and get them to fax a copy of Claire's photo to the local station here; we can pick it up and be back for his statement in an hour or so. OK?'

'Fine.' Carol went over to the bar and said to the young man: 'We need you to hang around for an hour or so. You're not planning on going anywhere, are you?'

'No, I'm on duty.'

'Good.'

Annie looked at him. 'Is this a part-time job for you?'

'Yes, I'm at art college. I'm doing a degree in fine art.'

'What d'you paint?'

'Portraits mainly.'

She smiled; hence the good memory of faces. 'We'll be back in an hour or so and we'd like you to look at a photograph, if that's OK?'

'Fine, I'll be here.'

Annie glanced at her watch as they left; it was five to seven. Hopefully, if they got things moving quickly, she could be back here in half an hour and on her way home by eight. She climbed into the back of the squad car with Carol and said to the driver: 'Metropolitan Police, Pimlico, please.' Then she sat back and listened to what Carol had to say in detail about Rob Meredith.

*   *   *

An hour later, Annie abandoned the idea of getting a good faxed photo of Claire Thompson. They had had four attempts, and despite her mutterings about crap technology, there was nothing they could do; it still wasn't clear enough to be able to use for identification purposes. She telephoned the bar, took the young man's address and asked him to be available tomorrow morning for a statement and to look at a photo of the woman in the bar. Then she left Pimlico nick with Carol Pinto and asked the driver to take them home.

'Unless you've got other plans, Carol?'

'No, home, supper and bed for me, boss. I'm shattered.'

'Me too,' Annie said. So this was the lot of a female detective, she thought: home alone and in bed by ten. It was all rather sad. She glanced out of the window at the grey urban landscape. 'Let's hope tomorrow will be worth the early night,' she remarked.

'Let's hope so.'

'You did well today, Carol,' Annie said. 'Thanks for your input, I was impressed.'

Carol Pinto smiled. 'Just doing my job,' she replied, but it made one hell of a difference to be thanked for it.

Annie let herself into her small, heartless house at ten past nine. The first thing she did was pour herself a large vodka. She added a splash of orange juice and took her drink through to the sitting room. She ignored the packing cases – untouched – kicked off her shoes and sat down on the sofa, shoving the papers – unread – on to the floor. She took a hefty slug of her drink and closed her eyes. It was always like this; in the middle of an investigation the tension was only just bearable. The vodka helped, it eased things, loosened her mind. Annie Taylor was an intuitive police officer, but she only worked with intuition when there was some solid ground behind it. She might have started with a gut feeling, but then she went on to test a case from every angle, to note down every relevant point, from the most insignificant little fact to the things that were glaringly obvious. So now, standing to pour herself another drink, she picked up a pad of paper and a pen, made a heading and decided to jot down her thoughts on the case, in meticulous detail. In her small, bare kitchen, she added more tasteless spirit to the orange juice and reached up into the cupboard for a packet of crisps. The front door bell rang and she glanced out of the window on to the drive. She didn't recognize the car, so at least it wasn't her mother. She opened the door with the chain on.

'DS Coulter.' She was surprised, and it showed. 'Is there a problem?'

Coulter stood with his hands in his pockets. 'No problem. I came to apologize to you. I don't think I've been behaving very well recently. Look, can I come in?'

Annie hesitated. Her instinctive reaction was to make an excuse, but she knew how bad that would look and how DS Coulter would take it. She took the chain off and opened the door wider. 'I was planning on an early night,' she said. 'I'm knackered.' She had no desire for company, particularly not difficult company.

'I won't take up much of your time, I promise.' He smiled nervously. She stepped aside and he came into her hallway.

'Look, DI Taylor, I realize that I've not made things very easy for you recently, but it would seem that this investigation is hotting up. I'm sorry, I thought you were wasting our time, trying to pull rank and assert yourself, and I was wrong. I apologize.'

Annie looked at him. 'Fine, apology accepted.' She put her hand on the front door latch. 'Is that all?'

He looked at her. 'I don't know.' He shrugged. 'You did offer me a drink a week or so ago. Is the offer still on?'

Annie sighed. Tricky one. No, the offer wasn't still on; she was tired, she was stressed and she wanted time alone to think, but – and there was always a but where men were concerned, she thought – if she refused, it looked mean and unprofessional, and the last thing she wanted was to make matters any worse than they had been between her and DS Coulter.

'Go on in,' she said. 'I've got vodka and orange juice or vodka and water, no ice.'

'Vodka and orange would be great, thanks.'

She went into the kitchen, took a glass from one of the boxes and poured him a drink, then took it through to him in the sitting room.

'Nice place,' he said.

'It's OK. Sorry about the boxes, I haven't had time to unpack. Seat?'

'Thanks.' He took a sip of his drink. 'We've got off to a pretty bad start, haven't we?'

'Yes, you could say that.'

'I admire the way you've handled things. You took no shit and just got on with it.'

Annie raised an eyebrow.

'No, seriously, you had a hunch, you acted on it and it looks as if that hunch was right.' He smiled. 'Instinctive policing.'

'I don't think it was exactly just a hunch, DS Coulter. I had some pretty strong evidence working in my favour when I decided to investigate Claire Thompson's disappearance.' Annie took another gulp of her drink and suddenly felt the vodka hit her bloodstream. Shit, she didn't need this, she wanted to get pissed in solitude. 'When I investigate a case, DS Coulter . . .'

'It's Jerry, please.'

'Jerry. When I look at a case, I evaluate all the facts, and if some of them don't add up then I look a bit harder at why not. I wasn't working on gut feelings or a personal whim with the Thompson case; I was acting on certain facts not adding up. I wanted to know why.'

'And do you?'

'Do I what?'

'Do you know why they didn't add up?'

'Not exactly, but we're getting there.'

Jerry finished his drink and put the empty glass down on top of a packing case by Annie's notepad. He glanced at it. 'Do you ever stop working, boss?'

'No, not when I'm in the middle of a case. And it's Annie, not boss, out of hours.'

'So what do you do to relax and unwind, Annie?'

'I sit and make notes on my case and get plastered.'

'Alone?' He shook his head and smiled.

Annie looked at him. He was attractive, there was absolutely no doubt about that, and he was the sort of attractive that Annie liked – strong, masculine, not groomed, not in the least self-conscious. Suddenly she smiled back. Another time and another place, she thought. 'Yes,' she replied. 'Almost always alone.'

'Pity.'

Annie smiled again; the vodka had relaxed her. She glanced down at his glass and said impetuously: 'Would you like another drink?'

Jerry took a moment to consider, and Annie liked that. 'Is this the almost?' he asked.

'Yes, I suppose it is.'

'Then I would, thanks.' He picked up his glass. 'Shall I help myself?'

'Yes, do. There's another carton of long-life orange juice in the cupboard if the one in the fridge is empty.' She sat down on the sofa with her own drink and pulled her notepad on to her knees. This has nothing to do with the fact that I find him attractive, she told herself; this is purely professional. She meant it too; Annie wasn't swayed by things emotional.

Jerry came back into the room carrying his glass, along with the bottle and a new carton of juice. 'Packing cases make great tables,' he said, putting everything down on one of the unopened cases of books.

'I will probably have them here so long that my mother will end up putting floral cloths over them all,' Annie said.

'And one of those glass tops, to protect the material.'

Annie laughed. 'Exactly.'

'Your mother should meet mine,' Jerry said. He pulled another case of books over and sat on it. 'And great impromptu chairs. So where are you up to? Obviously Meredith did it, so how do we prove it?'

Annie sighed. 'I'm not so sure he did.'

'Sorry?'

'I think it all hinges on whether or not he was having an affair with Claire Thompson, and that I'm just not convinced about.'

'Despite everything in her diary?'

'Yes, despite everything in her diary.'

'You really don't think he did it?'

'I don't know.'

Jerry shook his head. 'But I don't understand. Doesn't everyone think we've got our man? I mean, I know the diary insertions are a bit wild, but everything as far as I can see points to them having an affair. Didn't he have problems in his relationship with Langley? Didn't she say that she wondered if there might be someone else, that he wasn't very committed?'

'Yes, she did.'

'Then there's all the other facts that add up, like a sighting of Meredith's car in Shorebridge where the purse was found . . .'

'A possible sighting.'

'No alibi for the night Claire went missing, a sighting of them in a bar in London . . .'

Annie put her hands up. 'Whoa! Hang on a minute! Who've you been talking to? We've only just found that out, and it's inconclusive. We won't get a positive ID until tomorrow.' She put her pad down on the sofa. 'Innocent until proven guilty, Jerry. Remember that?'

Jerry stood up. 'That's half the problem, isn't it? Proving the buggers guilty. I mean, you know it and I know it, but does that make a difference?'

'But I don't know it, I know nothing of the sort!'

'Oh come on, Annie, it's staring us in the face!'

'Not me it isn't.'

'Another hunch?'

Annie sighed. She was too tired and had drunk too much vodka to be bothered to argue. So what if he thought she acted on hunches, so long as she got results? 'Maybe,' she said. 'More of a gut feeling, the thing you're so fond of accusing me of.'

Jerry smiled ruefully and drained his glass. 'Well, let's hope you're right.' He dug his hands in his pockets. 'I should be off,' he said. 'Thanks for the drink, and . . .' He held out his hand; Annie took it. 'I'm glad we patched up our differences.'

She stood. 'Did we? I thought we'd just uncovered more of them.' She smiled to show him that she was joking, but they both knew there was a bit too much truth in what she said. She followed him to the door and stood in the hallway to watch him drive off. When he'd gone, she collected up her drink from the sitting room and poured the rest of it down the sink. She was too tired to even drink it. She left the carton of orange juice and the bottle of vodka where they were, and went upstairs to bed.

Chapter 22

Nothing is ever easy, Daisy thought, as she filled a kettle with water and placed it on the range to boil. It was heavy and it cost her a good deal of effort to lift and settle it on the hot plate. She sat down for a few moments to recover, and looked out at the blue sky above the ponds. She scratched at a mosquito bite; she had several of them, despite the net over her bed, and they seemed to be worse this year than they had ever been, one of them weeping with pus. Of course the place was swarming with mosquitoes; the water and the woods meant that the night air was thick with insects. Daisy hated insects; she hated insects and the damp and being alone. And she was alone here, for the first time ever in her life she was completely alone, not a sound in the night except the hum of mosquitoes above her head, not a sound in the day except the birds on the water. There was nothing but silence, and it was eating away at her, minute by minute, eroding who she was.

Daisy was eight months into her pregnancy, and Henry had married. The day of his wedding she had lain in bed and wept, unable even to lift her head off the pillow. Now she was resigned to her loneliness, to her misery and jealousy. Every day she felt it and every day she had to beat it back so that she could face dressing and preparing herself some food to keep alive. She ate very little; if it hadn't been for Ethel, who came every day, she probably wouldn't have eaten at all.

She waited for the kettle to boil, then stood and took the tea

303

jar from the shelf, the tea pot from the side. It was a beautiful pot, bone china, chosen by Henry, and Daisy loved it. It felt good in her hands, like it belonged. She lifted the kettle with both hands and poured boiling water into the pot to warm it. She swirled the water around, holding the pot lovingly, then emptied it and spooned in the tea. She was just pouring the boiled water on to the leaves when Ethel came into the kitchen.

'That's my job,' Ethel remarked. 'You shouldn't be lifting heavy pots up at this stage!'

Ethel came across and took over, shifting the tea pot aside to get at the cups and saucers. It pained Daisy to see the rough treatment of such a lovely thing, and she said: 'Do be careful, Ethel, please.'

'Yes, milady,' Ethel replied, and Daisy felt a rush of embarrassment. Ethel had taken to calling her that recently, and it hurt. She said nothing, though. Ethel was her friend, the one person who had come to help, and without her she would have had no human contact at all. Daisy sat down and watched Ethel make the tea. She was quick and efficient, but her movements were graceless and Daisy thought her china deserved better.

'There!' Ethel said, plonking the tea pot down on the kitchen table. 'Tea in here is all right, isn't it?'

Daisy would have preferred it in the small sitting room – the range in here was hot and the hard, straight chairs caused her back to ache if she sat on them for any length of time – but again she said nothing. The headstrong, opinionated, intelligent Daisy said nothing. How had she come to this?

'I'll make you some lunch in a minute and leave it for you to have later,' Ethel said, coming to sit down. She was a large girl and her bulk filled the chair. She poured the tea, slopping some on to the tablecloth. 'Deary me, aren't I clumsy?' She smiled at Daisy, and Daisy caught the slightest hint of disregard.

'I'll get a cloth,' Daisy said. She stood and went across to the

304

linen drawer, taking out a cloth and laying it over the tea stains to soak up the worst.

'You'll have it for the wash tomorrow,' Ethel said. 'I know how you like to keep things spick and span.'

Daisy stood for a few moments and looked out at the water. Her back ached from sitting even a few minutes in that chair, and she had pains down the inside of her thighs. She had her back to Ethel as she said: 'Henry will be back soon, it's just a few more days, a week at the most.' Ethel didn't answer her; she didn't expect her to. Daisy talked about Henry a great deal to Ethel, but Ethel never made any comment. Daisy had supposed these last few months that she didn't like to comment, but she knew Ethel must have an opinion; Ethel always had an opinion. She turned and said: 'You don't ever say anything when I talk about Henry. You don't approve at all, do you, Ethel?'

What had made her ask? Was it a perverse streak of self-pity; was it real curiosity? Later Daisy couldn't remember why she had even mentioned Henry in the first place. She looked at her friend. 'Do you approve, Ethel, or do you think it too awful, to be a mistress, living here?'

Ethel's mouth pursed and she looked away. 'It's not for me to say, Daisy.'

'Really? Why not? You always used to say.'

'It just isn't, that's all. It's not my place!'

'But you're my friend! Surely you can confide in me?'

Ethel stood suddenly and began to clear away the tea things. 'I must get on with lunch,' she murmured.

'No,' Daisy said. 'Please, Ethel, tell me what you think of me. I need to know.'

Ethel stared at Daisy, at this once beautiful, strong, confident girl who had become only a quarter of who she used to be. 'I can't,' she answered.

Daisy stared back. She could see what was in Ethel's eyes,

the pity, the lack of admiration, and she knew that she had changed beyond redemption. 'Tell me,' she said again.

Ethel looked away.

'Why won't you be honest with me?' Daisy suddenly cried.

'Because it's not my place,' Ethel answered.

'Not your place? Why not?'

'Because I work for Mr Henry and it is not for me to comment on his domestic arrangements!' Ethel blurted.

Daisy clasped her hands in front of her belly. 'You work for Mr Henry? What do you mean by that? I thought you worked for Lady Chatten!'

'I do,' Ethel said. 'But Mr Henry pays me extra to come here every day and keep an eye on you . . .'

'He pays you?' Daisy took a step back. 'He pays you to come here?' She shook her head; she couldn't believe it! Ethel, her friend, her ally, was paid to be here?

Ethel hung her head. 'He asked me to make sure that you ate properly and that you were looking after yourself while he was away.'

'He pays you . . .' Daisy murmured. 'He pays you to be my friend? So alone and so cast out am I that he has to pay you to be kind to me.' She slumped down into the chair, knocked back by this knowledge. 'Do you think so little of me, Ethel, that you had to be paid?'

'I don't think much one way or the other, Daisy. You made your bed, now you have to lie in it.' There was an edge of hostility in her voice that Daisy picked up on.

'You must think something,' she said. She couldn't let it go; her self-destructive streak had taken over. 'You always think something, Ethel, you have never been short on opinions and you've certainly never been shy about making them known.' It was said to wound, and Ethel's temper flared.

'All right!' she snapped. 'Yeah, I do think something, Daisy

Burrows, I think that you got what you had coming. If you's lonely and miserable then I got no sympathy for you, you deserve it. I come here 'cause I'm paid to, and I wouldn't come if I weren't paid. What would I want with a woman of disrepute?'

It was more than Daisy had bargained for, and she struggled to answer. 'A woman of disrepute? Is that what I am?'

'You're no better than one of them ladies of the night!' Ethel spat.

Daisy gasped; the insult was like a slap round the face. She put her hands up to her cheeks. Ethel watched, unremorseful. She felt no pity, she was bitter and resentful. Why should she have to come here and wait on someone who was no better than herself? What right had Daisy Burrows to this lovely home and money and love? For what? For opening her legs and getting herself in the family way. She should have been in the work-house where she belonged. She should have been sent there years ago, instead of being taught things that could never bring her anything but unhappiness. She was a misfit and she deserved the misery that she had.

Daisy, paralysed by Ethel's hatred, heard Ethel turn and leave the room, but she couldn't look up. The front door slammed and still she sat, motionless, her breathing laboured. Finally, she dropped her hands down from her face and stood, the pain in her back more intense for sitting so long. She walked across to the range and stood near it, needing the warmth. She was cold, chilled to the core, and she wrapped her arms round herself. She felt sick, and pain swelled inside her, rising in her spine and burning down through her body to her uterus. She rubbed her back, then her belly. It felt good, the physical affirmation of her emotional pain. She urged it on, wanting to have something that took her mind away from the shock and fear of her utter lone-liness. She lifted the kettle to fill it again, and as she did so she felt a wetness between her legs. A pain shot across her womb,

307

and she dropped to her knees, fumbling between her legs, under her skirts, touching warm, thick wetness. It was blood. Another pain shot through her, and she curled her body up and began to cry.

It was over. Before her time, too early, too quick. Daisy lay on the kitchen floor, her skirts soaked in blood and urine, the smell of death and excrement seeping from between her legs. In her hands she held a perfect, tiny body, still attached to her, the cord pulsing with life blood, wasted life blood. She couldn't look at it; she held it, and her shaking fingers slipped over the head and the shoulders, wet and sticky with white vernix, then down over the body to the crease, the tiny crease and folds of flesh that told her it was a girl. She was exhausted, bathed in sweat and tears, trembling with pain and grief. This thing, this wet, bloody, life-less thing, was her child.

She let it go, let it drop on to the floor between her legs, and fumbled with her skirts to cover it. She could hear a fly buzzing, that sickening sound of filth; flies, big black bluebottles waiting to eat and lay their eggs. She moved, struggled to some sort of half-sitting, half-lying position, and reached for the bread knife on the table. She cut the cord and the pain came again. It washed over her with no relief, one huge tidal sweep of gut-wrenching pain. Her womb shuddered, contracted and closed up, expelling the last of her baby. The placenta slipped down the birth canal and out of Daisy's body, making the tears and wounds of her vagina bleed all over again.

She must have lost consciousness then, because the next thing she knew there were more flies; she heard the noise like a drone of bees and sat up suddenly, frightened and sickened by it. She scrambled back, swatting at the five or six that ate up the air above her, and got to her knees. She saw her then, she saw her frail, beautiful daughter, forever asleep, peaceful and no prisoner of her mother's sin. Daisy picked her up and held her. She tucked the still, lifeless body safe inside her shirt, close to her breast, and felt the milk seep out, as if her whole body wept. She got to her feet, mustering every last atom of will and strength in her body, and taking a clean white linen cloth from the drawer, she walked out of the lodge and into the copse. Every step she took hurt. She walked deep into the woods, to the place she had discovered by chance, and found it with ease, as if she were meant to be there. She knelt, took her stillborn from her breast and wrapped her, folding the cloth lovingly as she would have done a blanket around a sleeping baby. Then she kissed her, held her child against her lips and murmured the Lord's Prayer. A moment later she dropped the body into the well. She waited for the small echo of it hitting the water, and stood up. Then she turned and walked away.

Mr and Mrs Henry Chatten arrived back in London two days after Daisy lost her baby. The ship that had carried them across the English Channel docked in Southampton at eight in the morning, and they were in the drawing room of the Chattens' Kensington townhouse by lunchtime, having taken the steam train directly to Waterloo. Lady Chatten was there to greet them.

'My darlings! Here you are! You both look wonderful!' She embraced Isabella first as they came in, thinking how radiant she looked, then kissed Henry on the cheek. In truth he did not look wonderful; he was drawn, tired and on edge.

'We feel wonderful,' Isabella said, glancing at Henry. 'Don't we, darling?'

'Yes, yes, of course.'

'I am so glad. And from your letters we read that you had a marvellous time!'

'It was the best honeymoon anyone could have had. I don't want it to end,' Isabella said.

'Well we shall extend it, then, with a few days in London,' Lady Chatten announced. 'Sir Lionel is here with me and we will entertain you until the weekend. There are some very good shows in town, Isabella, I thought we might . . .'

'Mother, I cannot stay,' Henry interrupted. 'I'm sorry, but there is just too much to do back at Bicester, getting myself ready for the interview with the bank and sorting out all the unfinished business from Cambridge. There's no reason why Isabella can't stay on with you, if she'd like to, but I simply must return to Bicester.'

'And I simply must come with you!' Isabella said, smiling. 'I would love to stay in town, but where you go I go, Henry.'

Henry smiled, but Lady Chatten saw no warmth in his eyes. 'You'll stay one night, I hope, at least,' she said.

'Not even one, I'm afraid,' Henry replied. 'We will leave after lunch. We are booked on the three ten from Victoria.'

'I see,' Lady Chatten said coolly. 'Well, I shall have to go and tell Cook to move luncheon forward to one, then.' She swept out of the room and Isabella went across to Henry.

'Try not to look so anxious, darling,' she said. 'I am sure that the interview will be fine and we will be back at Bicester before you know it. Your mother is pleased to see us; let us be good company for her at lunch. Hmm?'

Henry nodded and kissed her hand. She was so good, so kind and understanding, and yet every time he looked at her he wanted someone else. He wanted Daisy. 'Of course,' he replied. 'I shall be charm and wit and good company personified.'

Isabella looked at him and willed him to look back at her in the same way, but he dropped her hand and moved away to the window. It will come, she told herself, staving off disappointment; he will learn to love me if I am patient and deserve his love. She turned as Lady Chatten came back into the room and fixed a smile on to her face. She had no reason to be unhappy;

she was married to a man she had fallen in love with, a gentle, caring, honourable man, and if he was distant, then she would wait.

Henry and Isabella returned to Bicester that afternoon. They arrived in time for tea, which they took in the drawing room, then Henry excused himself, telling his wife that he had many things to attend to and that he would see her at dinner. Again Isabella was disappointed; she had not expected a separation so soon, had wondered if Henry would take time to show her round the estate that he so dearly loved, had thought that they would be together. She smiled, as she always did, and agreed to his suggestion that they see each other in the drawing room at eight thirty.

She watched from the window of the drawing room as he walked off across the parklands, and wondered where he was going. She would ask him later, over dinner, but she knew she mustn't pry. There was a way, she thought, of handling all this, a way of seeming indifferent but interested, caring but not possessive. There was a way of handling it right, and Isabella hoped to God that she would find it.

As Henry struck out for Ludwell Ponds, he found his whole body moved with an urgency that he hadn't experienced for weeks. He didn't mean to hurry, he wanted to look at the estate on the way, take time, view the changes that had occurred over the summer, but his strides increased in pace, and as he neared the copse he knew that his entire being ached with longing for the woman he loved. He ran through the woods, he ran along the side of the ponds and through the gap in the hedge. He fumbled with the gate, too anxious to open it, his fingers slipping on the catch. Then he sprinted up the garden towards the the terrace of the lodge. He slowed, then stopped dead. He watched her unseen, watched her

311

head bent in concentration over her sewing, saw her hair loose, that long velvet curtain of hair, as it fell half over her face. She removed a hand from her work, a slim white hand, and it reached up to tuck the hair back behind her ear. He moved forward slowly now, until he was standing just a few feet away, and he said her name. 'Daisy?'

She looked up. She dropped her sewing on to the table and smiled at him. 'I knew you would come today,' she said, 'I just knew it.'

She put her arms out and he came to her, bending to enter into her embrace. He closed his eyes and ran his hands down over her breasts and the plane of her belly. He pulled back. 'What? What happened? Did you . . .' He stopped, seeing the blankness in her eyes. Then she looked away and shook her head, a small, almost involuntary movement. He dropped to his knees, a sudden overwhelming pain in his chest, and laid his head in her lap. 'Oh God, Daisy, no . . .' he murmured, over and over. She stroked his hair to comfort him, even though her own sense of loss engulfed her. When he looked up at her he saw how much she had changed, how much pain she had suffered and how far away from him she had slipped. He cried and she held him, but all the time she did that, she gave nothing of herself to him. She had nothing more to give.

It was dark when he left her. He had made her some supper, tried to talk to her, tried to get through, but it was useless. In the end they had sat in silence, their bodies touching, but their hearts separate. He slipped away, unable to say any more that would make sense to her.

Henry walked back to Bicester far later than he had intended. He had lost track of time. Isabella had waited for him in the drawing room, then cancelled dinner when he still hadn't returned at nine. She sat by the drawing room window that looked out over the parkland and the drive to the house, and watched for him. It was raining when he walked up the drive; he was soaked, the night was black and cold and he noticed nothing. He was numb inside and out. When she spotted his figure, Isabella ran out of the house with a lantern and a blanket, oblivious to the rain, and met him halfway up the drive. She put the blanket over his shoulders and embraced him, trying to warm his icy flesh with her body. She had no idea what had happened to him, but she could feel his agony and it was her agony. He kissed her, held her face in his hands and tried to see something in her eyes: a spark of life, an affirmation that all was not lost. They stood like that, in the wind and the rain, illuminated by the lantern, two people loving hopelessly, joined and separated by that love.

From the edge of the parkland Daisy saw them. She had followed Henry, hardly conscious of her action, and she saw them from afar, locked in an embrace, hungry with need, husband and wife. She bent double with the pain of it, struggling for breath. Finally, when she was wet through, she recovered enough to stand straight. She turned into the driving rain and darkness and walked back to the lodge alone.

The following day Henry went to London. He left early in the morning on the train and Isabella got up to see him off. He had an interview with a bank for a job and she tried to put his strained appearance down to that. But she worried, she worried all day because she knew something was not right. The man who had returned to the house last night was not the same man who had left hours earlier; Isabella knew that something had happened to him but she had no idea what.

He returned very late. He had missed dinner again and Isabella had sat alone in her room, having asked for something on a tray, then gone early to bed. When he came in just before midnight, Ethel was waiting for him in the entrance hall, her

313

hat and coat on, her face white and stained with tears. Mr Maekins stood over her, like a prison guard.

'Sir? Might I have a word?'

Henry looked at Ethel and the blood in his heart froze.

'Ethel here, one of the parlourmaids, would like to speak to you, sir. I've asked her what it pertains to but she won't tell me. I've also asked her to come back in the morning, but she is insisting that she wait for you. I apologize, sir, I have put her on a warning for this, I . . .'

'It's all right, Maekins,' Henry said, 'I'll deal with it. Please, don't worry yourself about it.' Henry went across to Ethel. He glanced over his shoulder at Maekins, who took the hint and shuffled away towards the servants' quarters.

'Mr Henry, I'm sorry, but you've got to come to the lodge, now, right away.' Ethel grabbed his arm. 'You gotta come now, sir, please. Oh God, I can't believe it, you gotta come, quick!'

'What is it, Ethel? Calm down and try and explain. What's happened?'

'It's Daisy, sir, it's . . .' Ethel put her hand up to her mouth and stifled a sob. At that moment, Isabella appeared on the stairs in her nightdress.

'Henry? Is there something the matter? I tried to speak to the girl earlier, but she wouldn't answer me. She's been here since nine o'clock. What's happened?'

Henry looked up. 'I don't know,' he replied truthfully. 'Go back to bed, Isabella, please!' His tone was harsh and she flinched. Turning on the stairs, she glanced back at him, but he had already dismissed her. He opened the door, took the lamp that Maekins had left and walked out, followed by Ethel. Isabella went on upstairs to her room, but she didn't go back to bed; she dressed and sat waiting for Henry to return.

At the lodge everything was in darkness. Henry had hurried the whole way, stopping every now and then for Ethel to catch up with him, and losing his patience when she fell behind. He thought of nothing, his mind blank, fear having emptied it. Approaching the back door, he held the lantern in front of him and let it cast its halo of light on the ground before him. He went inside, but he didn't call out; somehow he knew that no one would answer him.

He turned to Ethel. 'Where?' he asked.

'In the bedroom,' she said. She had told him nothing, she couldn't bring herself to; her guilt silenced her. If only she had been kinder, not walked out, not left it several days before she came to make it up. If only. Ethel stayed outside in the darkness, shivering with cold and fear. She couldn't bear to go in and see it again.

Henry went into the bedroom alone. He shone the lantern on the bed and saw it soaked in blood. Sheets, torn and ripped from the mattress, white linen stained with dark red blood. It was everywhere, and the smell and the flies made him run from the room, emptying his stomach in the gutter outside the house.

When he had finished, he wiped his mouth on his handkerchief and went to find Ethel.

'Go back to the house and tell Maekins to send a boy for the police. I will wait here.' Ethel looked at him. She wondered how a man of twenty-one could look so old and so near death. 'Go!' he cried. 'Go now, Ethel! Go!' He gave her the lantern and she hurried away, down the muddy drive to the lodge and out on to the main road. As she ran, it started to rain, and against a background of falling water the night was split in two by the horrific scream of human agony.

Isabella was right to wait up. Henry returned in the early hours of the morning, freezing cold, shivering with shock. He was helped upstairs by Maekins and then Isabella took over, undressing him *and wrapping him in warm towels by the fire. She gave him weak tea and brandy, and she rubbed each of his limbs in her hands to try and bring the circulation back. He felt, she thought then, as if he had died; there was no life left in him at all. She asked no questions; she didn't want to know the answers, because she thought they would probably destroy her. In the morning, having fallen asleep for a few hours on the bed, while Henry dozed in a chair by the fire, she was woken by the police, who were insistent on speaking to Henry and searching his room. Isabella let him go. She sat alone and waited. She had been married just two months and she felt she had used a life in waiting.*

The police found Daisy's nightdress, soaked in blood, ripped and cut with a knife, in a drawer in Henry Chatten's room. They found a knife, stained with blood, hidden in a cupboard. They spoke to the staff of the house and in the course of the day the truth, half truth and quarter truth all merged to create something that bore no relation to what had really happened at all. Unknown to anyone, Henry had spent the day in London looking at different areas of the city where it might be possible to live his secret life with Daisy. He had told no one and had no witness to his actions. It was all speculation and hearsay, a bloody nightdress and a blood-stained knife that no one, least of all Henry, could explain. Although Daisy's body was never found, the Crown won the case, while Isabella lost the husband that she loved, Lady Chatten lost her son, and Henry lost every living moment he had spent believing in truth and honour and God.

Chapter 23

Charles sat and stared blankly at his screen. It was Monday, five thirty a.m., he had been at his desk all night and had written as much as he was capable of. He was stuck. It wasn't just a case of writer's block, the words unable to come out, it was a fundamental flaw in the work and he was unable to see a way past it. How had the nightdress got into Henry Chatten's room? Who could have been involved? Was it Maekins? Ethel? How big a part had jealousy played? Could it have caused the mild and loving Isabella to murder her husband's lover? And if it had, how had she found out about the affair? Surely she would have wanted to protect Henry, if she loved him enough to kill to keep him, not set him up. Charles had thought that somehow in the research and the writing these things would miraculously unravel, and that the answers would come to him with ease. But he had found quite the opposite. In writing he had found himself convinced of Henry's innocence but at a loss as to how to prove it. And now, after his own police interview and a community of doubt stacked against him, he realized that innocence was something intangible, reliant entirely on opinion, on the way things were viewed, interpreted, and the way facts added up or didn't. He decided that to make sense of it all, he had to go back to the lodge at Ludwell Ponds.

* * *

Gordon was shaving when he got a call from his lawyer. He had run out of shaving foam, something Lotte always dealt with, and was having to use one of the tiny little tubes from an airline comfort pack. It wasn't particularly nice, it was highly scented and he could already feel his skin beginning to itch. He grabbed the phone in the bedroom, covering the mouthpiece with slime in the process, and snapped: 'Hold on, will you?' When he came back on the line he had wiped his face, knowing that he'd used the last of the gel in the Virgin pack and had only shaved his chin and one cheek. He was extremely bad-tempered. 'Who is it?' he growled.

'Gordon, it's Lorry Keen, from Millard, Fraser and Tims.'

'Yes?'

'Sorry to call so early, Gordon, but I got your message late last night and came straight into the office first thing this morning to see what I could do about it. I've been on the case, so to speak, since six o'clock and I think I've got some good news for you.'

'Good news, eh? I could do with some good news, I can tell you. So what the hell are you going to do about the theft of half my things?'

'Nothing. Mrs Graham's lawyer has an excellent reputation and he's done his homework, that's for sure. From what you told me it looks as if Mrs Graham has taken only what belongs to her, so I think we should write that off and put it down to experience.'

'Experience? She takes off with half my bloody house and I'm supposed to put it down to experience? I don't think so, Lorry. Lotte is going to pay for this little humiliation if she decides not to play ball this afternoon. What about the figures I gave you?'

'I've been looking at all the figures you've given us and

it's still much as we outlined in our first letter to Mrs Graham, with a few subtle alterations that should make you feel more comfortable. To start with, the house is yours. You made the down payment with a lump sum of your own equity and you've paid most of the mortgage. No judge is going to insist that Mrs Graham has it, so I would suggest that you split the value down the middle, with you taking out the sum you originally put in, which is not an insubstantial amount. Of course the easy way round that is to buy Mrs Graham out, and that would be my recommendation. It would save on fees and be the easiest all-round solution. I suggest that you pay a small maintenance sum for the children, say fifty pounds each a month, and that Mrs Graham can continue to work part time. All the capital investments and your pension will, of course, stay with you.'

Gordon felt himself relax; he sat down on the edge of the bed in his towel. 'Good, nice to see you're earning your fee, Lorry. Now there's something else I'd like you to look at for me. I'm going to see my wife this afternoon to tell her that I'm thinking of considering a reconciliation, but there might be a slight possibility that she will be difficult and I want to cover myself just in case. I'd like you to look into me having custody of the children.'

'Custody? But I thought in our initial meeting you didn't want to apply for custody.'

'I don't particularly. Let's just say it would be my bargaining tool. I'd like you to look into the whole thing and particularly into Mrs Graham's fitness for sole custody. And I'd like you to prepare a letter to her to that effect.'

'I see.' Lorry Keen was known as a sharp matrimonial lawyer, one of the best, but he never played dirty. He didn't like the sound of this. 'Are you sure this is the best way to approach a reconciliation?'

'I think that's my business, don't you? I'll approach a reconciliation with my wife any way I choose, Lorry.'

'Of course, it's just that in my experience . . .'

Gordon cut him off. 'I'm not interested in your experience, only your legal expertise. Please do as I've instructed.'

'Fine. I'll get on to it right away,' Lorry replied, without enthusiasm.

'Excellent. Can you courier a copy round to my office this morning?'

'Of course.'

'And have one ready for Mrs Graham, which I'd like sent registered post, should things not work out the way I planned.'

'Right.'

'Thank you, Lorry.' Gordon hung up. He stood, glanced at himself in the full-length mirror on the wall, and straightened, throwing his shoulders back and sucking his stomach in. He wasn't bad-looking for his age, he was certainly virile – so Eve always told him – and he still had all his own hair. Lotte would be insane to turn him down this afternoon, it was almost unthinkable. Still, if she did, then he was ready. He smiled, checking his gums, then went into the bathroom to shower. His mood had definitely improved.

Half an hour later he was dressed and ready to go, deciding to get his breakfast on the way. He left the house humming, and it was only when he got to the sandwich bar in the City and ordered his toast and coffee to go that he realized he had only shaved one half of his face.

Leo arrived early at Lotte's because he hadn't been able to get her on the mobile and was worried about her. Meg had told him not to fret, but he knew that was her acting cool, so he dressed and had left the house by eight, telling her that he'd grab some toast with Lotte or might even take them all out for breakfast to the transport caff on the side of the A361.

When he got there, the lodge was in darkness. He knocked, knowing that Freddie and Milly never slept late, then went round the back to see if he could find any sign of life. He could smell a bonfire, heard shouting and wandered down to the end of the garden where the smoke was coming from.

'Hello? Lotte?' he shouted. 'Anyone home?' He walked around a clump of bushes and saw all three of them seated on logs around a small bonfire.

'Hello, Leo! No, no one's home, we've all had to abandon home because the cooker's broken down, the shower leaked and came through the wall, making my bedroom all damp, and we've been bitten to bits.' She smiled resolutely and pointed to three red lumps on her face. 'My mozzie net must have had a hole in it because the buggers had a feast last night. You should see my bum! Come and sit down, we're cooking sausages.'

'So I can see.'

Freddie and Milly both held long sticks spearing sausages that they were supposed to be holding over the flames but inevitably had let sink into the hot coals.

'We've got eggs too, haven't we, guys?'

'Yes,' Milly said. 'It's like being a Girl Guide.'

Lotte pulled a face behind her back that indicated she hadn't a clue how Milly could possibly know what being a Girl Guide was like, and Leo laughed. This Lotte, this sensible, coping, smiling-in-the-face-of-disaster Lotte, was hardly recognizable from the woman he once knew.

'You must have been up early,' Leo said.

'The damp,' Lotte said. She glanced over her shoulder and lowered her voice. 'Also, I heard a car.' She looked uneasy for a few moments and Leo picked up on it.

'So?'

'It was Phil, the chap who helps Lady Beatty on the estate. He was down at the water and, well, it gave me the creeps a bit, to be honest.'

'He was probably fishing,' Leo said. 'I should think he's got fishing rights as part of his job.'

'Of course, I should have thought of that.' Lotte was suddenly visibly relieved. 'So you think that's what it was, fishing?'

'Yes, I'd have thought so; fishermen often get up at some godforsaken hour to catch the first bite. Never understood it myself, wanting to leave a nice warm bed for a damp, cold stool by the side of a river or lake or whatever, but then perhaps they're not married to Meg.'

Lotte smiled. If she ever did the marriage thing again, although it was highly unlikely, she would look for someone like Leo. 'Breakfast,' she announced, 'I'm starving.' She took a frying pan from her basket, and a small pan stand, which she placed on the fire. She melted some butter in the pan and opened a box of eggs. 'So what brings you down here, Leo?' she asked, cracking an egg into the pan. 'At eight thirty in the morning?'

'We couldn't get you on the mobile, I think your battery must have gone, and we were fretting. Or rather I was, Meg was quite calm.'

Lotte smiled, reached out and squeezed his hand. 'Thanks, Leo. One egg or two?'

'One, please.' Leo sat down on an upturned log. 'Lotte, I had a call from Gordon yesterday.'

Lotte stopped what she was doing and faced him. 'And?'

322

'And he asked for your address here. I'm afraid that I had to give it to him. He got a bit shirty.'

She put her head down and concentrated on cracking the eggs into the pan.

'I'm sorry,' Leo said, 'I just didn't think that I had any choice.'

'No, you probably didn't. His lawyers'll be sending another letter, then, suing me, or taking me to the cleaners.' She looked up and Leo saw how genuinely upset she was.

'You would have to face it some time, Lotte, better sooner than later.'

She shook her head. 'I was just hoping for a bit of a let-up, that's all, until I found my feet, felt a bit more secure.'

Leo patted her shoulder. 'Looks to me as if you've more than found your feet, Lotte. Don't let Gordon get you down; get to him first.'

'How? How on earth would I ever get to someone like Gordon?'

Leo looked at her. 'Find his weakness. Everyone has one.'

Lotte shrugged. 'If only,' she murmured. She took a spoon from the basket and basted the eggs with the fat. 'Right, I think they're ready.' Taking the pan from the fire, she arranged some slices of bread and butter on three plates, then slipped an egg on to each one. 'Sausages!' she called. Milly brought her stick over and Lotte forked the sausage off it on to her plate. She cut it up, then passed it to Milly. 'Freddie?' Freddie came over with a rather burnt offering, and Lotte said: 'Hmmm, looks yummy, Freddie.' She cut it up for him and put it into a bowl, then took a bottle of ketchup from her basket and squirted some on to his sausage. 'Bread and butter, darling?' He nodded, and she cut a piece into small squares for him. He carried his bowl very carefully back to his little seat and she served Leo and herself. The remainder of the sausages Lotte had cooked for herself on a stick and they were fat and juicy.

Leo, never allowed fried eggs at home, tucked in with relish. Between mouthfuls he said: 'Lotte, you know I never asked, but Meg did tell me that the woman Gordon was having an affair with worked for him, is that right?'

Lotte had lost her appetite and moved the food aimlessly round her plate. 'Yes,' she replied. 'Although how he got away with it I have no idea. His firm are particularly stuffy about that sort of thing, I'm surprised he . . .' She stopped. Senior partners having affairs with junior staff, opening themselves up for misconduct, for breach of client confidentiality, for sexual harassment allegations; it was a sackable offence. She looked up at Leo. 'Gordon's work is his life, and yet he risked all of it for an affair.' She shook her head and suddenly smiled. 'You didn't come here this morning just because you were worried, did you?'

Leo waved his hand in the air dismissively, but he did grin.

'You're a genius,' Lotte said. 'That's his weakness, that's Gordon's Achilles heel. You've seen it, haven't you? No one knows about him and Eve Francis, not a single person, except me. But of course, if they did, if one of the other partners got to find out that she'd had a rather rapid rise within the firm, then Gordon would be in deep trouble. Actually, he'd probably be sacked.' She speared a piece of sausage with her fork. 'And nothing on earth could be worse!'

Meg was washing up the remains of last night's supper when she heard Leo's car pull up in the drive. He had been gone quite some time and she'd been worried. She went to the front door and saw Lotte climb out of the car. She was

324

grubby, her clothes were creased, she had some nasty bites on her face and she looked completely exhausted. Here we go again, Meg thought, we're going to have to bail her out again. The children climbed out after her and ran up to Meg. They were dressed, but their clothes were damp and they too were dirty and scruffy. 'Come on in,' Meg called, 'I'll get you some breakfast.' The children ran inside and Leo followed them, kissing Meg on the way in.

'We've eaten,' he said. 'Lotte cooked sausages over a camp fire, with fried eggs and bread and butter.'

Meg raised an eyebrow. 'She did?'

Lotte came after Leo carrying a file in her arms. 'Where's the rest?' Meg asked.

'The rest of what?'

'Your stuff.'

'Back at the cottage,' Lotte answered. She looked at her mother, then said: 'I'm not stopping, Mum. The lodge may be damp, cold, mosquito-ridden and bloody uncomfortable, but it's home and we'll get used to it.' She went into the hall. 'Leo said I could use the phone, d'you mind?'

'No, of course not.' Meg looked questioningly at Leo as Lotte disappeared into the office.

'She's getting her life back,' Leo said, 'bit by bit.'

'Maybe,' Meg remarked.

Leo shook his head. 'There's no maybe about it, Meg. I don't know what it was that kick-started her, but now she's on a roll, nothing will stop her.'

'Except Gordon.'

Leo turned to her. 'No, not even Gordon,' he said, and this time Meg really believed he might be right.

Gordon knew the presentation was going well; he could feel it, feel the energy in the room. He was in his element, in control, he had every single person in that meeting eating out of the palm of his hand and it felt good. It felt very good indeed. Gordon got off on power, he knew how to win it and how to keep it, and as one of the top fee-earners in the partnership, he also knew how to assert it. He pressed the buzzer on his intercom, this time holding his finger down for a good ten seconds, before looking round the table and saying: 'My secretary doesn't seem to be answering her phone, but if you'll excuse me for a short while, I'll just go and fetch the relevant file and we can get right up to date on those latest figures.' He smiled, then left the room.

Outside in the corridor, he took a deep breath to try and calm his sudden irascible anger, then stormed into his secretary's office and demanded to know why she had just spent half an hour on the phone.

'That's company time and money you're wasting!' he said coldly. 'And I've had to interrupt what I was doing and come out here and speak to you personally because your telephone was permanently engaged.'

'The exercise'll do you good,' Jesse, his secretary, muttered under her breath. She didn't like her boss; he might be brilliant, but he was a bully, and she didn't let men like him get the better of her.

'I'm sorry?' Gordon snapped. 'If you want to address a comment to me, then please have the courtesy to say it loud enough for me to hear. If you don't, then keep quiet!' He had walked across to her desk and was rifling through her papers.

'Excuse me?' she said. 'Can I help you?'

'I'm looking for the UTAH file. It should have been in with the other files for this meeting but it wasn't. Where the hell is it?'

Jesse stood. She leant across her desk to an in-tray marked *Urgent* and picked the top file up off the pile of papers. 'I put it out for you this morning. I'm sorry you missed it,' she said.

Gordon took the file and headed back to his meeting. 'By the way,' he said from the doorway, 'if you do have to make personal calls, then do it in your own time. Using company time for private conversations is tantamount to theft.'

'This wasn't personal,' Jesse said. She smiled; she had been waiting for this moment since she'd put the phone down. 'This was business. It was your wife on the phone.'

Gordon's face drained of all colour. 'My wife? Why didn't you let me know?'

'Because she wanted to speak to me,' Jesse replied. 'Don't worry, Gordon, I've always been a loyal employee. For the moment, my lips are sealed.'

'What the hell . . .' The phone rang and cut Gordon off. Jesse answered it and said: 'Oh, Miss Francis, yes, of course he's here, hang on a moment, I'll transfer you right away. Gordon would hate me to keep you waiting.' She glanced up as Gordon went into his office and slammed the door after him, then she smiled again. Revenge is sweet, she thought, and God bless Lotte.

Annie Taylor was not in the office for the policy meeting at nine that morning, and DS Coulter made a note of it. It wasn't that she had overslept; indeed, she had been up at five and at seven had taken a drive on to the university campus, where she'd parked the car and had a good look at a local map. She had started at Claire Thompson's hall of residence and walked the indirect route into town, down by the canal. She'd wandered round town, looking at the

327

sorts of places that the students at the university hung out at, then she'd gone back to the canal path and carried on walking it. If I were drunk, she told herself, a bit stoned and pretty out of it, I think I'd probably just keep walking. Annie wasn't a prude; she'd smoked the odd joint in her time, and she certainly liked vodka enough to know what the bottom of the bottle felt like. She walked on, convinced that that was what Claire would have done, down past the warehouses, the offices, the electronics factory, and finally sat down on a bench opposite the lock. She had been putting off until now the idea of dragging the bottom of the canal, but it had to be considered. Claire could well have slipped and fallen; she could have been pushed, but that wouldn't of course explain the appearance of her purse in Shorebridge.

Annie took out her map and looked at it again. She thought about what Jerry Coulter had said last night, about how everyone assumed that it was Meredith and it was only a question of being able to pin the crime on him, and it made her blood boil. Well, she wasn't assuming anything; she was going to make damn sure that she'd covered every angle before she charged a man with murder. That was why she was here at eight forty-five this morning, trying to rethink a crime, trying to re-evaluate all the conclusions that had already been drawn. There was very little evidence: a blood-stained purse; a few witness statements; a possible siting of Meredith's car in Shorebridge; a possible siting of him in a bar in London with a woman, maybe Claire, maybe not; a lack of alibi. What did that all amount to? It would seem to her colleagues, guilt. To Annie it amounted to more hard work.

She put the map away and had a good look round. This whole place was dismal, dark and depressing. What if Claire, too drunk and stoned to think clearly, too depressed by drugs and loneliness, had simply taken her own life? Annie decided to walk on, see where the path ended up, then head back to the office and break the news that she wasn't happy. There was going to be trouble, she thought, standing, but it was better now than in six months' time when their case fell apart or they'd convicted the wrong man. The next step was a reconstruction down here, then a possible door-to-door of the area. Someone, somewhere had to have seen Claire Thompson on the night she disappeared, on her own or with Meredith. Shit, the Super was going to love that! Annie walked on. Bugger the Super; while there was a chance, no matter how slim, that Claire Thompson was still alive, the case deserved every ounce of her commitment.

After she had made her calls, Lotte took the children home. She had been promised a new cooker by Lady Beatty that afternoon, and she now had some ammunition for dealing with Gordon. It was a good morning's work, she thought, pulling up outside the lodge, and by the looks of it, with Phil Granger's car already there, it was about to get better. She climbed out and unstrapped Milly, leaving a sleeping Freddie where he was. She went into the house, put Milly down and stopped. She had expected Phil to be in the bathroom, fixing the shower, but a movement from the bedroom put her on alert. She took a step forward and saw a shadow. 'Phil?' She felt a rush of panic. 'Phil? Is that you?'

Phil emerged from the bedroom and Lotte said: 'What were you doing in there?'

'Nothing,' he said. He was flushed and avoided her eye.

'Nothing? Then why were you in there?' Lotte was suddenly angry. 'Please, Phil, answer me. What were you doing in my bedroom?'

'I was checking the damp on the wall from the shower,'

Phil mumbled. His hands shook and he shoved them into the pockets of his jeans.

Lotte calmed. She walked into the bedroom and saw that the bed covers had been ruffled, as if someone had stood or sat on them; the damp was directly behind the bed. 'OK,' she said, coming back into the hall. 'Fine. Any luck with the leak?'

'It wasn't the shower, it was one of the water pipes, it had a hole in it, and when you were running the bath the water was seeping out. It's taken a couple of days to come through the wall, that's all, but it's fixed now. The plaster has to dry out, and when that's done I'll put a fresh coat of paint over the damp.'

'Right, well, thanks.' Lotte was uncomfortable; she wanted Phil out of her house. 'I'll let you get on,' she said. 'You must be busy.'

Phil shrugged. He stared at her and she felt herself begin to blush. Willing herself to speak, she took a deep breath and said: 'I must get on myself, Phil. Thank you, I won't keep you.' She went to the front door and opened it a bit wider, standing there waiting for him to leave.

He shuffled towards the door. 'I'll have to come back to fit the cooker,' he muttered.

'Fine,' Lotte said brightly. 'I'm sure Lady Beatty will let you know when she's bringing it up.' She closed the door behind him and leant against it, letting out a huge sigh of relief.

'What's the matter, Mummy?' Milly asked.

'Another small step for man,' she answered, 'but a giant leap for Lotte.' Then she smiled.

Annie Taylor called a policy meeting as soon as she got back into the office. She assembled her team, having called

330

them earlier to give them some indication of what she was thinking, grabbed herself a coffee and sat down in the meeting room.

'Carol's in London, is that right?'

DC Allen Gorden said: 'She left at eight with an up-to-date photo of Claire. She should be calling in about now.'

'Great.'

'You don't sound very convinced,' DS Brown said.

Annie didn't expect a positive ID on Claire from the bar in London, but she was willing to be surprised. 'Let's wait and see, shall we?'

'Sounds to me like you've already written Meredith out of the investigation.'

Annie looked at him. 'Do I detect a note of criticism, Steve? Is there something you want to share with me?'

Steve Brown hesitated for a moment, then said: 'I think you're wrong going in another direction. We've all been talking and Jerry Coulter said that you're acting on gut feeling, on instinct, that you told him as much. I'm sorry, boss, but I think, I mean we all think Meredith's the man and you've lost your grip on things. You think that because Meredith is educated, middle class that he's not capable of abducting or murdering a young girl, don't you?' Steve was angry, his voice choked with antagonism.

Annie took her time to answer. How could she have been so bloody stupid? So Coulter had come to apologize, had he? In reality he'd come to get a quote that he could bandy around the nick to make her look irresponsible and unprofessional. God, she was an idiot! She took a deep breath. No, she wasn't an idiot; he was a jealous, resentful git who had set out to undermine her, and people like that were single-minded and ruthless in their pursuit. 'I don't think anything yet,' she said calmly, 'and I don't rush around doing things on whims or gut feelings, Steve. I would hope that you of all people would know by now how thorough I am.' She clasped her hands together; they were shaking. 'I am trying another route, that's all. Everything is as it was.'

'Then why haven't we brought Meredith in again for questioning?'

'I haven't ruled that out.'

'Haven't you?'

'No.' Annie sat back in her chair. 'Look,' she said, 'I don't know who's fed you this duff line about me going off on another tangent, but I think we need a reconstruction and I think that we need a search of the area backing on to the canal walk that Claire took. If anything, that will give us more evidence against Meredith, make the case stronger, not weaker.'

'How do you know she took it?'

'I don't. Let's say it's an educated guess. I've been down there this morning, it's a rat run for the students into town and I don't think Claire, stoned and a bit pissed as she was, would have taken the main road. I want to investigate it, that's all, and until we've established where Meredith was on the Tuesday in question, I don't want to bring him in again and batter him. So for the moment we're stuck. We need to wait on Meredith, all right?'

Annie's voice was clipped and DS Brown put his head down. He would have argued further, but DS Coulter reckoned they should go higher if they weren't satisfied, said he'd already spoken to the Super himself.

'Right then, actions. I want to know as soon as we get anything from Carol, and I want the blood samples chased. I am going to speak to the Super about a reconstruction for this evening and I want everyone involved in that. OK?'

Annie stood up. 'We'll meet again at lunchtime,' she said. 'Call me when you hear from Carol.'

Annie had to wait to see the Super; he was in a meeting and she had to take her turn. When she did see him he was dismissive.

'I can't see why you want a reconstruction at this point, Annie. Shouldn't we wait until we know exactly where we stand with Meredith?'

'And if Meredith didn't do it, sir,' Annie said, 'then we've lost valuable time. Claire Thompson might still be alive. I don't think we've got time to waste.'

The Superintendent shook his head. 'You think Meredith's innocent, is that right?'

'I don't know yet, sir.'

'Because there are several members of CID who aren't at all happy about this, Annie.'

'Tales out of school?'

'Loss of confidence. The one thing you cannot do is work without your team, and this is the second time on this case that I've had to speak to you about it.'

'The first time I was right, though, wasn't I?'

'Yes, but . . .'

'But this is an expensive mistake, we're sure we've already got the right man, your team don't agree with you . . .' Annie shrugged. 'I know all the arguments, sir, but it's important that we do this, because if Claire did take that route then someone is bound to have seen her. It was a spring evening, light, and the perfect dog-walking time. I'm not convinced about Meredith, I'm not sure that first impressions, which is what we're all going on, are right. I need more.'

The Superintendent said: 'OK, you've got more. Make

sure that you get results, though, DI Taylor, or I'll have egg on my face.'

Annie smiled as she left the room. Somehow the image of the Super with egg on his face didn't quite add up.

Carol Pinto sat with the barman in a small interview room at Pimlico nick and asked him to take one last look at the picture. 'Sometimes it helps if you turn it over, clear your mind for a few minutes, then turn it back,' she said.

'Right.' There was a short silence, then the barman flipped the photo of Claire back over and stared at it again. He shook his head. 'I'm sorry,' he said. 'It does look like the woman in as much as she's got shoulder-length brown hair and she's quite attractive, but I couldn't be absolutely certain it was her. It was dark, it was nearly two weeks ago, she was drunk and it's amazing how different women look with all their make-up on. Erm, no offence, Officer. Sorry, but I'm just not sure.'

Carol nodded. 'Would you mind making a statement to one of the officers much to that effect while I just pop out and call my boss?'

'Of course not.' The barman picked up the photo and held it. 'Shame. Pretty girl. Sorry I couldn't be more helpful,' he said.

DC Pinto shrugged, then she left the room and called DI Taylor.

Annie was on her way out to the streets adjacent to the canal walk when she got DC Pinto's call.

'Could be Claire,' she said to DS Brown. 'The barman thinks it could be her, but he isn't sure. He wouldn't like to say for certain.'

'Cop-out?'

334

'More the other way, I'd have said. He doesn't think it's her, but he doesn't want to disappoint anyone. If he dismisses the picture out of hand as not her, he gets sent home right away; if he's not sure he gets more attention. Basic human psychology.'

'Basic human cynicism,' DS Brown said.

Annie glanced sidelong at him. She didn't retaliate, but she did reckon on a quiet word with DS Jerry Coulter sometime in the near future, if she could stomach it. They drove on in silence.

Gordon decided to drive down to see Lotte after lunch. The partners' lunches were excellent, and as he didn't know where his next meal was coming from, it was best to stock up while he had the chance. He ate well, tucked the letter for Lotte from his solicitor into his pocket and left the office about two. He would get to Lotte around four thirty, and if he was lucky and things went as well as he expected, then he might even get her home by dinner time and look forward to his life getting back on a level again. It would certainly be nice to have some home-cooked food, and with this in mind, he set out to woo his wife.

Charles had put off going to see the lodge, and of course the woman whose name he still didn't know; he didn't have the nerve. He went to the gym instead – anything to fill the time now he wasn't working – had lunch in a café and finally set out for Ludwell Ponds mid-afternoon. He was lonely, miserable and afraid. His life had suddenly slipped further into chaos than he could ever have imagined possible, and all he could think about as he drove in the direction of Birley and out into the rolling open countryside was Claire Thompson; about her loneliness, her isolation and despair. All those months he had seen her in lectures, in tutorials, withdrawn, not socializing, and yet he had never given her any real thought or concern. Was he really that indifferent to other people's lives? Was he really that smug about his own? Had she felt like he did now, set apart, disliked, not trusted? Had she loved him like he loved this woman, this wonderful, wretched woman who wanted nothing to do with him? Had she worried that she might not have a future? Why hadn't he ever thought to ask her? Perhaps if he had he might not be in the vulnerable position he was in now. More importantly, perhaps if he had, he might have been able to save her.

Chapter 24

After lunch, a picnic in the garden, with Lotte thankful that the weather was holding, Milly and Freddie went down for a nap and Lotte had an hour or so to herself. Usually at home she got on with some work, or tidied – Gordon had been fanatical about a tidy house. The last week at Meg's she had spent the afternoons trying to keep on top of the mess that the children made so that it didn't upset Leo; but here, in her own small, scruffy home, she felt no urgency to do anything at all, no washing-up from lunch, certainly no tidying. She could just please herself, and that was exactly what she did.

She got a step ladder from the store at the side of the house, put it up right under the hatch in the ceiling that opened into the roof space, and, armed with a powerful torch, climbed up. She forced the hatch with both hands and it sprang open, sending a cloud of dust down. Lotte coughed, rubbed her eyes, tasted grit and spat it into her handkerchief. She climbed up a few more steps and shone the torch inside, her heart beating and her whole body poised to flee if she saw anything that frightened her. There was nothing. It was an attic space that been laid with flooring and filled with boxes and trunks, some of which looked as if they'd been there for ever.

Lotte climbed down, went to the kitchen and took the flashlight that she kept there, along with a couple of lanterns that she used for the garden. She went back to the ladder, climbed up it and laid the flashlight on the ground. She switched the lamp to diffuse rather than beam and it lit up the space. Then she lit the lanterns and put one at each end of the attic. It was dim in there, but she had enough light to see by. Having a really good long look all around first, to check for small furry friends or giant spiders, Lotte saw that she was alone, apart from lots and lots of redundant webs, and moved towards the first trunk.

It was pine, with a rusty brass lock, but it was open, so she lifted the lid. Inside were clothes layered with tissue paper. There was a smell: dust, obviously, but something faint, almost imperceptible. She sniffed. It was lavender, faded, crumbling, ancient lavender. Moving the first layer of tissue aside, Lotte took out the top garment, made from soft, yellowing lawn cotton, delicately sewn with lace. It was a baby's nightdress, pin-tucked on the bodice, long, with tiny hand-sewn sleeves. She fingered the work on it, the intricate, loving work, and it made her heart ache. Gently she went through the layers of clothes, all made for an infant, all unused, and she thought about how much pain and grief there was in this trunk alone and thanked God for her own babies. Then she replaced everything exactly as she had found it and closed the lid of the trunk, moving on to the next one.

It was a sort of plan chest. She opened it and lifted out the first tray of plans. She took them over to the lamp and put them on the floor so that she could see them more clearly. They were plans of the lodge, Victorian plans, with a detailed land survey of the ponds and the copse, all beautifully drawn by hand. They fascinated Lotte. She would take them downstairs and have a really good look at them now; she could go back to the attic tomorrow. Closing the hatch, Lotte replaced the step ladder in the store house and took the plans outside into the sunshine. She laid them on the garden table, securing each end with a stone, then bent over them and began to read.

For the second time in just twenty-four hours, Charles walked to the lodge at Ludwell Ponds on foot, retracing the steps that Daisy and Henry had taken, both together and apart. This time, though, he knew that what was there represented all that he wanted and couldn't have; the parallel with Daisy and Henry was almost ironic. It was a beautiful afternoon and that made it worse somehow, heightened his sense of loss. He ducked through the gap in the hedge and into the gardens of the lodge, and he saw her up on the small terrace, standing at the table, bent over, reading something, her body tense in concentration. She was beautiful, to him. He stood and looked at her. What is it, he wondered, that makes us fall in love? What small, insignificant, intangible thing is it about one person that changes everything? Why does it happen and why, when we are masters of so much, can we not direct this?

He stood where he was for some time, longing to speak to her and yet dreading making contact. Then he walked towards her, knowing that she alone could change his life if she chose to.

Lotte glanced up as a shadow fell across the plans.

'I'm sorry, I startled you,' Charles said.

She put her hand up to her eyes to shield them from the bright sun, but she didn't tell him that she had known he was there, that she had glanced sidelong moments earlier and seen him walking towards her. She didn't tell him that she hadn't known what to do, that she had wanted him to come, but was afraid of what he would bring.

'How are you?'

'Fine.'

'I hope you didn't mind me coming, I sort of had to.' Charles stared at her to see if there was anything in her eyes that might give him hope, but she looked away.

Lotte twisted a strand of hair round her finger and thought: why does he have such an effect on me? I hardly know him and yet when he looks at me I want to run, run as far from him as I can. And then she thought: but what if he didn't come after me?

Charles glanced at the papers. 'What have you got there?'

'I found them just now, tucked away in the attic. They're plans for the lodge and a survey of the land.' Lotte went back to them. 'They're amazing, so detailed and beautifully drawn. Look, here, I didn't realize that the land belonging to the lodge goes right down to the water's edge. There's a little boathouse here, just on the edge of the ponds.' Lotte pointed to the map. 'I've never seen it, I don't know if it's still there, but it must be smothered by rushes now. No one's lived here for over a year.'

'My God, it's fascinating.' Charles moved round the table. 'D'you mind if I have a look?'

Lotte moved aside, but only fractionally, and their bodies were almost touching.

'These are working drawings, they're dated 1896, the year that Henry and Daisy had their affair. Henry Chatten had some drawings made for alterations to the lodge for Daisy; these must be them.' Charles looked up at her. 'Where exactly did you find them?'

'In a plan chest in the attic. Why? Are they important?'

'I don't know if they're important, but they're certainly

340

a great find!' Charles looked at them again. 'I can't believe all this!' He shook his head, then turned to Lotte. 'I would thank you formally, of course, but I'm afraid that even now I don't know your name.'

Lotte suddenly laughed. 'That,' she said, 'is ridiculous. We spent the night together, you've been looking for me ever since and yet you don't know my name! How very remiss of me. I am sorry. My name is Lotte, Lotte Graham.'

She held out her hand, still laughing, and Charles took it. He held it for a few moments and felt the same weird sensation that he had felt the first time he met her. He held her hand and he knew that he didn't want to let go of it, that he could have held it for ever. 'I am very pleased to meet you, Lotte Graham.' He smiled. 'In fact, I'm delighted.'

Gordon had gone past the turning to the lodge several times and only just managed to find it on his fourth trip up the lane because he slowed to a crawl and inspected the hedgerow for any gap that might be a track. He drove up it in a thoroughly bad mood, in desperate need of a pee and a cup of tea. Halfway along he stopped. He could see directly into the garden and the back of the house and he could see his wife, his Lotte, standing with a tall and not unattractive man and laughing. Laughing, relaxed and beautiful. Of course she was beautiful, he would never have married an old dog, but why hadn't he seen it before? She was amazing, stunning: wild auburn hair and a smile that promised so much. He stopped the car, left it where it was and climbed out. He had a pain in his chest, an acute, sharp pain, and as he walked toward the terrace and heard her voice, as happy as her laughter had been, he knew the pain was loss, loss and jealousy.

'Lotte!' His voice was harsh with the anger that sprang

up out of his jealousy. 'What the hell is going on? Where are the children? Who is this man?'

Lotte's face crumpled. She turned away to cover the shock and embarrassment of being humiliated in this way.

'Children?' Charles said.

'Yes, children!' Gordon snapped. 'We have two children and I want to know where they are.'

'They're asleep,' Lotte murmured, 'having a nap. I've . . .'

'You've what? Forgotten about them? It wouldn't be the first time, Lotte, and it certainly won't be the last, that's for sure. I've got a letter here from my solicitors and they are seriously doubting your suitability for custody. In fact . . .'

'In fact,' Charles interrupted, 'I don't think you should be shouting like this. If your children are asleep then surely you don't want to wake them.'

'I beg your pardon? Who asked for your opinion?'

'No one, but if Lotte can't stick up for herself, then someone needs to . . .'

'Who said I can't stick up for myself!' Lotte suddenly cried. 'Hmmm? Who? I can stick up for myself perfectly all right, thank you very much, without any interference from you, so I suggest you bugger off and leave me to it!' She turned to Gordon. 'And as for suitability for custody, I don't think you have a leg to stand on, Gordon! You can't cook, you can't clean, you certainly can't work the washing machine. You have no idea what Milly likes to eat or read or play with and you've never changed a dirty nappy in your life, so how in God's name would you look after Freddie? But apart from all that, apart from your complete ineptness as a father, husband and person, you have been humping one of your team for three years; all the time I was pregnant and having Freddie you were out getting your leg over, and I have to say that I don't think that

342

makes you fit to even speak to the children, let alone look after them. Plus . . .' Lotte was out of breath. Never, never in her life before had she said so much, with such venom, to her husband. 'Plus, if you're sacked, which you may well be if I decide to inform some of the other partners about Miss Francis's rapid promotion in the firm, then you won't have time to look after the children, because you'll be looking for work. Don't threaten me with custody, Gordon, because if you do then I will threaten you right back!' She stopped, her face crimson, her eyes wet with tears. She looked at Gordon, at Charles, then she turned on her heel and walked into the house, slamming the door behind her.

Charles hung his head. He dug his hands in his pockets and felt completely sheepish. He waited for a few minutes to see if Lotte reappeared again, but when she didn't, he turned and walked away. He heard Gordon leave too; he heard his car start and drive off, and he loitered for a few minutes more, out by the pond, wondering whether to go back or not. He decided against it – she wouldn't want to see him anyway – and set off for his car. So, she had children. Charles was stunned. In all his thoughts on love and the nature of relationships, in all his longing for this woman, he had never once given a moment's consideration to the fact that she might have children. Absolutely not. He had expected love, then perhaps to have to win her over, but Charles had never, ever expected children. And now he'd got them, he wasn't sure how he was going to deal with them.

Annie Taylor was down by the canal with two uniformed officers, making arrangements for the reconstruction. They had decided to re-enact the scene twice, once in about an hour, around six; and once later, at the time that Claire would have been walking into town, around eight thirty, nine o'clock. A WPC, dressed in the sort of clothes Claire's friend remembered her wearing, was hanging around, chatting to a couple of other officers while Annie and DS Brown worked out the logistics of the operation with the team. Annie was convinced this would jog a memory somewhere; she had to be, a lot was riding on it.

Cat Collins was walking her children home from swimming lessons; they swam Monday nights, and like everything else, she walked them to the pool and back because Jeff had the car. She stopped in town to pick up a bit of shopping and saw a friend.

'Did you come by the canal path?' the friend asked.

'No, not today. It's a bit longer and the kids are knackered.' Cat glanced at her children, engrossed in bags of Frazzles, and smiled. 'Why?'

'The police are down there doing a reconstruction. Apparently a student's gone missing and they think she's been abducted. It was in the paper at the weekend, didn't you see it?'

'Nah, I never read the paper, haven't got time.'

'She went missing from the canal path, they think. Poor girl, she's only eighteen apparently.'

Cat shuddered; that could be her daughter. She never used to be like this, but since she'd had the kids it was the first thing she thought of when she heard something terrible. 'When did she go missing?'

'A couple of weeks ago. One of the PCs down there was talking about dragging the canal next.'

'God, poor girl. Poor parents.' Cat reached out and stroked Kylie's hair. 'Who was she? Was she local?'

'No, a student up at the university. Claire Thompson. I can't stop thinking about her, it makes me . . . Cat?'

Cat was striding off. She had taken both children's hands in her own and marched away as fast as a five- and a seven-year-old, two swimming bags and two bags of Frazzles would allow her.

'Cat? You all right?' her friend called after her.

Cat waved and carried on walking. They made it home in ten minutes, a record, and she dumped everything in the hall and scrambled frantically in the coats cupboard for her scarf. She found it, pulled it out and looked at the name tape on the bottom right-hand corner. Claire Thompson. Of course she'd know the name; she'd been wearing the scarf for the past two weeks. She went to the phone and immediately rang the police.

Annie was on her way back from the canal when the call came through. She diverted to Cat Collins' home address and was there five minutes later. The squad car pulled up outside a neat semi in one of the grottier housing estates in town and Annie climbed out. Curtains twitched.

Cat opened the door, Annie went in.

'So you found the scarf in the pub you clean, is that right?'

'Yes.'

'Can you remember when?'

'A week last Wednesday. I found it and took it. People rarely claim things like scarves from pubs.'

'Of course not. The pub is called the Black Ferret, is that right?'

Cat nodded.

'Can you confirm the address?'

She gave the address of the pub.

'Do you clean there every day?'

'Yes, every morning before the kids go to school.'

'And the scarf wasn't there on Tuesday morning?'

'No.'

'Are you sure of that?'

'Yes. I do a thorough clean every morning. I found the scarf on Wednesday morning and I reckoned it'd been dropped on Tuesday night.'

'Right, thank you, Mrs Collins, I appreciate you coming forward with this.'

Annie took the scarf and dropped it into a bag. It would be useless, of course, but procedure had to be followed. She left the house and got on the phone in the car.

'Steve, I want you to check out the pub and the whole area. Interview the landlord and his staff, take a team with you. The pub's also next door to the electronics factory, as far as I can remember from this morning. Check out the factory and see if they've got any CCTV for security. There might be something on it. I'm going to get Meredith in again for questioning now and I want to search his car.' She hung up. 'Back to the nick,' she told the driver. 'I have a feeling it's going to be a long night.'

Charles was at his desk when he heard someone at the front door. He went to the window, saw the squad car outside and slipped his shoes on before going to answer the door. He had been expecting this.

'Mr Meredith?'

'Yes.' Charles was older than both of the officers, but it didn't give him any superiority; quite the reverse.

'Would you mind accompanying us down to the station, sir?'

'No, that's fine. Hang on, let me switch off my PC.' As

346

he went into his study, he glanced behind him to see one of the officers just in the doorway, watching him. He switched his machine off.

'Would you mind coming with us in the car and giving your keys to PC Ryan here. He'll drive your car to the station, if that's all right; we'd like to have a good look at it.'

Charles swallowed; he hadn't been expecting this. Keep calm, he told himself, panic makes you look guilty. He handed his keys over and left the house with the two officers. Minutes later he was on his way to the station.

Chapter 25

Charles was shown into the interview room where DI Taylor and DC Pinto were waiting for him. He took a seat and DI Taylor cautioned him on tape. She asked him if he'd like a solicitor present but he declined. She then told him that he was entitled to one telephone call, which he made to Leo Chandler.

'Please go to the lodge, Leo, and ask Lotte to come down to the station. Tell her I need her to verify that we spent the night together on Tuesday the second of May.'

'Lotte? Charles, have you got the right person?'

'Yes, I have. Please, Leo, Lotte will explain it all. I need her to come down now.' He hung up and sat back down again ready for his interview.

Annie switched the tape on again. 'Interview commencing at . . .' she glanced at the clock on the wall, 'five forty-five p.m. Professor Meredith, can you tell us where you were on the night of Tuesday the second of May?'

Charles looked directly at her. 'Yes, I can. I had a row with my girlfriend, Mia Langley, and I drove up to London in a temper. I stayed the night at my brother's flat in Dolphin Square, but I wasn't alone.' He stopped and cleared his throat. 'I met a woman in a cocktail bar up the road from Dolphin Square, Gaffers it was called; we had too much to drink and I took her back to Rob's flat. We were kissing and had gone into the bedroom to make love when my brother Rob called from somewhere across the Atlantic and asked me to look some stuff up for him on his PC. It was urgent so I did this, and when I got back to the bedroom the woman had fallen asleep. We spent the night together in the same bed but nothing happened. In the morning when I woke up she had gone.'

Outwardly Annie kept her cool, but she was raging. If this was true, then why the hell hadn't he said before? 'Do you have the name of this woman?'

'Yes, it's Lotte Graham. She's on her way in now to verify what I've just said.'

Annie stood up. 'Interview interrupted at five fifty p.m.' She went to the door. 'Excuse us, please.' She motioned to Carol and they left the room.

'What the fuck's going on?' Annie said in the corridor. 'Why the fuck didn't he tell us this before? Jesus! What a fucking waste of our time. If Professor Smart Shit was in London all night, then that puts him firmly out of the frame.'

'Unless Claire was with him?'

'Not if this Lotte woman shows up she wasn't.' Annie shook her head. 'God give me patience!' She re-entered the interview room.

'Professor Meredith, might I ask you why you didn't mention any of this before? You do realize, don't you, that I could prosecute you for wasting police time?'

Charles stared down at his hands. 'I'm sorry,' he said, 'I didn't realize it would be important. I've been very confused. I've only just found out who the woman was, I didn't know her name and I had no way of tracing her. I didn't mention it because it didn't seem plausible.'

'But if it was the truth, plausible or not, Professor Meredith, you should have told us.'

Charles looked up at her. 'Sometimes the truth isn't any use, DI Taylor; no one believes it anyway.'

Annie left the room. What was the fucking point?

Up in the office, she spoke to the team dismantling Meredith's car, but there was nothing. Then she called DS Brown.

'Nothing from the pub, boss, but the factory's got hours of CCTV and they're trying to find the tape for that Tuesday. They have cameras at the front and the back, so we might be lucky.'

'Bring the tape in as soon as you've got it, OK?'

'Will do, boss.'

Annie looked at Carol Pinto. 'What now?' she asked.

'Mia Langley? What was Meredith doing in Shorebridge?'

She sighed. 'You go and ask him, Carol. I don't think I can.'

Leo drove his car right up to the lodge and climbed out. He saw Lotte in the garden, picking up toys, and called out to her.

'Hello, Leo!' She was surprised to see him. 'Is everything all right?'

'I don't know. I've just had a call from Charles Meredith.' Leo watched her face; she blinked twice, then glanced away. Lotte was too honest by nature. 'He's with the police. Apparently they think he's involved in the disappearance of one of the students up at the university, but he's told them that he has an alibi for the night she went missing. He's told them he spent the night with you.'

'With me?' Lotte turned back to Leo. 'That's ridiculous, Leo. When was this supposed to have been?'

'Tuesday the second of May. The night Meg had the children to stay. I looked it up on the calendar.'

Lotte said nothing. From inside the house Milly called out.

'They're in bed, I should go and see what's the matter.' She moved past him but Leo caught her arm.

'Lotte, Charles said he needs you to verify that you spent the night together. He is being questioned by the police. He's in trouble, Lotte, and he said you would explain it all!'

Lotte pulled her arm free. 'I can't, Leo, I just can't!' She hurried towards the house as Milly cried out again.

Leo waited. What the hell was going on? Christ, he hadn't been aware that Charles even knew Lotte, let alone had some sort of relationship with her. Was that why she had left Gordon? Was that what she was doing here? Lotte came out of the house and Leo said: 'What is going on, Lotte? Is Charles the reason you've left Gordon?'

Suddenly Lotte threw her hands up in the air. 'That's exactly it!' she cried. 'That is exactly why I won't admit to anything! All of you, everyone jumping to conclusions, the wrong conclusions! Have you any idea what Gordon would do if he knew I'd spent the night with someone? Someone I didn't know and didn't ever intend to see again? I made a mistake, that's all. Admittedly it was a mistake that made me realize that I was wasting my life with Gordon, but what if he found out? He's threatened to take the children away from me, Leo! He left a letter here this afternoon from his solicitor. I'm going to fight him, but God, I can't let this get in the way . . .' She wiped the tears that ran down her cheeks on the sleeve of her sweatshirt and left dirty stains on her face. 'I can't get involved with this, I just can't. So far I think, just about, that I've got the upper hand, and I can't afford to let that go. Please, Leo, you must understand that.'

Leo shook his head. 'Lotte,' he said, 'I don't understand

anything at the moment. I don't understand what you're doing in this insect-infested swamp, I don't understand how Gordon could have been such a stinking idiot and I don't understand one bit of this thing with Charles.' He looked at her. 'But I do understand the severity of Charles Meredith's situation. He's an innocent man and he needs you to prove that.'

'I can't.'

Leo closed his eyes for a moment. He felt suddenly very tired. 'Please, Lotte, think about it . . .'

'I can't, I just can't do it.'

He sighed. Then he turned and walked back to his car. What the hell was he going to tell Charles? He honestly had no idea.

Annie Taylor walked back into the interview room and sat down. She turned on the tape, gave the time and who was present, then said: 'Ms Graham has declined to verify your whereabouts on the second of May, Charles. Mr Leo Chandler just came in to inform us that she refuses to give you an alibi.'

'Then go and interview her!' Charles suddenly snapped. 'She was there, we were both there, we spent the night together!'

'We intend to do exactly that. We've got an officer on his way there now. But just supposing she has nothing to say, just supposing she still refuses to give you an alibi because there isn't one. What then? How are you going to prove you were in London and not out with Claire Thompson?'

Charles looked down at his hands. If he had felt the loss of Lotte hard the first time, then he felt it doubly hard now. 'Can I talk to her? Would it be possible for me to telephone her?'

'No, I'm afraid not. That could be considered coercion.'

Charles dropped his head in his hands. 'What now?' he murmured.

Annie Taylor looked at DC Pinto. 'You tell us, Professor Meredith,' she said.

Lotte parked the car and helped Milly carefully out of the back seat, then she leant in for Freddie and lifted him up on to her hip. She wondered why children always seemed to weigh more when they were asleep. She lumbered into the police station and up to the front desk, and said: 'I've come to make a statement about where Charles Meredith was on Tuesday the second of May.' Milly stood patiently beside her.

'Wait a moment, please.' The duty sergeant called up to CID. 'Could I take your name, please?'

Lotte sighed, knowing that she was about to open herself up to all sorts of recriminations. If only she didn't have to give her name. 'Lotte Graham,' she said.

'Has our officer not been out to see you, Miss Graham?'

'No, and it's Mrs Graham.' She was asked to wait; someone would be along to take her statement in a few minutes.

Charles was released at seven p.m. Lotte was waiting for him in reception. She was carrying Freddie, who had woken grumpy and disorientated, walking him round to keep him quiet. Milly lay across the plastic seats, crying and whining in a small, tired voice. Lotte looked up at him and he said: 'Thank you, for coming here, I . . .' He broke off, afraid that he would lose control of his emotions.

'I had to.'

'Did you?'

Lotte looked directly at him for the first time. 'Yes, I did.'

Freddie started crying and Lotte jiggled him up and down to calm him. Charles bent to Milly, stretched out on the seat, and gently touched her hair. 'What happened to her arm?'

'Broken, don't ask how.' Freddie's cry moved up a gear to a wail. 'I'd better get them out of here, they're exhausted.'

'Of course.'

'D'you need a lift? The sergeant said they'd impounded your car.'

'Thanks, but actually I don't really want to go home alone.' Charles couldn't look at her. 'I don't suppose I could come back with you for a drink or something, could I?'

'I have to get the children to bed.'

'Can I help?'

Lotte hesitated. 'OK. Can you carry Milly? She's dead beat and I don't think she'll make it to the car.'

'OK.' He wasn't sure quite how to carry out this request. Lotte said: 'Scoop her up and carry her across your arms.'

He did as he'd been told, fumbling with sprawling limbs and over-balancing a bit, but eventually he righted himself and stood straight. 'Where's the car?'

'Follow me.' Lotte opened the doors and went out down the steps to the car park.

'I've never done this child thing before,' Charles said, placing Milly not very comfortably on the back seat.

'You'll learn,' Lotte said. She stood straight, having strapped Freddie in, and looked directly at him. 'If you want to, that is.'

They climbed into the car and Lotte started the engine. As she went to shift into gear, Charles said: 'They told me you wouldn't agree to an alibi. What happened? I don't understand.'

'Gordon, my husband, has threatened to go for custody

354

of the children, and I was frightened to come forward. He could use this against me.'

Charles touched her arm. 'So why did you change your mind?'

Lotte took a deep breath. 'Because I knew that if I wasn't going to be true to myself, then I could never be true to anyone else.' She turned to him. 'It's a long story, but I wanted independence and I'll get it. I will not let Gordon bully me any more. I've told the truth and that matters. Besides, if he wants to fight me for my children, then let him. He hasn't seen half of what I'm capable of yet.'

Charles shook his head. 'Poor Gordon,' he remarked. And suddenly Lotte smiled. Now that she had said it, Lotte realized just how much she meant it.

'Yes,' she agreed. 'Poor Gordon indeed.'

An hour later, although he had never anticipated children as part of the parcel of love, Charles had surprised himself. He had bathed Freddie, after Lotte had first done Milly, filling the bath with boiled water from fifteen kettles because the heating and hot water had gone off; he had struggled with, and overcome, a Pampers Stay-Dry nappy, managed to fasten the poppers on what looked like a sleeping bag with arms and legs, and read two children Bob the Builder without cringing. He also filled another bath with fifteen kettles' worth for Lotte and rung the local tandoori to order them both a curry to be delivered at nine. He couldn't say that he had enjoyed the experience, but he'd done it. Charles Meredith, the man who had never wanted children, had found that what you want and what you get aren't necessarily the same thing.

That, he reckoned now, sitting with a glass of sherry – not because he liked it, but because he needed a drink and that was all he could find – was what life was all about; coming to terms with that fact. He could see, from every movement that Lotte made, every word that she spoke, that she was right for him. It was indefinable as to why, it just was; it couldn't be explained. But could he reconcile that with who she really was and the fact that the children came with her? He didn't know, and the nice thing, he thought, tipping the sherry away, was that for now he didn't really care.

'Is there anything else at all to drink?' Charles asked, as Lotte came into the small sitting room, barefoot, in jeans and a sweater. 'I could run down to the off-licence in your car if there isn't. I'm insured third party for other cars.'

'I think I might have a bottle of wine in one of the boxes I took from the house. Hang on.' She went to the corner of the room, to a pile of boxes stacked up there, rummaged around for a few minutes, then lifted a bottle out.

'Here!' She took it over and handed it to Charles. 'No corkscrew, though.'

Charles dug in his pocket and took out his Swiss army knife.

'Now I would never expect you to have that!' Lotte announced.

'True boy scout,' Charles said. He went into the kitchen, found two glasses and popped the cork on the wine. He poured and put the lot on a tray, carrying it back to Lotte. 'Shall I make a fire?'

She smiled. 'That would be wonderful. Granger put some wood in the porch.' She took a sip of her wine and watched Charles as he set about laying a fire. He was calm and measured, he took time with things. I like this man, Lotte thought, I am glad that he's here. The wine was delicious; it slipped down so easily that she had poured herself another glass by the time the fire was lit. She knelt down in front of the fireplace and looked at the flames taking hold.

'Are you OK?' he asked, turning to her.

She nodded.

'You know, what you did today was very brave. Proving my innocence.'

'Brave?' She shrugged. 'I've never done anything brave in my life. I've been a weakling and I've lived to regret it.'

Charles took her hand. 'There is no weakling inside Lotte Graham. You are strong, Lotte, but you are vulnerable too and that's what makes you so . . .' He stopped, then smiled cautiously. 'So attractive.'

Lotte took her fingers back. 'Thank you.' Then she moved away from him and sat on the sofa. It wasn't a rejection, more a warning. Get close, but not too close. Charles stood.

'Those plans you had earlier, can I have another look at them?' he asked.

'Of course.' Lotte reached over and took the papers out of a box. He came to sit beside her and spread them out on the floor. 'God, these really are amazing. They give me such a sense of who Daisy and Henry were, what this was all like. Look, plans for a bathroom. Henry must have put that in for Daisy, and another bedroom. That bedroom used to be a pantry, see?' The plans were in perfect condition and Charles wondered if the scribbled notes had been written by Henry Chatten. He went on to the next plan, of the sitting room they were in, and looked at the drawings for the fireplace. 'Look, Lotte! Henry had this made for Daisy, carved with the words *Verbum Tuum Mea Veritas*.' Charles stared at the words. 'It means, I think, something like "my word is truth" . . . No, hang on, "your word is my truth", that's it. "Your word is my truth."' He looked at her. 'That's amazing, isn't it? He must have really loved her.'

Lotte stared at it. 'It's so sad,' she said, 'that a love like that ended so miserably.'

Charles stood up. 'So this fireplace was put in when Daisy lived here.' He was looking at it, running his hands over the blackened stone. 'Here are the words; they're hardly visible now, because of the soot.' He looked at the drawings again. 'Look at this, Lotte. Does this look like it's been designed so that the mantelpiece comes off?'

Lotte peered at the plans. She shrugged. 'I've no idea, I've never been any good at design technology.' She glanced up at the fireplace. 'I honestly couldn't tell you. It looks solid enough.'

Charles stood again and ran his fingers along the edge of the mantelpiece. He couldn't find anything and at that moment the door knocker went.

'Curry,' he said. 'Let's eat.'

Lotte stood up as well. Feeling the full effects of two glasses of wine on an empty stomach, she was a bit unsteady on her feet. 'How did they find the place?' she asked.

'Very explicit instructions and the promise of a large tip,' Charles said. Lotte laughed and went into the kitchen to find plates and cutlery.

DS Brown stopped the CCTV tape. He rewound it, replayed it and let out a shout. Then he called DI Taylor. 'It's here, boss! I've got her, Claire Thompson, outside the factory on Tuesday night! Yup, that's her, a car pulls up, she leans in, then opens the door and climbs in. It's a blue . . .'

He stopped as Annie Taylor strode into the viewing room. 'Brilliant, Steve!'

DS Brown rewound the tape again and they watched it together. Annie phoned down to the CAD room. 'Hi, it's DI Taylor. Can I have the registration details of a blue Ford

Orion.' She gave the registration number. 'I need it urgently, OK?' She put the receiver back and they watched the tape again. 'She's out of it,' Steve said, 'completely out of it.'

Annie shook her head. 'Poor girl.' The phone rang and she snatched it up. 'Great! Thanks.' She looked at DS Brown. 'Come on, Steve,' she said, already on her way out of the door. 'Let's go and find Claire.'

Phil Granger was watching TV in his room when three squad cars pulled up outside his house and six police officers got out. His mother opened the door to them and followed them into a bedroom she hardly ever set foot in.

'What you done now, runt?' she called out from behind them.

Annie turned. 'If you'll excuse us, please, Mrs Granger.' She shut the door, despite the foetid air in the room. 'Philip Granger, do you own a blue Ford Orion . . .' She read out the number.

'Yeah, why?'

'I'd like you to come down to the station with us, please. Philip Granger, I am arresting you on suspicion of abduction. You do not have to say anything, but it may harm your defence if you do not mention when questioned something which you later rely on in court. Anything you do say may be given in evidence.'

Granger pushed himself up the bed until his back was against the wall. 'What the fuck's going on? What've I done?'

'Up, please. We can do this nicely or we can do it the other way. Your choice.'

Granger stood up and one of the PCs snapped some handcuffs on him. He walked out of the bedroom, past his mother and down the stairs.

'What's he done? Where you taking him?'

Annie ignored her. Downstairs she said: 'Car keys, please.'

Granger gestured towards his pocket and the officer retrieved some keys.

'One of our forensic will be driving your car to the station, where it will be impounded for investigation.' She followed everyone out and closed the door on Mrs Granger, who by now was ranting abuse at them from upstairs.

In the interview room, Annie and DS Brown sat opposite Granger and a legal aid brief. DC Pinto and a uniformed officer stood behind him. The tape was running.

'Let's just go through that again,' Annie said. 'You have never met Claire Thompson, you never picked her up in your car and you've never been to the Black Ferret. Is that right?'

'Yeah, that's right.' Granger didn't look up; he picked his nails under the table and flicked the dirt on the floor.

'So how do you explain the CCTV recording that shows her climbing into your car on Tuesday the second of May? That's two weeks ago tomorrow, just to remind you.'

Granger shrugged.

'For the benefit of the tape, Mr Granger is shrugging his shoulders.'

There was a knock on the door. DC Gorden put his head round. 'May I have a word, boss?'

'DI Taylor is leaving the room,' Steve Brown said. Annie went out into the corridor.

'They found Claire Thompson's student union card in the boot of the car, boss.' Annie shook her head. 'Along with various DNA. It's gone for testing.'

'Thanks, Allen.' She went back into the interview room.

'DI Taylor is back in the interview room,' DS Brown said.

Annie sat down. 'Well, Phil,' she said, 'we've just heard

that Claire Thompson's student union card was found in the boot of your car. Isn't that a surprise? Are you still going to maintain that you don't know her, because if you are, then we'll go ahead and charge you anyway. I think we've got enough to convict you.'

There was a silence, then the solicitor said: 'May I have a word with my client, please?'

Annie stood up and left the room with her team. A few minutes later, they were called back in.

'Interview resumed at ten thirty p.m.,' Annie said.

'My client would like to explain,' the solicitor said.

Granger chewed a fingernail, then said. 'I sometimes go to the Black Ferret with me mates, and I sometimes give students a lift home in my car. I don't know this Claire Thompson, but she could have been any number of girls I've taken home in the last month. I'm always finding things they leave behind, most of them are pissed anyways when they get in the car. I wouldn't have a clue whether it was hers or not.'

'So you may have given Claire a lift home on the night she disappeared, is that right?'

'Yeah, I might of.'

'But you can't remember.'

'Nah, nothing specific. Like I said, I take loads of 'em home from town.'

'How kind,' Annie said. She turned to the tape machine and said: 'Interview terminated at ten thirty-five p.m. Mr Granger is free to leave the station.' She switched off the tape and stood up. She could feel the shock in the room. 'If you'd like to go down to the front desk, Mr Granger, I'll arrange to have your car ready for you in about ten minutes.' She walked out of the room and waited upstairs for the place to erupt.

As DS Brown hurried into the office, she held up her hands and said: 'I want surveillance on him from the moment he leaves here. Claire Thompson is out there, and from the level of Granger's nerves, I'd say she's still alive. She's somewhere on the estate where he works and I want her found. Get on to surveillance and set it up immediately.'

'What about the Super?'

'The Superintendent isn't here, so I will take full responsibility for this decision. OK?'

DS Brown shook his head. 'You sure do earn your fucking money, boss!'

Annie raised an eyebrow. It was half a compliment, and half a one was better than what she was used to round here.

Lotte was sleepy. She had drunk more than half the bottle of wine, eaten far too much curry and was lying on the floor in front of the fire, her eyes closed, listening to Charles rustle the papers as he studied the plans yet again.

'You know, I'm convinced that there's a compartment in this fireplace. The plans look as if Henry had some sort of safe built into it.'

'Why would he do that? It's a bit James Bond, isn't it?'

'For security, perhaps? Maybe he wanted a safe place for Daisy to put her money and valuables. She was here on her own, after all, in the middle of nowhere.' He stood up and Lotte opened one eye to look at him. He'd taken out his pen knife and began to score under the ridge of the mantelpiece. 'You know, I've only just met you, and already I know you're insane,' Lotte said. Charles continued to try to dislodge the top of the mantelpiece and Lotte closed her eyes again. She must have drifted off into a doze, because the next thing she knew she'd woken with a start at a loud bang just beside her ear.

She sat bolt upright. 'What the . . .' She rubbed her eyes.

'It's come off!' Charles burst out, dropping a long slab of stone on to the ground. 'Lotte, the top's come off and . . .' He stopped. He lifted out a book, a leather-bound book tied with red ribbon, and held it gently in his hands. He was shocked. Lotte stood up as he untied the ribbon and looked inside the book.

'"This is the diary of Daisy Burrows,"' he read, '"*in the year of Our Lord, eighteen ninety-six."*'

He was silent, just holding the book in his hands. Lotte touched his arm. 'Are you OK?'

He shook his head. 'I'm stunned,' he murmured. 'It's like she's spoken to me.' He opened the book at the first page and glanced down it. 'It's all here, every moment, every word, every emotion . . .' He handed it to Lotte and dropped his head in his hands.

Lotte turned to the last few pages. She read the words written in a neat, well-formed hand, and said: 'She's here, Charles . . .' She bent, took up the lodge plans and held them up. She followed the lie of the land with her finger and found what she was looking for. 'She's here,' she said again to Charles. She pointed at the plans. 'She's been here all the time.'

Phil Granger wasn't stupid; he knew he was being followed. He watched the car headlights in his rear-view mirror, certain that he'd lose them soon enough. He was sure of the land where he was heading and he had ingrained knowledge of it. He drove carefully, watching all the time, then as one car turned off and before another pulled out, he took his chance and dipped into a field. He turned off his headlights, climbed out of the car and ran for it. He was half a mile away before they realized he'd gone.

Annie took the call in the CAD room.

'Oh fuck!' She slammed down the receiver and said: 'Get the maps out, Steve. He's done a runner and he's somewhere on the Bicester estate.'

'D'you want the helicopter?'

'Does the Super want to have kittens? Let's hold it for now. He's headed for somewhere specific and if we're clever we'll find out where.' She looked at her team. 'He's hiding her, so we're looking for any physical feature that gives cover. OK?' She stood up. 'Get on to it.'

Claire was asleep when he burst in. Her body ached and she was in pain, her fever was high and she drifted in and out of consciousness, in and out of sleep.

'Get up!' he shouted. 'Get up now!'

She struggled to her feet, just managing it. He dragged her forward and she stumbled, hitting her head on the door frame. She was going to die, she knew it; somewhere in the deepest recess of her mind the fear sprang to life and shot through her body, making her shake uncontrollably. He dragged her on, pulling her by the rope around her wrists, and she staggered through water, freezing cold water, sharp rushes cutting her legs. Then on to solid ground that was easier to cover, but more painful to fall on to. Finally he stopped, and she sank to her knees. She began to cry and called out several times. He hit her across the face.

'Kneel up,' he said. 'Kneel up and move forward.'

She raised herself, but instead of kneeling, she squatted, pressing her hands down hard on to the ground, and inched forward. She turned then and looked at him.

'Don't look at me!' he suddenly cried. 'I don't want to

do this but I got to. Don't look!' He lunged towards her and pushed, and she kicked her legs out from under her and fell, feet first, not head first as he'd wanted. She felt her body weightless for a few moments, then her shoulder hit something, a wall, her hip smashed and she screamed with pain. Then she hit the bottom. She crumpled, as a rag doll would do, and lay whimpering in pitch black and half an inch of water.

Granger ran. He ran down to the ponds and along the edge of the water. He didn't know where he was going or what he was going to do, but he was going to survive. All these years he'd survived, and he wasn't going to give in now.

Lotte stood by the French windows and looked out at the ponds. She had heard a cry and it made her shiver. Charles came across and stood with her, and she said: 'I hear voices, Charles, I know it sounds weird, but I think it's Daisy.'

Charles stared out at the darkness. 'It's not weird, I hear them too. It's as if she's calling to me, drawing me towards her.'

'I wonder why they never found her, why they didn't search the estate.'

'I don't know. All I can think is that the police didn't do their job properly. They thought they'd got their man; everything pointed to Henry having murdered Daisy so they didn't bother to look any further. Christ, it's terrible, isn't it, this travesty of justice?' Charles shivered. He turned to Lotte. 'I want to go to her, Lotte, now, tonight. I have to. I have to go and see if she's actually there. I need to see her grave, put her to rest.'

'No, not now, Charles, it's pitch black out there, you don't know the lie of the land, it's too dangerous.'

'No it's not. I've got a flashlight and I've got the map.'

'No!' Lotte stared at him. 'I won't let you go out there at this time of night! Do it in the morning, not now.'

Charles put his hands gently on her shoulders. 'I have to go. I've been thinking about it since I found the diary. I have to, Lotte. I know that sounds odd, but I've had these people in my head for years and I need closure.'

'Charles, please, don't. It scares me.'

'Why?'

She shrugged him off and stepped away. 'Because it does.'

'But why?'

'Because I don't want anything to happen to you, all right? There, I've said it now.'

He smiled. 'Yes, you've said it now.' And he leant forward and kissed her, lightly and gently on the mouth. Then he turned, took his jacket off the back of the chair and patted his pocket to check for his mobile. 'Nothing will happen to me. I have a phone, a strong light and a map. I will be fine, I promise. He pulled on his jacket and took the plan from the floor. 'Is the flashlight in the kitchen?'

'Yes.'

He found it and went to the door. 'Thank you, Lotte,' he said.

Grudgingly, Lotte smiled. 'Go and finish your book,' she said. 'And come back as soon as you can.' She watched him go across the woodland, his torchlight visible shining up to the dark sky, then she turned back inside to wait for his return.

Charles had only been walking a few minutes when he began to realize how difficult it was going to be to find the well in darkness. He stopped, looked up at the sky and wondered if he could get a sense of direction from the stars.

The night was silent, totally silent, not a sound. He held his breath to take it in, a silence so complete that it was rare, and then he heard it. It was a faint cry, a human cry. He called out.

'Hello? Is anyone there?' It came again, and he held his breath once more to try and hear it more clearly. He walked on. 'Keep calling to me!' he shouted out, 'Please, please keep calling to me . . .'

It came again, louder, nearer. He looked at the map. It was here, the well was here, it had to be. He dropped on to all fours and started running his hands over the ground, the beam of the flashlight concentrated down on to the grass. 'Keep calling!' he shouted out. 'Please help me find you . . .' He was suddenly panicked. 'Please, talk to me . . .' The cry was faint, more like a whimper, and Charles moved more quickly over the ground. As he put his hands out again, one of them slipped; he fell forward and pulled himself back just in time. He'd found it. He snatched up his flashlight and shone it down the well.

'My God! Claire?'

He heard her begin to cry.

'It's all right, Claire, just hang on in there, you're going to be all right.' He kept the light on her and felt in his pocket for his mobile. Pulling it out, he dialled 999. Moments later he was giving his details to the ambulance service; a few minutes after that, they put him through to the police.

Granger heard the medical air rescue before he saw it. He was taking cover in the rushes, knee deep in water, when he heard the helicopter. He looked up and knew he had to run for it. The place would be swarming with police in an hour. He waded through the water in the direction of the lodge and made it through the bog up on to the dry land at the edge of the garden. He looked up at the house; the lights were on, she was still up. He swore under his breath. Creeping along the side of the garden, he made it up to the house unseen. She was standing in the window, looking out, her arms folded across her body. She was an easy target.

Granger walked out from the bushes and silently in through the kitchen door. His wet shoes left a trail of water over the floor, but he made no noise. He moved into the sitting room. Her back was to him, she had no idea he was there. He pounced. Lotte was on the ground before she even had a chance to turn round.

The squad car with DI Taylor in pulled into the track that led up to the lodge and stopped. The house was lit up like a Christmas tree, lights blazing in the kitchen, the sitting room, the bedroom. Annie looked at Steve in the back.

'Odd?'

'Very.'

'Reverse,' she told the driver. 'We'll go up on foot.'

Lotte was kneeling, her body pressed against the window. He had tied her feet and was looking for something to bind her hands with. She looked out at the black expanse of lawn and saw a faint beam of light cross it. A car. The light disappeared, and she dropped her head down; she would never escape being a victim. She heard him enter the room and her whole body tensed. She shifted her glance to the side, to try and see what he was up to, and she saw the slab of stone. It was up against the wall where Charles had placed it; it was two feet away from her, and she couldn't reach it. She felt him approach her, and jerked round.

'Don't move!' he shouted. 'I need them to be able to see you in the window.' She turned her face towards the glass; she could see his reflection. 'You stay there till I've got the kids!' He started to rifle through the boxes, looking for rope. He was scared, she could see that, scared and volatile. Moments later he kicked a box over. 'Where's the fucking rope? Where is it?'

'I don't know . . .' Lotte bit her hand. She took a deep breath. 'I don't know,' she said a moment later, trying to keep her voice calm and low. 'Shall I help you look for it?'

He stopped and stared at her. He was momentarily confused, then shook his head. 'I told you, you can't move . . .' He came across to her and touched her hair from behind. 'We could have been friends,' he murmured. 'If you'd just given me a chance, we could have been friends . . .'

Lotte clenched her teeth. 'We still can,' she said quietly. 'If you leave the children where they are, we can be friends, good friends. Just you and me . . .'

Suddenly Granger yanked her head back with a clump of hair. Lotte cried out. 'D'you think I'm stupid? Eh? Do you? D'you think I'm fucking daft? We can't ever be friends now, not after what I've done! I've got to get away and I need you to help me. They won't touch me if I've got you and the kids . . .' He reached forward and put a knife against her throat. 'They won't touch me if they know I could kill you . . .'

Lotte closed her eyes and willed herself to be strong.

Annie and Steve used a torch, but kept the beam down low. Annie sensed something was wrong; she could almost smell it in the air.

'Take the front,' she murmured. 'I'll take the back.' She came round the side of the house to the back door. It was open, she saw water on the floor, footprints. She backed off, shone the torch up into the air, and seconds later Steve was beside her. 'He's here,' she whispered. Steve nodded. She stepped forward and slipped in through the door, with Steve right behind her. They stopped at the sound of low talking in the next room; she glanced back at him and moved into the house. As she stepped forward, she trod on a toy; it squeaked, then snapped in half.

Granger pulled back. He heard the noise and jerked away from Lotte. She didn't think, she didn't have time to. She lunged forward and grabbed the slab of stone with both hands, rearing up and swinging it with the full weight of her body. She hit him in the ribs. He let out a scream and fell back. Lotte scrambled forward, kneeling over him, the slab of stone in her hands. He screamed again, then Annie dived across him and wrestled the stone out of Lotte's grip.

'Police! Stop, police!' she shouted. Lotte fell back against the window, shattering a pane of glass, then slumped on to her side. She began to cry.

DS Steve Brown snapped a pair of handcuffs on the injured Granger, yanking his hands forward to do it and making him cry out in pain.

'Philip Granger, I am arresting you for the abduction of Claire Thompson,' he barked above the noise. 'You do not have to say anything . . .'

As DS Brown recited the familiar words of the caution, Annie dropped the slab of stone and knelt by Lotte, gently untying her feet. Still weeping, Lotte sat up. She covered her face with her hands. 'I didn't see anything happen here tonight, OK?' Annie said. Lotte managed to nod. 'You were incredibly brave. Are you all right?'

Finally, Lotte looked up. Annie dug in her pocket for a

tissue; it was a bit crumpled, but she handed it over and Lotte blew her nose. A minute or so later Lotte raised her head, then got to her feet and wiped her face with the back of her hand. 'I'm fine,' she answered. She was no longer a victim; she had fought back. Lotte looked right at Annie, and knotting her hands together to stop them from shaking, she said: 'I'm OK, and I'm going to be fine. Just fine.'

Chapter 26

The deli across the road was not used to big orders, so when Annie phoned and asked for fifteen cappuccinos and nine large espressos, along with twenty-four Danish pastries, she knew it was going to be a bit of a wait. At seven thirty it all arrived, only fifteen minutes after she had placed the order, and she was impressed. She called a meeting in the office and handed round the drinks.

'This is from me,' she said. 'Thanks to all of you involved in finding Claire Thompson. She's in hospital, out of intensive care this morning and on the ward. Well done; for a bunch of hicks, I am very impressed.' There was a great deal of laughter and some jeering. The mood, despite no sleep, was jubilant. Finding an abducted teenager alive was something they were all going to celebrate. It was an up side of the job, and in CID you didn't get many of those.

Annie left while the party was in full swing. She was wrung out and she needed more than coffee to hold her together. As she went, DS Brown shook her hand and she said: 'A full compliment, Steve, thank you.'

'You deserve it, boss,' he replied, and Annie thought that perhaps the move had been worth it. Perhaps. DS Jerry Coulter, she noticed, had left his coffee untouched; he was nowhere to be seen.

*   *   *

Lotte Graham pressed the end button on her telephone and held it for a moment. She had ended the call; ended her marriage. Her solicitor had said: 'Mr Keen, of Millard, Fraser and Tims, has just rung me this morning to put forward verbally a settlement offer from Mr Graham.' He had then outlined something that was, if not generous, then just about fair. There was no mention of Lotte not having custody of the children. She went back into the bedroom and climbed very carefully into bed, trying not to wake Milly and Freddie. She lay awake in the double bed that Lady Beatty had insisted she have, with her children either side of her, the sun streaming in through the window of the lodge, little hands tucked into her own and little bodies pressed close. Lotte was alive, she had saved herself and her children; last night she had faced pure terror and she had survived it. She knew now that she could survive anything. She turned her head on the pillow as Milly woke, and smiled at her daughter.

'What're you smiling at, Mummy?' Milly whispered.

'Nothing and everything,' Lotte whispered back.

'Good,' Milly said.

'Is it?'

'Oh yes.' Milly snuggled in closer. 'You haven't smiled for such a long time.'

Charles had almost finished his letter to Mia; it was one of the hardest things he had ever had to do. He knew it was cowardly to write, but he also knew that there was so much pain involved that they both needed some privacy to cope with that. He asked if he could meet her next week to see if she was all right, and he tried, although he was sure that he failed, to explain in some way how he felt.

How *did* he feel? He wasn't honestly sure at that point,

it was all too raw, too close, but he did know now for certain that love was something that happened without prompting, without knowing why or how. It was arbitrary, all-consuming, and it moved people to do things that they would never have believed themselves capable of. It could create and destroy. He knew that he loved Lotte Graham and he thought that his love would have to be tempered and shared and that it would always involve compromise. He was prepared for that and he was also prepared for loss. Charles Meredith, the thinker, the reasoner, the academic, had carried the idea of love through to its ultimate conclusion. If you loved, then you would always have to experience loss. One could not exist without the other. Not for him, or for Lotte or Henry Chatten or Daisy Burrows. There was only one way past loss, and that was death. It was the way that Daisy had chosen; it was the only way she would ever achieve the union with Henry that she wanted.

He laid down his pen and took up Daisy's diary. To conclude his story, he would have to let Daisy speak out about love and loss in the only right and fitting way. In her own words.

Chapter 27

7.15 a.m. I am alone. I have no future, I have no baby, I have no hope. What am I to do? I have come to a decision in the night, another long and lonely night, and that decision, in the cold light of this watery dawn, has held firm in my heart. I will do what I have to do. It frightens me, but I know that I have no choice. I cannot bear the pain of this loss and yet I know that I will lose more, I will lose him.

10.30 a.m.
I have cut myself, I have opened a small wound on the flesh of my hand, just below my thumb, and I know it will bleed profusely – the original wound bled for hours. It pains me, but I need the pain to make me feel alive. I am so cold and numb with grief and I think every minute about my little girl, my darling girl in her icy, wet grave. I cannot go on.

11 a.m.
I have bound the wound now with my nightdress and it is soaked with my blood. I have had to bind it again with linen on top of that. I will take the path down by the ponds towards the house and walk across the gardens. It is mid-morning. I know the hours of the house so well, so many times have I used its small detailed movements for my own deceitful gains. The staff will be cleaning and preparing and no one will ever notice me. I will put this bloody thing where they will find it and I will take my love to

the same point of pain and grief that I am at. We will be together, we will join the eternal life together.

12 noon
It is done and I am not sorry. Can love be so unforgiving? Is this love in my breast or is it anger and revenge? Surely I cannot have anger and revenge without love? I do not know how long it will take once I have cut into the veins; I think that I can leave the bed as witness to my pain and still make it to the well to lie with my baby. I pray to God for the strength to do that because I do not want to die on the way there and I do not want to leave my child alone for all eternity.

2 p.m.
There is no pain, only relief. I will wait with my child in my arms for my love, and we will face the afterlife as we were meant to be: as one.